ANNE LEE

A Gathering of Blood and Magic

Era of Ruin and Reunion Series

To Mom and Dad, in loving memory.
This book would not have been possible without your
support, belief, love, wisdom, and encouragement.

Contents

Chapter 1

He could hear the creatures in the forest now.

Captain Garridan's breath plumed in the night air. His muscles tensed to ward off the unwanted temperature drop and strained not to give in to the shivering they longed to do.

Or perhaps that was fear.

Garridan's two-dozen men slipped into position behind trees, treading cautiously on the foliage and grass. Those who could climb stealthily enough did so, nocking arrows while waiting for the enemy to arrive.

From the forefront of the force his men created, he crept as deep into the forest as he dared. Sparse new leaves clung to the skeletal branches of the trees that reached out like gnarled limbs and fingers. The leaves on the ground, dead remnants left after winter's thaw, were crisp and dry. Every slight movement crackled in the air.

Garridan stood behind a large oak. One hand rested on the hilt of his sword. Past his own beating heart, he could hear the sound of the monsters coming closer.

The pale bodies of Erepos, eerie and ghost-like in the still of early morning, wove through the trees. Bare feet shuffled over the leaves and dirt. Bald heads gleamed in the fading moonlight. Garridan could not see their faces clearly due to the distance, but his memory filled in the blanks.

Murky eyes sat in sunken, pale faces; dirt ground into their skin covered them in patches like the discoloration of disease. The beings loped about, sometimes on all fours, their backs hunched as if in pain—but that was a ruse, like a bird feigning injury; they gained speed at an alarming rate.

He could hear their faint grunts. Wordless cries and shrieks were their only methods of communication. As far as Garridan—or anyone in his country, for that matter—knew, they possessed no language. And by no means were they skilled; apparently they lacked the higher brain functions to master any weapon. Once upon a time, they'd used only their hands and teeth, but in the past few decades, they'd picked up swords and knives. What they lacked in strength and skill, however, they more than made up for in speed and numbers. Even though they could almost match Garridan and his men in physical size, they were not difficult to kill.

A twig *snapped* mere yards away. Garridan stared hard ahead. The northern moon, Naula, was a thin slice low in the sky. Its wan light barely penetrated the gloomy forest floor.

Garridan waited.

Faint movement to his left caught his eye. He discerned the outline of a familiar figure leaning against a tree trunk. Darson, his lieutenant, appeared deceptively relaxed.

The captain tilted his head toward the noise.

Darson nodded in affirmation.

Garridan then raised his arm for the rest of the men to see. As he did so, the trilling call of a bird cut through the bitter air.

Arrows flew with synchronized hisses, slicing past bare tree limbs. Seconds later, shrieks began, destroying the hallowed silence of the forest as the Erepos broke into a run.

Garridan drew his sword and stepped out of his refuge.

A pale, white form rushed at him, its gaping maw screeching as its feet pounded into the dirt. Garridan thrust his sword and buried it deep into the Erepo's shoulder, and then pulled it out swiftly as the monster screamed in pain. He then swept the blade in a smooth, wide arc toward the creature's neck. The head thudded to the ground. The body collapsed after a moment of unsettling suspension.

His sword met the curved blade of another Erepo with a reverberating clang that sent shock waves up his arm. The Erepo didn't parry so much as swing wildly for a few seconds while snarling at Garridan with rotted, blackened teeth. Disgusted, the captain wasted no time in running him through, feeling his sword meet resistance in flesh.

He slashed the throat of another foe, and warm liquid sprayed his face. Garridan kicked the pale body away and hastily wiped his hand over the dark splatters, careful not to smear any of it near his lips.

Something heavy pounded in the dirt behind him. He whirled.

A blade sunk into his right shoulder.

Garridan's breath seized. He didn't react as quickly as the Erepo, who immediately abandoned the weapon and leapt on him. Its momentum threw the warrior to the ground. For a sickening few seconds he was falling, with the weight of the strangely warm, sinewy body on top of him. Then the ground rushed up and caught him in a rough, painful embrace.

The Erepo clung to the captain like a spider, its fingers digging into his sides. It shrieked in his face, spraying him with spittle. Garridan's stomach rolled with nausea and bone-deep fear as he brought his hand up to the Erepo's head, clutching its skull and forcing it away from him. Scrambling, it grabbed Garridan's hair, fighting for control.

With his free hand, the captain blindly searched the ground for his sword, a weapon, anything. His fingers felt cool metal as the Erepo struggled and writhed on top of him. Garridan's hand closed around the hilt of his own sword. He brought it up swiftly, slamming it into the monster's skull with as much force as he could muster.

Bone gave a satisfying *crack*. As quickly as it had launched itself onto him, the Erepo fell off. Garridan stumbled to his feet, grimacing as a slight rotation of his right shoulder sent shooting pain through the torn muscle. He took in the surrounding area, making note of a soldier fighting one last Erepo. When it was dead, silence reigned once more save for the harsh breathing of his men.

"Everyone all right?" he called. Positive responses greeted him from more than a dozen voices, but Garridan was not satisfied until he called every name under his command and received an individual response.

As a precaution, he sent one of his men to scout further to ensure there would be no other unwanted visitors.

"Find as many bodies as you can and drag them to the plains," Garridan ordered. "We'll do a sweep at sunrise for any we missed."

The work was not long, although his shoulder screamed with pain by the time all the bodies were collected. Dawn scrubbed the air clean of the sooty gray leftover from the night, and visibility improved. The men trudged back to their original campsite. Garridan looked into the faces of tired men. Men who just wanted to go home.

"Break camp soon, Captain?" a soldier named Averi asked.

Garridan nodded. "After inspection. The horses?"

"Spooked, but all accounted for, sir."

Good. Tethering the horses a few yards north of camp proved to be a blessing, he thought. As his soldiers attended wounds and cleaned weapons, a wave of exhaustion gripped his bones with a great, heavy pull. He didn't bother to push the feeling aside—he let it take him to the ground. He sat on the cold dirt and took a deep breath; the movement jarred his shoulder wound. Gritting his teeth, Garridan reached with his good arm and used his fingers and teeth to tear the bloody fabric of his shirt away from the pulsing injury.

"You ever intend to get that looked at, Captain?"

Garridan glanced up as Darson crouched down.

"When Thyme has a moment."

The lieutenant pointed at the gash, visibly wary of touching it. "You're bleeding all over your shirt. And you have blood on your face."

"It can wait until he's seen to the others."

Darson sighed, dug up a rag from his pocket, and threw it at Garridan to wipe off his face. He called for Thyme, the group's healer.

"In a moment!" the man called in a hoarse voice that was first sharp and cutting before the last syllable disappeared into nothing. "I got two dozen a' you to look over, get in line!"

Darson lifted up his hands and gave Garridan an affronted

look.

"He's ready to retire," Garridan said, almost apologetically.

"Oh, I had no idea. He only reminds us every day."

The groused mutterings of a healer who'd stayed too long in the field wafted on the breeze to the two men. Garridan took his focus off the pain that radiated from his neck down into his arm and shifted it to the aging healer's verbal discontent. Thyme commandeered the soldiers like a stern, impatient father would deal with young, petulant boys. Shirts came off; wounds were prodded and inspected to satisfaction. It would be a shame to lose such a talented, experienced man. One of these days, though, the old man would make good on his daily threats of retirement.

". . . four hours from home, creeping up like vultures. Don't have the decency to wait till morning, nasty little—oh no, must have a snack. Strip down, son, quick now."

Darson gestured to Garridan. "He's the lame one, not me."

"You're standing right in front of me, boy. I need to get you out of the way, too. Faster you go, sooner I can see the cap'n."

Darson rolled his eyes at the disgruntled healer and obediently pulled off his shirt.

"Report?" Garridan asked Thyme.

The old man sniffed. "Lacerations, knocks, bruises. Nothing fatal. Foster wrecked his knee over a tree log and one of their disease-ridden blades. He'll be needing the infirmary to nip off an infection." The old man sniffed. "Clumsy boy. Averi, too—tore his back all to hell. Goddamn trees as deadly as Erepos to you lot."

"Now that's not fair," Darson argued. "It's been a long tour. Am I finished?"

Thyme waved his clearance. "Let's have a look at you, Captain. Are we dealing with anything serious?"

"I'm actually not sure, sir."

Thyme knelt down, knees cracking. Hair resembling a hawk's crown of feathers bobbed softly with the movement. Eyes squinted at the drying blood and torn skin.

"Shirt off."

With a baring of teeth, Garridan carefully removed his shirt and assessed the damage right along with the healer.

Darson hissed in a breath, and Thyme muttered a few choice expletives at the jagged, six-inch gash in Garridan's right shoulder. The skin around it flushed an angry red. Garridan couldn't see any exposed muscle, but the light was poor; blood flowed freely, and it throbbed like a mouthful of infected teeth.

"Boy, I don't have the supplies this kind of mess needs. I'll clean and bandage it, but you get yourself to the infirmary the minute we get home. You'll be needing stitches. Two months, I ain't had to stitch nothin' bigger than a cut—hours from home, I got three of you."

The captain winced and ground his teeth as Thyme's fingers probed the bloody wound and then smothered the injury with a mixture of egg yolk, rose, and pine oil to reduce the inflammation. The smell overwhelmed his nose.

"Hurt like hell for a few weeks," the old man continued to mutter. "Won't be able to use it much. Damned lucky you weren't bit." He wrapped Garridan's shoulder with a clean bandage and gave him a drought for pain that tasted like oil and rotten fruit.

Garridan felt the drought take effect moments after his scout came back and reported no other signs of Erepos. The fierce pain dulled to a low, rumbling ache, and his right arm was no longer stiff. The air continued to lighten, heralding warmer temperatures, as the sun eased its way up to break on the horizon.

As the sunrise saturated the sky with dazzling color, Garridan and his men performed one last sweep. No bodies were left behind in the forest for other scavengers to find. In an empty field of frost-tinged grass, four-dozen Erepo carcasses were piled atop one another in a mound of dirty, pale limbs, torsos, and ruined heads.

With the horses packed and the wounded looked after, the men mounted their steeds for the last stretch home. Garridan sent the majority of the troops ahead as Averi prepared to light the pile, knowing the wind would blow the smell of burning, diseased flesh in their direction.

"I haven't seen a group that big in months. A nice surprise for our productive tour," Darson remarked sarcastically as he helped ignite the heap.

"The king won't be too happy," Averi agreed. He grimaced and cursed after chucking a merrily burning branch deep into the bodies, and then he stretched his back.

Garridan raised an eyebrow at the soldier as smoke began to rise. "How's your back?"

"Colorful and sore," Averi explained cheerfully, gesturing to his lower back. "Monster knocked me right on a tree branch. We danced for a bit, and then I beheaded him. Anyway. Worry not, Cap. The mission wasn't a complete loss. A lot more alive than dead, just … not the person the king sent us for."

Darson snorted. "Not that anyone *wanted* that sack of—"

"Dar," Garridan sighed. "At the very least, gentlemen, this

particular group won't be bothering the capitol. Let's be done here."

The mound began to blaze.

The men ignored the bright yellow bonfire in favor of the brush strokes of purple and pink that streaked the sky and illuminated the presence of the large planet Parna and its thin, delicate rings.

They headed north. It was time to go home.

Chapter 2

The city of Laurus rose from the flat plains in walls, spires, and towers, a patchwork of concrete, fieldstone, and limestone. It was a lone bright spot in a calm sea of scruff grass and farmland. Arcing around the farmland, half a mile out from the city walls, stood an unfinished barrier, a slow work in progress stalled time and again from lack of raw materials. From a distance the barrier looked abandoned, a remnant of a much larger city halved in size.

The city gleamed gloriously in late springs past. This early morning, as clouds crept in to cover the sun, Laurus's beauty was dimmed but not lost. The brilliant blue flags fluttering in the breeze atop the ramparts were still warm and welcoming for the soldiers coming home. The pale gray clouds and grass not yet touched with the sustenance of spring rains washed out the pale limestone, giving it a dingy white cast that briefly, and uncomfortably, reminded Garridan of the pallid flesh of Erepos.

He couldn't shake the troubling comparison as the heavy gates opened to let in the troops. No one awaited them. The king's royal unit did not operate on predictable time schedules, and none of his men's loved ones would know of their return.

The long, narrow courtyard Garridan and his men rode into was sparsely populated, as the city folk rarely bothered loitering near the front gates unless it involved food replenishment. Some twenty years ago, the decorative pools of the capitol's courtyard underwent a conversion to feed the growing population of the haven city. Now, the green waters of the pretty stone pools housed trout, perch, and cod. Water chestnut and watercress floated along the edges. Each pool belonged to a specific neighborhood—Garridan's own area of dwelling possessed a pool in the far left corner—and individuals designated by the king's cabinet regulated the supply of fish and vegetation to ensure fair distribution. He never understood why those pools gave him such comfort, but they never failed to settle him when he watched the calm waters ripple with the life teeming underneath.

Garridan coaxed his mare to stand in front of the group of gathered men. "Gentlemen, this was a successful tour," he said. "Despite running into circumstances out of our control, we still had the opportunity to assist two towns in need; we ensured their safety and aided their ability to continue trading and feeding their families. I'm proud of the way each and every one of you conducted yourselves, and deeply pleased that we are all home healthy and uninfected. Enjoy your leave."

The men cheered. The captain heard Darson extend an open invitation to celebrate at a tavern in the northeast corner of the city. As the men began to leave and make their way down the cobblestone streets that branched out to different parts of the city, two young women seated on the concrete lip of a nearby pool rose, beaming in the direction of lingering soldiers.

Darson leaned in Garridan's direction from his horse. "Enjoy telling the king that his package died before we could get to him. Ladies!" He dismounted cheerfully, accepting a hug from one of the maidens. "What a happy coincidence to see you here."

"Do not flatter yourself," the dark-haired young woman laughed, lowering her pail of water chestnuts and brushing a kiss across Darson's cheek. "It was our turn to gather fresh stock for the market."

"Don't crush my hopes that you waited here every day until my return."

"Consider them crushed, Lieutenant."

Darson looked up at Garridan. "Do you see the welcome I get?"

"Better than none at all," Garridan answered with a half smile.

"We need to find the captain a lady friend," Darson told the young women. "Not having one to welcome him back makes him ornery." The moment he finished his sentence, the soldier realized what he had said. Darson's eyes widened, and contrition filled them. "I meant that entirely in jest."

"I know." The captain smiled tightly, unable to quell a dull ache drummed up from the harmless teasing. The memory of a young woman he remembered all too well flashed across his mind. Fortunately, the passage of time had made it easier to push her back into the recesses of his mind. The longing, however, was not so easily banished. He forced a light, equally teasing tone. "You should escort these ladies to the market and then go bother your poor mother. I'm sure she's dying to have her agitating son back from the fields."

"She'll want a visit from her insufferable pretend son, too." Looking thoroughly unhappy with himself, Darson appeared to swallow his apology, and patted the flank of Garridan's horse. "Coming out later?"

"Not with this shoulder."

The lieutenant winced. "I can stop by and play nursemaid."

"You're not pretty enough for me to enjoy that."

The maidens laughed, and Darson ruefully raked back his hair. "Get that looked at; I'll see you later."

Garridan nodded and pushed his heels into the mare's side, wordlessly acknowledging the continued apology coming from his friend's expression and body language. His shoulder was stiff, but the pain draught made the discomfort bearable. He headed for the main road, which snaked through the heart of Laurus like a wide river with streams and rivulets of cobblestone branching off throughout the city, only to slow to a halt as a man hailed him from the courtyard.

Garridan's guard rose as Radley, the captain of Laurus's home unit, moved to block his path.

"Welcome back," Radley said. "On time, I see."

"Thank you."

"I happened to notice the lack of a certain council member."

Garridan fought the urge to sigh. "I noticed as well. Dead long before our arrival to Espen."

Radley grimaced. "Damn."

In that, we are in full agreement, Garridan thought. "Did Callum's troops return from the south?"

"Yesterday afternoon. Four soldiers dead. Two turned. Three farms found burned, their families massacred."

Damn. "I see."

"The Marshal instructed me to inform you he will debrief

you this afternoon. The king wishes an immediate audience. You'll find him in his study."

Well. The stitches will have to wait. Nodding, Garridan bid Radley farewell.

He headed toward the large wooden stables not far from the gates to the king's castle. Garridan barely paid heed to the bustle of the city market to his left, which opened from the main road into a large stone square. Wooden stalls stood in rough rows. Men and women threaded among them, trading with vendors.

He'd known these streets and that market, the largest in the city, most of his life. From the stories his parents and grandfather used to tell him, the commotion he was familiar with could not compare to the days of the previous generation's youth, when vendors from other cities came to trade.

Reports from other towns and cities were scarce, as Garridan and his men had repeatedly discovered during their excursions through Aliquis. Most notably concerning the town of Espen and a specific task bestowed upon them by the king.

Which had ended in failure.

It was this very lack of information that set so many on edge. Unease continually rippled through the masses at the prospect of what the next week would bring, or what sort of grim news the next military official would deliver. The people here were still largely sheltered from the horrors that lay beyond the white stone, but they were not ignorant of it.

The smell of sweet hay, horse, and manure accosted Garridan's nose and brought him back to the present as he entered the huge wooden stables. A few stable boys groomed two horses out in the aisle.

"Need help, Cap'n?" one of the boys called.

"Could you take her for me, son?"

The boy smiled, dark eyes flashing to the captain's mare. "Yes, sir."

Garridan dismounted, patted the horse's flank, and handed the reigns over. He slid a hand into his pocket and, dismayed, realized he did not have any silver. He always slipped the stable help a few. Garridan vowed to remedy that later.

Weariness settled in as he walked, a reminder of the sleep he didn't get the previous night. He wasn't pleased at the lack of time to clean up before having an audience with the king, and he wiped some of the grime off his hands onto his pants. The hell with it. The king wanted him now; he would have to deal with the filth.

The king's castle was an imposing stone and wooden structure more functional than attractive. Garridan walked past the guard stationed at the large wooden doors, nodding at the guard's salute, and strode through the nearly empty grand hall. Servants wiped down the scarred surfaces of the meal tables in the southern section of the great room; more carried buckets of water and linens down the hallways.

When Garridan reached the study, he knocked softly.

A muffled "Enter" came through. Garridan let himself in, closing the door behind him.

Open bay windows reaching the room's vaulted ceilings let in the late morning light. Golden tassels bound thick, velvet drapes to each side, luxuriant and fine to the casual observer, if one didn't inspect too closely and find ragged ends and frayed threads. Shelves bearing books, small bronze statues, and carved wooden boxes lined every wall; the large tomes and small volumes lent a musty, antiquated smell to the room. A fire crackled in the fireplace carved into the center of the right wall.

The king of Aliquis stood before the fire.

Hair white with age swept back from an impressive, regal face, touching the collar of his red tunic. The gray eyes studying Garridan were still sharp and wise, if a little tired. "Welcome back, Captain."

"Thank you, Your Majesty." Garridan made a sweeping bow, which proved to be a terrible idea. The pain that lanced through his shoulder stunned him. He took a deep breath as the king bid him to wait. The monarch approached a wide, polished wooden desk and retrieved a bottle of wine and two glasses.

While Garridan waited, he looked around. A newer rug, swirled with grey and green, soft and thick enough to sleep on, spanned the room, and reminded Garridan of how dirty his boots were. He was positive he'd tracked in more dirt than this room had ever seen.

He was also positively not looking forward to informing his liege of the demise of his councilman. The two-month tour for the king's private unit included many tasks and assignments carried out successfully, but Garridan wasn't able to accomplish the retrieval of the councilman.

These things happen, he reminded himself. Mortality rates were high. He wasn't particularly bothered by the death itself—he hardly knew the man beyond his somewhat unsavory reputation—but the king had been mysteriously adamant on Mathias's presence in the capitol.

King Edric returned holding the two glasses of red wine. Garridan took the offered glass and murmured his thanks.

"Have a seat, Captain."

Garridan followed him to two high-back chairs waiting on either side of a table of rich dark wood. He sank gratefully into the deep golden cushion. Edric sat, and they both paused to drink deeply. A low hum of appreciation announced the captain's pleasure at the full-bodied taste of a no-doubt expensive, increasingly rare wine.

When Edric finished, he pointed one ringed finger at Garridan. "You are quite filthy."

Garridan ran his tongue over his teeth to savor the lingering aftertaste of plum and chocolate. "When am I not?"

"Indeed. Report? How fare Pithe and Espen?"

Garridan briefly summed up his unit's activity over the course of their absence, including the morning's confrontation. Pithe was a town too close to the border for anyone's comfort, long left to the Erepos by most citizens except a stout few. Garridan's unit had overseen a full evacuation of those remaining to the nearest town. Another town's trade routes with a neighboring village had become compromised, and they assisted with a reroute, erecting new barriers for safe cargo transportation. The manual labor alone took weeks. Espen, on the other hand …

Edric didn't give him a chance to ease into it. "Mathias has passed, hasn't he?"

Garridan mentally sighed. "Yes."

"On the return home?"

"No. When we reached Espen, his family informed us Mathias had died the week previous. An infection of some kind. I am sincerely sorry, Your Majesty. Had I thought to travel to Espen beforehand, we might have been able to rush him here for treatment."

Edric shook his head, weariness aging his features. "And he probably would have died regardless. Mathias has not been in good health for ages. It is a tragedy, and playing at 'what if' will not solve anything. We will carry on without him. I will contact his family and send condolences."

"Are there any other council members you require in his stead, for whatever purpose?" Garridan kept the question light, fishing a little for the reasoning behind the request for the outlying councilman. He never outright questioned Edric's assignments for them—there was never a reason to—but curiosity got the better of him.

"Not at this time, Captain. I could use an ear, however."

"Of course."

"The attack this morning … quite close to our city. Closer than they have come in some time. And a great deal of them."

"It was a rather large group, and they are edging closer to the capitol, yes. It is slightly troublesome."

The king chuckled humorlessly. He looked away from Garridan and out the window for a long moment. "Slightly troublesome. I try not to forget how much death you see daily. How commonplace it is for you. How it should not be, but there it is. It is how we have lived since before my time, but we are ever searching for better ways to … get around it.

"Their boldness, I suppose you should call it, worries me. It is a constant worry. I have been thinking heavily on this matter for the past few months. No." A brief, sad smile touched his lips. "Years. Since I became king. How can our people continue to lead lives as normal as possible, as structured as we can give them? How can we keep them safe, and provide for them?"

Garridan didn't answer. The king rarely laid his true

thoughts bare. After years in his service, Garridan was well versed in reading the burdens and frustrations between the lines on his monarch's face.

How difficult it must be to represent the hope for a nation held captive by an evil no one understood.

"Garridan, I would like to hear your thoughts on how to remedy this growing predicament of ours, and perhaps I will share with you some of mine."

The captain straightened in his chair. He went to lean his elbows on the table, and then his shoulder reminded him what a poor decision that was. He improvised by leaning his arms against the edge of the table to steeple his fingers.

"Some of the larger cities are adjusting well enough to becoming self-sustaining," Garridan said slowly. "Protecting what crops they can grow, maintaining sanitation. Water access is a challenge, since the Erepos make it so difficult to travel far from the safety of city walls. Population control in larger cities is another thing, but continuing to encourage smaller towns to develop their own methods of protecting their borders has helped. The citizens are still vulnerable. There are not enough willing to receive proper training to defend themselves, and there are not enough of us to help them do so. We're stretched thin as it is."

Garridan did not mention that he had to continue to lead soldiers into the increasingly hostile territory of their own lands. Throughout his military career, he'd watched countless men die not because of poor strategy, but because of being overwhelmed. No one envied the soldiers in Aliquis; the position was dangerous, soul crushing, and largely thankless. Rewards, other than decent pay, came rarely, and a violent death was almost always guaranteed. Those who chose the life either possessed a streak of audacity the size of a small country or had personal reasons for joining.

Garridan shook his head in frustration before continuing. "And for every Erepo we kill, ten more take its place. The spread of their infection shows no sign of slowing."

The captain looked into his king's eyes and saw Porphys reflected back at him. Five months ago, the southeastern border town had been nothing but an assignment for the eastern unit—a unit the king paid particularly close attention to from the moment his grandson joined its ranks.

The compassion of one soldier for an abandoned child had been the town's demise. The ensuing forty-eight hours had been … horrifying.

"We will not let self-preservation supersede our humanity," Edric said abruptly. "I have made my position clear on the matter."

Garridan noted the waver of emotion in his king's voice. He conceded with a nod. "I understand."

"Porphys was an avoidable catastrophe."

Garridan nodded once more, internally wincing. Edric's tone once again allowed no room for comment or argument. Garridan held his own beliefs about how it could have been handled, but he held his tongue. It was difficult to argue damage control methods to a king who deeply personalized such an awful incident.

The death of a grandson would do that to any grandparent.

The words nearly stuck in Garridan's throat. "I agree." Defending the choices of his brothers-in-arms would only anger a king who already did his best to maintain order, save lives, and preserve the highest quality of life for the people of Aliquis.

"Fortifying the border and river towns has been a priority simply because of their location," Garridan said, continuing in the same light tone while Edric's eyes still reflected the grievous matter. "A priority progressively becoming harder to keep. The more ground we lose, the further we are from Virtus and Ferox, which hurts any chances of mutual assistance in the future, if it ever becomes feasible. Ferox is still in shambles."

The king had reached out to Virtus and Ferox before, but both neighboring kingdoms—the only other inhabited realms on Hylla they could turn to—had their own problems outside of Erepos. Garridan had never been to Ferox despite its close proximity to Aliquis. He knew the kingdom held great architectural wonders and art from the multitude of cultures it absorbed from its long history of conquering territories and smaller countries, but its deterioration had begun long before his birth. Those wonders had no doubt fallen into disrepair once Ferox began to crumble from its own size and unstable government. They had received no news of the massive kingdom for years; he could vividly imagine the kind of hellhole it would be now.

Virtus enjoyed order somewhat similar to Aliquis—but endured problems that Garridan did not want his people to inherit; illness outbreaks and food shortages among them. "Virtus has never had a substantial military force, and there is the misfortune of their ailing king." Along with a belief system that chose to look at the spread of Erepos as heavenly retribution; for what, Garridan did not know. The overarching religion in Virtus was far older than the primary religion in Aliquis, which branched off almost a thousand years prior to remove the shackles of a harsh, restrictive, and archaic belief system.

"The king's son is shouldering much of that burden," Edric agreed. "Prince Hadrian has much to contend with as of late, and they haven't the resources to give."

"Neither do we," Garridan pointed out.

"No. We cannot afford to lose much more farmland to fire or languish." The king leaned back and rubbed his forehead wearily. Worry lines cut in between his brows and around his mouth.

Garridan usually didn't allow himself to think about every obstacle humankind faced. Forcing it into the light was difficult.

"As it stands now, and as I said before …" Garridan hated even saying it. It was redundant, and obvious, but there was no other way to face the situation. "We are losing territory to Erepos; we are shrinking. And they are leaving more victims alive instead of feeding on them." Animals killed and ate their food; they did not have the foresight to leave their victims intact enough to increase their numbers. The newer development itched the inside of Garridan's mind relentlessly; he could not reconcile a behavior that spoke of intelligence with the habits of the Erepos.

Intelligence and organization. Who was responsible for the change? Were they evolving? Or did they have help?

"I would be more than willing to hear your thoughts," Garridan admitted. "Because I have exhausted every resource I know."

"There is more available to us than you are aware of," the king replied cryptically. "Since …" The unspoken recall of Porphys's demise hung in the air. Edric cleared his throat. "I have given it serious thought over the past six months.

Struggled with it for years. My father and his father never followed through with this idea. But as of late, I feel it is time to truly *exhaust*, as you say, every viable resource at our disposal, conventional or not."

Edric hesitated, his lips a thin line as he stared pensively at his half-full glass of wine. His fingers traced the rim and then stroked the table. Abruptly he stood, grasping the glass, and began to pace slowly as he visibly struggled to speak his mind.

Garridan watched him curiously.

"I have reigned for thirty years," the man said quietly. "In that time we have lost countless towns. Thousands dead. Infected. The remaining cities are crowded. My people run the risk of going hungry. Laurus has been blessed; the people here, they are fortunate, and sheltered from the way some have to live elsewhere. The inequality tears at me. I am failing them."

Garridan wanted to find the words capable of soothing the king's anguish. But with his own throat tight, his fingers interlaced in his lap, he couldn't find them. There was no silver lining here. And he didn't know where his king would find it.

"It is not entirely wise. But it is a chance I am unwilling to set aside if it has any hope of helping us. I am going to ask for outside aid."

Garridan's head tilted to the side. Surely, that was not the answer. They had already discussed the neighboring kingdoms.

Edric saw the confusion on Garridan's face. "Not Ferox or Virtus."

"Perhaps a more direct response would aid this discussion, so I may provide the input you seek," Garridan said somewhat dryly.

The corners of Edric's mouth ticked up in a faint smile. "Very well. I am going to approach the fae."

Chapter 3

Garridan stared blankly at King Edric. "I am—I apologize. I do not believe I heard you correctly."

"Your hearing is perfectly fine."

"I beg to differ, Your Majesty."

Edric laughed. The pleasant rumble filled the room. "I do enjoy your company, Garridan. Please, tell me how you really feel, instead of letting your face do the talking."

Garridan shifted in his chair, cleared his throat, and took a drink of wine. His expression was almost pained. "I have always been under the impression the fae were fairly … unconcerned with humans."

"It hurts me to watch you try to say it nicely. Speak your mind, that is why you are here."

"No one has *seen* them in ages, Your Majesty," Garridan said. "Far longer than any living memory can recall. They have been relegated to stories. Cautionary tales for mischievous children. My father used to frighten me inside after dark by saying a faerie would snatch me up and keep me because they kept all naughty children."

"I have told my granddaughter the same."

"Ancient relics or not, you are considering reaching out to the immortals. Are we so desperate for help that we will ask beings of folklore for assistance? While we are at it, we might as well ask the elves."

"I have considered them," Edric said honestly. "But they are too far north for safe travel. I have been informed that, regardless of distance, they are also a lost cause. The fae are much closer in proximity."

Garridan laughed weakly. "The last known record of elven existence predates the fae. And we have never had dealings with them. I do not ..." The elves were not just relics, they were dead myths. How could faeries—or mystical creatures of any kind—solve their problems? Clearly those other beings had not found a way to eradicate Erepos. And the fae had shown no interest in human affairs for over a thousand years. The elves? Never. Ancient records held zero accounts of elven encounters.

"Neither fae nor elven existence is in dispute," Edric added.

Garridan smiled ruefully. "For you or me, perhaps, but for the greater population, mythology is all they are. We know literally nothing about the elves. What I know of the fae, I learned from Lieutenant Darson."

"His mother," the king said with interest. "Idavida is a historian, is she not?"

"Yes. She is the only person I have ever come across who speaks of them in the present tense. Are you sure the fae still reside in the same lands?"

"I am sure," the king replied firmly. "My source of information is incredibly accurate."

"Who is your informant?" Garridan asked. "How does this person know the elves are a lost cause and the fae would be willing to help?"

"He deals almost exclusively with the faerie kingdom,"

Edric answered. "He has no connection with the elves. Here. Let me show you something." He raised a hand in a gesture that told Garridan to wait, and then moved across the room.

His voice drifted behind him as he retrieved something from a large writing desk. "I have had extensive talks as of late. …" A drawer opened and then shut. Edric returned with something cupped in the palm of his hand. "With Eyad."

"The sorcerer?" Surely Garridan had not heard that right, either.

Edric offered a small glass jar filled with a rich, brown, fine substance to Garridan. "Take it. Smell it."

Garridan uncapped the top and breathed. His eyes widened at the sweet yet savory smell. He reached in and carefully placed the powder on his finger and touched it to his tongue. It held little flavor, but the aroma was still divine. "What is this?"

"Cinnamon. From the rain forests in a southern country of the fae realm—a realm very much alive and thriving. Eyad gifted it to me recently. Their borders are well protected by extremely adept military forces. Their population flourishes under that protection.

"Imagine the vast amount of knowledge and expertise you could develop in eight hundred years, Garridan. Many fae are even older than that. Eyad is almost positive they will not turn us away if we approach them. His counsel is the main reason I am giving this serious consideration. We have nothing to lose at this point, and I do not want to dismiss the possibility of aid because the majority believes it is unattainable. Especially in light of my meetings with Eyad."

Garridan's eyes narrowed. "Little is known about the

sorcerer himself. May I ask how long you have been meeting with him?"

"Long enough."

Although he realized he had nearly overstepped his boundaries in this strange conversation, Garridan could not help but add to it. If he was already digging a hole, what were a few more shovels of dirt? "I am only trying to say—respectfully, Your Majesty—that we cannot let wishful thinking cloud rational judgment. Your points about our dwindling resources are valid, but if this happens the way you wish it to, if we reach out to them for aid, we are indebted to them. Are we willing or even able to pay whatever price they demand in return?"

"Yes, Captain." Edric's expression grew severe. "We have food *now*, and water, barricades, and soldiers left to defend *now*. But when my granddaughter is grown in thirty years, in fifty, one hundred, there will *be* no food. There will be none left willing to fight off the Erepos, and we will be prisoners wasting away in our fortresses. Our people will die, and the Erepos will keep growing. I am not willing to wait until the eleventh hour when we are reduced to poverty and scavenging like crows to eke out an existence. And as the kings before me never tried, I do not believe any of my potential successors will, either. So it falls to me. If it is not attempted now, it will never come to be."

Garridan sat back in his chair. Humbled, once again, by the fierce commitment the elderly man had to his people, he could think of nothing to argue against the logic.

The king and captain stared at one another in silence. Garridan could see Edric's conviction waver in the edges of his eyes, revealing the desperation and weariness underneath.

"I do not enjoy throwing us at the mercy of another species."

Garridan tried hard to keep in mind that the whole thing was a leap in the dark on the king's part, blind hope to avoid the inevitable that was based on the word of a sorcerer Garridan was not sure he trusted. The king was willing to attempt some sort of alliance with an ancient race that had closed its borders a thousand years ago; Garridan was still unconvinced.

A headache began to pulse at the base of Garridan's skull. He closed his eyes and tried to see the potential Edric envisioned. "I imagine the benefits we are hoping for would involve trade agreements and military aide."

"The benefits are potentially huge. But let us not get ahead of ourselves. We have to make contact first. I appreciate your concerns, Garridan, and trust me when I say I am keeping all of this in mind if this moves forward."

If. Garridan shook his head. "Forgive me, Your Majesty. Neither you nor the sorcerer has spoken to anyone in the faerie realm yet? Have you discussed this with the council?"

"Not yet. I wanted to test this on someone I trusted first, someone aware of the depth of our plight, to see the sort of reaction I would receive." Edric's tone turned dry. "So far, you have not disappointed my expectations. I only hinted at some of my ideas to Mathias the last time he visited, and he was supportive. It was encouraging. Unfortunately, that's now water under the bridge."

Garridan finally understood Mathias's importance for this council meeting. He couldn't decide if the councilman's demise would prove to be a blessing or a curse. "And my concerns?"

"The faeries are everlasting, as you pointed out. Their

concept of time differs from our own. They may request aid decades down the road. Perhaps not even in our lifetime. By then, God willing, we would have ample time to replenish our fighting force and crops."

Garridan sat back in his chair, silent as he struggled to process the past half hour.

Edric smiled in sad appreciation. "I want you to think on this. That is all I ask. As the captain of my guard, it is important to me that you understand why I am pushing for this. I am no longer willing to send the young men of my kingdom out for slaughter if there is help out there to be had. Nor am I willing to have my people starve when resources exist, unorthodox as they may be."

The returned resolve and strength in Edric's voice gave the king's words more weight. This was not a man making a rash, premature decision, but one who consistently earned the trust of his people by refusing to let their society deteriorate in the face of adversity. And in reality, if Edric wanted to do this, it was going to happen whether Garridan agreed or not. He appreciated that the king was willing to hear his opinion on the matter.

"I am hesitant to agree, but you have my support, as always," Garridan said grudgingly.

The king smiled. "That is all I can hope for at this time. I will need that support when we face my advisors on the matter." Garridan laughed, and then sobered when the king's word choice sunk in.

"You want me to come to that meeting?" His tone made the king chuckle. Garridan did not think anything was funny.

"I need every ally I can get, not just Eyad. Three days from now, ten in the morning."

"I'm—"

"And in the meantime, speak with the Marshal—and get that shoulder looked at by the healers. You look like you are in pain. If this is approved, I will need you in good health."

The king made a shooing gesture. Garridan stood, perplexed. He barely remembered to bow to his king before turning to leave.

"Oh, and Captain."

Garridan stopped, afraid of what he was going to hear.

"Let us keep this conversation to ourselves, shall we? No use working the masses into a state prematurely. We both know Darson is incapable of ignoring a potential scandal."

Garridan nodded.

"Good man."

* * *

An hour later, the captain, still shell-shocked, stood at the doors of the infirmary. He didn't quite remember the walk there. His mind was still floating somewhere in that study, replaying the last half of the conversation. Trying and failing to process the unpleasant task he'd been given.

He was supposed to be on leave. And why was it necessary to drag him to an advisors' meeting? Honestly, as if his presence was going to sway the minds of men whose stubbornness rivaled that of a group of angry, obstinate goats. Even if they did come around and agree to send a request for assistance to the faeries—who made it a point to have nothing to do with humans—the chances of help actually happening were so ridiculously small that ... well, he wasn't sure numbers that abysmal even existed.

He would bet his wages for the next five years they'd send *him* to test the waters.

"It will never work," Garridan said out loud. He received an odd look from a woman passing by on the path, and he smiled weakly at her.

The infirmary was nestled next to the outer stone wall of the city, an antiquated old building of board and batten brown wood. The space inside was open and accessible, with raftered ceilings and a scarred wooden floor. A handful of patients were scattered among the narrow, low beds lining the walls. He spotted Foster asleep in one of the cots, along with a few more of his men.

Old and young women alike moved steadily about, hair tied or braided behind their backs and hands filled with bandages, fresh linens, and medical supplies. They wore simple long dresses and lace-up boots that made the floorboards groan with their steps.

A young nurse slowed to a stop a few feet from him, one hand holding a basket of small towels and the other fussing with her hair. She looked from the top of his head to his boots, and a faint blush covered her cheeks. It took her a moment to make eye contact with him.

"May I help you, sir?"

"I need the assistance of a healer, my lady," Garridan said politely. The girl flushed more deeply before dropping a small curtsy. He smiled slightly as she walked away on quick feet, still touching a hand to the top of her head to smooth back her blonde hair. Normally, Garridan would be flattered. He was distantly aware that a disturbing number of women tended to do that around him: flush and look down, or sometimes edge closer. God only knew why; he doubted he smelled pleasant half the time. Now, he was just sore, tired, hungry, and full of a long mental list of complaints.

As Garridan sat in one of the wooden chairs by the main doors to wait, feeling his shoulder twinge in protest, he began to realize how little time he spent in the city. He only recognized a few of the healers, those who had treated his wounds before. Everyone he passed outside earlier, he couldn't place. For the past five or six years, Garridan's life had revolved around his job; he hardly had the time or—truthfully, the inclination—to return a pretty girl's smile or pursue the hint of attraction he felt for someone every so often.

"Captain?"

Garridan looked up and schooled his pensive expression. The head healer stood before him; she was a tall, imposing woman with long blonde hair threaded through with silver.

"Hello, Helena," Garridan said, cheering up his tone to match his smile.

Helena didn't try to disguise the urge to roll her eyes. She did embrace him carefully. "I suppose I should just be grateful that you're still alive."

"You and me both."

"Let's take a look at you." She waved him along, and Garridan followed her to an empty, clean bed in a corner of the infirmary's main hall. He sat obediently and didn't bother keeping his face blank as she cut away the bandage and probed the wound.

"Still bleeds," Helena muttered to herself. The broken skin was crusty and reddish brown with drying blood, and dirt still managed to cling to the torn edges.

Helena took a good look at him and realized the grime

was everywhere. "You're filthy."

"You are the second person in an hour to notice."

"I'm sure more people noticed. They were just too polite to say anything."

"No, they just stared a lot and pointed."

She frowned at him, ignoring the attempt at humor. "Why don't you get cleaned up before I stitch the wound. Use the wash in the back, change into a fresh pair of linens—you can return them later."

He got up and did as he was told, which admittedly was quite wonderful. Cleaning off proved to be more therapeutic than a massage, even though his shoulder ached tremendously afterward. He walked out of the washroom with wet, clean hair, wearing one of the patient linens and smelling better than he had in a long while.

"Good," Helena said. "Let's get you fixed up."

Receiving twenty stitches wasn't pleasant, but the company was. He liked Helena; he didn't necessarily care for how thorough she was at sanitizing all wounds, but he was certain he wouldn't have liked anyone else tending his. After the six years of their acquaintance, this woman knew more about him than anyone else in the city did. She handled the delicacy of the first situation that had brought him to her with the utmost discretion. Long after it was over, she continued to heal both physical and emotional wounds as a mother would for a son. He never knew how to repay her for the kindness she had shown to his then small family.

"I'm not sure how to interpret that vaguely satisfied look on your face," Garridan commented with another wince as she threaded the needle through his skin. "Sometimes I question your reasoning for becoming a healer."

"Didn't I tell you?" Helena replied absently, eyes engrossed on her task. "I became one to legally inflict pain since I couldn't join the military. It had nothing to do with income."

"We have something in common, then."

The comment startled a laugh out of the older woman. "I'll bet you just kept hacking away within an inch of your life after you received this."

"Naturally. And the Erepos weren't even digging into my shoulder with their fingers."

"Quit your bawling," she chastised. "Heard nothing but complaints from any of you today. Your boy Foster thinks he's just about lame with that knee of his. You'd think it was sawed in half."

Garridan chuckled. "He didn't say much earlier, but he has a different audience now. Did Averi stop in for his back injury?"

Helena's eyebrows drew down as she frowned. "No. I haven't seen him today. I can check the records, but your brood came in around the same time, and I wouldn't have missed that cheerful loudmouth."

Of course not. The captain held in his exasperation. Thyme didn't recommend the infirmary for the hell of it; if Averi needed to go, then it stood to reason he'd risk an infection or further injury by ignoring it. He might pay the soldier a visit in a day or two.

Garridan jumped when she swiped a corner of the gash with the wet cloth after finishing a stitch, and then stared at her when she swatted his arm. "Your bedside manner is one of a kind."

"I get the job done—when my patients don't wriggle like a fish on a hook. One more. Here, Tabitha." Helena stopped the young blonde nurse and handed her a wrapped-up towel containing used cloths from cleaning the wound. "Dispose of this for me. Change that bandage frequently, Garridan, and keep the wound clean, understand? It's not something to trifle with, given the condition of their weapons. The last thing you need is metal poisoning."

"Yes, ma'am."

"Are you telling me that to shut me up, or do I have to send one of the ugliest nurses I have to remind you?"

"You don't have ugly nurses," Garridan said, and winked at Tabitha as she took her sweet time to dispose of the materials. The nurse smiled and looked away shyly, hurrying off. Garridan and Helena shared a chuckle.

"Turn these girls upside down, every time you come here."

"As filthy as I get? Hardly."

Helena scoffed as she put her equipment away. "You could come in covered head to toe in mud, and they'd offer to wash it off you. Let's get your arm secure." She took a wide, square cloth, folded it, and leaned in close to wrap it around him to cradle his injured shoulder. "Still keeping that little cottage to yourself?"

His lips quirked, already clued in to her verbal prodding. "Of course."

"A lot of nice, smart young girls working around here."

"I do not doubt it."

"I'm sure homecomings would be even sweeter with someone welcoming you back."

Garridan, still amused, made eye contact with her. "Don't I know it. But time is not something I have a lot of here at home."

Helena fussed with the sling until his arm looked secure

enough. "Been five years since she passed," she murmured.

He looked down to the floor as he stood. "I am aware."

She sighed a little. "I know what you lost, but don't let that—"

"Thank you for your assistance, Helena." He kissed her cheek and gave her a watered-down smile. "I always appreciate it. I'll be back to get the stitches out."

"Be gentle on that arm."

After receiving a draught for pain, the captain left the infirmary and dragged himself home, more exhausted after Helena's well-intentioned conversation than he'd felt after the morning's battle. He didn't care to dwell on the details of his love life—thinking about it twice in one day was more than enough.

Garridan's small cottage came into view. The cottages around his were decorated with colorful curtains, beds of flowers, and curling vines climbing up trellises. He was never home enough to tend to his own place, so the front was left bare.

Years back, a mutt of a dog would have welcomed him with slobbering kisses, a woman with kisses of a different kind; now, nothing but cool darkness greeted him. When she disappeared, their short, furry companion—her birthday gift all those years ago—had to go, too. He no longer had the time or the heart to care for the puppy.

Garridan bypassed the eating area entirely, despite his stomach's growling protest, and instead made a beeline for the most inviting bed he'd seen in two months. Although it was only late afternoon, he fell asleep minutes after pulling his off his boots and propping up his shoulder.

He dreamed of the family he'd once had, long out of his

reach.

<h1 style="text-align:center">Chapter 4</h1>

Naula, the northern moon, gave Laurus's stone walls a ghostly white glow, pitching deep shadows in narrow pathways that wound through darkened cottages. The moonlight fell over the deserted courtyard market, vendors having long since packed up their wares and left for home.

A lone stable boy led a pony into the stables, where warm golden light and a bed of hay beckoned. The boy murmured softly to the animal, his calm crooning and the soft clip-clop of hooves a tranquil harmony in the night air.

Soothing light also glowed dimly from the infirmary. Inside, a young nurse walked quietly past the patient cots, checking the breathing of an ailing elderly man, listening carefully to the congested cough of a young girl, smoothing blankets and feeling for fevers.

The head healer sat at a desk situated by the front doors, massaging the small of her back as she finished filling in the register of a patient on her list from earlier in the day; Captain Garridan, needing stitches for a shoulder wound. She was thankful that was all he needed, considering how long he'd been in the military. Was he thirty-two now? My, how time flew. The boy—man—had worked himself to the bone for years to keep the kingdom safe. Helena smiled to herself as she remembered the fuss among her nurses when he appeared; the young captain was a favorite. And why not? Tall, broad shouldered—cleaned up, his skin held a nice warm tan and looked as smooth as a baby's, where it wasn't scarred. Her long married heart had given its own flutter and fuss when he came back to her after washing up with his dark-brown hair swept back from his face, leaving his handsome features bare and bringing the focus to his startling blue eyes. She already knew he could find any sweet young woman to share a life with, but God knew how long it'd take him to try it again.

Helena sighed and attempted to move on to the next patient on her list, squinting at her own words for the umpteenth time. Reading by lamplight was increasingly difficult as of late. It was about time to give in her daughter's nagging and invest in a pair of spectacles. Rubbing at her eyes, Helena squeezed them shut and pushed back from the desk. This could wait until morning. Callie had everything under control; it was time to go home.

Helena stood slowly, biting back a groan. She stretched and caught Callie's eye as the night nurse made a round past her.

The young woman smiled and nodded, a silent go-ahead to leave. The healer waved good-night and rounded the corner of her desk.

Wood creaked, loud and startling. The main doors swung open, bringing in a rush of fragrant air.

A tall figure leaned in the doorframe, its pale arm and hand braced on the door to keep it open.

Helena breathed through her nose, pushing back the mild

irritation at her now-delayed departure. She couldn't quite make out who it was—though it was definitely male. When the individual didn't move, she called out. "May I help you?"

The man seemed to rouse himself. He withdrew almost wearily from the door, walking slowly. He dragged his feet as if moving was painful. Seeing his difficulty, Helena went forward.

"Don't need you passing out in the doorway, now," she admonished. She clasped a hand on the cold, clammy skin of his forearm. Flu perhaps—or, she thought once the smell of alcohol hit her, a case of too much drinking. Once she got a better look, her eyebrows rose in recognition. "Averi? You look terrible."

The soldier attempted a weak smile. Glassy brown eyes met hers but appeared to look right through her. "Say the sweetest things." His voice was slurred and faint, and he was making a visible effort to expel the words.

Helena sighed. She wrapped an arm around his waist and helped him inside, grunting softly when he leaned more weight on her than she expected. She felt the muscles in his stomach and back spasm at her touch; heat radiated from his upper body.

"Nauseated, my dear?" she asked.

Averi groaned. "I can't eat anything. Just comes right back up. What's wrong with me?" he asked miserably.

"My best guess is too much alcohol."

He shook his head, his sweaty hair brushing against her neck. "Felt off all day. Only had a few, then went home. Got worse."

Helena's lips pursed. "Might be flu. God knows the places you boys stay in aren't the cleanest. In that case, I'll move you to a room. Can't have our recovering patients catching a nasty bug from you."

"Just need to sit down," he mumbled. His head leaned on the top of hers, surprising her. She felt a twinge of sympathy. What an awful illness to catch the day back from a long tour.

Averi was nearly dead weight by the time Helena got him through the open door of a sick room sequestered off to a corner of the infirmary. He breathed shakily, and his free hand clutched his stomach. The soldier collapsed on the lone cot in the middle of the tiny room.

Helena pressed the back of her wrist to the hot, sweaty skin of his forehead. Out of habit, she smiled when his tired brown eyes rolled up to meet hers. A trembling hand came up to lightly rest on her arm.

"Sorry." His teeth chattered now. "… so late."

"That's what we're here for," she countered. "Sit tight. If you need to vomit, use the bucket. I'll be back." She patted his hand and turned to leave.

Averi's hand suddenly convulsed on her smaller one. The grip was surprisingly strong, considering how sick he appeared to be. She turned to stare at him. He gazed back, almost as surprised as she.

Helena smiled as unexpected tension rippled up her spine.

Averi let go of her hand with a mumbled apology.

She pulled the garbage bucket over to the cot and left, shaking off the unease his sudden movement gave her. She searched the infirmary for the night nurse, eyes darting over the sleeping forms of other patients.

She spotted the girl walking toward her from the far end of the room. "Callie," Helena called softly. "Mix a stomach tonic for me, please. Got one who might have the flu."

The girl glanced sympathetically at the dim light cascading out of the sick room. "I'll boil some water, too."

Helena grabbed a blanket and pillow from the storage closet along with a small cloth she dampened with cool water. Returning to the room, she found Averi curled on his side, clutching his stomach, emitting low, quiet moans. A quick glance inside the bucket told her he hadn't thrown up.

"When did it get this bad?"

It took him a moment to answer. His voice finally came out, cracked and pained. "Few hours ago. Started … afternoon. Ate … felt sick. Went out, thought it'd stop … had to leave. Tried sleeping. Couldn't. Threw up. Just … awful. Like—" Averi gripped the bed weakly and pulled himself up enough to hang his head over the side. He dry heaved, torso contorting as the sound hit the air.

Helena used the opportunity to slip the pillow under his head. She laid a hand on his back and rubbed soothing circles as he retched. Liquid sloshed into the bucket and she peered over his hunched form to take a look.

Blood mixed with stomach acid spattered the inside of the wooden bucket, raining down the side and staining the wood. Another retch from Averi, and more scarlet drops hit the bottom. Helena realized she needed to reevaluate his illness.

"Averi, what did you eat and drink?" she asked.

His response was a long, low groan as he shifted to lie on his back, his eyes closed and breathing labored. Sweat glistened on his forehead and neck in the lamplight.

Helena took the dampened cloth and laid it over his searing forehead, murmuring comforting nothings as she watched his entire body tense and relax intermittently. After assessing all the symptoms, she became more uncertain of her initial diagnosis.

She took a closer look at his skin. The color had positively leeched out of him; that was obvious even in the golden lamplight. Blue veins stood out in stark relief down his arms, in his hands, and at his temples. His teeth clenched. Wheezing breaths whistled out of his nose.

A memory from earlier that day churned up suddenly. "Averi, weren't you supposed to come in about a back injury?" He didn't answer, but Helena wanted to check, nonetheless. Perhaps that would provide some answers.

She pulled up his shirt and then swallowed a hiss at the raw, scraped skin of the lower right section of his back. A salve, presumably applied by the unit healer, glistened over the torn flesh; blood wept in a rash-like pattern where the tearing went into deeper tissue. Foolish boy, she thought angrily. Any manner of infection could have snuck its way in on the journey home, or anytime that day.

Helena let the shirt fall and waited for Callie; when the nurse entered the room, she needed to fetch another ointment to give that wound a deep clean, bandage it, and then make him comfortable. They'd do what they could and then pray it made a difference.

Averi vomited again. The healer braced a hand on his shoulder to keep him from pitching off the cot. Dread curled up in her stomach as more blood and some digested food hit the bin. Whatever this was, it was starting to look as if he might not make it through the night.

She cupped one sweaty cheek and then lifted his right shut eyelid and peered closely into the glassy iris. The pupils were bloodshot, the whites completely overtaken with a shiny pink haze, and wispy red lines surrounded the dark iris.

Fear jumped in Helena's stomach. No; it meant nothing. He was just a sick boy. Aggressive vomiting would do that.

But the fear that gripped her wasn't for him. It was for herself.

What is wrong with me?

It couldn't be—

No. Helena wrestled the ludicrous notion away. Impossible. All soldiers were checked thoroughly before reentry. It was not possible for that to come here, to invade these city walls. He'd picked up a nasty infection out in the field. The king's boys trekked all over the kingdom, eating at poorer villages where illness from rotted meat was as common as a cold. Or the injury had something to do with it.

"Averi?" she asked quietly. Motion in the doorway caught her eye. Relieved, she beckoned the nurse in. "Callie is here with something to help settle your stomach."

There was no response as Callie came in carrying a small black pot of steaming water, the freshly brewed tonic tucked underneath one arm. She set the pot and a dry cloth on the wooden counter and uncapped the brew.

"We are going to sit you up so you can drink this."

It took both women to lift the nearly unresponsive soldier to a sitting position. His head slumped forward, and Helena lifted his chin up, feeling the tension in his jaw as his teeth clenched.

"His shirt, Helena. Perhaps he should change."

The healer looked down. Dried vomit clung to the bottom of his shirt.

"All right, then. Let's get this shirt off, Averi, we'll get you something clean in a minute."

Getting him out of the shirt was slow going; they pulled it over his head when he barely responded to their commands. A fine sheen of sweat covered Averi's chest and arms. His eyes rolled about, barely registering the women, before his eyelids went down again. Callie braced him with a hand on his bicep.

Helena grasped the young man's chin when his head began to slump forward. "All right, Averi. Stay awake long enough to take the tonic."

Something firm and warm grasped her wrist. The healer jolted when she realized it was Averi's hand. His fingers clamped tightly around her arm.

"I need you to open your mouth for me," Callie said calmly. "This will soothe your stomach." She held the tonic, hesitating, dark eyes watching his reaction carefully.

The night nurse's placid voice continued in a murmur, and Helena stayed silent as she watched Averi, hyper aware of his grip. He did not respond to Callie's voice, but his entire body went rigid. Sweat glistened as it rolled down the side of his neck. The grip on her arm tightened, and she swallowed convulsively.

She thought of the injuries on Averi's lower back again.

"Callie, hold his chin," she said absently.

Helena used her free hand to squeeze in between their adjoined limbs. She gingerly pushed down the waistband of Averi's pants to reassess the wound, her eyes straining in the dim light.

"Should have come in earlier," she murmured with a shake of her head. She stared at more of the same chafed skin, redness, and speckles of blood.

Low on his hipbone, though, the outer bruising was ugly.

A small abrasion, no larger than half a gold piece, oozed puss. Fresh. Not a blade injury. Rounder, with some kind of small, dark indentation. It looked like—

"Is this a bite?" she whispered.

Callie gasped. Helena's head whipped up.

Averi jerked his chin out of Callie's fingertips. A snarl rumbled from his chest. The man's body thrummed with sudden tension, and his head turned to the warm-blooded body leaning into him.

Helena did not feel the teeth tear into the soft, tender flesh of her neck until Callie screamed.

Blood poured from her neck. The breath tore out of her throat in gasps. Her hand fluttered to her neck like a haphazard butterfly, grasping weakly, fumbling for the dark head at her shoulder. Callie's screams were distant and down a long tunnel.

I'm bleeding, she thought. *I am going to bleed to death.*

The world barreled back in—Callie's shrieks were in her ear, raw like an exposed nerve. The noises coming out of Averi's throat were hungry and obscene.

Helena's throat gurgled as she tried to scream, terror pumping hot as the blood coursed down her neck. Averi worried at her flesh like a vicious dog with a piece of meat, and Helena reared back, panicked and desperate to fling him off, but he gripped her tighter. The man's teeth remained fastened as his weight fell on her, and they both tumbled to the ground.

* * *

Helena's blue eyes stared sightlessly at the ceiling, and Callie couldn't pull her eyes away from the obscenity in front of her.

It took tremendous effort to stop screaming once common sense pushed its way past utter hysteria. Callie could not control the sobs hitching in her throat. In the sudden quiet of the room—other than the execrable sounds of Averi *eating* Helena—Callie became painfully aware of her proximity and his speed. Hands shaking, she dared to look away from him at the partially open door.

Shouts of alarm sounded from the greater part of the infirmary, but she didn't hear them. The dull, wet snap of Helena's neck as Averi tore into it with his teeth and hands made Callie flinch and swallow another cry.

Averi finally let go of Helena's broken neck, and his head fell back, a piece of flesh dangling from his lips. For an eerie moment, as Callie's breath shuddered and her body tensed to flee, the room was deathly quiet. He sat crouched on the prone woman's chest like an animal with its prey. Blood ran down his chin, splattered onto his pale face. His eyes gazed at the ceiling, and a trembling grin touched the painted, scarlet mouth.

A keening, alien howl tore out of Averi's throat.

Callie's terror instinctively answered with a cry of its own.

The man's gaze snapped over to her.

She darted for the door as Averi shot off Helena, flying on all fours around the cot after her.

She sprinted as the turned soldier closed in fast. Callie wheezed and sobbed, feet pounding on the wood as she passed patient beds in her race for the doors. *You can't go outside*, her mind shouted, *he is sick, you will lead him to the people!*

The little girl in the cot closest to the healer's desk sat huddled in her bed, clasping hands over her ears and crying. Callie heard her and almost hesitated in her trajectory. Two patients climbed out of bed, shouting, and a few more ran for the infirmary's back door.

As Callie rounded a corner and her side clipped a chair, the wood slammed into her waist and sent her stumbling. A heavy weight hurtled onto her back and knocked her to the ground.

"No! Oh, no, please *please*, stop! Stop!" Callie's terrified pleas ended in wailing as Averi held her down and began to feed.

Horrified yells and screams of agony rang in the air outside the infirmary.

Naula shone down indifferently.

Chapter 5

The heavy *bam!* of a fist pounding into wood cracked sharply in the still, early morning.

Garridan's eyes opened drowsily.

The fist pounded into his front door again in rapid, urgent succession.

He sat up in bed and flung off the covers. A cry of pain escaped him as his shoulder screamed at the movement. Bare feet fell to the floor, and he sat, teeth grinding, as the torn muscles throbbed from the rude awakening. The pain shocked the fatigue out of his system. Trying to ignore it, Garridan grabbed a dagger from the bedside table with his good hand and tucked it in the waistband of his sleep trousers. Hand hovering over the weapon, he went to the front door.

"Can I help you?" he called.

"It's me."

Darson's curt tone made Garridan swiftly open the door. The other man's expression was grim.

"Get dressed."

"Why?"

"I'll explain, but time is something we are lacking."

Garridan realized he needed to undo the sling to change

shirts, and set about the surprisingly difficult task. When Darson saw his fruitless efforts, he breathed out of his nose impatiently and began the task of removing the sling to help Garridan dress.

"I woke up around half an hour ago," Darson said as he loosened the white cloth. Garridan hissed as he tugged the shirt off one-handed, minding the taut arm.

"I heard a racket next door, at the neighbors'. Went to see what the trouble was." He yanked out one of Garridan's drawers and grabbed a clean white shirt, then helped Garridan pull his bad arm through the sleeve.

Garridan was alarmed by the troubled look on Darson's face. The man was carefully weighing his words before he said them, as if worried about how Garridan would take them.

"The infirmary came under attack a few hours ago," Darson finally said.

He momentarily forgot the pain in his shoulder. *"How?"*

"Someone was bitten."

The news punched Garridan's heart. His mind raced in a flurry of awful imaginings, filling in the blanks with macabre images. He knew the horror of attacks out in the field; he could not imagine confining all that blood and terror in an enclosed space. With ill victims.

Frantic now, he grabbed at the cloth for the sling, but Darson kept his grip on it and told him to stand still before putting the sling back into place.

Garridan's mind searched to make sense of it. How did a bitten individual get in?

Oh, God.

Of course.

"Who?" Garridan demanded as bile and acid churned in his stomach.

"I do not know," Darson admitted as he tied the cloth at Garridan's shoulder. "I couldn't glean much from a very choppy, emotional explanation. I came to tell you before heading there." He paused. "The neighbor who woke me is Helena's daughter."

It hurt to ask. Each syllable added a weight to his chest. "Helena?"

Out of the corner of his eye, he saw Darson nod.

Grief closed a fist around Garridan's heart.

"I'm sorry," Darson said quietly.

Garridan closed his eyes, and for a moment he allowed the sorrow of her passing to course through him—and then felt it shift to anger and confusion over the incident. *How did this happen to her?*

"I am assuming, otherwise you would have told me, that the infection did not leave the infirmary," Garridan said tonelessly.

"I cannot absolutely confirm that," Darson answered. "Which is why we must go."

Garridan followed Darson quickly down the path from his cottage and farther into the heart of the city. Many homes were still dark; birds chirped in the pre-dawn air. Thin ribbons of deep purple and scarlet stretched along the horizon.

He could feel Darson sneaking looks at him as they drew nearer to the infirmary. He didn't push it, though, and Garridan silently thanked Darson for exercising some restraint. It was far easier to slide into the mentality he reserved for battle and traveling through Erepo-infested terrain; that was an alert, cold space that kept him vigilant and alive. He could not think of Helena now, or the other victims. He trusted the home guard had already taken precautions, and he hoped those had been enough; otherwise, they had a hell of a problem on their hands.

God, let it be under control. What happened at Porphys could not happen here.

Raised voices reached them from the next block over. Words were unclear, but the thread of panic, anger, and grief in each tone was apparent. The men accelerated their pace. The infirmary came within sight, and Garridan braced himself for the worst.

Laurus's home guardsmen stood and barricaded the infirmary doors. A group of civilians crowded them. Family members of those inside were shouting while soldiers tried to calm and control them.

One of the guards spotted Darson and Garridan, and his face lit with recognition. He turned to speak to another soldier behind him, who then disappeared.

"What happened?" Garridan demanded flatly as they approached the guard.

The infirmary door opened, and Captain Radley stepped out.

"I was in the process of sending for you. The bitten was one of yours. I am rounding up your men as we speak."

"It stayed within the infirmary?" Garridan asked.

"We are fortunate enough for that. One of your injured is responsible for keeping it within the walls." Radley's face was stony; exhaustion showed in his eyes. He looked vaguely sick. "Barred the doors from the inside and beat the infected to death with the broken leg of a chair. I am not discounting that, Garridan; if he hadn't acted that quickly, we might have lost the whole city by this afternoon.

"We need to speak to Thyme, seeing as he missed something pretty damn important. I need you and your lieutenant here inside and checked over by another healer."

"I can arrange …" Garridan began to offer help, but then shut his mouth at the look Radley gave him.

"I would love for you to handle this. However, it is at the front door of *my* jurisdiction, so your problem is now *my* problem."

Garridan tried not to let Radley's biting tone offend him—this was not the time to let petty competition and dislike control his emotions—but that did not stop frustration from whispering its pestering nothings in the back of his mind. "What *can* we do?" he asked patiently.

"Submit to a search so we can make damn sure the crisis is over."

Darson's face filled with confusion. "The incubation period—"

"I do not care if we are past the incubation period," Radley snapped. "Every member of the unit *will* be searched again. A handful of patients fled before the doors were locked and cannot be found. We don't know if they were bitten or not. I spent an hour going through the patient log, figuring out who was missing—we are still tracking them down."

Guilt and regret soured Garridan's stomach. He tasted the acid in his mouth. "You are absolutely correct. Every man needs to be accounted for. Who was infected, and who killed him?"

"Foster. The infected was Averi."

Darson cursed. Garridan felt horror worm its way through

him. Thyme had cleared Averi. Well hell, he'd cleared all of them. How could he have missed it? Never had the man made a mistake like this, not in all the years Garridan had served in the royal guard, or beforehand, to his knowledge. He could not reconcile Thyme's unblemished service as a healer and … *this*.

He recalled his conversation with Helena. Averi never went to the infirmary, at least not before the incubation period had ended. Or did he? There was a whole afternoon and evening unaccounted for, and for all he knew, Averi went in—but was he thoroughly checked? Helena or one of her nurses would surely have caught it.

Should have tracked him down and made him go, Garridan thought, feeling both helpless and angry with himself.

Radley, visibly spent, tugged a hand through his short hair. "The marshal is going to want answers. I want this to go as smoothly as possible, for everyone involved. Your cooperation would be greatly appreciated."

"You have our cooperation, Captain," Garridan said. Darson remained quiet.

Radley turned on his heel, expecting them to follow him inside.

They could smell the blood at the doors.

The home guard captain stepped to the side. Garridan and Darson's eyes immediately fell on the blood streaking the bright wood floor. Red splatters speckled the lower right wall opposite Helena's desk. A broken chair lay on its side in the aisle. One of the legs lay discarded by the front door, no doubt jammed through the handles of the doors to keep the infection in.

Patients sat up in their beds, visibly shaken, some crying.

Soldiers attempted to calm the sick, and a few military healers ensured their conditions were not aggravated. Garridan noticed two beds were missing near the front.

"Averi attacked two patients before Foster could subdue him," Radley explained. "The beds were…soiled. The bodies have been moved to the sick room where it started. While we wait for your unit, I am moving you to another room to be examined."

"I would like to see Averi first," Garridan requested solemnly.

Radley looked at him for a long moment, then nodded tersely. He opened the door to a small stone enclosure where garbage was disposed and then later carried off; the two missing beds were by a large trash bin, frames broken, mattresses stained with blood.

Two bodies wrapped in cloth lay prone on the ground, guarded by another grim soldier. Radley pointed to the one closest to the beds.

Garridan crouched down. Radley ordered the soldier to pull back the cloth and, with a neutral expression, the soldier did so.

Only years of intimate encounters with such a sight kept Garridan from heaving up the contents of his stomach. He regretted squatting so close, and braced his position with a hand on the ground as the smell alone dizzied his senses. The acerbic bite of blood choked the immediate air around him; the bitter taste coated his tongue.

Darson made an unintelligible noise. Garridan sensed more than saw him turn away, and he heard the man quickly suppress a gag.

He could not see Averi in that ruined face. The dirty, blood-matted blond hair gave him the faintest clue; beyond that, the caved-in mess of tissue, bone, and torn skin turned his soldier into any number of doomed men who died violently. A rush of emotion closed Garridan's throat. He placed his hand on a tuft of blond hair and cast out a mental prayer for Averi's soul and his family.

Garridan's shoulders tensed when Radley moved behind him. Hearing a rustle of cloth, he turned his head, and his gaze fell on the body of a young nurse. He looked away sharply, took a deep breath, and forced himself to take a longer look at her ruined body. If Radley saw this fit enough as punishment—and oh, but did that vindictive action burn a hot fire in Garridan's gut, due or not—then Garridan would swallow his pride and take his medicine.

Her pretty features had endured the attack, her brown eyes half lidded as if roused from sleep. Below the chin, however, the slim neck was split and spread open in a crude mimicry of a dissection. Instead of the neat cut of a knife, teeth marks ravaged her skin, bits of tendon and muscle pulled out in strings like fingers dug into a chicken's breast for the tender meat.

"She knew what was happening when we eased her passing," Radley said, going for neutral and failing. "She cried, apologized, and asked where Helena was."

Garridan's flat hand on the stone became a fist. The rough surface needled the skin of his knuckles. More needles slid into his heart.

After an age, Radley asked, "Ready?"

The captain rose slowly, fixed the other man with a flat, steely stare, and wordlessly trailed back into the infirmary, unsurprised that Darson had already retreated to the door.

The lieutenant looked at Averi and the nurse as the other soldier covered their faces again with cloth.

Radley led them to a guarded door across the room and ushered the pair inside.

The room was not empty.

Foster sat on a cot, back hunched as he curled forward with his head in his hand. The bloodied hand clutching his sandy-blond locks shook. Every so often, the tremor would move through his entire body.

"Why is he in here?" Garridan asked quietly.

"To be debriefed by Illiad," Radley responded, referring to the marshal who oversaw all military divisions.

"He's not under quarantine, is he?" Darson asked, and then cleared his throat when the words came out rusty.

"It is standard procedure," Radley said flatly. "Foster, your captain is here," he called.

The young man's head shot up. He looked terrible. Tear tracks stained his face. His gaze did not rest on Garridan for very long; it darted from Darson, to Radley, to the floor, and then jumped back to Garridan. Foster was a resilient, exceptional soldier. This shaken, pale young man was a far cry from that.

"Why is he still in those clothes?" Darson asked, unable to contain the censure in his tone.

"How are you, Foster?" Garridan asked.

Foster's mouth opened and closed without a sound. He shook his head and then ran fingers through his hair that left pale red streaks. The front of his shirt was stained scarlet. He finally found his voice, and it came out rough. "Captain. He got—Averi got to Helena and …the nurse, I can't remember her name. I can't … and two other patients before I could bar the door and get him down on the floor. Couldn't let him leave. One was a little …" He shook his head again fiercely, as if to shake the images out. "My knee buckled on my way to him, before I could stop it."

"It's fine." Garridan lifted his hand in a placating gesture to stop the babble tumbling out of the man's mouth. "You did well. You acted fast, and you saved the lives of a lot of people today."

"Not fast, even when I heard screaming. I didn't even see Averi come in. I didn't know it was him until after I …"

Darson squeezed past Radley and Garridan and went to Foster, easing down on the cot. He spoke softly and firmly to the soldier. His eyes shot up to Garridan, questioning.

"This is your show, Radley," Garridan said, implying Darson's unspoken question.

The home guard captain sighed heavily. "I will fetch my unit's healer to check you both out. Stay put. I mean it, Captain."

Garridan watched as Radley left.

Images of the young woman's face and Averi's remains surfaced in his mind's eye. *Short of checking every man yourself, you would not have known,* he told himself as the guilt surged forward again.

How did so many obstacles get thrown in the way of the bite getting noticed? It *was* Porphys all over again: the perfect storm of misinterpretations, neglect, and timing. Half a dozen points of entry to halt the slow slide to slaughter, and every one of them bypassed by fate.

Do not go down this road.

He focused on Darson's voice and heard, "Rather than focusing on what lives you could not save, I need you to think about who you *did* save. Over a dozen patients. And everyone outside these walls."

"I know. I just … Helena was … she didn't deserve that. And the nurse, when she—Callie. Her name was Callie. Should never have come to them, you know?"

"I know."

"Not a single one of us died in two months, and I just bludgeon Averi to death."

"It was not Averi anymore," Garridan said, knowing it was an inadequate response. Garridan knew firsthand how awful it was to take down a comrade and kill him before he feasted on someone else. How soul crushing it was to give the command to do so, much less be the one holding the weapon. He walked over and made sure Foster was looking at him. "We all know the risk we run on those tours. It was everyone's misfortune the bite was missed. But I can promise you this will never happen again. How is your knee?"

All three glanced down at Foster's left leg. Blood soaked through the cotton at the kneecap. Garridan smothered a sharp response.

The door opened, and Radley entered with the home guard's healer.

"The rest of your troop is arriving. I am moving them to the back sick rooms to be examined," Radley told him.

"If Foster has been cleared of infection, I believe he can be moved back to a regular patient bed," Garridan said.

"I will need the both of you to strip to your undergarments, please," the healer said with the fleeting hint of a professional smile.

"Oh, for God's sake," Darson muttered. "I think I would either be showing some symptoms or dead by now."

"We will," Garridan said before Darson could get another word in. "But not before Foster has been seen to. His knee injury has been severely aggravated."

The healer looked at Foster with a frown, and then nodded sharply. "Certainly. I will move him and retrieve help to assess him. Only a moment, Captain," he said in response to Radley's impatient expression. He helped Foster to a standing position, and the soldier leaned heavily on the lanky healer and hobbled along with his injured leg hanging mostly limp. "When I return," the healer called behind him as they left, "I expect you both to be in your undergarments."

"Why has Foster not been seen since the attack?" Garridan asked mildly. Underneath those calm waters, his insides had begun a slow boil. "Because it appears he was denied medical assistance for the injury that brought him here in the first place. Forcing him to sit in his bloody clothes with an exacerbated injury is not only irresponsible, it is unnecessarily cruel."

"Forgive my oversight," Radley said, a trifle mockingly. "It has been a difficult morning. In the chaos, Foster was simply overlooked, not maliciously denied."

"Choosing his room to put us in did not jog your memory?" Darson retorted.

Color splashed Radley's cheeks. He worked his jaw but remained silent.

He still had not responded when the door reopened and the healer came in. With a touch of exasperation, the healer said, "And we are still clothed. Gentlemen, please."

Darson fairly snarled at him and then viciously pulled off his shirt. It flew through the air, landing at Radley's feet. Trousers followed, landing with a heavy thump at the toes of the home captain's brown boots.

Radley looked down with a raised eyebrow before stepping on the trousers as he left the room.

Garridan turned to his comrade. "You are making this more difficult. Don't do that again."

"I'm sorry," Darson said, "But you saw the way he treated Foster. You know I can't stand him. He's a churlish maggot."

"I …" Garridan stopped, decided he couldn't form an appropriate response, and settled for sighing loudly.

Fifteen minutes and two thorough examinations later, the pair began to dress. Garridan took his time, selfishly wanting to avoid the situation that waited for them outside the door. Radley's words still rang in his head as he thought over the entire night's hellish events. He imagined Helena's terror and pain, and that poor young nurse surviving such a brutal attack only to be quietly killed for her injuries. He saw her face again and again. Averi had been in such good spirits yesterday morning, healthy and looking forward to seeing his father and sister. He was a joy to work with, optimistic by nature. He and Foster were good friends.

"Do you need some help fastening your pants like you did your sling? You seem to be having trouble. I can call Radley back here, and I'm sure he would be glad to help. You're just about his favorite person right now."

Garridan closed his eyes. "Dar, now is not the time. Averi is unrecognizable."

Darson sobered. "I know. Believe me. Let me continue coping through inappropriate humor. It's better for everyone. The other option is violence, and I think everyone here is frightened enough."

"When did you see Averi last?" Garridan asked. "Did he

go to the gathering at the tavern?"

"He was there, but not for long." Darson thought on it, and then shook his head with frustration. "I can't recall any odd behavior from him, other than his departure."

"He was supposed to stop at the infirmary as soon as we arrived," Garridan said quietly. Darson looked at him curiously. "His back injury. I don't know if he ever went. I cannot help but think …"

"Don't do that. The worst thing you could do is play that game. There are no winners. Let it be enough that he never made it out of the infirmary."

The door to the sick room opened, and both men looked up. A soldier looked in.

"Captain, your presence is requested in the palace."

His head began to pound. No doubt it was the marshal, and perhaps the king, wanting answers. *I'm not ready for this.*

The guard added, "Your troop has been cleared of infection."

"Excellent," Darson said brightly as Garridan looked on in dismay. "Can *I* go?"

"No. Captain Radley wishes to speak with you, Lieutenant."

"Oh, this day just gets more magnificent by the minute."

"Do not get yourself in trouble," Garridan warned.

Darson walked out with Garridan. The captain made the mistake of glancing into the first sick room.

Three bodies lay on the floor, white sheets draped over their forms. Blood saturated the white cotton at the stomach area of one and the upper body of another. The second was painfully tiny. A healer crouched by the third figure. She slowly pulled a sheet over the body, almost reverently. The material billowed softly in the air as it dropped. Garridan was momentarily mesmerized by the serene movement of the sheet as it fell and settled on Helena's face, hiding the features and long blonde hair.

Sorrow ached dully in his chest.

"Garridan. The king," Darson reminded, his voice unusually kind.

Garridan looked away and passed Radley without comment. A few of his soldiers called to him, and he acknowledged them without thinking before the infirmary doors closed behind him.

Chapter 6

Garridan stood at the foot of the palace steps, tired, stomach twisting, and grossly underdressed.

With a grudging sigh, he ignored the voice coaxing him to turn around and just go back to bed, and walked up the steps. He stopped at the door. One of the guards gave him a peculiar look as Garridan stood staring at the elaborately carved wooden entrance.

The more he thought about it, he realized it could very well be an emergency meeting he would walk into. It was naïve to think the king's most trusted advisors were not alerted of this incident. Precautionary measures had to be taken immediately; the public could not know what almost happened to them. Those who did know must be coerced into keeping their silence to avoid the spread of panic. It was a slippery slope, but Garridan had seen the disastrous results of a population in the grip of hysteria; that needed to be avoided at all costs in a city like Laurus. The king's advisory council functioned as the cogs that kept the wheel of the capitol turning smoothly, and their influence would be evident by midday.

Walking into a room full of the king's advisors would be the equivalent of dropping into a den of angry snakes. Garridan was the perfect shade of guilty for them at this point. No one liked to be woken up to hear that a disaster of apocalyptic proportions nearly befell a walled city; he sure as hell hadn't.

Garridan could only imagine what they would have to say when *he* walked in.

"I am quite certain the doors are not going to open for you, no matter how long you stare at them, Captain."

Garridan turned at the deep voice, disconcerted that he did not hear the stranger's approach. The newcomer, an aging gentleman of perhaps fifty, appraised him with a smile. He had brown hair sprinkled with silver and white, and was sharply dressed in a high-collared tunic and pristine trousers. He looked like a remnant from another time untouched by this generation's troubles.

It wasn't the man's fine clothes and carriage that gave away his identity; a combination of his convenient arrival and the odd sort of energy surrounding him did the trick. Garridan had only felt it once before; a faint hum of power disturbing the air around the man, like heat rippling over hot stone. Not unpleasant, but not altogether…human.

"Eyad," Garridan said evenly, mildly pleased with himself that he managed to smother his total surprise and absolute bother at being snuck up on.

What was the sorcerer doing here?

Did he know about last night? How would he, if he was not already in the area? Unless he was called here. But how does one go about calling a Craft member?

"A pleasure to see the captain of the king's division," the man said lightly. "From the way you are dubiously eyeing that door, I am guessing you were invited to this meeting, as well."

So it is a meeting, he thought. Wonderful. "It appears that way."

"I will accompany you, then. I, too, received a message from your king."

The information rankled. Why? The attack was a Laurus matter that should not concern a sorcerer—Garridan could not help but feel offended and highly suspicious. He did not want this man involved with their affairs in this capacity. Why would Edric want his counsel?

Eyad watched him with that disquieting smile. For a surreal moment, the captain wondered if Eyad had heard his thoughts somehow.

Garridan eyed the sorcerer. "May I ask a somewhat personal question?"

The sorcerer gestured in the affirmative.

"When did you arrive this morning? Your timing is uncanny."

"You are referring to last night's events."

Garridan's face settled to a nice, empty blankness. *Event* indeed. "Yes, I am referring to the purpose of this gathering."

"I was called here after the fact."

Somewhere between the hours of two or three in the morning and barely dawn, then. *Where were you, sorcerer, that your arrival is so prompt?* Garridan kept his peace as the guard ushered them inside the castle, but he held himself stiff next to the peculiar being. He recalled the only other conversation he ever had with the Craft member; almost three years ago, when he was promoted to captain of the royal guard. The reference to a *craft* actually meant very little to Garridan—he had no idea what in the world that entailed, where they lived, their numbers, or the capabilities a sorcerer possessed. Eyad could turn people into horses for all he knew, or command the elements, or awaken the dead. The only hint of otherness on the man was the aura he wore like cologne.

The only concrete reason for Eyad's presence involved something entirely different, which should not take place for a few days, unless Edric saw this as an opportunity.

Garridan's eyes widened. He couldn't look at Eyad as the notion blindsided him.

Surely the king would not bring up the faerie issue this morning? Of *all* days?

"You are here because the king wishes to approach the faeries for help," Garridan said slowly, almost to himself, tasting the words as the reality of them set in. "Aren't you?"

Surprise showed on the sorcerer's face in the form of one raised eyebrow. "Well, my boy, that would further explain your presence. He told you? And you do not agree?"

Garridan didn't bother trying to discern how Eyad came to that conclusion. He merely shook his head as they walked. The morning bustle of the castle's inner workings carried on around them in a subdued manner; quite a few conversations between palace staff took place in hushed tones. They watched Eyad and Garridan closely as they passed.

"Would it sway your opinion to know," Eyad said in an undertone, "that those wonderful creatures are immune to the bite of an Erepo?"

The captain stopped walking as it felt like a lead weight slammed into his chest. "Excuse me?" he demanded.

Eyad smiled faintly. "The fae cannot be turned; only gravely injured."

They could take a bite and live? Moreover, *not* spread the

infection? Envy and disbelief staggered Garridan. These creatures were humanity's mortal enemy; an enemy that imprisoned its prey behind wood and stone, cut them off from one another, nullified safe travel, and forever changed entire economies and ways of living.

And these faeries went untouched by it all because Erepos could not destroy them as completely as they had done humans. No wonder King Edric was so adamant about allying with them.

God clearly declared a favorite, Garridan thought bitterly.

"What is your role in this?" he asked after Eyad gestured to him to continue walking. "Do you send word to their leader? Do you speak to them on our behalf?" What *are* you to them?

"The easiest way would be just that," Eyad admitted, "approaching the queen and her princesses on your behalf myself. Unfortunately, I am bound by the restrictions of my stature. My level of involvement has to be as little as possible; the effort has to come from you."

Garridan's eyes narrowed.

"As I told the king, the best method is a small convoy bearing his message with my seal of approval," Eyad continued, hushing his voice when a few servants passed. "I was hoping, Captain…"

This was the sorcerer's idea of helping? Garridan thought incredulously. Planting the seed of the idea, and then stepping back without finishing the job? *What* restrictions?

Eyad turned to Garridan as they stopped by the thick, glossy wooden doors of the meeting room. Raised voices drifted to him from beyond the closed doors; not one sounded happy. "Knowing your skill and experience, I was initially planning to ask you, but seeing as you are injured, your health prevents that. In your place, I would like to ask if you have an idea for a few members of your rather elite unit to take on this unprecedented task. Should the council come to an agreement, and I am confident they will. I can think of one soldier in particular."

An elite unit that nearly flattened the entire city in one night, Garridan thought dourly, uncomfortable with the turn of phrase. At first, he could not think of whom Eyad was suggesting, mentally combing through his troops.

Then it hit him. Who, of all his men, had any prior knowledge of the faerie race?

Garridan stared into the sorcerer's sharp gray eyes, and realized they both knew the answer.

"Come," Eyad said. "Let us convince these men to pursue their salvation."

* * *

Garridan returned to the infirmary when the meeting ended at noon. Darson was gone, as were most of his men, with the exception of Foster. He checked on the soldier who, while still pale and shaken, looked cleaner and more composed. The torn ligaments and muscle in his wounded knee would take over six months of recovery to even obtain half of its use, let alone enough to return to active duty. Garridan did not voice it, and Foster did not ask, but the captain could see the despair in the man's eyes at the prospect of losing his career in the king's division.

With a heart that weighed as much as stone, Garridan left Foster to heal, promising to routinely monitor his progress, and spoke with Radley to see about assisting with the situation. Radley plainly told him that Garridan could do no more; the home guard had the infirmary locked down, and family members spoken to in order to keep the nature of the attack from leaking to the public and taken home. He cited Garridan's injury and dismissed the captain. Garridan was too exhausted to argue.

His feet led him home while his mind wandered. He was not surprised to find the front door unlocked, but he was a touch annoyed. He had hoped to take more of the pain draught and sleep for a few hours before having this conversation.

God knew he needed a few days to process how drastically their lives might change after the last few hours.

Darson sat at the dining table, sipping tea.

"What are you doing here?" Garridan asked tiredly.

The man peered at Garridan over the rim of his cup. "Waiting for you."

Garridan wanted to do anything but tell him of the meeting. "What did Radley want?"

"Help. That is the last time he will have the enjoyment of using me as an errand boy. Not that I minded helping; I only minded the way his lip curled after every order. Another hour and he'd have had me wiping down the floors." Darson rose, finishing the cup and going to a cupboard Garridan used for storage. A kettle of hot water and a tin of tea leaves sat on the cupboard's wooden surface. "Tea?"

"Yes, thanks. There's some liquor in the cabinet, by all means."

Darson's lips twitched as he pulled out another cup and poured. He handed it to Garridan.

"What did our king have to say about this morning?"

"Quite a bit."

Darson raised an eyebrow. He studied Garridan's face. "You're going to say something I won't like, aren't you? Did *you* get fired?" Anger blossomed over his face like a sudden storm. "Did they blame you for last night? I swear—"

"No. Not outright, although they enjoyed raking me over the coals when I initially got there. As I left, the king sent for Thyme; I intend to see him before the day is over, as well. They proposed additional inspections at the city gates, and quarantine stations for incoming soldiers."

Darson shook his head. "How long has the marshal been suggesting that, and Edric's council never let it pass?"

Garridan shrugged. "They always assumed the unit healers were enough; so far, they have been. I say it is about time."

A pregnant pause filled the small room. Garridan's throat was suddenly dry, and his hesitation dragged out too long. Darson looked expectant.

"So that took four hours?"

Garridan shifted his weight. "No. There was one other topic of discussion."

Silence again. Garridan's jaw began to tic.

Darson drummed his fingers on the wooden cupboard. "Something to do with Thyme?"

"No. All right." It did not matter how ridiculous it sounded; it had to come out. And yet he still could not put it into words. The large gulp of tea burned hotly in his throat. "Edric proposed a radically different approach to the Erepo plague."

"Virginal sacrifice?"

Garridan promptly lost his thought. "It…no. Stop it. Eyad was there this morning."

Darson looked startled. "The sorcerer? Are we going to *hex* the Erepos to death now?"

"No." Garridan stopped himself, feeling a flush of frustration creep into his face. "Edric wants to reach out to the fae for an alliance."

Darson choked on his tea. The choke turned into a coughing fit. When the fit cleared, the lieutenant remained posed with his fist by his mouth, frozen as he tried to grasp what Garridan told him. The man mouthed *fae* a few times, and then *faeries*, stared at Garridan almost accusingly, and then struggled to find his voice in half a dozen starts and stops.

"You said the fae," he repeated slowly.

"I did."

"As in faeries."

"I would think so."

"The king wants an alliance with them," Darson said, enunciating each word carefully.

"It appears that Eyad has been in the king's ear for quite some time. The fae have abundant crops and an excellent military, supposedly."

Darson acted as if he did not hear. He then glared at Garridan again. "What is Edric thinking?"

Here we go, Garridan thought. He summarized the meeting as best as he could: how the advisors reacted—poorly; their misgivings—many; the tale Eyad spun to turn their opinion around, the king's determination. "They eventually voted yes," he finished. "They are willing to give it a try."

Darson stared at him, brown eyes unreadable. He bent down and opened the door to the cabinet in the corner, next to the cupboard.

"You are not done yet, are you?" A cap twisted. The liquor went into the tea.

"They asked who would be good candidates to send on the first convoy." Garridan paused, guilt tugging at him. "The convoy he suggested would travel to the fae kingdom and deliver the king's request. With your background, Dar, considering your mother's position and knowledge…your name came up."

Darson did not look surprised.

Garridan searched his mind for anything to soften the blow of this new task. "Eyad assured us this would be a peaceful mission."

"As peaceful as a trip to the infirmary?"

Garridan winced. "I know anything can happen. We will work with Eyad on a route through the calmest areas we know."

"Why can't Eyad deliver the letters?"

"I do not understand that any better than you," he replied. "He gave me a thin excuse about the boundaries of his position and direct intervention. The message had to come directly from citizens of Aliquis."

His heart pounded as they stared at one another. They both knew Darson could not outright say no.

"I am going to humor your ridiculous proposal long enough to ask exactly *how* they want this expedition to go."

"Eyad insisted the convoy must be small, nonthreatening. Two men."

Darson laughed humorlessly. "You are *joking*."

"The sorcerer will be watching you." Garridan heard skepticism in his own voice and was disgusted with himself. "He says he has ways of ensuring the way remains clear. Eyad did not detail how, but if he truly wants this thing to work, I do not believe he would be inclined to lie when it came to your safety."

"Because you know this being so well," Darson said sarcastically.

"You will carry a token from Eyad as a peace symbol," Garridan continued, ignoring him, "as well as the letter of proposal from Edric. Both of you will be prepped by Eyad before you leave."

Darson mulled over the plan, head bowed. He lifted his cup to take another drink, eyes flashing briefly to his captain and closest friend. He chose his words carefully. "You realize that this…" He waved his free hand around in an all-encompassing gesture. "Thing … excursion … is seriously jeopardizing our six year friendship. How can I possibly remain friends with a complete idiot?"

Garridan would have laughed if not for the edge in Darson's voice, a note that did not speak of humor. Cautiously, he said, "I know it does not seem feasible."

"Does not…" Darson chuckled cynically. He uncrossed his ankles and folded tanned arms across his chest. "It is suicidal."

"When has that ever stopped you?"

Darson's voice cut the air in a swift, angry slice. "So naturally, because I have a talent for putting myself on the line, you assumed I would agree to this? Enough to let me be volunteered before approaching me?"

"I had little choice in the matter," Garridan snapped back. "*They* volunteered you."

The man shook his head. "Edric is completely daft."

"He feels as if he is out of options." And now, so was

Garridan. "You know as well as I do what it is like out there." Garridan's voice lowered, dark with memories and persuasive with the desire for a solution. "This is *our* home, these are *our* lands. Those creatures are getting bolder and more organized. You said it yourself months ago; they've started listening to someone. Learning and grouping together when we know they do not operate with any intelligent mindset under normal conditions. That group yesterday was enormous, and they never traveled in packs that large until a few years ago.

"If there is a chance the fae know more than we do, this opportunity should not be discarded. It is tenuous and uncertain, but we *need* to follow through with this."

Darson's sigh was aggravated. "Garridan …" He shook his head with a laugh that had a curious note of finality to it. "We are talking about the fae. It's just not done."

"According to whom?"

"Why do you think there have been no relations between the races in oh, I don't know, a thousand years? They are all but eradicated from our history books. Ask anyone on the street and they will tell you they do not exist."

"You know different."

"*I* do. Ninety percent of the people do not. They do not remember."

"They're totally ignorant of this expedition; what does the general population have to do with it?"

"They don't remember, but the fae *do*." Darson gave him an impatient look, and suddenly Garridan realized Darson was worldlier than he had given him credit for. "The faeries remember everything. They are *old*, and you cannot forget that little detail. They remember every wrong humans have ever done them."

"Eyad briefly touched on that. What wrongs?"

"You never thought to question why they would cut themselves off for this long? Did any of you? Did Eyad really portray it like a thousand years of zero contact has no bearing on how they will receive us?"

Darson's words gave Garridan pause. No, he had not stopped to think on the massive communication rift, given that he'd known about this plan for twelve hours. "A thousand years—"

"Doesn't mean a whole lot to them. I read the same texts my mother did, and there is a lot more in their pages than you would believe. We do not have a good history with them. There are not many details, which is no surprise. Granted, it's not as if we have never glossed over events we are ashamed of, but it was ugly. We used to lynch them, Garridan. Among other things."

The captain did not know what to say. That kind of violence, while not eradicated, happened rarely. It did not take much imagination to envision why. Prejudice and hatred were age-old evils, and a foreign species would most certainly ignite feelings that severe in more than a few.

"It is why they have not bothered with us in all this time. Why they have never offered aid. They couldn't care less what goes on here."

Garridan remembered Eyad's words. "Eyad said if the queen saw the benefit in an alliance, there is a good possibility she would offer assistance. The mere fact that we are willing to beseech them first and meet them on their terms might be enough."

"They could also slaughter us for trespassing on their lands, without asking why we're there. But wait!" Darson's eyes went wide and he slapped a hand to the side of his face in mock surprise. "Edric wants us nearly defenseless and cowering like dogs on our bellies, so naturally, everything will work out for the best."

"Did you stop to think why Eyad is also pushing for this?" Garridan asked.

"As a matter of fact, I have," Darson said. "Why is he suddenly interested in our economic well being?"

"He has nothing to gain if this fails, and far more knowledge of the present day faerie race than anyone else outside of them."

"But he has something to gain," Darson countered. "It's not an altruistic move on his part. And you trust this?"

"What he proposes has very little chance of causing us any more harm than we are already experiencing," Garridan said. "He would not even offer it if there was not potential."

"And he can single-handedly change their perception of us and thaw their hearts to our plight? What do the fae have to gain by caring for their pathetic, short-lived neighbors? How could we possibly change their mind after all this time?"

"Why are you fighting this so hard?"

"Because the king is grasping at straws!" Anger threaded Darson's words and darkened his face. "And you are taking up the cause. He is asking us to walk into unknown territory and risk our lives for almost certain denial. They will reject us no matter what the Magic Man wishes for, and what little hope we have will be crushed. It is an unnecessary risk that could cost lives. Like mine."

Garridan narrowed his eyes. "And if we do not, we gain nothing, and we keep sending young soldiers—like *you*—out to battle and then bringing them home to their families as lifeless corpses. Or worse, turned, where they'll be unleashed on the public like Averi was hours ago."

Darson's expression darkened further.

"I do not like this plan anymore than you do. But Averi and Helena were alive yesterday. I don't give a damn if the faeries tell us to go to hell, but I give a damn if we do not even try. I will always wonder years down the road, when we come across another village burned to the ground and everyone maimed beyond recognition, if they would have said yes. If we should have tried, if they would have listened. If it could have prevented us from being overwhelmed in another battle. I will not have that on my conscience."

The room fell into another tense silence. Angry now, Garridan turned away from Darson, pitched the remainder of his tea in the basin next to a waist high storage cupboard. He braced one hand on the top of the cabinet, willing his mind to wash out the images his words conjured.

"That is fantastic for you," Darson said dryly behind him. "Except you are not the one going. Clearly, *I* am whether I wish to or not—oh, come off that look, Garridan. When is it?"

"Dar—"

"Captain."

Garridan's voice went flat at Darson's chilly tone. "Three days from now. And keep your mouth shut about this."

Without another word, Darson set the cup down and stormed past Garridan. He stopped halfway to the front door, turned, and shot Garridan a cold look.

"I will give this to you, only because I would rather see this done right than by some fool soldier who would pitch us neck deep in a war with beings that would wipe us out indefinitely. I think you and our king," he spat, derision curling his lip, "are too blinded by that sorcerer to see how very wrong this could go. I get where it is coming from; I even understand why you might support it. I just do not appreciate being thrown, blindfolded, in the same corner."

The door slammed behind Darson.

Garridan dropped his mug down with a crack and sought out the pain draught.

Chapter 7

A lively wind whipped through the city, rattling shutters and windowpanes. Wispy clouds like stretched cotton chased each other, streaking through the hard blue sky and around Parna, the round behemoth a deeper cobalt. The previous night's light rain ceased with the dawn, and droplets of water shook free from awnings and hanging leaves.

A man walked alone with a small white bag in hand, head bowed against the wind, rich brown hair whirling around his handsome face. He stopped in front of a residence of russet wood and smooth stone, herbal plants and wildflowers dripping from the windowsills.

He let himself in, and a whistling tunnel of air shut the door behind him. The bright cooking area was empty. A steaming kettle of tea hung above the dying embers in the small hearth.

Darson set his bag of food on an oval wooden table. He took a cup and poured the hot tea, feeling the tight set of his shoulders finally give a little after three nightmarish days.

Helena's mourning service drew more people than the church's courtyard could handle. Averi's was smaller, but for Darson, immeasurably more painful. As far as the city knew, the deaths were not related; Averi died of a sudden infection picked up from the field and Helena suffered from a heart attack at the end of her shift. Averi's victims would not be cremated for another two weeks to eliminate speculation, as if they succumbed to their illnesses after the fact. He could not argue with the council's decision to hide the truth of what had happened. It would spread like a brush fire in a rain starved forest; the panic and mayhem would be monstrous.

By this afternoon, Darson would leave the city and travel to territories unknown, acting as the king's emissary to a race of beings so far removed from human contact that most of Aliquis remained ignorant of their continued existence.

He still wasn't quite ready to let go of the anger toward Garridan, although he never could stay upset with him for long. His captain had earned his trust and friendship at some point during a two week siege that trapped half a dozen members of their unit in an abandoned jail until the Erepos sought dinner elsewhere. If *that* kind of experience didn't forge a camaraderie, he didn't know what would. And the captain was blessed with a guileless nature that, after awhile, made Darson feel like he was punishing a puppy for remaining cross. He understood that Garridan had no choice; an order was an order. Even if it was a ridiculous one that Darson could scarcely wrap his head around.

Faeries.

If the king wanted to waste the time, effort, and money indulging in wishful thinking, he was more than welcome to. I'm happy to collect that pay, Darson thought. *If I return at all.*

He sipped the tea and headed past the wooden stairs and

down the hall to the room Darson and his father repurposed for his mother before his father died. It was only fitting, after all, for one of Laurus' esteemed historians to have an archive of her own.

Wooden shelves lined the tall walls on three sides, cramped with rows upon rows of books collected by Idavida through the years, as well as those passed down within her family. The volumes were well cared for, covers and spines carefully treated, pages unbent and smooth. Heavy drapes covered the two windows along the right wall; his mother had always been mindful of how light could damage fragile paper and binding. Only a pair of lamps burned on the wooden desk situated in the center of the deep room.

Idavida sat at her desk behind an open volume, her back hunched as she leaned forward. As if the closer she sat to the words, the faster she could absorb them.

"And so the ruination of your spine continues," he mildly chastised. "I thought we splurged on those lamps so you would not turn into a decrepit old hunchback."

She didn't take her eyes off the pages. "The delivery of your concern is so charming."

"Breakfast is on the table," he told her. "You are unable to give these books a rest."

"This is for you, my heart, not me. Come; I want you to read this."

He sidled up next to her, bending forward and resting an elbow on the desk for a better look as he set the mug down. At the light touch of his hand on her upper back, Idavida straightened, shooting her son a look out of the corner of her eye. He hid his amusement when she couldn't help but roll her neck, smothering a wince.

Darson glanced at the passage she tapped with her finger. The writing was faint, wispy, and somewhat difficult to read.

> *And they appeared out of the grasses as if by supernatural means, not having walked, but dropped as if from the heavens; soundless. A pair, their garb not unlike our own, but eyes of infinity, heated like flame and unforgiving like stone. We complied with their demands without a word passing their lips, leery of their unnatural grace. Frightened, but not for our lives. Their features were unbearably striking, but hard as granite; they were not happy with us having wandered. We were not allowed far, but we were not harmed. Their hands were cool and firm, but gentle. One spoke our language in a voice as lovely as a songbird's, as chilling as a hawk's: "Do not roam this way again." We left, turned, and found them disappeared, as if they never were. We brushed against the infinite that day. We are changed.*

"This was written two centuries ago by the scholar Taramind, who was traveling the northeastern borders with his son," Idavida said. She could not hold on to a pedagogical tone for long; animation and wonder seeped in, trickles that would turn into a stream of excitement. "I have long sought out actual encounters with the fae, not just folklore. This is the most recent account I could find. He goes on for pages, mostly detailing their appearance, the area, and his own speculation of our past relations with them. Rather than rely on his theories, I wanted to see if our volumes held any older accounts. I know you might not find it necessary, but I also know it's important for you to build your knowledge of a thing before you proceed."

"I wonder where I get it from," he said dryly.

Idavida's mouth quirked into a smile. "Yes, I do wonder."

She picked up an ancient, bound text, its sage-green leather curled and yellowed at the corners. As she opened it and carefully turned to her marked pages, Darson's eyes wandered past the map Eyad had given him two days prior—Idavida had gleefully confiscated that for further study the moment he brought it home—to an open volume of poetry lying by Idavida's cup of tea. "I haven't seen you read Kavya in a long time," he remarked.

"Well, it is not her poetry that I was interested in per se, although I adore her work. I thought perhaps that my mother—Kavya was among her favorites—would have kept her essays. I wanted to bring some of them to the king today."

Darson did not think he heard her correctly. "To whom?"

She hummed in agreement. "King Edric. With this brave attempt of his, I thought I would offer some information and history. I have a meeting with him after yours, so I may take him some of these texts." A faint smirk widened her mouth at the disbelief on his face. "And here you thought I was going to merely see you off at the door."

Looking smug as Darson shook his head, Idavida tapped the book of poetry. "The most pertinent piece of information about Kavya is that she was alive and writing during the last fifty years of fae and human alliances, when faeries actually traveled frequently to Aliquis. When public opinion began to sour on the fae, she remained a staunch supporter, and wrote wonderful pieces on prejudice and what she feared was the end of a golden age of harmony."

"She is not a small name among the classics," Darson said thoughtfully. "How have her ideas been lost?"

"Copies of her essays were confiscated by the monarchy after we inherited a king who did considerable damage to fae relations. The connection was buried, and many fae supporters were quieted. Kavya disappeared not long after, but she left a stack of unpublished poems and short stories in her wake, many of which found their way into my family's collection," she added with no small amount of pride. "Unfortunately, I have not been able to locate some of those essays quite yet. I thought it would tickle you to know that most of the love poems in that volume were written for her faerie lover, not a human man."

Intrigued, Darson motioned to pick up the book of poetry, but Idavida guided his hand instead to the sage-green volume. "What I really want you to read is the historical account I *did* find. I was up half the night poring over Folant's journals, because he was also writing around the same time. He was a member of King Ignacio's council, and a former judge. A very intelligent man, and quite verbose, he kept daily journals that give us a stunningly in-depth view of Aliquis's culture from a thousand years ago. If memory serves me correctly, I knew that long-winded man would touch on the fae at some point, since it was King Ignacio who nearly put Aliquis at war against the fae. I was right; in 5413, Folant wrote of the last meeting between the king and Emilia, queen of the faeries."

Darson began reading the text where his mother pointed a finger.

Mair 7, 5413

His Royal Highness deigned to convene with the Faerie Queen as the sun reached its zenith. I, having risen with the sun, cogitated a course of action in the early hours, to no avail, for as the rendezvous approached I grew more affrighted of the outcome. His Majesty Ignacio deliberated well into the night, and on the morn as I approached the golden field surrounding our great city and came upon our monarch, I witnessed the weight of those long hours on his countenance. He would sever ties with yon creatures, but could he do so without bloodshed?

I did not know. These beings, that do not hold God in their hearts as we, or perhaps adhere to the same God as we, operate in a manner I cannot grasp. I never held ill will toward the fae—I marveled at their beauty as one marvels at the splendor and skill of a wild wolf, careful to keep my fingers from those sharp teeth—sympathized, yea, with the ageless bodies nailed to posts and burned, as ignorant masses would try to burn the eternity out of their flesh, but I had not a voice strong enough to undo the vast damage of the past decades. His Majesty's eyes filled with the bitterness of the northern raids, and he wanted their queen punished, the perpetrators hung like common criminals, and the Faerie Queen Emilia would have raised her hand to strike in retaliation in such a way that Aliquis would have dearly suffered.

The queen cameth to the field garbed in blue and green, a terrible beauty, surrounded by formidable soldiers. At her side stood Renaud, an oddity I have never understood; he spoke little throughout the proceedings. His Majesty Ignacio stood strong in the face of her bewitchment, and declared the charges against her people. Such a quiet fell upon the field when he finished, and I feared for my people as the queen remained unmoved. When she did then speak, it was not words of condemnation spoken in righteous anger, as His Majesty had done, but with a calm that filled me with such a fright, for I did not come to the field this day to die, and I witnessed our demise in her impassive face.

And yet it ended, and we did not perish. His Majesty wanted their absence henceforth, and the faerie sovereign had preempted King Ignacio with the removal of her peoples from Aliquis lands. The fae would leave our lands evermore, and with them, the trade that so sweetly filled our cupboards.

"The faeries could have killed them all," Darson said in disbelief. "And Aliquis would not have been able to retaliate. Why didn't they?"

"They had their own reasons for not wanting to risk open war," Idavida replied. "The fae enjoy everlasting youth, but they can be killed. They are made of flesh and blood, and they have deficiencies as surely as we do, just not as many. Our ancestors unfortunately found many ways to exploit that.

"However." She shut Folant's journal. The fervent light in her eyes dimmed. "Let us not forget that we were not the only ones perpetuating violence. They did their fair share against us, as well. Children went missing; bands of faeries retaliated against groups of traveling humans, and faeries of ill repute found their mortal ilk and enabled appalling business practices between both species. The trade of illegal substances. Conspiratorial murder. Slavery."

"And we want to ally ourselves with them again?"

Idavida laughed. "You will find corruption wherever you go. Please do not think it was all terrible. Wonderful things came from our interaction, too. The food and produce from their kingdom was unparalleled. There were festivals, celebrations of the arts and culture, and their military force was an incredible asset. Folant mourned that loss. When they left, they took everything—the trade, the culture, the knowledge. Part of the reason there is so little written about them is because they preferred it that way. I only have the materials I do because my ancestors presaged the division between humans and faeries and hid what they could. I am rather curious as to why the sorcerer waited so long to suggest a renewed alliance to the king."

Darson wrinkled his nose. "What do you know about Eyad?"

"Oh, very little." Idavida took a drink of her tea, grimaced, and then, to Darson's amusement, grabbed his and drank. "The Craft are an entity unto their own. They greatly discourage outsiders from learning anything about their culture. From what I pieced together out of references in writings from kings and advisors that dealt with sorcerers in the past, their kind are unique to specific family lines. They are more human than anything else, but after generations of cultivating that sort of power, they set themselves apart from humanity. I am not sure what it is they are protecting—I know next to nothing of their history—but I have postulated before that they are simply protecting themselves from the same prejudice the fae faced. I believe the Renaud Folant mentioned may have been a Craft member, and I have seen suggestions that they maintain a council of their own. From what I understand, Eyad is on that council. I do not know Eyad personally, so I am afraid I cannot be of more help to you than that."

Darson's throat was dry. He swallowed and mulled over her words silently. "Everyone's hopes are so high for this all to work. It feels presumptive."

"And it may be. Whether or not their desire to help will override the past remains to be seen. But I admire the king for trying. Throwing oneself at the mercy of another people is a humbling act and a large leap of faith. I know you do not carry the same faith."

Darson's light brown eyes met his mother's blue ones. "Do *you?*"

Her eyes shone. "I can only hope. It would be marvelous to open the doors of communication between our races. With what humanity is facing in this day and age, people could use a dose of wonder and hope. A promise for a better future. I wish for you to recognize what an unprecedented chance you are being given by receiving this honor. To 'brush up against the infinite,' in the immortal words of Taramind."

He wanted some of her conviction to coat him like a fine dust, but his heart barely moved. "Forgive me if I do not find it much of an opportunity for anything. Other than total humiliation at the hands of a race *certain* people do not understand."

"Darling."

He sighed and closed his eyes. "I am not angry with him. And I did not intend to react so harshly. I could have used more tact." He opened one eye to glance at his mother. "You never defend me like you do him. And *I* am your son."

Idavida rolled her eyes. "You do not need me to defend you. I am fond of Garridan, I consider him partly mine. I do not like him alone in that cottage, or in that area."

Darson snorted. "I assure you he's perfectly safe, and that part of town is not as bad as you think. He locks his door. I also heard he is trained in combat."

She swatted him on the shoulder for the sarcasm, and they grinned at one another. "The way you tease me is awful," she laughed. "Now. I want you to be extremely careful—do not roll your eyes at me. Taramind was a scholar, a civilian. You are coming to them as a military representative. I imagine their response to you will be different. It is very important they do not perceive you as a threat. And remember: a great many of them *do* understand our speech. Vinculum has been the common language among our kingdoms for longer than our dealings with the fae. Watch what you say; their hearing is greater than ours."

"I can hardly contain my excitement," Darson said humorlessly. He took his map from her desk, smiling when she frowned at its loss.

"Well, let us eat before you leave, and then I will see you off," she said.

Mother and son ate together and as Darson cleared the plates, he reached for small glass dish on top of one of the cupboards. Nestled in it was a silver ring with a small, lone ruby that had belonged to his father. He put the ring on his right ring finger and then paused to study his mother, who suddenly appeared melancholy. "Shall we?"

She tucked her arm in his as they walked through the windy

streets. The courtyard in front of the king's castle was empty except for a small handful of men and two saddled horses in the eastern corner. Idavida spotted the king in discussion with a man she did not recognize.

"That must be Eyad," she said.

"Yes. He is supposed to give Mourin and me directions and some sort of protection before we leave. I have no idea how helpful it will actually be."

"Do not sound so skeptical. If you can believe in faeries, then believing in a sorcerer's magic should be no trouble." Idavida smiled brightly when she spotted Garridan. "Hello, my dear!" She left a disgruntled Darson with a light kiss on his cheek and rushed forward.

Garridan smiled with genuine delight and hugged the smaller woman to him.

"How are you, Idavida?" Garridan asked.

"Fair—better if I could keep my son in one spot for longer than a few days."

"Don't let her lie to you. She has seen plenty of me the past few days." Darson came up behind his mother and smiled ruefully at Garridan. "So what kind of etiquette did Edric have in mind for this? Do I have to get down on my knees and offer myself at their mercy?"

Garridan hesitated, not entirely sure if Darson was still cross with him. Eyad interrupted before he could speak.

"Oh, I do not think groveling will be necessary," the sorcerer said. He clapped a hand on Darson's shoulder, who smiled even as his teeth ground together. "I do wish to speak with you and Mourin, if you have a moment."

Darson nodded sharply.

The captain turned to Idavida, who stood alone watching

Darson walk away. "He will be all right," he said gently. "He is more than capable."

"I know," Idavida said. "I am truly happy for him to have this opportunity. What I would not give to meet a member of the fae myself. I cannot help but—well." She smiled at Garridan, her eyes suspiciously bright. "As a mother, of course I will worry. For you, as well, every time you leave these city walls."

Darson heard Garridan soothe his mother as he met with Mourin, who smiled eagerly at him. Mourin was of the hardy, lean stock common in the farm towns of western Aliquis. He and his family had been evacuated some ten years ago; an evacuation that did not save his parents, brothers, and sisters. Mourin joined the military as soon as he was of age. Darson did not converse with him much, but trusted his abilities and valued his quiet, steady presence during previous missions. His level demeanor during harrowing situations was probably the deciding factor in his inclusion for this task.

"Eyad tells me we'll be traveling to jungle terrain," Mourin commented. Anticipation sparkled in his eyes.

"Wonderful," Darson said automatically. He turned to Eyad, who watched him with amusement. Oh, I'm glad you find this entertaining, he thought darkly. "I've familiarized myself with your route. I have traveled a good deal of the portions of Aliquis you have us in, but I do have a question. Why does our route veer so far north?"

"I was wondering that, too," Mourin admitted. "From what I understand, their borders stretch farther south than that."

"So they do," Eyad agreed. He pulled a map from a pocket in his tunic and held it out so the three could look at it. It was identical to the copies given to the soldiers. He traced the unmarked border east of Aliquis and the Wild Territories, tapping his finger on two areas south of the route's ending point. They were not labeled, but suggested more plains and deciduous areas. "There are two other fae countries you would reach if I let you travel due east. However, it is preferable for you to travel to the northernmost country along this border. The princess there is a trusted friend. Darson, where does your knowledge of the Wild Territories stop?"

"At the eastern border past the town of Lisle, two days' ride northeast. I have not ventured far into the territories."

Eyad traced the remainder of the route with his finger. "From there, as you travel northeast, you will hug Aliquis' borders and move briefly into the wild territory east of Virtus. You will gradually move farther east until you're parallel with fae borders. Once the terrain becomes tropical, you will be close to the country of Miranda, which you will enter. I have sent word to the princess to expect guests, and that is all. There is one thing I would like for you to keep in mind when you reach the faeries' borders."

The sorcerer's good humor vanished like a cloud covering out the sun. "Fae country is infused with the magic that runs through their world—it keeps them hidden. You will begin to feel things you may not understand, and it may be alarming. You will feel as if something is wrong. As if you need to turn back. That is not a coincidence, and it is not coming from *you*; it is coming from the magic that protects their borders."

Mourin and Darson exchanged apprehensive glances.

"You must push past that feeling. Resist the urge to leave.

You will know you are through the barrier when the anxiety vanishes. They in turn will know when you enter their borders. They *will* be on the other side. Make note that the magic acts as a veil. They can see you, but you will be unable to see them until you have crossed through."

A mild chill trailed down Darson's spine.

"Will they bring us to the princess?" Mourin asked.

"Most likely not. They will not allow you to travel beyond the border."

The sorcerer instructed them about what to say to the border guards, and then handed Darson two sealed envelopes, one stamped with Edric's royal seal. "Request that these be given to the commander. My letter is for the princess. The king's letter is for the queen's eyes only. The faeries will search you and confiscate the letters, but I am confident those letters will go immediately to the intended individuals."

Would you want to wager on that? Darson thought dubiously. He wisely kept his thoughts to himself about how very wrong this could go, and waited patiently for the sorcerer to finish.

"One last thing." Eyad raised his arms. He laid his hand on Darson's forehead, and then on Mourin's, as if administering them a blessing.

A trill of uncertainty and something *other* jolted up Darson's spine as Eyad uttered a few words in an unintelligible tongue; his fingers felt warm and dry on the lieutenant's skin. Darson's heart swelled like a kettle boiling over, and for a moment he could not catch his breath. Then it was over, and Eyad retreated from the two soldiers.

"Go with my protection," he said solemnly. "I will ensure your safekeeping as you travel."

Darson let out a breath and shared another look with Mourin. His heart still drummed a rapid beat from the sorcerer's touch.

King Edric walked over from where he had been speaking to Idavida and nodded at Eyad as he approached.

"Your king and your kingdom are proud and fortunate to possess soldiers such as you to carry out this task." Edric looked at Darson and Mourin with satisfaction. "I am confident of your success, and we will all be praying for your safe venture forth and back. You carry the name of Aliquis with you, and I have no doubt you will represent her well."

The soldiers bowed low to their king, and he touched a palm to each of their shoulders before stepping back and allowing for last farewells. Idavida embraced Darson tightly. After dropping a kiss on her forehead, Darson's eyes sought out Garridan.

"If I remember, I will try to bring back a souvenir," he said.

"I will consider your return souvenir enough. I'm sure you will have plenty to tell me," Garridan replied, unable to lighten his tone as Darson had.

The lieutenant rolled his eyes and then clapped Garridan on the back. "That's quite enough self-deprecation for one morning. Just look in on my mother while I am gone—she thinks you're lonely. And that I should be nicer to you."

Garridan smirked, relief lifting some of the weight in his eyes. "I can think of a lot of people you need to be nicer to."

"Do not ruin my generous mood," Darson said flippantly. He turned to the saddled mare and patted her spotted flank. "I am forgiving you before I ride off into an unknown fate so you are not plagued with guilt all the rest of your days thinking I died upset with you."

"Generous to a fault, you are."

Darson grinned. "Absolutely. See you in twelve days, Captain."

"Travel swiftly and carefully, Lieutenant."

Chapter 8

The first two days of travel were uneventful, with clear skies and empty paths, which caused Darson to give serious consideration to the protection Eyad bestowed on him and Mourin. Parna hung high in the heavens like a shining ornament of deep blue, greeting them along with the sun and urging them forward. Wrana, the pale golden disc of the western moon, traveled across the morning sky.

Their route wove along the Rausa River, which meandered through the eastern part of the kingdom before curving north into the Territories. The men were flanked by the bank of the river on one side and flat plains on the other, and they stopped every so often to replenish their water supply. Across the river sprawled a forest that swallowed a large chunk of northern Aliquis. The barest hint of buds speckled some of the trees. A warm snap continued to hasten spring's arrival, and pleasant currents of air accompanied the soldiers.

Once, as Darson nocked an arrow, a rabbit in his sights for supper, he caught flashes of movement across the water. Something with pale flesh traveled between the trees.

The horses galloped past a handful of small towns along the

way, isles of civilization set among the sea of short, scruffy brown grass and barren, abandoned farmland. Only a few towns still held inhabitants; the majority were ghost towns, with weather-beaten cottages and empty roads.

They rode into the night at the close of the second day, guided by the constellations. The pair stopped only when Naula was in its zenith. Rather than sleep in the open, Darson and Mourin decided to stop at one of the deserted towns to rest; it meant better shelter for the horses, and a less nerve-wracking night watch.

The Wild Territories lay before them on the third day.

The land was unremarkable and unclaimed by any kingdom. Once upon a time, kingdom borders encroached farther in, drawing jagged lines of ownership in larger chunks. As the Erepos grew more numerous, however, the borders shrank back. The soil within the heart of the territories was rocky and thin and unyielding to most crops, as stripped as the discarded dwellings and towns.

Darson's mother had told him once that outlaws from all three human kingdoms once attempted to build their own small towns out here, to raise sheep and cattle, but no one ever knew what became of them.

Evidence of Idavida's words stood to the west; over a series of small hills, Darson saw a few wooden structures. They left the buildings alone. Taking refuge in an abandoned town within Aliquis was one thing; chancing a visit to a town in unchartered territory was another. Meeting others out here might prove to be just as dangerous as stumbling across Erepos.

And yet they had seen little of the creatures. Darson inwardly marveled at that, and could not help but wonder again at the intricacies of Eyad's so-called protection. Was it merely luck, or was the sorcerer's magic actually affording them safe travel? How did it work?

Darson and Mourin spent the third night in a small grove of trees crowded around large, misshapen rocks. On the fourth day, the sun began to bake the land and the temperature rose to impressive heights. It didn't seem to bother Mourin, but the heat sapped every shred of patience Darson possessed.

The terrain was changing to a land beaten into submission by the sun. Small, hardy trees grew haphazardly, nearly swallowed up by tall brown grasses and patches of tough, short vegetation the color of rotten greens.

The end of the day did little to alleviate the heat; the ground soaked in the sun as if it anticipated winter to suddenly fall on the land and steal the warmth away. Darson slept badly among the scratchy, coarse grasses and ate little when morning came; the oppressive air robbed him of his appetite.

Mourin remained in decent spirits the next day, and Darson hated him a little for it. Darson's body reacted badly to the ragweed cropping up among the fields. He was usually better at adjusting to the elements and irritants—he had slept more outside than inside for most of the past year—but the prolonged heat, so premature for spring, took his energy faster than he could replenish it. Without forest cover, so easily attainable in Aliquis, there was no relief. He wanted a cold bath and a nap.

And Mourin would not stop talking.

"What do you think they look like?" The snap and crunch of Mourin eating an apple followed the question; Mourin chewed obnoxiously loud.

The tart smell of apple barely registered to Darson's clogged nose, but the noise registered loud and clear. "I imagine they look remarkably like us," Darson answered tonelessly.

"What do you know about *jungle?*" Mourin wiped his chin with the back of his hand and continued chewing. "I've read very little on it."

"It will be hotter."

"Well, I gathered that. Do you know what sort of animals it has?"

"No," Darson said sharply. "I have no idea, but we'll find out, won't we?"

Mourin raised his eyebrows at the lieutenant, but kept mercifully silent.

Darson closed his eyes. It pained him to urge his mare to a brisk trot through the dry, drab brown and faded green fields. His thoughts could only lightly touch on their impending meeting with faeries, distracted as he was by his physical reaction to the grasses. He tried to amuse himself by thinking of Garridan and how he would have fared on the journey, crippled as he was, but images of Averi and the nurse crowded Garridan out. Darson's mood plummeted further.

The wretched fields went on for miles, and Darson worried that the tall grasses did not have an end. As they edged east and Sorya, the southern moon, began her late afternoon climb across the sky, the environment finally began to change. The grasses lost their choked, brown color, and began to look healthier and even taller.

Unhindered by clouds, the sun continued to punish, frothing sweat from the horses' flanks and drying the men's throats. Here and there, more spindly, squat trees grew, branches curving to the sky and sprouting lush green leaves, unusual for the time of year. Golden grasses swayed in the breeze, imitating the pleasant sound of rustling leaves as the air rippled through them.

Darson and Mourin slowed the horses to a walk so they could survey the land and take a moment to gather their bearings. Darson consulted the map.

"I believe we'll be all right if we continue north," he said slowly. "We're as far east as we need to be, I'm sure of it."

"Are we still in the Territories?" Mourin asked, doubt in his voice. The area was disarmingly beautiful for as flat as it was. The grasses smelled sweet. Every so often a wind would swirl through the air and relieve some of the heat.

Darson was quiet a moment. "I don't know."

Something stirred through them minutes later. Like the rising and falling wind churning through their guts, shaking down their very nerves.

The sun's intensity pierced their eyes. Darson wiped a thumb across his brow. He felt his heart working harder at pumping blood through him, gearing up for what, he did not know. There was no danger here. The grasses were empty of all but them.

We should not be here, he thought. *This place is not safe.* What he'd thought of as beautiful a moment ago was suddenly ... unwelcoming. The horses slowed to the barest of walks, hooves grudgingly kicking up soil as they were urged forward. Darson's mare began huffing, pawing at the soil more than walking through it.

"We don't belong here," Mourin said abruptly. "We really should turn around, Dar."

Darson caught himself nodding in agreement, digging the heel of his boot into the mare's side and tugging at the reins to turn her around. She willingly complied. Mourin eagerly followed suit.

No. No, wait ...

Eyad's words echoed in his mind—"You'll inexplicably begin to feel as if something is wrong, as if you need to turn back."

You need to turn around and go home, Darson told himself.

He—was that him? Was that ... his thought? His, or—? *Is this right? I don't need to turn around, I need to keep—*

Turn around and go home.

"It is not coming from you; it is coming from the magic that protects their borders."

We are at their borders.

The thought dashed away the disturbance rattling around in his mind. Darson nearly gasped. Mourin was far ahead of him. "Mourin! Wait! We've arrived. This...come back here."

Mourin's horse stopped, and he looked back reluctantly. "Dar, we can't be here."

"That's—" Darson shook his head, trying to slough off the growing unease. "That's the border. The ... magic that lines their border."

It took Mourin three tries to get the mare to move forward and deeper into the grasses. "No, this does not look like a jungle."

"I know," he said. "I'm not saying we enter here, but—"

Darson stared at the fields in front of him, and a kind of wonderment filled him. *Here* was the proof of all of his mother's research, all the stories she'd told him as a child. He felt it now; the stirring of excitement Idavida effused so naturally.

It was truly real.

His head spun as his body thrummed with the urge to leave and his heart pounded with the desire to go forward, just to see. For a moment, he thought he would be sick.

What is it protecting? What could be beyond this bizarre line in the dirt? If I stuck my hand through, would it disappear? Stuck it through what? Does it look any different on the other side?

"Lieutenant."

Darson came back to himself. He shook his head to clear it. "We'll stay back far enough so the … energy, or barrier, doesn't interfere with our travel, but now we know we are definitely heading in the right direction. This is as good an indication as we are going to get."

Mourin breathed a sigh of relief. He followed Darson's mare half a dozen yards west of the barrier, and they resumed their travel. They had no choice but to traverse a field stretched out longer than either cared to trek, forcing the horses to trudge though grasses that tickled their bellies.

Darson watched the stalks carefully, still feeling some of the unease of drawing close to the barrier. The low whine of countless insects irritated him, as did the multitude of them rising up from the ground in puffs of small, buzzing clusters, flying around his ears, arms, and sweat-dampened hair.

The insects fell away from his attention when he saw something much larger move in the grasses.

He stilled his mare and motioned for Mourin to do the same. He stared hard at the section of field three yards ahead and to the left. He had expected to see glimpses of pale skin, something lower to the ground and quick. What he got was a tall thing, not an Erepo at all; not low to the ground like a wolf or with the delicacy of a deer, but a very dark entity that went from motionless to slow, deliberate movement and gave the impression of heavy muscle.

Darson reached for his bow and an arrow. Jaw clenched, Mourin did the same, lips pressed in a firm, thin line.

As Darson nocked an arrow, his gaze remained fixed on the spot where the movement stopped. He lost his view of it as the breeze played with the golden stalks, and his stomach muscles tightened. When the wind shifted, the grasses fluttered again. *There.* Between the swaying grasses, he could just make out mottled flesh and bunched muscle.

What is *it?*

His eyes narrowed as he decided to hell with it. From what his eyes could piece together, it was a predator, and it needed to be put down. He had no intention of dying in a wild animal's jaws. His arm muscles locked, straining as he aimed for what he assumed was the creature's flank.

The creature in the grasses emitted a low growl. Mourin's eyes widened. The warning was deep, as if the throaty notes could shake the very ground the creature stood on. It sounded *big*. Darson held his breath and exchanged a look with Mourin. In the silence between them, they agreed that a confrontation might not be the best course of action. Darson's body tensed.

The growl burst into the air again, and this time, the horses reacted. Snorting, both shying and backing away.

The creature exploded into movement.

Darson let an arrow loose; the creature let out a harsh snarl. *Oh, no, this animal will not be stopped by a simple arrow.* "Go!" he ordered Mourin, and did not have to urge his own mare to flee as Mourin obeyed.

Darson's heart hammered in his chest as he urged her on, casting glances behind to catch glimpses of what followed them. Could they outrun it? He did not know what it would take to stop whatever monstrosity used the fields to hide its full form, but how long could they keep this up?

It followed them, weaving and ducking—he still couldn't see the entire animal, just flashes of sinewy muscle, dark fur, and the grasses it disturbed as it traveled. It acted like a great beast skulking through water, only rippling the surface. Darson's hand hovered over the sword strapped to his saddle. His mind scrambled for the best course of action; dismount and slay it? Risk halting to shoot another arrow and have it take down his mare?

He had forgotten how close they still were to the barrier. When the same rolling nausea and sense of wrongness hit Darson, he had an easier time ignoring it as panic, brought on by the more immediate foe, screamed through his blood stream.

"Darson," Mourin gasped, the wind tearing through his hair, face frightened and unsure.

"Push forward!" he shouted. He no longer cared what was on the other side. Maybe the barrier would slow the creature down; maybe it would feel the same trepidation and slow its course.

Maybe safety lay on the other side.

Another roar ripped through the air, and Darson pushed the mare further, heading straight for the invisible wall his body and mind tried to avoid.

Stomachs churning, minds screaming, he and Mourin charged through the invisible veil at the same time.

Chapter 9

Warm, dry dirt scraped Darson's cheek. His eyelid twitched as something small and fast scuttled across his forehead. The urge to brush it away cleared some of the cobwebs of sleep.

The fact that he couldn't move his hands to do so revived him faster than a flash of lightning. His entire body froze.

Where was the creature?

He opened his eyes only to find a world of darkness, even though the sun enveloped him and baked his skin. He was blindfolded; some kind of whisper-soft material. The same material bound his hands behind his back, and his muscles throbbed at the awkward position.

But he felt no immediate, consuming pain. Clearly, whatever chased them over the border had not killed them.

Yet.

Panic injected itself directly into his veins, and Darson fought valiantly to keep his breathing steady. He struggled to *think*, to remember the sequence of events that brought him to this point, on the ground like a pig trussed for supper, and could not. His last memory was crossing that invisible border on his horse—*where is my horse?*—moving through that sea of discomfort with their unseen foe nipping at their heels. And then nothing.

Where is Mourin?

Where is that creature?

Alarms clamored in his head, and he tried to smother it before the fear grew too loud to think straight. It was already hard to untangle and organize his thoughts. Maintain your breathing, he ordered himself, numb fingers squeezing together. *Focus.*

He listened carefully.

Far off, field bugs droned in a low whine. A cricket chirped nearby. Another many-legged visitor tickled its way along his collarbone, and the compulsion to crush it was maddening.

Soft-soled shoes glided over the ground nearby. Hairs on the back of Darson's neck rose at the unseen presence. Whoever it was did not speak. Sweat prickled under his clothes.

Where is Mourin?

Were we taken to another location? Did the faeries defeat the creature?

Another possibility dawned on him. Was the animal some sort of protective guard utilized by the faeries, tasked with attacking any human who drew too close to the borders? Did it stalk them with purpose and fulfill its function?

Darson swallowed and used his tongue to moisten his painfully dry mouth. He kept his movements minimal, unwilling to provoke the individuals who had knocked him out.

He tried one more time to wet his throat for speech, and then took a chance and called, softly, "Mourin."

He knew the soft inquiry would not go unnoticed.

No answer.

Cautiously louder this time: "Mourin."

He sensed a person come close. Darson's muscles coiled tight as he felt … something … hovering near his exposed ear. He was almost positive it was a weapon of some kind. He inhaled carefully through his mouth, absently noting the pleasant, faintly sweet taste on his tongue. *Did they drug me? How much time has passed?*

Darson used every ounce of restraint within him to keep his voice calm and controlled. Eyad's words left his mouth. "We are messengers on behalf of the kingdom of Aliquis. We mean you no harm; we were chased onto your land by an unknown beast. We come bearing a message of peace. May I inquire about my companion?"

He gritted his teeth when he received no response. "I respectfully ask if—"

A hand landed on his bare arm. He hissed in a breath when it gripped and pulled him upward with enough force to bring him to a seated position; the movement made his arms and back scream. Darson shifted his body to ease the pain, mildly surprised to find his feet only loosely tied together. Dizziness briefly muddled his senses.

Fingers slid through his hair and tugged at the blindfold.

Sunlight seared his brain with the heat of a sword pulled fresh from forging. Darson squeezed his eyes shut, and then blinked rapidly as moisture filled them. Through watery, blurred vision, he saw nothing but their two horses— *thank you, God, our transportation has not been eaten*—a few yards away, calmly munching on tall grasses. They shared their bounty with two other horses, one mottled gray, another golden.

Darson's head pounded. More pain nestled down behind his eyes. He sought out Mourin, and the worry eased some when he spotted his companion's unconscious and apparently uninjured form ten feet away, cheek in the dirt. Strangely, he was *not* blindfolded.

Movement rustled behind him, and a tall figure stepped into his line of vision. Dark leggings tucked into leather boots came into view. Darson didn't bother looking up. The figure crouched.

He gazed at a faerie for the first time in his life.

No matter how close this being resembled a human, Darson knew he would never mistake it for one despite their similarity in stature. Eyes the color of nightfall stared at him with unwavering intensity. Its features were an unreadable, perfect mask, smooth and angular and unsettling in a way Darson could not describe. He thought of figures in classical paintings imbued with the embodiment of beauty, beguiling predators, demigods brought down to Hylla.

The only movement in the otherwise motionless creature was tawny brown hair stirring in the breeze. The hands resting lightly on bent knees were free of weapons—although Darson knew those relaxed hands could easily *become* weapons. He idly noted the absence of his own sword and daggers and wondered if he would ever see them again.

He noted the absence of his ring. Anger stirred in his gut.

They stared at one another for an indeterminate amount of time, a stalemate the faerie appeared comfortable to maintain for an age, before Darson spoke.

"Do you understand me?"

Nothing.

Behave, behave. "My companion and I sincerely apologize

for entering your lands. We did not mean to trespass; we realize we are not supposed to be here. We were pursued by a creature, and our intrusion was not deliberate. We would gladly retreat and continue our mission, given to us by King Edric of Aliquis. Our orders are to seek the country of Miranda, bearing a peaceful request from King Edric. We have been sent forth with the sorcerer Eyad's blessing."

The faerie's left eyebrow quirked upward. Darson absurdly felt like he got somewhere with that comment. Either that or the faerie had an itch.

"There are two letters in the left pocket of my breeches," he continued, pleased his voice sounded so steady. Idavida would have been proud. "One letter is from Eyad, addressed to the princess of Miranda. The other is from my king, addressed to the queen of the faeries. We are acting as messengers for the king, bearing words of peace. We merely wish to deliver the letters to the proper authority."

The faerie shifted minimally on the balls of his feet, his head tilted to the side.

It was a male, Darson suddenly realized. He had not immediately attributed a gender to the faerie, but in hindsight, he felt as if he knew it all along. The faerie's graceful features lent him a beauty Darson found distracting.

Talk, you silent bastard.

More footsteps made him straighten. He fought the urge to break eye contact with the stone-faced faerie to see who was coming. Two more faeries walked past. A slim broadsword gleamed against the male's hip. Darson then noticed a small hut, like a guard station. A handful of trees, clustered to the right of the horses, sheltered a barren fire pit. A few hammocks were roped between the trees.

One of the passing faeries turned to him. A tail of long, shining brown hair trailed behind a thin, pale face. A tunic was tucked into the waistband of a simple skirt over leggings and boots. A female. He was not entirely surprised that women participated in the military in this world.

The male in front of him stood, and Darson's head snapped up to follow the movement. He wanted to say more, but—well, what else *could* he say to get any sort of answer? He'd already stated twice what he and Mourin were doing here, and all he had to show for it was a sore derriere.

The taciturn faerie turned toward the female and spoke in a lyrical tongue, the cadence fast and pleasantly husky. Darson couldn't venture a guess at what he meant, since no hand gestures or eye contact accompanied the words. The trio of faeries ignored their captives.

He didn't try to engage the faeries any longer, surmising that they were waiting for a superior to arrive to figure out what to do with these two humans trespassing on their lands.

He shifted again as the numbness spread from his fingers up his arms and the sun grew uncomfortably hot. He had no idea how much time had passed since they'd fled into faerie territory; one brief glimpse at the fiery orange ball in the sky and its small, red companion, the southern moon Sorya, told him it was now late afternoon, close to early evening. Some four hours had passed.

Disgusted and sweltering, he stared at the surroundings beyond the border guards and horses.

When he and Mourin first wandered into the plains, the land was flat and generally unremarkable—a simple beauty. Now, it was as if he'd never seen it at all.

Water flowed in a silvery blue ribbon through the fields

between small clusters of squat, oddly shaped trees and tufts of yellow underbrush. Gently sloping hills rose and fell farther out, rippling with swaying wheat fields. Wild grasses grew, peppered with tiny wildflowers of shocking yellows, brilliant blues, and vibrant purples.

Small herds of deer-like animals grazed casually, strolling on thin, delicate legs. Dark, slender horns swept skyward, and their beige coats blended with the golden stalks save for striking black markings around their eyes and on their sides. A few began to gallop, springing into the air with the speed and poise of trained dancers.

The quality of air was different, cleaner than any country air he'd smelled before. It possessed an atmosphere that, while they all waited in silence, had a curious effect on him. What had made him sick and uneasy at the border took on a different temperament, as if it were alive; vibrancy thrummed along his skin, dancing with the wind to create a charge that reminded him of everything good and lovely about spring. He felt renewed and pure. He inhaled, and a deep pleasure of just being trembled at the edge of his discomfort and worry.

A groan from the ground captured Darson's attention. He looked to Mourin. It did not escape his notice that the trio of faeries also turned to study the blond intently.

The soldier's face screwed up in a grimace, and his eyes opened. He went rigid. His gaze darted to the faeries, then wildly around, and finally to Darson, who immediately knew Mourin's next move.

He finished uttering the first syllable of Mourin's name right as the younger man sat up and attempted to hoist himself to his feet.

"No, Mourin!" Darson hissed. He looked frantically between the scrambling man and the faeries. As the female faerie shot forward, Darson clumsily maneuvered to his knees, still helpless, shouting, "Wait! Mourin, stop!"

Mourin made the noise of a trapped animal when she lunged and grabbed him by the biceps. She dragged him back from the meager few feet he moved, not without struggle; he flailed like a dying fish. She didn't appear to handle his thrashing well, but got him on the ground a few feet from Darson. One of the male faeries pulled his sword and glowered at both men, but the tawny-haired one did not bother, observing the whole scene with a harsh, clinical air.

"Forgive my comrade," Darson said, barely able to keep the pleading note from his voice. "Please do not take his fear as a threat of any kind. We only want to continue our peaceful mission and be on our way to deliver *letters.*"

One long look from Tawny-Haired and his voice died.

"Don't, please," Mourin implored hoarsely, arms trembling as the female faerie remained close, studying him with narrowed eyes. "Leave me alone!"

Mourin's shaking did not stop as he engaged in a wordless staring match with her. When her lips curled in a cruel smile, Mourin's eyelids fluttered, throat working, and he looked away.

She glanced behind her at the other two faeries who watched, paused as if reluctant to comply, and then rose and walked away.

As Darson's galloping heart attempted to slow its breakneck speed, he eyed Mourin with growing confusion and anger. "Why would you do that? We don't know if that creature is gone; or what *they* will do, for that matter."

"They'd kill us if they could," Mourin said softly.

"I don't doubt it," he replied tightly. "We were prepared for a situation like this."

Sweat rolled down Mourin's face, and he kept his eyes on the ground. "It was a bad idea, coming here."

"Mourin, we had no choice."

"No." He shook his head. "We don't need this."

Although it pained Darson to say it, he had to respond, "It is too early to tell."

"Not for me." Mourin paused. When his voice returned, it was small and low. "I woke up earlier. I tried to get free."

Darson looked at the soldier more scrupulously and didn't like what he saw. Mourin's fair skin was soaked with sweat and splotched red from all the hours they'd spent outside, and his eyes were glassy, on the verge of tears. The lieutenant finally noticed an odd patch of substance on Mourin's shirt. Drying vomit.

"You were still unconscious," he added softly.

Dread curled uncomfortably in Darson's gut. He was painfully aware of the faeries watching them a few yards away. What did they do to him?

"The girl speaks our language," Mourin continued. "She got in my head. She showed me things."

Darson hazarded a glance at the woman. His tingling, heavy limbs were forgotten when he found her staring at him. Her attention made him uneasy, but he held it defiantly. A faint smirk played at her lips in return. "What things?"

Mourin never answered him. He seemed to withdraw into himself, become smaller, huddling in the grass and dirt like a terrified child.

"They're not our friends, Dar," Mourin whispered.

Jaw clenched, Darson never took his eyes off the faeries, and continued waiting for whoever would come continued.

The sun sank lower in the sky; Parna glittered prettily next to it, a vibrantly blue. Tawny-Haired approached them only once to give them water and allow them to stand. He did so without emotion. Darson felt the resentment in the faerie's unnervingly strong grip as he made Darson walk in a tight circle to work some of the stiffness out of his limbs. It made him feel like a horse.

When the faerie tried to do the same to Mourin, the soldier grew visibly distraught. Tawny-Haired forced him to stand, but Mourin, limbs shaking, scarcely moved. A barely audible sigh escaped the faerie; the first real hint of emotion Darson had seen all afternoon.

Some two hours later, the three fae stood at attention to greet a new arrival before Darson was even aware of anyone coming. Then he heard it—the faint pounding of hooves, muted but increasing in sharpness and proximity. He could feel the earth vibrating.

A gelding glided across the flat plain, a deeper tan than its slight, deer-like cousins. Its easy gallop slowed to a trot, and the trio of border guards relaxed. The rider dismounted with a movement as smooth as a cat's leap for its prey.

This was who Darson needed to contend with to get them home alive. Not the guards. Here was their superior, come to deal with the problem himself. Adrenaline shot into his muscles as he readied himself for whatever was to come. He caught Mourin's eye and issued a silent warning. To the soldier's credit, he remained quiet, his face grim.

The newcomer stood a few inches taller than the rest, bearing a build closer to a human male rather than what

Darson had seen thus far in the other two faeries. For a higher rank, he was dressed quite casually in a simple dark green tunic of thin weave, with brown boots over tan-colored breeches. He exchanged a few words with Tawny-Haired, the latter showing more signs of life with gestures and something close to concern pinching his fair, pretty features. The officer looked at them, and then at the brunette female faerie standing idly by the horses, who in return fixed the newcomer with a blasé stare.

The new faerie then turned and approached Darson and Mourin, looming larger as he drew closer. Tawny-Haired walked with him. And then spoke.

"This one says he has papers in his pocket."

Perfect Vinculum.

Darson fumed.

The newcomer crouched in front of Darson, resting elbows on his knees. Darson found himself being appraised as if he were recently acquired livestock rather than a trespasser. Grave, dark-green eyes bored into his brown ones; sandy-blond hair tousled around a sternly handsome face. Darson fought off the urge to rear back and put some distance between him and this … being. Energy radiated from the powerful physique. This faerie made him think of quick deaths and swift blades, and those thoughts robbed his throat of all the precious moisture he had gained from the little water they gave him. He could not help but swallow.

The male faerie's eyes flickered briefly to Darson's throat. "Parched?" he asked in a voice as level and smooth as the stream in the grasslands.

Darson blinked. "No," he said tightly. Then remembered to add, albeit grudgingly: "Thank you."

The male did not outright smile, but amusement touched the depths of his green eyes. "Comfortable?"

How did he answer *that*? Darson shoved back the urge to bite out an answer. He settled on, "Comfortable enough." The prickling in his forearms and shoulder blades had begun to stab like needles.

He would try this one more time. "We did not mean to trespass on your lands," he said, his speech slow and even. "We—"

Faster than Darson cared to track, the faerie moved; warm hands gripped his arms and lifted. Darson sucked in air sharply as the faerie rose and pulled him to his feet with startling ease.

"Sir, we mean no harm," Mourin blurted from the ground, distress breaking apart his carefully erected calm. "We're messengers. We meant no offense by stepping on your lands, we were chased—"

"Shhh."

The sound was more frightening than an Erepo screech.

The imposing faerie shot Mourin a mildly reproachful look, tempered with enough implication that both men knew he was aware of Mourin's attempts to flee.

Darson ground his teeth and concentrated on staying upright while his calves cramped and more needles stabbed at nerve endings. Standing, Darson discovered the smug faerie was the same height as he, and his iron clad grip made Darson realize the faerie could break him in half. He suddenly remembered the female faerie and Mourin's near breakdown. Is he going to do the same to me? he wondered. *Will he put things into my mind, too?* A shudder worked its way up his spine.

The faerie let go of his arms and moved behind him. Mourin watched with dread, breathing rapidly.

The faerie's deep voice, alarmingly close to Darson's ear, lilted in a question. "Pocket?"

Darson's heart pounded. "Left."

He inhaled harshly and arched forward in a feeble attempt to escape as the faerie's hand slid into the back pocket of his breeches and deftly pulled out the letters. Darson's heart fluttered wildly. The faerie's breath warmed Darson's ear. "Word of advice: there are better locations to store documentation. Better for you, at any rate."

Darson's face was stone when the faerie appeared in front of him again, head bent to examine the envelopes. He gave himself a moment to temper his tone; he didn't want to offend the faerie and draw more trouble down on their heads. "I am sure you were informed by your soldiers who we are and why we are here." He stopped as the faintest hint of fear trembled in his voice. The sandy-blond faerie acted as if he didn't hear a word, but Darson knew better. "May I ask your name?"

"Arrian."

Arrian the Ass. "I understand that we entered lands we are not supposed to be in, and we are gravely sorry for doing so—no harm was intended. Our orders, from King Edric of the kingdom Aliquis, are to deliver peacekeeping messages to the queen of your realm through the country of Miranda. If we may be allowed to continue to our intended destination, we would be indebted for your benevolence." The words tasted like ash in his mouth.

Arrian looked at him for the longest time, as if he knew what it cost Darson to continue. "No," he said.

Darson breathed out through his nose. *No* to what? "We were to deliver the letters in person to the highest ranking officer in Miranda. One is for the queen, and the other is for the princess of Miranda."

Arrian shook his head. "You will not be doing so."

Darson and Mourin looked at one another, unease rippling in the air between them. A nagging voice in the back of Darson's mind asked what he didn't dare say: then what would they be doing? How did these faeries handle messengers who were coincidentally trespassers?

He looked beyond Arrian to the other three. Their main focus was Arrian, but the female kept smirking at them. Darson suspected Arrian held great authority, and that his and Mourin's fates rested on whatever he fancied to do with them.

"There is some creature close to your lands," Darson said quietly. "I did not fully see it, but it would have killed us had we not ventured this way."

Arrian paused from examining the front of the letters. "I am aware of what caused you to cross my border," he said just as quietly. He looked up and met Darson's gaze. "You said the name Eyad earlier."

The male nearly spat the name *Eyad*, and if Darson had been in any other situation, he would have appreciated the sentiment implied.

Darson nodded. "The sorcerer is assisting my king with the attempts at contact."

Arrian raised an eyebrow with the nearest thing to surprise Darson had seen on the faerie's face. For long minutes, no one moved as Arrian considered this information. A breeze whistled through the encampment, ruffling strands of Arrian's dark-blond hair and slapping damp strands of Darson's own hair against his sweaty neck. Songbirds called to one another far off in the grasslands; leaves murmured welcomingly.

"May I ask the name of your country?" Darson inquired, as politely as he could muster.

"You may not," Arrian said mildly. "Feel free to ask Eyad." A disparaging tone accompanied the sorcerer's name again; Eyad did not appear to be well liked in this part of the world, either. "For your information, Miranda is nearly a day north," he pointed behind him, "that way." He paused, and then tapped the letters with his free hand. "You have already traveled a long way to bring these."

"Yes."

"Are we what you expected?" The question held a provoking edge.

Darson's eyes narrowed. "No."

Arrian's eyebrow rose again. "No?"

He was being toyed with, and Darson didn't know why, or where it was going. Simultaneous questions about what was going on, and *damn Edric and damn Eyad for this* clashed in his brain.

Mourin answered for him, his voice faint. "We did not know what to expect."

Arrian looked at him and then back to Darson. "I give my soldiers very specific instructions on handling trespassers. Shall I tell you what they are?"

I am almost positive we are going to die, Darson thought. He did not know how to respond, so he merely stared at Arrian, waiting.

"Given your circumstances, however," he continued mildly,

"I will make an exception. What is your name?"

At the last second, Darson decided to leave out his rank. He imagined rank in a human guard would be a laugh to a being like this. "Darson. My companion is Mourin."

"How long have you served?"

The lieutenant frowned at the unexpected question. "Eight years."

Arrian smiled then, the solemn lines chased away by a more approachable, warm expression. And then it was gone, his features settling back into total solemnity. The enigmatic faerie had not done or said a single thing that gave Darson any clue as to how this would turn out.

He couldn't help his curiosity, though. When would he ever have the chance to ask again? "And you?"

Arrian tucked the letters in the waistband of his breeches and walked toward Darson, stopping inches from his face. Metal flashed as he pulled a six-inch dagger from his belt. Darson's stomach jumped.

Mourin gasped, naked fear on his face. "Arrian, please—" His wide eyes stared at them, and flickered occasionally to the other faeries close by and then back.

The blade winked in the sunlight as Arrian reached behind Darson. The lieutenant's breath came out in rapid, short bursts as he waited for the blade to meet flesh. He jerked when Arrian's arm flicked upward. The knife bit into the cloth binding his hands. The material gave, and his hands fell free.

Arrian fought off a smile and stepped back from Darson.

"Longer than eight years," he finally said. "Do not wander from your path again." He saw the argument on their faces before they voiced it, and added, "You will not be bothered by the animals in the grass. We are aware of the problem. You may return to your king with your mission satisfied."

They stared at him, still grappling with fading terror, unsure if this was a trick.

"I will deliver the letters." He gestured to the tawny-haired guard, spoke rapidly in Fae, and gestured toward Mourin. The faerie went to free him.

"Off you go."

Darson's tingling hands trembled faintly. Mourin got up on shaky feet, and both men froze, afraid to move lest the faeries change their mind.

Arrian's eyes narrowed as he sheathed the knife. "Do not make me repeat myself again. Gather your horses and go."

Darson and Mourin did not need any more prompting. They retrieved their horses and weapons. Darson nearly mounted before he realized one item was still missing.

No. He could not leave without it.

"I want my ring back," he said, turning to look at the group of faeries again.

Arrian looked sharply at his soldiers. The female smiled. She sauntered toward Darson, pulling the ring off her finger. She palmed the piece of jewelry and offered it to him.

Darson plucked it from her palm, acutely aware of Mourin's discomfort. Arrian watched the exchange, and Darson did not know what to make of the pointed look of censure the blond faerie gave the female. Without another word, he slid the ring on his finger, the metal still warm from the thief's skin. He turned and mounted his horse, eager to put distance between them and these creatures.

He knew instinctively what direction to take, and could feel eyes burning into his back long after they left the faerie camp. Neither man spoke as they coaxed their horses into a trot, eager to put space between them and a faerie that might or might not change his mind about their safe departure.

Both men knew the moment they left faerie territory and entered the ordinary world. It pulled at their bones, whistled through their lungs as the sweet air was sucked away and replaced with dry, common air. A tingling rush ran over their skin, then evaporated.

The world lay still. Mourin's breathing shuddered quietly. Darson's eyes roved over the countryside, paying close attention to the grasses, looking for movement.

The sun beat down on empty fields and parched grass. Nothing moved but leaves, wheat stalks, and tall thrushes. Any sign of life had vanished.

Except for the red, irritated marks circling Darson's wrists, if not for the missing letters, it was as if nothing had happened.

An odd ache nestled in Darson's heart as Mourin said nothing. He gently dug heels into his horse, spurring her on.

He couldn't help but ask, "What did she show you?"

Mourin's gaze remained fixed ahead, shoulders slumped a little as his fingers played with the horse's reins. "It doesn't matter. Edric shouldn't do this. No good can come from beings like … that."

Curiously, Darson felt he could not fully agree. He abruptly remembered the silent faerie giving them water, and Arrian's silent condemnation of the female faerie's theft. "Mourin, despite what just happened—which was not exceedingly awful or cruel, in hindsight—we have to keep in mind that Eyad wouldn't have suggested this if they were wholly evil."

"We don't know what we're dealing with," Mourin argued.

"No," Darson agreed. "But even if everything works out the way Edric wants it to, I am almost certain you will never see her again. Take heart in that."

Take heart.

He needed to heed his own advice.

Because he could not banish Mourin's words from his head.

She showed me things.

Chapter 10

Garridan's steps were slow and measured as he left his small cottage. The sun was beginning to set, and the barest brushstrokes of indigo and scarlet appeared as night claimed the sky. He paused a moment on the cobblestone, away from the stream of horses and locals passing by him, to gaze at Parna. After a while, he stopped seeing the colossal blue orb sitting prettily in Hylla's skies. Parna's beauty hit him with a gentle fist; the deep, shimmering blue against the evening sky, the faint, icy rings curving delicately around the orb. Naula moved slowly across the heavens, a white half moon waltzing toward her enormous, elegant partner.

His injury had narrowed the scope of his activities over the past few weeks as he put rehabilitation at the forefront of his duties. He had attended funeral services for all of Averi's victims. Stopping by the household of Helena's family had stung like a fresh wound, but he made himself go to them a few times to help Helena's daughter and grandchildren cope with the loss, even if it was just to lend a shoulder for tears.

Garridan's visit with Thyme a week ago still sat unpleasantly in his mind; his memory was tinged with regret at the aged appearance of the discharged healer. Thyme would suffer no harsh punishment for his mistake, given his length of good service in the military, and no one would know the reasons for his sudden retirement, but Thyme knew of his folly. He could barely meet Garridan's eyes during the short, painful visit.

He grimaced at the memory and tried to empty his mind. As he ambled up to the Fair Lady's Tavern, a few women—regulars in this section of town—called to him in a beguiling manner. He smiled a little sheepishly, shaking his head when they beckoned him closer.

Damn Darson for insisting on visiting this area enough for him to become a familiar face.

The tavern, a battered wood building painted a faded green, sat on a corner at the edge of his neighborhood, squeezed in between an apothecary and a blacksmith shop. Garridan never came here of his own accord, frequented as it was by farmers stripped of their farms and out-of-work tradesmen, but Darson fancied it for some reason.

This was not where Garridan wanted to spend his last night before heading into the faerie realm.

The Faerie Queen had sent a letter to King Edric via a messenger bird two weeks after Darson and Mourin's return. She invited him and a small convoy to the country of Miranda for a "meeting of minds" with her and the princesses of the realm.

He was to meet and speak with *immortal* beings.

Even his fertile imagination had a difficult time processing that.

For all the talk of faeries by the king, the sorcerer, even Darson, for all the advocating *he* did even when he did not fully support the cause himself, it was still a surreal notion, akin to hearing *the Erepos have been eradicated*. Truth be told, deep down he never expected a response from the faeries. The prospect was a nice thought and a lofty dream.

Darson and Mourin would liken it more to a nightmare, from what they had reported. Garridan could not help but remind Darson, an hour into his impassioned diatribe on the horrid experience, that the faerie soldiers he'd encountered had acted tame appropriately toward a pair of foreign soldiers. Darson had agreed, but Garridan knew the entire incident would no doubt remain forever colored by Darson's initial misgivings about the mission.

And Mourin. He still wondered about the soldier's reaction. Darson could not give him many details and seemed confused about the incident, since it had happened when he was still unconscious. The only thing he *could* tell Garridan was that faeries could do things Eyad had not disclosed. That they were perhaps gifted in the way Eyad was gifted.

The thought left him uneasy, but he wasn't positive Mourin's negative reaction to the experience wasn't fueled by plain terror. For so long, their enemy had been the mindless Erepos; meeting a sentient, superior foe with undisclosed abilities would be an experience anyone might take badly. It nearly smothered the faintest twinges of excitement that had been racing through Garridan ever since the king summoned him, Darson, and Mourin to his study two days ago, where the king, the sorcerer, and a letter waited. He had almost envied the pair their opportunity to meet immortals. Now, he was not sure if he was all that thrilled to do the same.

Garridan realized he was loitering outside the tavern as he considered recent events. He rolled his healing shoulder before opening the warped door. The sling had come off two weeks ago; daily exercise with the muscles of his arm and upper back gradually strengthened them, and he could tolerate longer practices with a sword. His initial rehabilitation had been with Foster, who needed the practice to strengthen his knee. So far, the soldier's progress was slow, yet promising. It gave Garridan hope that he had not lost a fine soldier after all. Sparring matches with Darson over the past ten days put the healing, unused muscles to active use, and he was finally waking up to less soreness.

Which was all for the best, as it would be put to good use by the morrow.

Smoky air, faint with the smell of cooking meat, curled around Garridan as he entered. Muddled voices clashed in the boxy room, mixed with wheezing laughter, bird-like shrieks, and growling complaints. He scanned the room, his eyes skimming over hunched backs, ruddy faces, and narrowed, inquiring gazes from regulars to find, he was sure, the youngest pair of patrons. A smattering of women coiled around some of the men noticed him, much to his chagrin.

Mourin's blond hair, burnished gold under the lamplight, caught his eye. Before they saw him, though, he hung back and observed the two men he would depend on for the next three weeks—or more.

At first glance, Mourin looked fine, albeit a little pale, as though recovering from an illness, but Garridan had known the man for five years, and easily read the discomfort he was trying to hide. Wearing that slight defensiveness with a frayed edge allowed him a harmony with the crowd that Darson could not match.

No matter how basic the lieutenant's clothes, he would

never fully blend into a throng like this. His words often betrayed his education, and that ruby ring on his finger gave away his social status. Darson's indifferent attitude to that social status and ability to adapt won him more friends in vastly different places than most in his mother's circles would believe to be true.

Garridan weaved through the scarred tables to the round table in a corner.

"Cap'n!" A tavern patron shouted.

He saluted with two fingers toward the gravelly voice, earning raucous laughter and an unintelligible shout.

Darson heard the call and spotted him. He pushed a pint of ale in front of the empty stool.

"You could think of no place quieter?" Garridan asked as he sat, raising his voice so his soldiers could hear him.

"The quieter it is, the harder people listen," Darson said. "We also have private tables."

Ah. The majority of taverns and inns around the city still utilized long trestle tables; in Garridan's dim recollection, the owner of the Fair Lady had a furniture maker build the smaller, round tables. He appreciated the little privacy they afforded.

"Are you not thrilled?" Darson asked acrimoniously. "We are to be a part of history over the coming weeks. Granted, no one will know it; history texts rarely note the *help* in these matters."

"A good portion of the meeting concerns the military," Mourin said, almost hesitantly. "Would they not at least reference the captain?"

"More than likely," Garridan admitted reluctantly.

"I don't even know why they want me back," Darson said.

"I spoiled everything. And Edric let me know it in half a dozen ways."

"Redemption," Garridan answered. He waved off the rude gesture Darson made at him and took a swallow of ale. "In all seriousness, Edric has managed to keep this a secret from almost everyone in the city except the council and us. It is far easier for him to send the two of you than to start over with new soldiers."

"Even for safety measures? I cannot comprehend why he's only sending three soldiers. *Three.* Do you understand what that translates to? Constant vigilance. Do you realize that, as the royal unit, we have not been tasked with guarding the king's person in over four years?"

"He never leaves the city," Mourin pointed out.

Darson swung his gaze over to the blond. "I *understand* that. Damn that man for forbidding me to discuss any of this with the rest of the unit," he muttered. *"In all seriousness,"* he said mockingly, "having only three soldiers guarding the king is unheard of."

"From what I gathered, the Faerie Queen insisted on only three," Garridan said. "Not that it makes it easier to understand, but it isn't a random number the king decided on."

"There's more out there than Erepos, Captain," Mourin said, as quietly as the noisy tavern would allow.

"If we come across too many of those creatures, we are outmatched," Darson added soberly. "And I don't know if I trust Eyad to be any help. Garridan, that animal was massive and fast; we were easy prey until we crossed the fae border."

"What choice do we have?"

Darson sighed and took a drink. "None. I just hate how

little we know. And I hate that wizard."

"Sorcerer."

"Silence, Captain." Darson stared moodily at the scarred wooden table as Garridan chuckled a little. He looked back at the captain, a new thought brightening his demeanor. "I have something to tell you. I learned of a new development today."

"I don't want to hear it."

"As if you have a choice. You will never believe who we have to endure during this trip."

Garridan looked at Mourin. The blond shook his head and drank his ale.

Darson finished his pint. "Guess."

"No."

"*Captain.*" Darson sighed significantly. "Do not ruin my last night of freedom."

"Do you anticipate a lifetime of indentured servitude after today?"

"This man will be intolerable until we get him soused," Darson informed Mourin, who smiled. "He hates this place, and he is being a lout on purpose. Now *drink.*" He pushed the mug closer to Garridan, who rolled his eyes skyward and drained the rest of his ale.

Darson's name was shouted from the bar. Clapping his hands, the lieutenant sprung over to the wide wooden counter, and then came back with a small wooden serving platter of food and three more pints. Strips of cured and salted beef between rye bread, a block of sharp yellow cheese, ears of toasted corn wrapped in the husk filled the platter.

"Now, let us try this one more time," Darson said cheerfully as he plucked out an ear of corn. "What miserable bastard on the advisors' council would be the absolute worst man to have with us?"

Garridan frowned after breaking off a chunk of cheese. As far as he knew, the members attending were Kiryk and Silanus. "Who is unable to go?"

"Silanus."

Well. That was not so bad—he was relieved Kiryk, the most levelheaded and good-humored of them all, was still accompanying them. "I can think of a few who would be poor substitutes," Garridan said.

Mourin looked troubled, deep in thought as he chewed slowly on the meat and bread. "Tiberius," he finally said.

Darson lifted his ear of corn in triumph. "*Excellent deduction, Mourin.*"

Tiberius? Garridan felt the food in his stomach curdle. He could not say there were many people he came close to hating, with so many worse things to truly hate, but that man possessed every personality defect Garridan hated in another human being. He was exceedingly arrogant, greedy, bullheaded, narrow-minded, and treated women like a lesser species. He had a fondness for women forced into prostitution to feed their families, and his methods for keeping those relations out of the public eye were deplorable. Every man at the table knew just the kind of depths he would sink to, and short of killing him, nothing they had tried put a stop to any of it without the threat of repercussions.

Yet the advisor's position on the council was never questioned. Edric simply did not see that side of the man. Tiberius covered his tracks quite effectively. Being well connected in Laurus helped considerably.

But why would a misogynist like him consider negotiating

with a matriarchal society? Garridan wondered. Unless he planned to sabotage the efforts by thoroughly insulting them or whispering in the king's ear. In that case, he would require close watch indeed.

Garridan lost his appetite. "How did you come about this information?"

"I was collecting my mother at the castle. She and Edric have become fast friends, apparently," Darson said drolly, "and he has met with her a number of times to discuss the faeries. My mother is beyond ecstatic that I am going back. She wants me to keep a journal that she will no doubt confiscate when I return."

"Are you going to ask the faeries to sign your diary?" Garridan asked innocently.

Darson snorted, and then gave him a dirty look. "Eyad was at the castle." He paused to take a drink. "And I finally found out the name of the country Mourin and I ran into. It's called Hesperia. Eyad seemed to find that incredibly amusing, and I wanted to hit him. Then the king saw fit to tell me that Silanus was unable to attend due to 'illness,' and Tiberius would take his place. He did not sound happy, but he did not elaborate, either."

"Perhaps we could leave Tiberius with the faeries," Mourin suggested.

"That would be a fitting end, would it not?" Darson smiled wickedly. "If his whining during the journey doesn't force one of us to put him out of his misery."

"The king could think of no one else to replace Silanus?" Garridan asked, but even as he said it, he knew the answer.

"Edric has never removed his blinders regarding some of his advisors. Most notably Tiberius. Remember the prostitute debacle?"

Mourin looked pained. "Do you have to call it that?"

"I was trying to be polite."

None of them could forget; the trio exchanged glances but did not discuss the matter further. The names of the missing women still surfaced in Garridan's mind every so often, reminding him that corruption still thrived in their world. Tiberius would never pay for what he did to those women, but the three soldiers worked to ensure it would never happen again. Garridan was the only one who knew of Tiberius's abhorrence of the entire faerie matter, but they all knew enough of his character to guess that he'd engineered the change to suit his own ends. If he didn't choose to sabotage it, he could possibly ensure the meeting's success if he liked what he saw and heard on fae land. A man like him could not stand to hear things secondhand; he wanted to be an arbiter of change, for good or ill—if it suited him.

Garridan sighed. "We will handle him," he said confidently. "We will guard him, and deal with him, as we've always done. Tiberius is the least of our worries."

Mourin did not look convinced. He looked as if his food was not sitting well, either. He excused himself and left, heading toward the front door to exit and relieve himself.

"How is he?" Garridan asked once they were alone.

"Better. Almost normal the past week or so. We are headed for a different country, with different faeries, so he feels more secure. *I* don't; I can't see how royal faeries will be any better than their border soldiers, except maybe haughtier and better dressed."

Garridan made a noncommittal noise, focusing instead on eating more beef and some corn as his appetite returned.

Darson eyed him suspiciously.

"You don't agree," he said. "Are you looking forward to this?"

"I am a little curious," Garridan said defensively. "I might not like it, but I have to find the bright side somewhere. If they come to no agreement, we won't have anything more to do with them. I would not mind seeing something spectacular in my lifetime."

Darson looked disgusted. "You are not missing anything."

"You can't possibly know that," Garridan argued with an abrupt chuckle. "You met a handful of faerie soldiers at the border of *one* country. Your mother would be so disappointed in your attitude."

"You were not *assaulted* by a member of their military, either."

Garridan laughed.

"I hope you meet him someday, and he treats you like a barn animal, too."

"A man can only dream, Darson."

"Of what?" Mourin asked as he rejoined them.

"Getting treated like a barn animal," Garridan answered.

"I have walked in on the wrong end of a conversation," Mourin said.

"A toast!" Darson raised his pint. "To Captain Garridan, swine of Aliquis."

"To a safe journey," Garridan corrected, gesturing rudely at Darson. "A fruitful mission and a promising future."

Darson groaned.

"Quit it and toast." The trio clinked mugs. Garridan, satisfied with his comrades, smiled. "Let us enjoy our final night at home."

Chapter 11

The wilderness never pressed so thick, the air never so heavy and humid. It collected on their backs like stifling weights, clogged in their throats, and stole the air from their lungs in great, thieving pulls. Light, dying as the day neared its end, barely shone on the dirt path. The sky was not a never-ending blue but a pressed, murky green. Big waxy leaves, plump vines, and twisted limbs pressed together to create a lowered, living ceiling to the world.

It smothered Garridan.

The closest he'd ever come to a terrain this dense and oppressive was the swampy cesspools of the outermost region of southeastern Aliquis. The soggy bogs stretched on past their borders, and Garridan never desired to explore them during the few times his unit needed to wander that far. They were nearly inhabitable, with deceptively calm waters hiding sinkholes and all manners of serpents and insects.

The jungle was surely its louder, denser sister.

After five days of wide fields, plains, and sloping hills, Garridan keenly felt the loss of long-range visibility. The close quarters agitated him like the incessant buzzing of a fly in his ear, and put him on edge even more than having the king out in the open did.

The tight expressions of Darson and Mourin confirmed they felt just as he did. Grim faces, all around; even the advisors were sullen and subdued. The sorcerer assured them their travels through the jungle would end before they had to spend the night among the screeching birds and roaming, slithering creatures, but as the slivers of daylight waned, Garridan was not sure he believed him.

They had not seen a single faerie.

The last Erepo sighting had been nearly two days ago.

The latter was a relief; the former a constant worry flitting through Garridan's mind, having nowhere to go but bang around his skull as his eyes constantly lit on any movement in the dark foliage. Eyad's presence and assurance that the foreign forest was friendly territory did not keep him from being in a state of high alert.

He knew eyes watched them. No guard unit worth its salt would allow outsiders to roam free in their territory for an entire day. The fact that Garridan could not detect any sign of their movement or whereabouts was a testament to their skill.

There was no doubt in his mind that the country's forces watched and waited as they slept outside of the border, within a few yards of the strange, invisible barrier signaling fae land.

Garridan started when a spider dropped from a tree onto his bare arm, and he smacked the spindly, striped creature away, barely suppressing a shudder. Never in his life had he seen spiders and mosquitoes so grotesquely large. If they were ever forced to sleep in the jungle, he would lie awake all night for fear of the next beetle the size of his palm camping on his face.

"They sleep under netting to protect themselves from the mosquitoes," Eyad said conversationally to the group at large, embracing the role of guide. Garridan had only half listened to him prattle on about the ecosystem of the jungle, gleaning only what would be useful as they traveled; he'd missed the change of topic to the native faeries. "Those that live in the trees and small settlements, that is. The palace is not the only stone structure—there are other cities—but they are scattered throughout. Miranda does not lack for running water, so every portion is habitable."

"I beg to differ," Tiberius said gruffly.

"I am not far behind in agreement with Tiberius," the king said with a breath of a laugh.

Garridan watched the monarch for a moment. The aging leader was handling the trip well, but the humidity seemed to be wearing him down. Sweat slicked his long, pepper-gray and white hair and beaded on his forehead. No matter what they found at Miranda's palace, he was glad Edric would have a chance to recuperate from the journey.

"They are long used to the living conditions," Eyad said. "Many prefer it. And the food here is divine. Fruits you would not believe. Chocolate, coffee ..."

The captain perked up at the thought of coffee. The delectable drink was such a rarity in Aliquis. He'd not had it since his youth, when his mother had traded for coffee beans in the village of Garridan's birth. The trader passed through their village once a year in early fall, and his mother exchanged homespun blankets and sturdy trousers for coffee and cocoa beans, cheeses, and nuts. She would sweeten the coffee with cream and share a cup with him in their tiny kitchen, especially on chilled winter evenings when his father was away on duty. He could smell the coffee, hear his mother's laughter and the crackle of the fire in their hearth.

Garridan's heart ached.

"…what of their customs?"

Kiryk's voice intruded on Garridan's thoughts. He latched on to the other advisor's words—anything to put memories of his mother safely away.

"I imagine we greet the princesses as we would any monarch," Kiryk continued.

"Oh, yes," Eyad said. "You should bow; you may notice that the princesses greet each other with kisses to the cheek; some of the friendlier ones may even extend this to you as meetings progress. I do not recommend reciprocating, but they are not unfamiliar with a kiss on the hand, and that would be an acceptable response. When we arrive at the palace, you will be ushered to your quarters. I will have to leave you there, as I have obligations elsewhere with the faerie monarchy."

"And so we sit and wait until one of them deigns to retrieve us?" Tiberius sounded less than happy, which was not a surprise to Garridan; the man had done nothing but complain since they'd left Laurus.

"Do you expect them to play nanny to us?" Kiryk asked.

"It is true that you may not see much of the palace," Eyad responded. "Not many faeries beyond those with governing power are aware of this meeting; it all depends on the outcome. I will be moving back and forth between both parties." His tone grew conciliatory. "You will all be well taken care of, I promise."

"Will the king and advisors be given their own rooms?" Garridan asked.

"I believe so," Eyad said. "There are separate quarters for military, but I think they would rather keep all of you in the same area."

Garridan shook his head. "Eyad, I will have to insist that we remain with the king and advisors." He then turned to view the advisors, side by side on the trail behind him. "Gentlemen, Your Majesty—for security purposes, I highly recommend that Kiryk and Tiberius share quarters. We can better protect you if you are not separated. We *will* designate a watch each night." He looked at Eyad, who gazed back with a neutral expression. "Friendly or no, my men and I will not negotiate that point."

Eyad nodded slowly. "Understood."

"Very well, Captain," Edric agreed.

"If I can endure Tiberius's snoring on the journey here, I am sure I will survive another week and a half," Kiryk said dryly. Tiberius cast him a stony glare.

Garridan looked past the advisors to Darson and Mourin, raising an eyebrow inquisitively. Darson raised his hand in an "all-clear" signal.

"The question is, does he want us in the room with them?" Darson whispered to Mourin. "If he does, I might suffocate Tiberius in his sleep."

Mourin coughed to cover a laugh, then winced and slapped his neck. He rubbed a fresh mosquito bite. "I don't recall there ever being a need for mosquitoes the size of dogs," he muttered.

"Might not have been that big before he started with you."

"That's disgusting, Darson."

"Feeling lightheaded? A bit woozy, perhaps?"

"Entertain yourselves quietly, men," Garridan called to

them. "Where we are not forced into your conversation due to close proximity."

Kiryk chuckled. "Now that is the politest way I have ever heard someone tell others to shut their mouths."

Darson smirked at Garridan when the captain looked back, and then continued to cautiously watch the jungle, as if staring hard enough would peel back the vegetation and reveal a land more familiar. The horses were uneasy as well, ears pricking at every close noise, nostrils flaring when a stray, particularly pungent scent wafted to them. A fine mist crept along the path, weaving through the wild forest.

Darson eyed a slender snake, striped bright yellow and brown, slithering through the limbs of a nearby moss-laden tree. The noise level in the jungle was ridiculous; with the constant low murmur of cicadas, the throaty croaking of frogs, buzzing insects whipping past and tickling his skin, birds trilling and cawing to one another in mildly sweet notes and piercing, sharp cries. Strange animals hooted and shouted warnings with high-pitched shrieks and low, ominous growls from deep within the thick trees.

Any number of predators could lurk in the foliage, or perhaps above in the maze of limbs and leaves. Darson found himself longing for the open, flat lands of home and even godforsaken Hesperia. Even the birds were difficult to keep track of; they were mere flashes of vivid colors flitting past the eye.

The king broke the quiet of the group. "Would it be safe to say, Eyad, that the Erepos have not traveled this far north? Or could there be another reason for their absence in this region?"

"The borders are quite fortified," the sorcerer replied. "And even Erepos find this sort of terrain unpleasant and difficult."

"Too much work," Darson agreed, more to himself than the group. Large plants with leaves the size of saddles sprouted from the ground and brushed his breeches as they passed.

"How do they live in this humidity?" Tiberius wondered aloud, his voice strained. He adjusted his weight uncomfortably as he wiped his hand across the back of his hot, sweaty neck. "Land alive, a week here's going to be the death of me."

"Could be beneficial to you, Tiberius," Kiryk quipped. "What sort of meat do they eat, Eyad?"

"Humans," Darson said automatically.

Eyad chuckled along with the king and Kiryk. "It has been quite a while since they had contact with humans," the sorcerer said. "Meat is not as prevalent here as in other fae countries or Aliquis; they consume quite a lot of fish. Wild boar, alligators, certain amphibians and insects. Snakes."

Darson felt ill at the mention of snakes. Would they be forced to eat anything like that? He would rather starve.

"My grandmother used to tell me stories," Tiberius said, eyeing Eyad suspiciously. He blew out a breath and then reached down for his leather water bag and took a drink. "She heard tell they kept humans as pets, namely children. Raised them and kept them for their amusement. Any truth in that, sorcerer?"

"I have never met a faerie who did so."

That is a terribly ambiguous answer, Darson thought sourly, noting Eyad had evaded the human meat question as well.

"Will we not see any faeries until we reach the palace?" Tiberius asked. "Are there none in this part of the jungle?"

"They are not far," Garridan said over his shoulder. "I have no doubt they are very aware of our movements."

"The captain is correct," Eyad said. "They were warned ahead of time to allow us passage without presenting themselves."

The trail widened, allowing for more breathing room and easing the claustrophobia of the jungle. Garridan rearranged the placement of his men; Eyad took the lead, with the king in between Mourin and Garridan, and the advisors riding alongside Darson.

"I'm sure they have their rope and blindfolds handy as a precaution," Darson said. "They appear to be fond of that combination."

"Hesperia's soldiers are very … thorough. And suspicious," Eyad said. "Some of the best trained in the kingdom."

"Trained to be sadistic," Darson muttered. "Trained to play mind games. Trained—"

Garridan sighed. "Lieutenant."

"Captain." Darson stared moodily at a shiny black beetle perched on a sloping leaf. Yellow markings slashed its carapace in random streaks. "You didn't have the pleasure of meeting that superior."

Garridan gave him a look that quelled Darson's desire to continue.

The convoy fell into silence. It wasn't until an hour later, when they traveled under an awning of sun-dappled leaves and great, waxy white flowers shot through with purple veins that Eyad held up a hand. His eyes took on a faraway look as he smiled. "We will have company momentarily."

Garridan's gazed at the sorcerer. Mourin stiffened and Darson's hand strayed to his weapon.

Eyad waved off their reaction. "You needn't worry."

The footfalls of a horse, softly clopping on the dirt path, reached Darson's ears. Eyad quietly encouraged them to make room on the path. Darson urged Kiryk's and Tiberius's horses to the left and positioned himself behind them to encounter the traveler first.

The misty film along the dirt path whirled as a lone horse approached their party from the rear. The mare, a chestnut with a high, reddish sheen, trotted slowly, head held high, mane fluttering. She shifted to one side, slowing to pass the group.

Darson looked upon the rider, and all else fell away.

He suddenly understood why the poet Kavya's pages of lyrical devotion to her faerie lover were among the greatest love poems ever penned.

The faerie's sun-kissed hair swept back from a lovely face into a careless bun. Olive green draped over warm golden skin, the sheath-like material embroidered at the hems with red and ivory whorls and delicate, unfamiliar markings. Her golden eyes watched them with friendly curiosity, yet retained sharpness, as she appeared to commit each face to memory. When her attention lighted on Darson, he stared unabashedly back. He could not believe the true gold of her irises; they were the color of sunlight striking autumn leaves.

One eyebrow rose higher, letting him know she was perfectly aware that he had yet to show proper manners.

Hand to chest, Darson inclined his head. With her attire and demeanor, he would bet every ounce of silver in his savings that she was royalty or close to it. She all but confirmed it when she looked away from him as if dismissing him.

But why was she alone? He did not believe royalty

anywhere traveled alone—unless Miranda's hidden soldiers kept an eye on her. Or maybe this realm truly was as safe as Eyad proclaimed. It pleased him that, regardless of the land's protection, a fine looking wooden bow and a quiver full of arrows hung from her saddle, close at hand.

"Who is that young faerie coming up the path?" Eyad asked in a manner that suggested long acquaintance.

The exquisite female's vaguely pleased expression dwindled to nothing. A cool blankness took its place. "Hello, Eyad." Her dulcet voice, in perfect, faintly accented Vinculum, carried the same distance—a perfunctory politeness. "Wonderful to see you."

If wonderful meant *awful*, Darson thought, intrigued. He recalled Arrian from Hesperia and his similar reaction to Eyad's name. And now *another* faerie less than thrilled with the sorcerer's presence. *We don't like him, either, you gorgeous creature. Tell me all about how much you hate him—I will hang on every word.*

Eyad turned to the men and said, "King Edric, gentlemen, this is—"

"Liana," she cut in smoothly, and then smiled. "From the country of Creo. Welcome to the kingdom."

Neither advisor seemed to know what to say. Their eyes struggled to comprehend the immortal being before them. Kiryk had turned a curious shade of pink. The king thanked her and said, "It is a fine pleasure to make your acquaintance, Lady Liana."

"The pleasure is mine, Your Majesty. I hope your expedition thus far has been uneventful."

"You are the liveliest surprise we have received," Eyad said. "Otherwise, without incident."

Liana paused. The words she spoke next felt like a substitution for something else. "I imagine the rainforest is quite a change for you." She directed the comment to the king, although her eyes included the advisors and soldiers. Darson felt a thrill when her gaze swept over him once more.

"*Warmer* than we are accustomed to, my lady," Kiryk responded. "Crowded with life and greenery."

She did not smile, but her eyes warmed. "I, too, am more comfortable in open spaces. And I must say I find the humidity quite tiresome. My country is drier."

Her countenance suggested that she was moments away from excusing herself and leaving, having engaged in a sufficient amount of pleasantries. Darson freed his tongue from the roof of his mouth and, heart beating wildly, asked, "What sort of terrain does Creo possess?"

Her gaze penetrated him in a way that assured him she saw the fluster underneath his attempt at a cool exterior. "Sand."

"The desert," Kiryk mused. "Fascinating."

Before he could continue, the faerie nodded, and then said, "Perhaps we shall meet at a later time and discuss further. For now, I must take my leave, gentlemen." She inclined her head to the king. "I hope you find your stay pleasant. We are pleased to have you."

She bid them good-bye despite protests from Eyad and Edric—and Darson's silent objection—and disappeared up the path.

"If our God is kind, they are all as ravishing," Kiryk said when they were alone. "Remind me again why we cut ties with them?"

"For every reason under the sun besides physical beauty, I am sure," Edric said somewhat dryly. "But she is certainly lovely."

"Would her appearance indicate our closeness to the palace?" Garridan asked Eyad.

"Yes. We are very close."

* * *

When they continued, Garridan could not help but marvel over the exchange. The reality of the faeries' existence blindsided him, and the effect lingered like a fragrant perfume long after the sound of her horse's hooves faded away. She looked no different than a human, yet she possessed the luminescence of a dream-like creature formed out of the imagination of a poet. The sun spun itself in Lady Liana's hair and eyes; the green of the earth wove through her dress. She truly looked as if the desert itself created her.

"Was she royalty?" he finally asked, aiming the question at Eyad.

"Yes," Darson answered confidently.

"Indeed," the sorcerer replied. "I do not believe she wished to conduct formalities on the path. Liana governs the country she mentioned."

"You appeared to know Lady Liana well," the king said.

"For many centuries. She is no stranger to the human lands."

"When has she traveled through our kingdoms?" Kiryk asked.

"It was well before your time," Eyad said blithely.

Garridan waited for more information, but Eyad did not seem inclined to provide any. Was it possible that the blonde faerie had been alive during the time of interaction between the races? His mind could barely conceive of such an age.

He was almost disappointed that they saw no more travelers on the path. Snatches of darkening sky appeared more frequently, and the rainforest's umbrella-like covering began to thin here and there; the thick jungle spread out and relaxed its tight embrace. The coming sunset, splashing brilliant red and orange where light was allowed in, increased Garridan's apprehension. He did not think staying a night in the jungle was a worry any longer—he knew they were close to their destination—but the total lack of visibility worried him.

* * *

After another forty-five minutes of travel, weariness and heat dug grooves in the King's face.

"Eyad." Edric's unspoken question hung in the air.

"We come upon the palace gates, Your Majesty. Minutes away."

And it was suddenly before them. The gate rose from the earth, as natural as the trees, shimmering gold against deep, vivid greens. The men stopped and drank in the impressive sight towering at least two dozen feet in the air, yet still dwarfed by the immense trees surrounding it. The slim, gold bars expanded into the forest; leafy vines intertwined with the effervescent metal. Naked tree roots, as tall as their horses' flanks and arching above the ground as a spider's legs might, formed an additional protective layer outside the boundary.

"Is that real gold?" Tiberius whispered.

Garridan wanted to reach out and touch it; he had never seen so much gold in all his life. He did not think such a gate could exist. Or if it *should* exist. That much gold would feed an entire city for untold seasons. How did this much wealth sit here, protecting a palace already well protected by its unforgiving surroundings?

"Princess Aaclyde, sovereign of Miranda, has fortified this country for centuries," Eyad said with a touch of a pride, "and it has many gifts and resources to give. She makes it shine, and guards it well."

Sunset broke through the clearing, setting the golden gate afire and piercing through the mist gathered on the forest floor. They could not see beyond the bars, only that it was lighter there.

Foreboding prickled along Garridan's skin, awed and dumbfounded as he was by the grandiose gate and what lay beyond it. He braced himself for the unexpected, and he knew his soldiers did the same. They waited.

The gate shivered, and then opened, silently swinging inward.

More jungle lay ahead, mists hovering protectively over the dirt, the lowering sun stinging their eyes and banishing the previous shadow. Darson and Mourin both knew the vision before them could be as big a lie as a deceptively empty golden field.

"Welcome, gentlemen," Eyad said, "to Princess Aaclyde's home." He swept a hand forward. "Shall we?"

Chapter 12

The procession entered slowly. Garridan tried, and failed, to anticipate what would happen; the anticlimactic answer of *nothing* did not ease him. It only mounted the strain and stretched it further, like a taut wire, as more of the same jungle surrounded the company for the next few minutes. No one greeted them, and no buildings came into sight. A large clearing scattered with trees lay ahead. Garridan suspected it was filled with no more than fauna and birds.

And then, to Garridan's shock, the nature of sound shifted from the wild calls of animals and insects to musical voices. The clearing was *not* empty. Eyad led them down the path, and ahead, the elusive faeries were gathered.

Figures appeared from behind thick tree trunks, up pathways now made of stone rather than dirt. Over a dozen, beautiful and unreal. Males wore high-collared jackets or long robes, some wearing leather belts with scabbards. The females wore tunics with skirts, wide-sleeved robes, high-collared dresses, all spun from silk in gleaming silvers and deep greens, the blue of a sea tide, glittering like stars or painted like the setting sun with beautiful embroidery. Their dark hair hung loose or braided with combs in their hair.

They watched the men with knowing, mirthful eyes. It surprised Garridan to see a few children walking through what he now knew to be a courtyard; cherubic young faces gaped at them with blatant curiosity.

Dirt became thick grass as the men and horses approached a large sandstone platform. The burnt-umber floor was smooth and expansive, stretching the length of the courtyard and curving into a half moon at the edges. The horses stepped up, hooves striking sharply on the stone. Two narrow, rectangular pools of pale green water ran up either side of the wide main walkway, the still surfaces scattered with flat lily pads large enough for a child to sit on, edges elevated like the crust of a pie. Flourishing white and pink flowers floated languidly. Sleek, colorful fish swam underneath. Potted ferns ran down the length of the pools, fanning the air with long, green fingers.

The tranquility of the courtyard transfixed Garridan. He looked down at the impossibly large, lazy gold and white fish curling around each other, flicking his gaze every few seconds to keep the king in his sights, until audible gasps rippled through the men and diverted his attention. His eyes followed the length of the pools up to the palace.

The structure, wrought of the same umber sandstone as the platform, stretched high into the fiery sunset. Long, wide steps rose to impressive red doors etched with shimmering veins of gold.

Gold in the door? They need it etched in the door? The gate was not enough?

Walkways stretched the expanse of the palace, protected by open square archways supported by red round columns five stories high, with fanlight windows decorating each tiered level. Pointed green cupolas mounted on pillars mingled with the overhanging leaves of the surrounding forest, spears of sandstone rising above the trees. The roofs were raised and curved at the corners, as if the roofs themselves reached towards the sun.

"Did you ever dream such a piece of architecture could exist?" Kiryk asked in a hushed voice.

"No," Garridan said faintly.

History permeated each pillar and eave, its sandstone, wood, and glass well cared for through time. Garridan felt the weight of the thousands of years of majesty before them. The king's castle was a dollhouse compared to the venerable and vast edifice. The entire company froze in silence before it.

Garridan heard the sound of a horse and tore his eyes away.

A gorgeous pale, gray-blue stallion cantered past, carrying another female faerie. He noted her state of dress; she did not seem like a monarch. Her deep teal tunic ended in an almost scandalously short skirt, and she wore knee-high black boots. The scabbard that hung from the saddle surprised him. He looked from it to her striking face and the unreadable expression that he guessed meant she was not too happy to see them. Loose, wavy black curls tumbled down her arms and back. Her eyes seemed to lock with his for a fleeting second, but then the moment was gone, and she looked at Eyad. She nodded curtly at the sorcerer.

Garridan watched her dismount nearby and walk to the palace entrance as a faerie led her horse away. Shaking out her hair, she ascended the steps but did not get far; one of the grand doors opened, and a lone male faerie slipped through.

He stopped his rapid descent, changed course, and went to her instead.

Eyad escorted the men closer to the steps, and they drew nearer to the female faerie and her new companion. After they dismounted, a young male faerie—to Garridan's eye no older than a boy of thirteen—approached and exchanged words in the Fae tongue with Eyad. He wore a comfortable looking long jacket held closed with small loops of fabric of the same silky material he saw on the faeries in the courtyard.

"They will care for our horses and take our belongings inside while we wait," Eyad translated. With trepidation, the men dismounted and allowed the faerie, accompanied by two new others, to take their horses. Garridan looked at Darson and Mourin, and the trio formed a rough circle around the king and his advisors. Garridan felt the tension radiate from Darson and the rising anxiety from Mourin, whose hand clutched the hilt of his sword.

"Mourin," Garridan murmured, his voice tinted with caution. Mourin relaxed and removed his hand from his sword with an exhale. Behind him, Eyad conversed with the king in low tones, their heads tilted toward one another.

Garridan looked back to the exchange between the two faeries on the steps. The female's back was to the men. The male faerie cut an impressive figure: windswept blond hair, handsome features, and a manner and stance that screamed military. His attire was comprised of more muted colors, earthy browns and greens; he, too, appeared to be a visitor here. Garridan could not quash his curiosity about what they discussed, and he wished he could understand the lyrical language.

Yet he questioned his own reasons for wanting to know.

Because the faerie was striking, and he wanted to know who she was? Did his curiosity stem from something that shallow?

"What are you staring at?" Darson asked, practically in his ear, startling him.

The lieutenant peered in the female faerie's direction without waiting for an answer. His eyes widened; he was as visibly taken aback as Garridan had ever seen him. Then his jaw tensed, and he swallowed. "Of course. Of *course* he would be here."

Confused, Garridan looked at the blond faerie. And then it clicked. "Is he the one from Hesperia?"

Darson gave a short nod. He crossed his arms and looked down, the picture of a man who wanted to sink into the ground and disappear. "Oh, yes. *That's* the ass that manhandled me."

"Careful," Garridan warned. "We don't know how good their hearing is." The faerie in question looked in their direction. The female turned, as well, assessing them—and locked eyes with Garridan again.

Recognition suddenly dawned on the blond faerie's face. To Darson's incredulity, the male began to laugh, head bowed as he enjoyed a moment of amusement at the lieutenant's expense. He said something to the female, and she broke her gaze with Garridan to listen to her companion.

Mourin watched the exchange, his face growing pale. He said nothing, and then turned his body away to stare at the palace doors as if he hoped to will them open.

"He appears to be laughing at you, son," Kiryk said to Darson. He seemed to appear out of nowhere and didn't bother to hide that he was eavesdropping. "This the one that trussed you up like a sow?"

Darson did not appreciate the reminder and had no compunction communicating that with his face to Kiryk. "No. This is their superior. His name is Arrian."

The name stirred Eyad. When he saw the faerie in question, he chuckled. "I still find it fascinating, Lieutenant, that of all the faeries you could meet on your journey, one such as he was the first. You should be honored. And worry not—the commander is utterly professional, and he will be an asset to our discussions." Eyad then dropped his voice and addressed the king. "As I mentioned before, the commander's role encompasses more than overseeing the military in each country; they truly function as second-in-commands to the monarchy. Arrian is considered one of the most formidable in the kingdom."

Darson hissed in a breath when Arrian looked at him again with a smile and raised a hand in welcome. "I am not feeling very honored," he muttered.

Garridan watched as Arrian led the female faerie away, one hand hovering at the small of her back. He could not speculate on them any longer, however, for the palace doors finally opened.

Eyad moved forward and blocked their view as he greeted the faerie that stepped out. "Princess Aaclyde."

When he bowed, Garridan glimpsed grey locks, a dark dress, and something shimmering, filmy and transparent, behind her head—was it *moving?*—before Eyad stood again.

"What a marvelous pleasure," the sorcerer continued. "Thank you for your generous hospitality, Your Highness."

The response was delivered in a smooth, feminine, low alto. "Thank you, Eyad, for escorting our guests."

Eyad stepped to the side and gestured to Edric. "May I present King Edric of Aliquis. Your Majesty, may I introduce Princess Aaclyde of Miranda, who has opened her home to hold this conference."

King Edric bowed low and raised his gaze to the royal faerie. He struggled to find his voice before the proper words came out. "It is an honor to make your acquaintance, Your Highness. My deepest appreciation for your kind hospitality."

A slim hand extended out in the human gesture of greeting. With no small amount of wonder did King Edric gingerly take the offered hand and kiss it gently, a smile lighting his wizened face. The smile was returned in kind.

"Long has it been since I looked upon the face of a mortal. I am pleased to see yours, Your Majesty. I am equally honored to welcome you and yours into my home."

Garridan was not close to her, but he could see the deep brown of her eyes, the limitless knowledge and weight of power in them. A sleek, short cap of grey and white hair fell to her gracefully pointed ears. A gold circlet graced her forehead, wrought with emerald ivy leaves. Her long, high-collared dress was radiant indigo, like the deep purple veins of the lush white flowers in the rainforest. But it was not her garb that took his breath away.

The wings fluttering at her back did.

As the other men of the party reacted with quiet gasps, Garridan drank in the sight his mind could not understand. He traced the outline of the nearly transparent wings with his eyes, and tried to process the reality of them as something *attached to her body*. Ocean blue and deep purple seemed etched into the delicate membrane, more prominent where wispy veins ran through the translucent, paper-thin skin. The wings curved upward from Princess Aaclyde's back and fluttered very gently every few seconds, like the twitch of a muscle or a heartbeat. The edges were not smooth but jagged, almost torn, until the wings met between her shoulder blades. They simultaneously astounded and repulsed Garridan.

"My God," Tiberius whispered from a few feet away, his face contorting as if he'd bit down on something horrid. Closer to Garridan, Darson stared too, with a perplexed intensity, as if his incomprehension of their existence angered him. Mourin's already pale complexion turned even whiter.

"The hour grows late," Princess Aaclyde continued, as if her appearance had not just changed them all in an inexplicable way. A smile touched her lips, lightening her serene countenance, perfectly aware of the reason for their distraction. "Tonight will be a night of rest for your weary company. The queen has retired for the evening, and she will see you first thing in the morning." At that, she turned and walked up the steps. The indigo dress draped low in the back, leaving her shoulder blades bare to accommodate the marvelous wings.

From the back they appeared larger, and Garridan repressed the urge to strain his neck to inspect where the wings sprouted—*sprouted*, like a plant; he could hardly believe it—from the skin of her back. Even the king stared, fascinated, yet also with mild repugnance, at the oddity.

Eyad led the men inside. They trailed in pairs once again, with Garridan protecting the king's back as they crossed over the threshold.

Garridan said to Darson, barely allowing sound to pass his lips, "You failed to mention *wings*."

"None of the soldiers in Hesperia had them," Darson whispered back fervently. "That's not a detail I would leave out."

The absolute splendor of the palace's cavernous foyer nearly struck Garridan dumb. Would the wonders *never* end? It was like walking into a mural infused with palatial strokes of vibrant greens for the plants, pale gold in the marble floors, all of it soaked in affluent finery. On the far left and right sides of the room, identical grand staircases rose to the second level, hidden behind the square cupola in the ceiling's center. The banisters and balustrades were a rich, deep wood, and ivory carpet lined each step. Crimson silk ribbons wove around each balustrade.

The vaulted ceiling curved, painted in golds and reds. A narrow ledge followed the curve of the ceiling, and flourishing green plants hung over it and drifted in the open air above the platform. A massive chandelier hung in the center, the glass and metal twisted to resemble slender tree limbs.

Garridan's travel-worn boots were filthy against the spotless floors. He wanted to apologize for coming in here, fouling up the perfumed air.

The group followed Eyad and the princess through a set of glass doors; the sorcerer and faerie princess had disconnected from the group, and they stood a short distance away, speaking in low tones. Tall windows lined the far sides of the lengthy hall before them. The right windows let in what remained of the evening light and filled the room with the dusky blue of twilight. Massive porcelain vases, set on either side of the princess's throne area, spilled over with a riot of feathery ferns and piles of exotic flowers of red, green, and gold. A single high-backed chair sat atop a lush, bloodred rug running the length of the raised dais across the open, airy hall. The chair was deep gold and run through with delicate carvings. A plush cushion the same shade as the rug sat empty.

Garridan wanted to touch it, if only to convince himself it was real.

The princess glided across the hall and veered away from her throne, leading them toward a large, arched doorway. Garridan mentally compared her to Liana, the only other faerie royalty he had seen, and found subtle differences that spoke of a difference in age. Liana carried herself regally, yet with an approachable, youthful air. Age and experience trickled from Princess Aaclyde's pores, to the point where she seemed far removed from the banal experiences that bothered lesser beings.

He made a conscious effort to tear his eyes from her, and noticed the hall was not empty; other faeries walked the floor or stood in small groups and watched the procession, their finery gleaming under the warm lighting. A few had wings like Aaclyde: one who looked closer to Garridan's age, her wings like spun sunlight with dew clinging to the veins and thin skin, and a male with wings the color of an early morning fog. Their wings would flutter, and a shudder would work its way up Garridan's spine. He looked away when they gazed back, scrutinizing him as he did them.

"Your home defies words, Your Highness," King Edric said, as quiet as if he were speaking in a holy place. "A true vision of artistry and elegance."

Princess Aaclyde graced him with a small smile. "Thank you for your kind words."

More children like the ones Garridan had seen in the courtyard lined either side of the doorway. Aaclyde gestured to them. "My helpers will show you to your rooms."

Helpers? Garridan and Darson instantly looked at one another, eyebrows raised.

"After you freshen up, should you choose to partake, there are refreshments in the dining area, which you will see on the way to your quarters. Feel free to help yourself to any food or drink before you retire. Breakfast will be served at dawn."

Eyad thanked the princess and then turned to the king. "I will retrieve you all in the morning for breakfast; then I will take you to meet the queen and the other princesses so our discussions may begin. I will leave you now so that I may converse with the Princess Aaclyde. Captain, I spoke with her about the sleeping arrangements; it is taken care of to meet your requirements."

"Thank you," Garridan said.

"Let the young ones take you to your quarters and show you where to find dinner. I will see you all in the morning."

Two escorts led them: an adolescent female with a long, dark braid moved to stand next to the king, and a young male faerie with a fall of black hair strolled along by the soldiers.

Garridan did not like Eyad's absence, nor did he like putting his trust and the safety of his king in the hands of small faerie children. He thought it odd that no one checked them for weapons, as would be the custom for any visiting convoy in Laurus or any other town. The princess had greeted them personally, without the presence of armed guards or any staff. Was it because they truly felt they had nothing to fear from these feeble humans? Were the faeries that confident? It made Garridan think that no matter what weapon he wielded, it would be useless against these creatures.

The thought plagued his mind as they walked down finely carpeted halls lit by lanterns in sconces. Murals of wild plants and vibrant flowers adorned the walls. The right wall eventually broke away in favor of a large pane of glass bearing the outline of a door; on the other side laid an outside courtyard, gray with growing nightfall. Stone paths wound through a garden, and somewhere in its depths, in spite of the glass, he could hear water gush and fall in pleasant patters.

Garridan felt as suffocated in here as he had in the jungle; the walls closed everything in, and the clutter of furniture and flowers in the halls filled the spaces to bursting. He had never in his life seen such an accumulation of *things*. He tried not to let that become a distraction as he mentally drew a map of their journey to remember the way out.

That proved to be more difficult than he expected. The men followed the faerie children for what seemed like ages, and he wondered if the children led them to their quarters in a manner to deliberately confuse their sense of direction. Garridan lost the thread of his internal map after the third staircase and the sixth turn into a new, twisting hallway. The boy pointed out the closed doors to the dining area, but by the time they reached the rooms, Garridan could not retrace his steps. His unease tightened the muscles of his shoulders, and he exchanged frustrated glances with Darson more than once.

Their quarters, a cloister of rooms down a T-shaped hallway, comprised one wing of the palace. The two guides showed them the communal bathing area, which were four doors down the hall on the left. Before allowing the king into his room, Garridan indicated to the little female faerie that he would search the room first. Ignoring her affronted look, he and Darson entered the king's quarters and inspected every nook and cranny of the room. A wide, four-poster bed took up most of the space; the king's belongings, collected with the horses earlier, sat in the travel bag on top of the brilliantly green satin bedding. Garridan combed through the bag and the bedding lest any nasty surprises awaited his monarch. He could not believe how incredibly soft and sleek the bedding was beneath his fingertips.

He idly noted little sculptures of a strange, plump animal that looked like a doughy cow. They were on the nightstand, carved into the bed frame, and depicted in small statues on the floor. He felt along the plush seats of the chairs, checked underneath the firm, well sown mattress, the armoire, closet, window latches—adorned with more carvings of the same odd, fat animal—and curtains.

The pair did the same for the advisors' room before letting the faerie child take them to their own quarters, leaving the advisors and the king to unpack.

Their quarters were far nicer than the three men had hoped for; there was a high ceiling, carpet, and a trio of double beds richly decorated, two to one wall and the third to the left of the door. A large bay window took over the entire far wall, and wispy golden curtains were pulled back to display a view of the jungle.

"There is the bell," the boy said in heavily accented Vinculum. He pointed at a silver bell hanging from the wall by the door. "If you need anything. Your room, it is good?"

"Yes, thank you," Garridan answered.

The faerie bowed, and then he paused as a new thought crossed his young face. He took a deep breath and said, "Do not be alarmed if you wake at night and hear … moving. It is normal. You… prefer them to clean at daytime, when you are not there? They prefer night."

All three men stared at him blankly. Garridan shook his head. "I beg your pardon?"

"Cleaning, like servants coming in?" Darson asked. "They would *clean* in the room while we slept?"

"Brownies," the child said, as if that explained everything. "You do not see them. They are…" his face scrunched as he searched for the word. "How do you say … careful? But if it troubles, we can have them clean when you are gone."

When Darson looked ready to ask more questions as Mourin paled again, Garridan hurriedly said, "If it isn't too much trouble, we would prefer it if they cleaned during the day. Thank you."

The young faerie smiled with relief that his message carried through. He wished them good night and then left.

"What is a brownie?" Darson asked.

"You don't know?" Garridan asked. "Resident expert?"

"My mother studies *faeries*. Have I ever given any indication I knew about the existence of a *brownie*?"

"You didn't know about the wings, either," Mourin added. "Should we worry about these brownie creatures?"

Darson gave him a dirty look. "I doubt it; they sound like maids. And for your information, my mother never mentioned wings. As I said, none of the soldiers in Hesperia had wings."

"Other than the princess, I saw two faeries with wings in the grand hall," Garridan said. "None of the children had them. Why is it so selective?"

"Why are you asking me? I have no idea." Darson thought about it and remembered how delicate the skin looked. "They don't look functional. Maybe it's a feature that was useful at one time, but now they have no need for it."

Garridan studied his friend. "Sometimes I forget how observant you are. You really should not hide that quality behind your idiotic tendencies."

"I am going to disregard that insult and remember the compliment, if you do not mind."

"It does not change the truth of both statements. Let us find the king and eat."

Chapter 13

When she smelled death in the courtyard, she knew the mortals had arrived.

Once again, she cursed the queen and the sorcerer.

She had wanted to arrive in Miranda without seeing the mortals' pale, aging faces any sooner than necessary. She *wanted* to put her troublesome new roan to stable—Breathitt was beautiful and promising, but trying after a day of travel—and slip quietly into the maze of Aaclyde's palace to retire after the long, hard ride in peace.

It took everything in her to keep from sneering when she had passed the huddle of human confusion earlier, staring at her people as if they were animals in a menagerie. It had taken a smidgen more willpower to acknowledge Eyad's presence among them.

She had been acutely aware of the sorcerer observing her with Arrian. She took heart when the Hesperian emerged from the palace. Watching him appear, as if summoned by her mind's pleas for respite, settled her warring heart like a comforting hand to the cheek.

And then he ruined everything by leaving.

She remained in the courtyard as the tan gelding and its

rider rode away from the palace and disappeared into the night. Her stance mirrored the pensive, troubled set of her face, eyes distant as Commander Arrian's words turned over in her head with an unpleasant portent for the weeks to come.

Commander Nevada let out a slow breath as time passed, and suddenly night had fallen. Flames flickered in sconces along the arcade walkway behind her, their light dancing on the smooth stone around her feet. The courtyard was nearly empty now, and yet she still earned curious glances from passersby.

The faerie rolled her shoulders, tight neck muscles rebelling, and turned toward the palace. She decided to obey her hunger and head toward the lone dining area that remained open throughout the night. She could not shake her distress as she walked and ruminated over Arrian's reason for departure: the appearance of an enemy not spotted near fae soil in over a century. Before last month, that was, when the humans had traipsed on their land.

The timing was peculiar. And she did not believe in coincidences.

Could they have brought the problem with them? It would figure. The humans' first foray into fae territory in almost a thousand years, and they brought unwanted guests.

And as competent a commander as Arrian was, he was not immune to injury or death. The past several years had forced the faerie to reevaluate her opinion on the matter of immortality.

Nevada worried for him.

The proximity of the sightings was troublesome, too, so close to the location of a gathering of every ruler in the kingdom. Granted, there was an entire mountain range in their way and the majority of Hesperia, yet she could not help but worry over the prospect of more than one crossing the border into Miranda and slouching toward the jungle.

For now, there's nothing else to be done, she told herself. Arrian will return soon with more information. The conference would be enough to occupy her attention over the next few days.

Already, her patience for this conference was fleeting.

Humans.

She snorted as she navigated the winding, carpeted hallways and took a shortcut through one of the gardens protected by a glass partition. In the courtyard, Nevada passed marble statues, ponds with small waterfalls, and night-blooming flowers bursting open with wide, vibrant petals. It had been many years since her last visit to Miranda's palace, but she recalled enough of its layout to allow her mind to wander as she walked.

The humans' boldness was surprising, but the reason why was obvious. She was not as willfully blind as many other faeries to the trials of mortals, of their shrinking borders and the increasingly desperate measures they took to survive. Proposing an alliance with her people was a shiny gloss attempting to hide the deep scars of a cry for help.

She wondered if the mortals even knew how much, once upon a time, they had been hated by the fae—and vice versa.

But why Eyad's involvement? What prompted him to strike up a relationship with the Aliquis king and convince the mortal to take this risk? Why this king's plight, versus all the others?

And Nevada knew enough about human nature to guess

they would hardly mention their need in the initial contact. The monarchy wouldn't know how to take all those hands held out for assistance begging for soldiers, food, raw materials, or medicine.

Build our walls, they would plead.

Train our men.

Stop the infection.

The list would grow now that they'd seen for themselves the sheer opulence of Aaclyde's country. Nevada recalled the wonder and awe in their faces in the courtyard. Never in their short lives had they believed such a place could exist, all while they rationed food and walled up their cities and lived in fear.

Would it deplete the fae's resources to help the mortals? No. Nevada certainly did not have the soldiers to spare, but it was possible for others. She only worried for the greedy reach of many hands — hands that had historically reached out to harm.

Nevada turned a corner and wound up a few doors from the dining area; her stomach groaned as her heightened senses picked up the sharp, sweet smell of fruit and wine. Marginally heartened, she quickened her step.

And heard the human voices coming from inside.

Her heart sank even as her feet carried her to the doorway. This was the last place she wanted an encounter with them. She hadn't yet crossed the threshold, nor been spotted by the humans loitering at one of the tables.

One of the soldiers chose that moment to look over at her. Of course.

To hell with him. Nevada backed up to go to the kitchens and eat alone, not at all interested in the spark of recognition in the human's blue eyes. The four-day journey had sapped her strength, and talking with Arrian had placed a boulder neatly between her shoulder blades, adding to the small mountain of stress balancing precariously at the base of her neck. She did not have a shred of endurance left to deal with them tonight.

Go home. Not all of us have excess riches to give you. We cannot fix your problems.

As she turned to leave, another voice, this time from an adjoining hallway in the opposite direction, reached her ears. Fast, furious, and masculine.

No.

As much as she looked forward to seeing this particular faerie, this was *not* the time and place to congregate. He probably just arrived, she thought, and had no idea of the changes made to the military involvement, or of Arrian's absence.

He will be so pleased to hear that nothing is going according to plan. Already.

"… if that miserable excuse for a sorcerer stayed out of our business, this seriously atrocious idea would not have come to fruition in the first place. I would like to know what he's been telling them."

Just turn and run, Nevada thought suddenly. Just sprint down the hall, and then stage another run-in at a safer location, where he could be fed up and angry far away from humans. Not that she disagreed—he was entirely on point about Eyad—but it was far too soon for the humans to find out that there were no bars separating them from the menagerie animals. And a panther was prowling his way toward them.

She'd already dawdled too long, and he would witness her mad dash and make the situation even more unbearable, so Nevada decided to head him off instead. She left the doorway and walked toward his voice.

"Liaison between humans and faeries," the male voice scoffed, seconds away from turning the corridors' corner. "I hope to Patris we are not paying him for that, since he has not mediated a damn thing between the races in seven or eight centuries."

The faerie attached to the voice rounded the corner with a long, purposeful stride, his hands in the middle of violent gestures and his head turned in profile. He was tall, with bronze skin and short, wild, dark brown hair. Breeches, with sand still clinging to the leather, and a simple, short sleeve shirt damp with sweat accentuated a lean physique.

Accompanying him was a much shorter, stunning redhead with wildly curly hair who appeared to be less outwardly affected by the ride in from their home country; dirt had a difficult time sticking to Princess Sunara. She did not bother giving him her attention, opting instead to stare impassively straight ahead. A flicker of relief in her patrician face rippled through the blankness when she noticed Nevada.

The male faerie turned his face in Nevada's direction, spotted her, and stopped walking. Surprise smoothed out some of the anger. His lips curved in a sincere smile. "Hello, Nevada. You look flustered."

He is too observant for his own good. Nevada smiled back. "Dacian. I was just so thrilled to hear your voice, I could hardly contain myself."

"Everyone tells me that."

"*Everyone* has different reasons for saying so," Sunara said.

She pointed to her companion and said to Nevada, "Take him. I am going to my room."

Dacian looked at his princess in astonishment. "Truly? The moons have barely risen. Aren't you hungry?"

There was no warmth in the vivid green eyes that met Nevada's gaze. "No."

"I can bring you some—"

"No."

She gestured to Nevada again in a way that suggested *he is all yours*, and then waved good-bye before leaving the male behind. He moved again, heading for the dining hall, and Nevada placed herself in front of him to stop him, demanding, "What did you do to your princess?"

"*Nothing.*" Dacian glared at her. "What is this monarchy doing to *us*? What are we doing here, Nev? Where is this surplus of soldiers with nothing better to do than be shipped out to a human kingdom? You cannot spare them, and I will be damned if I will send mine to the dark side of the world to live and work around humans."

"You are assuming too much before talks even begin."

"There are enough bleeding hearts ruling this kingdom to make it happen."

Nevada cocked her head to the side. "Really? We must be talking about a different group of princesses, because I can think of a few that are absolutely not all right with this. Not all—but some."

"Enough of them will not feel comfortable saying no, particularly if there are enough starving and dying children the humans can use as bargaining chips."

"*This* insight coming from a faerie whose concern with human affairs could not amount to a horse's interest in a fly," she said.

Dacian's voice lowered and acquired a new fervor. His hands sliced the air emphatically to punctuate his words. "You cannot tell me that our queen would allow them to come all this way, *knowing* what they will request, hear their case, and then turn them away. It would sully her reputation to ignore this opportunity if there is any kind of gain involved. Especially if it makes her look good."

Nevada hissed his name, unable to help the knee-jerk reaction to scan either end of the hall for any cherubic servants who would scamper straight to the queen. "She is *in* the palace, and you do not know who is listening. Save the slander for the open air, please?"

"She already knows how I feel," he responded flatly. "I repeatedly hold my tongue, Nevada, but this is ridiculous. Neither she nor any of us owe the mortals the time of day, let alone aid. And she'll offer it up on a platter."

Nevada wanted to take his words and infuriatingly accurate observations and set them on fire. She did not need this. What she needed was for this conference to be a quick, irritating blip, and then disappear, along with the mortals, into total oblivion. She was not ready to think about the long-term consequences of the humans' actions.

"And when this pact happens," Dacian continued, frothing himself back up to the lather he was in before running into her, "word will get out to the other mortal kingdoms. And guess whose door they will come to begging for scraps?"

"Enough." Nevada had to stop him and take him somewhere more secluded than mere yards away from a human-occupied dining room; they needed to be far from human ears and those of Aaclyde's staff before he really cracked open his chest of criticism. Or before she fired back and they had a spectacular row over politics. Again. "Let us discuss this somewhere else, or in the morning."

"I came here to eat. I'm starving."

"We can eat in the kitchens."

"Why? The food is right here, we can talk while I eat." He walked past her toward the entry, tossing back, "It has been a long day." He made it to the entryway with Nevada on his heels, and heard the laughter that trickled out. He halted and hissed in a breath like a territorial cat. "Perfect."

Nevada cupped his elbow to lead him away. "Kitchens. Leave them be."

He pulled out of her grasp, a new determination in his eyes. "I am not going to be chased away from a room because they are in it. The food is not labeled *mortals only*."

A flicker of doubt must have shown on her face, because he stopped advancing toward the doorway to give her a vexed look. "Nevada, I am going to get food, not terrorize the humans. Have a little faith."

* * *

Garridan had been pleased to see the raven-haired faerie from the courtyard standing in the hall, close to the archway entrance. She had stood motionless and looked vaguely uncomfortable at the prospect of entering. He then heard a masculine voice as someone approached her and she disappeared, presumably to greet the faerie she was talking with.

They spoke in the fae tongue; the male's speech rapid and displeased. The tone of her voice changed as well; the delivery grew sharper and then nearly desperate. It made Garridan nervous.

When the male faerie came into view in the archway, Garridan's guard rose. The faerie was tall, leanly muscled, and emanated a vibrant energy even from the hall. He didn't look happy, and his words, albeit indecipherable, left his tongue as fast as a spreading brush fire. The female stood by him, arms crossed, wearing an almost grim expression.

The topic of discussion was easy to guess when he tossed a hand in their direction.

"Do they know they have an audience?" Kiryk mumbled out of the side of his full mouth, craning his neck a little out of curiosity.

"They know," Darson muttered, watching the show as he ate a fried dumpling stuffed with pork in a violent sort of manner.

Garridan was ready to suggest the king enjoy the refreshments from his room, but remembered that the pair blocked the only exit.

"We will keep eating," the king told him, guessing the line of his thoughts. "They have every right to do as they please in their home. It is not directed at us."

"I wouldn't be so sure," Tiberius grumbled under his breath, shooting the faeries a scathing glance. "You do not have to be a linguistics expert to understand that when a word sounds like human, it most assuredly means human. The least they could do is go elsewhere."

Darson didn't look pleased at Tiberius' comments. He exchanged a glance with Garridan and discreetly scratched his ear.

Garridan nodded, understanding Darson's gesture. He

assumed their hearing was good enough to pick up even hushed conversation. Neither indicated as much thus far, but Garridan remained on guard. He couldn't tell how to proceed should the argument come into the room, or if either of the faeries addressed them. Diplomacy only carried so far; he did not know if they were here for the conference or if they merely lived in Miranda and worked in the palace. Eyad had not given them any indication of what topics were off limits or what constituted acceptable small talk in this country, if it came to that. There was a possibility the two faeries didn't speak Vinculum at all.

Maybe they would just leave the hall and disappear.

No sooner had Garridan completed the thought than the male faerie walked through the archway.

Chapter 14

He moved with a fluid grace that made Garridan touch his weapon for reassurance. The faerie didn't as much as blink in their direction, yet everything about his carriage suggested his complete awareness of the humans.

Kiryk continued eating, watching the faerie curiously. Mourin visibly tensed and appeared ready to leave his seat to stand by the king, but Darson touched his shoulder to keep him still. The lieutenant watched the newcomer, as well as the female faerie when she entered, with calculated disinterest. When her gaze swept over the men, Darson and Garridan nodded a greeting.

She hesitated, nodded back, and resumed watching her companion closely as he headed for the long table filled with platters of food.

Garridan was momentarily preoccupied with this closer look at the faerie he had seen earlier, notably her eye color: a vivid, entrancing violet. He had never seen that color outside of a flower or dye, and it transfixed him longer than he cared to admit. When he could look away, he noted the state of her dress again.

The deep teal material of what he originally thought was

a skirt appeared to be a short dress with no sleeves. Would this be a female warrior's attire? A uniform of some kind?

Maybe the more streamlined and form-fitting the uniform, the less it hindered them. Garridan wondered if the fae possessed the superior strength he assumed they did. Without the fear of infection from the Erepos, it allowed them to exchange the weight of protective armor for freedom, speed, and agility. And of course, this was the jungle; if she lived here, in this climate, he understood the lack of layers.

Garridan's attention returned to the male faerie's broad back, his nimble hand movements as he grabbed a plate and began dropping vibrant fruits and stuffed rolls on its surface.

The faeries' unintelligible argument hung in the room and left its mark on their beautiful faces. It was so quiet that Garridan cringed when Tiberius' chair screeched against the hardwood floor.

Edric cleared his throat politely and addressed the faeries. "Good evening."

The female smiled tightly at the monarch and, after a quick look at her companion's back, bowed slightly. "Good evening, Your Majesty."

Kiryk raised his wine glass to her, and Tiberius continued to eat, sneaking sullen glances at both of them.

"Are you here for the conference?" Edric inquired. "Do you hail from Miranda?"

Before she could reply, the male faerie clanked a glass against a plate hard enough to nearly crack it, startling everyone.

She glared at her companion.

"I am not from Miranda," she answered with a challenging note, apparently for her friend.

"And your comrade?"

Garridan's alert level went from mild caution to paranoid vigilance at Tiberius's question. The captain wanted to gag him. The advisor never could handle perceived or intentional slights of any kind toward himself or the king. He foolishly allowed the provocation to color his voice.

As the faerie's posture straightened and his shoulders squared, Garridan's fingers slid toward the handle of the dagger at his breeches—because the female also froze. He couldn't anticipate what the male would do, but judging by his friend's reaction, it could be a problem. Being on their soil subjected Garridan and his party to fae rules, and for all Garridan knew, a crown would not protect Edric—or any of them—if this faerie took offense to the Tiberius's conduct.

He suddenly wanted to remove the king from the room.

* * *

The silence carried on for too long, to the point where any response out of Nevada's mouth would sound stilted, and possibly exacerbate the excruciating atmosphere. But if she did not answer, Dacian *would*.

And if Dacian felt provoked …

"He is not native here, either," she answered for him. The tightness in her stomach eased a little when he did not rise to the bait, but instead casually returned his attention to the food. Nevada wanted to roll her eyes. Would not be chased out of a room, indeed.

"Does he speak Vinculum?" The large man loaded the question with a false tone of innocent curiosity.

Shut your mouth, Nevada mentally growled.

179

Dacian sniffed out the veiled belligerence. His head rose. "He does."

Nevada caught the gaze of the tall, dark-haired, blue-eyed soldier from across the room. He looked ready to move toward his king, but she gave him an imperceptible shake of the head. *No*, she willed silently. *Stay where you are.*

The soldier read her clearly and relayed it to the two other men with a slight movement of his hand.

"Do you have a name, son?"

Nevada's attention snapped to the advisor, and then immediately to Dacian. The patronizing epithet made her clench her hands into fists. An old prejudice crept its way into her heart. Minutes in their company, and one of them just reminded her of the many ways she had learned as a child to hate certain aspects of human nature.

"Tiberius," the king murmured in warning.

Nevada watched Dacian's jaw clench. He continued to show the humans his back while he finished eating hard bread loaded with wild mushrooms and cream cheese. When he turned, his gaze fell on his antagonist, and Nevada knew the moment the humans registered the jarring maroon color of his eyes.

"I am not your son," he said coldly.

Tiberius's face turned a ruddy shade of salmon pink.

King Edric attempted to recover the situation. "Please forgive the expression." He looked as if he would add more, but then cleared his throat and stood. "Gentlemen, perhaps we should retire. Let us allow our new friends to enjoy their meal, and we will be on our way."

"No, please," Nevada disagreed. "You were not yet finished. We will take our leave; stay and eat." Dacian stood next to her, eyes narrowed and focused as if memorizing each mortal down to the last hair.

The king smiled and thanked her; she returned the expression. She sighed with relief when Dacian walked with her to the open doors.

As they approached the exit, she heard Tiberius mutter, perhaps to the attractive older man with the silvering brown hair next to him, "Rudeness is universal, no doubt. No trouble disrespecting kings here, I see."

Dacian smiled humorlessly.

Alarmed, Nevada gripped the material of his shirt where the humans could not see, but he slipped out of her grasp. A reprimand sat unused on her tongue; she did not want to make the situation worse.

And then, finally, she decided on a simple, "Please."

"I am showing my respect," Dacian replied in Fae.

The blue-eyed soldier looked back at her when Dacian approached them. His eyes widened at Nevada as if asking her how to react.

Nevada shook her head a little to deter him from any heroics, but she must have looked more worried than she wanted to; the soldier spoke softly to King Edric and lightly gripped the monarch's arm.

Dacian reached the king and stood closer than Nevada was sure the lead soldier was comfortable with. Tiberius took a step back.

King Edric studied him calmly and waited with the patience of one without fear.

Nevada had to give him credit for that.

Dacian bowed.

He executed the motion without taking his eyes from the

king's, sweeping low with one hand over his heart in a parody of respect. When his head dipped close to Edric's chest, the human soldiers fiercely gripped their weapons.

After delivering a smile with all the warmth of an ice slick, Dacian turned and left the stunned party.

Nevada threw the king a sincerely apologetic look, heart pounding with distress, and followed.

* * *

"You did not need to do that," Nevada said tersely, easily matching Dacian's long stride.

"Do what?" Dacian asked incredulously. "I could have humiliated that mortal and relieved their party of him with a blade and a shallow ditch—they would have thanked me for it—and I all but ignored him. What more did you want?"

"I—" Nevada sighed explosively and stopped walking. She shut her eyes and pressed two fingers hard into her brow as a headache began to dance along the bone. "I do not know. I want this to go smoothly. We represent our race at this conference, and you *mocked* their king."

"I will not be talked down to in my own kingdom," he said fiercely.

"Not that I am defending him, but he was not aware of your rank, or our customs. I understand that does not excuse the behavior, but I wish you had refrained from involving the king."

"The king looks as if he can deal with it." He crossed his arms. "I refuse to relinquish my spine for the next week just to make things go *smoothly*."

Nevada raked her fingers through her dark curls and

pulled on the ends in frustration. "No one is asking you to. You are missing my point entirely."

Warm hands closed around her forearms. He lightly rubbed her skin in a silent apology. "I am a fast learner." His mouth quirked as he added, "I learned how to push your buttons within *hours* of meeting you."

Her eyes rolled, but the comment coaxed a smile out of her. It was hard to stay mad at him, considering what he'd done for her to make this trip even happen. She had meant to give him gratitude the whole way here, but that had slipped her mind with Arrian's leave-taking and that completely avoidable scene.

"Thank you," she said, "for sending that unit in my absence." She could not hold his gaze for very long, nor think of what lay in the unspoken space between them, so she stared at the sand that still clung to his boots. "I—*we* appreciated it. The princess felt better about leaving with the extra help. I have kept them quite busy."

"That was the point. That is also my point about this conference. I would rather send my soldiers to you than halfway across the world. But."

As if he also sensed her growing aggravation with the topic change, he switched again. "What is actually the matter?" he asked. "You were already upset when I first saw you."

She shook her head, avoiding his piercing gaze; again, he would not let her. With a touch of his hand to her chin, their eyes met. At the last second before the words tumbled out, she shifted her eyes and whispered into his left ear, "We are the only commanders here."

Dacian's brow furrowed. "Really?" When she nodded, he threw up his hands. "If I am not mistaken, attendance was mandatory. Not that I am wholly surprised with *certain* absences, but what about Arrian?"

She wanted to tell Dacian they could talk about Arrian in the morning, but again, her face gave away the truth.

His expression grew more severe—and troubled. *"Where is Arrian?"*

"He had to leave." Nevada held up a hand to stop the angry retort from bursting from his mouth. "Less than an hour before you arrived. I ran into him on my way in. He received a message from Hesperia."

She filled him in on what had been spotted in the grasslands just beyond the Hesperian borders. Dacian reacted appropriately with a flurry of Fae curse words and a few in the native dialect of his home country, complete with wild gesticulations. She let him finish before continuing.

"You know how he is—he needed to see it for himself. He said he would return in a few days."

"Those creatures are sniffing around fae soil? Then what are we doing here, Nev, wasting our time on a *conference?*"

"Arrian did not seem alarmed."

"Anything can happen in a matter of hours, let alone a few days."

"The queen is not going to call this off over a few sightings that one of her best people is looking into. He did not appear worried, and I am taking my cues from him."

"If Arrian is allowed to leave, I don't see why I need to be here," Dacian said.

"No. You are not leaving me here to field this on my own!" she burst out. "Half of this conference concerns military aide, and you would leave me as the *only* military representative of the five that should have been here."

"Easy." Dacian paused, searching her face with a mildly puzzled expression. "I was not serious, Nev. I'm not leaving you here by yourself."

"I am not in the mood for teasing," she said, feeling her face flush at the misunderstanding.

"I can see that." He pursed his lips and lowered his voice. "Go relax and get some sleep."

"I plan to. You should bathe. You're rank."

He grinned and ran his hand through his hair. "Later. I think I will train."

Her eyebrows shot up. "You traveled five days, and you want to train?"

"As far as I am concerned, it might as well be late afternoon. I will adjust easier to the sleep schedule here if I tire myself out."

Of course, she knew that; everyone in the desert countries kept opposite hours compared to the rest of the kingdom. The cool evening hours were their midday. Dacian's normal time of rest occurred when dawn colored the sky.

She thought of the pre-noon conference. "Early to bed for you; like turning in before dinner."

"If need be, I will nap after the meeting. I will see you bright and early, whether I like it or not."

He smacked her on the arm as he walked away with a last wish good-night.

Nevada smiled ruefully at the floor for a few minutes before remembering she was still starving, and then walked to the kitchens. She doubted anything warm would be available, but she knew the cooks always left out fruits and the remains of the night's dinner.

The kitchen was lined with glass windows facing a thick

outcrop of mangrove trees. Their naked roots looked both ghastly and gargantuan in the dark, visible only from the reflection thrown off the glass from the lanterns in the empty room. One section of the farthest wall that appeared to be a glass window was actually a door to the outside, where Nevada knew an herbal garden grew.

Three long, cleared-off wooden tables filled the center of the room; pots and pans hung from hooks in the ceiling. The fire pits were dark and cold, pots empty, except for one wooden stove and a single pan. The smell of freshly cooked food lingered in the air.

She immediately knew the culprit.

Nevada's steps lightened as she wove past the tables to find her sitting by the windows.

Here was the biggest reason she looked forward to this gathering.

The faerie sat on a tall stool, bare feet swinging lazily as she ate. She wore a simple green dress and her golden hair was tied back in a loose tail. A blue pendant hung on a thin gold chain around her neck. A plate of spiced rice and vegetables sat in front of her, and her attention was on a sheaf of papers lying next to the plate. A handful of small glass bottles stood in a row on the table, filled with what looked like turmeric, coriander, and mint.

"Thief," Nevada said affectionately.

Liana glanced up from the parchments, and her mask of concentration broke into a wide smile. The princess slid off the stool and hastened to Nevada, gripping the commander in a tight hug that belied her slender stature.

Nevada buried her nose in golden-brown strands and breathed in the smell of the faerie that was the closest she had to family. Two years was a drop in the ocean, but this separation had felt longer. Having Liana close and well was so strong a comfort that it brought a lump to her throat.

"Hello," Nevada said softly, unable to find the words to express the warm glow washing away the day's troubles.

"It is so good to see your face," Liana replied. She kissed Nevada's cheek, her golden eyes bright and shimmering with emotion. She squeezed Nevada's shoulders once more. "I could not help myself. Sit with me. I have missed you."

"And I you." Nevada's stomach rumbled. She nodded to the plate as they walked back to where Liana had been sitting. "Any good?"

"*I* made it. There is some left in the pan."

Nevada wasted no time finding a plate and helping herself. "What's in this?"

"Basil, cardamom, turmeric, a little cinnamon. Peppers, onion, asparagus."

Nevada started eating before she sat next to Liana, closing her eyes and humming with pleasure at the spicy flavor sweetened a little with the hint of cinnamon. "I am absurdly grateful you were hungry and cooked something."

"That and I needed to restock my coriander supply. How did your new stallion handle the ride? Breathitt, yes?"

Nevada nodded. "He was fantastic in the open fields; he has remarkable speed. His endurance focus leaves something to be desired, however. He also has a very lofty opinion of himself. High-spirited and finicky."

"You'll get along fine, then."

"When he learns who gives the orders, we will. Reminds me of someone we know. I ran into him earlier—along with the humans."

Liana blinked at her. "Dacian? He met the mortals?" She blew out a breath.

Nevada laughed and told her what had transpired. "In all honesty, it was not a confrontation, and the advisor *was* rude. Dacian behaved himself, aside from mocking their king. I do not know the man; it's been a long while since I paid attention to the affairs of the human realms."

The blonde swept a hand over the paperwork in front of her. "I was not familiar with him, either. I've spent the evening reading the information I requested regarding Aliquis and its past sovereigns. From what I have gathered, he is one of the better, fairer kings of late. I met him coming in; he was pleasant, with an honest look about him. And it sounds like the king handled himself well. We're going to run into clashes like that again and again throughout the week. I cannot imagine that the mortals did not prepare for cultural differences, too. And really, if the king was bad off enough to come here despite any misgivings from his cabinet—and I am sure there were plenty—he is willing to overlook a lot of prejudice to get what he came for."

"I worry over the 'get what he came for' part," Nevada said after a hearty helping of rice and peppers.

"We shall see. From some of the intelligence I have received, military aid might not be their only need. Their economy has suffered from losing whole villages to the disease the Erepos transmit."

"I am sure they will want to open trade routes."

"Possibly."

"I do not dispute they need help, but opening our borders could bring more trouble than it is worth—for both kingdoms. Not with the growing activity in the southern countries."

"I do not disagree." Liana stared at Nevada, who met her eyes for a moment before looking away uncomfortably. "Do you know who else I ran into when I met the king?"

Nevada grunted. "I know, because I saw him myself with them, in the courtyard. We did not speak."

"I did not have that luxury," Liana said. "By the time I smelled and heard them, I had nowhere to go but through. Eyad *fawned*."

She scowled, envisioning the sorcerer's cloying demeanor. As if his flimsy words made of spider's thread could repair a gaping tear in canvas cloth.

"We will be seeing more of him," Liana said.

Nevada rolled her shoulders and sighed. "I know. We have not had a reunion in, oh, five years." She could not keep the acidity from her tone.

"This one will go better," Liana stated wryly. "Tending to the mortals should keep him busy."

"Did you hear the slightest thing about this? Have you seen him at all lately?"

"No. I knew nothing until I received the letter from the queen. I tried contacting him, but he did not answer."

"Of course not," Nevada said bitterly.

Liana placed her hand over Nevada's and squeezed gently.

"I don't understand why he is doing this now," she said. Very few individuals understood her fractured relationship with Eyad; Liana understood better than anyone.

"I do not know, my love," the princess continued softly. "What he does, and what he has done for quite some time now, leaves me baffled. And I am beginning to think we may never understand."

The pair was startled by a sound coming from the doorway in the far left corner. As they looked over, Eyad stepped into the light. "Hello, my dears."

Nevada's heart pounded. She was not prepared to speak with him now—and when had he entered the kitchens? She had not heard a door open or close. She chanced a look at Liana and saw the same sliver of suspicion in her eyes. They were used to abrupt appearances from the sorcerer, but they had not suspected he was near.

Had he been listening to their entire conversation?

After a pause, Liana offered a polite hello. Nevada cleared her throat before dully echoing the greeting. She nearly jumped when Liana's hand lightly touched her back and rested there a moment.

"You have created a great deal of work for me," Liana rebuked Eyad lightly. "I had very little time to gather my sources and prepare for this meeting."

The sorcerer chuckled, but it sounded rusty, as if he had not laughed for quite some time. "You always worked best under pressure."

Liana slowly left her stool to greet him, as if it were a perfunctory obligation rather than a sincere motion. Nevada hung back, seated at her stool as Eyad embraced Liana and kissed her forehead.

Eyad made eye contact with Nevada, who shifted a little in her seat.

"It is wonderful to see you both again," he said softly.

I need to leave, Nevada thought.

Liana retrieved another plate, and Eyad took food and sat on a stool between them. He complimented the princess's cooking and began eating. His gray eyes found Nevada again.

"And how are you, Poppet?"

She squeezed her eating utensil. "*Nevada* is fine."

"There was a time you liked that nickname," Liana teased, trying to lighten the mood.

"When I was seventy, perhaps."

"As your former keeper, I reserve the right to use whatever silly nickname I wish."

He meant to tease, but Nevada tensed at the familiarity behind the words. She could not find it in her to reciprocate, nor do much more than endure Eyad until he tired of their company. Liana looked as if she regretted the man sitting between them.

Eyad, unaware of the tension and warring emotions of the faeries sitting next to him, changed the subject as he ate. "Quite unprecedented, this meeting. I have been hopeful for so many years."

"And we have you to thank for this," Nevada said with a wintry bite in her tone.

"It was rather unexpected," Liana said carefully. "I was not aware you had planned this for so long."

"I have wished for this for more years than I care to admit. This will be a marvelous opportunity to repair relations between you both," he defended.

Nevada rolled her eyes. "They are only interested in it to benefit themselves. Do you honestly think, if their little problem were ever solved, that they would be interested in keeping up relations with a race they used to—"

"Millennia ago," Eyad interrupted, waving off the comment. "Believe it or not, cultures are capable of change, and viewpoints can be altered with time and tolerance."

Nevada dropped her wooden sticks onto her plate. "Human nature does not change. They cannot war with one another because Erepos will eat them. Take away the Erepos, and the focus of their hatred will move toward each other or us, when we have outlived our use in their eyes. You thought of *none* of this when you convinced Edric to come to us."

"She has a point," Liana agreed. "A very cynical point, but one with seeds of truth."

"I understand what you are saying," Eyad said calmly. "But once you hear what *they* have to say, Nevada, you will better understand why this has to happen now."

Nevada's eyes widened.

Liana pressed two fingers to her mouth, swallowing her food painfully. "Eyad—"

"I am afraid I do not understand why it has to happen now." Nevada's voice hardened. "Not at all."

Nevada's stool scraped loudly as she pushed it back and stood. "I am exhausted." She stopped by Liana and rested a hand on her shoulder. "Thank you for the food."

"My pleasure," the princess said faintly.

Nevada shut the door behind her as she left the kitchen. Curiosity, however, kept her nearby. She rested her ear against the wood and heard Liana say, "You could have said anything. Anything at all. Yet you said the very things that would make it worse."

She heard Eyad sigh. He sounded tired. "I did not mean to, dearest. I thought it best to say nothing. I did not want to upset her."

"Do you not think she lives with the memories every day?"

"I do not have the power to ease that torment."

You bastard, Nevada wanted to scream. She could not listen anymore, so she turned and walked away, angry with herself for the tears welling in her eyes.

Chapter 15

Garridan wondered what Edric said to Tiberius in the morning. Whatever transpired dulled the advisor's disposition, and he conducted himself in a subdued manner, while the king appeared more at ease. This did not ease Garridan's mind, for if last night was any indication of the coming days, there would be more trials ahead.

Eyad arrived to escort them to breakfast one hour after the sun rose, and Garridan was not terribly surprised when Eyad told them Darson and Mourin could not attend because of their rank. They were to sit—supervised—in a waiting area nearby until the meeting was over.

As Garridan walked to the meeting room with the king and the advisors, he was once again struck by his inability to commit their path to memory. His only hope of building a map of the palace in his mind lay in marking his way like a lost child, but he had neither yarn nor bread crumbs to do so. He tried again to pay close attention to the colors and decorations, hoping a recollection of certain objects and hues would help him retrace his steps should he need to. He was fairly confident they were headed for the northwest corner of the palace, assuming his internal compass was not completely broken.

Most of the doors they passed were closed, but the few that stood open showcased more guest rooms and other sitting areas of the same meticulously embossed furniture and design found in their own rooms. He admired velvet fainting couches that gleamed like pearls, beds covered with pools of shimmering silver for blankets, and vases painted with native flowers in rich colors.

How long have these trinkets of old wealth sat prettily in these rooms? Garridan thought. How much of such worth sat unused and unnoticed?

"Today will be devoted to introductions and presenting the issues," Eyad explained as they walked. "We will not discuss much in depth; that will be for another day. You will learn more about the faerie kingdom, and they will learn about you. Now, the pomp and circumstance of human kingdoms is absent in affairs such as these. The princesses arrive at their leisure somewhere around the allotted time. The queen is usually the last to arrive. Once we enter, we take our designated seats and you are more than welcome to engage any of the princesses in conversation."

"When the queen arrives," he continued, "everyone stands and bows at the waist. Then, Your Majesty, you will have the opportunity to present your gift to her, and the pair of you will exchange greetings. Everyone sits when the queen takes her seat, but she will wait for you, so the pair of you will sit at the same time."

Eyad halted in front of a large pair of wooden doors. Delicate carvings depicting flowers, vines, and words in the fae language covered the surface of the deep oak. The guard opened both doors, and Eyad and King Edric walked in together.

The room's high ceiling soared above them, encircled and interwoven with swirls of gold snaking through jade-colored plaster. More burnished yellow threads rose and fell in patterns throughout the cream-colored walls, complimenting the red-cushioned chairs.

A pair of silent servants—not children like the others—led them to their seats, which were marked by place cards on the long, dark-amber table. Suddenly, Kiryk chuckled, "Look who is joining us today."

Curious, Garridan followed the advisor's stare.

At the right side table, next to a truly gorgeous young faerie with thick, curly hair the color of a fiery sunset, sat the male faerie from the night before.

God hated them, Garridan was sure of it. Or He laughed at their stunningly bad luck.

The faerie didn't look up at their arrival. The redhead, whose features were so exquisitely proportioned they took Garridan's breath away, spoke quietly to him. The faerie leaned his head toward her, his eyes on the glossy table surface. He was slouched almost casually with his muscular arms crossed over his chest.

Please let Tiberius hold his tongue, Garridan prayed as he sat. This faerie had to be a high-ranking military official to even be here, since only females were royalty. They did not need to make an enemy out of him.

As if he could read Garridan's thoughts, those eyes—Garridan could only liken them to the color of red wine—shifted right to the captain. Humor, and an all-too-knowing expression of how uncomfortable he made them, crept onto the male's face.

Garridan met his gaze for a long moment until the faerie's smirk widened. The captain finally looked away as more faerie royalty began to arrive.

The princesses drifted inside, clad in breezy dresses or long robes of chiffons and satins in cheerful shades. Garridan had to remind himself that each and every one of them led a country, since they all looked so youthful. He had a moment—a rather long one—where he could not believe he was surrounded by these immortal creatures. He felt out of place among the finery; basic and wanting in the presence of royalty more exquisite than any king Aliquis could produce.

Would they find them undeserving? Would pity, if they had any, move them? After a thousand years of silence, could Edric's words sway their hearts and minds? Did it speak only of their curiosity, he wondered, that they agreed to gather in the first place, and go to all the trouble of arranging this meeting on short notice?

One young princess, whose wavy brown hair fell on the shoulders of a bright blue dress, feigned reading papers in her hand, but her eyes sparkled with the excitement of a child as her gaze darted continuously over to them.

Another snuck around them like a ghost; Garridan caught a flash of long black hair and a flutter of apple red skirt as a small, petite faerie darted to her seat. Her youth—Garridan thought she could barely be out of childhood—shocked him as she smiled shyly at the king.

"Children are involved in this decision?" Tiberius grumbled quietly.

"Only a child in visage," Eyad reminded just as softly. "Do not be fooled by their features."

Garridan was relieved when the faerie he recognized as

Liana and the female from last night came in, even as the latter surprised him; he had not expected her to be here. She wore a sleeveless dress the color of green spring leaves, her wavy hair swept up in a complicated knot with dark tendrils framing her face. Her presence pleased him, for he felt that he'd made somewhat of an ally of her the night before. Even if she was a reluctant ally.

Perhaps these meetings would not be so grueling, after all.

Garridan observed the lone male faerie wave to the black-haired faerie and grin at her in an almost cheeky manner, a drastic transformation from the night before. She did not appear amused, and ignored him in favor of speaking in the youthful princess's ear, their raven hair and olive skin tones similar. He wondered if that was her ruler.

Princess Aaclyde arrived and spoke briefly with King Edric before taking a seat directly across from him. An exceptionally lovely blonde sat next to Tiberius. The ill-tempered advisor looked disconcerted and a bit self-conscious as the princess spoke to him in an animated fashion. The captain wished he could catch what she was saying in her low, pleasant voice.

The seat next to Garridan remained empty as all the others filled. A servant offered goblets of wine, and he took one. As Garridan stared pensively at the empty cushion, he caught Liana, who sat two seats away, studying him out of the corner of her eye.

"Hello, Captain." She turned as she greeted him, her eyes dancing. "I told you we might meet again."

He inclined his head. "You spoke true, Your Highness. A pleasure to see you once more."

Garridan felt a measure of relief at her familiar face—even

though the familiarity consisted only of the brief exchange on the jungle path. She was friendlier now, less aloof than before; he was curious to hear what she would have to say over the course of the conference.

"What is your name?" she asked.

"Garridan, Your Highness."

"Liana, please. Before we are through, we will all be on a first name basis."

Her tone did nothing to ease his curiosity about this meeting. He knew he would never remember the names and faces of the dozen or so present, so he decided to focus on those who contributed the most. He wondered who the dissenters and greatest supporters would be, and eagerly awaited the queen's words and reactions and her response to the opinions of her vast cabinet.

The queen of the fae. He could scarcely imagine what to expect when it came to her, and the prospect of meeting the queen filled him with more trepidation and anxiety than he felt before some of his unit's assignments. He glanced at his king and found Edric composed, leaned leaning toward Eyad and saying something to make the sorcerer laugh. Tiberius was still bewildered at the fair blonde princess's attention, and Kiryk looked around with bright eyes, as if he were on a holiday instead of appealing to these monarchs for aid. Garridan rarely felt self-conscious, but the sensation hit him now, making him well aware of the many eyes that fell on him due to his proximity to the king.

When a hand clasped his shoulder, Garridan knew his neighbor had arrived.

A sultry voice accompanied the small fingers clutching his sleeve. "Thank you for your assistance, sir."

He looked up; the faerie squeezing her way in between him and the chair was all of five feet. Her long, thick, dark brown hair nearly hit him in the face, and it filled his nose with the scent of warm vanilla. She set a wine glass down on the table and slid onto the seat, wearing something that masqueraded as a dress, with no sleeves that bared her shoulders, the only adornment above the neckline a brown beaded necklace.

Once she settled in, she swung one leg over the other and tossed her fragrant hair back. She gave Garridan a dazzling smile, her impossibly dark eyes looking into his.

"You are a sight," she said. "Would you be one of the advisors?"

Garridan cleared his throat and reminded himself to keep his gaze above neck level, as well as to keep a straight face; her breath smelled like fruit soaked in drink. "Captain of the king's guard, Your Highness."

She looked delighted. "Dashing and trained in combat. Marvelous."

A door Garridan did not even realize was an entrance into the room, hidden as it was by the room's wallpaper, opened. Two male faerie soldiers, scabbards at their hips, entered and stood at either side of the door.

"Rise for the Queen."

Garridan stood with everyone else as Eyad escorted the king toward the doorway.

Queen Emilia glided into the room with the faintest whisper of silk. A dress as blue as a summer sky, embroidered with threads of silver, hugged her curvy figure. Lush, curly hair the color of a raven's wing swept to the shoulders of the grand gown. A pair of sparkling blue wings sprouted from her shoulder blades.

The Faerie Queen's entrance was without much "pomp and circumstance," as Eyad had called it, yet Garridan's heart hammered as she turned to the king, her pink lips curving into a welcoming smile. In her pale, serene face, a pair of bright blue eyes twinkled with the eternity of the stars—vibrant with life, yet ancient as the land itself.

Her beauty made his heart ache.

King Edric bowed, eyes fixed on the monarch. "Queen Emilia of the Faerie Kingdom. We are eternally thankful and beholden to you for doing us this great honor."

"You honor my people and myself with such a humble request," the Queen responded in a voice like soft velvet. "Welcome to my kingdom. I hope you have enjoyed your stay thus far."

"Enjoyed and more. Your lands are breathtaking visions of perfection, as are your people. As a token of our deep appreciation for this opportunity, please accept these gifts of gratitude. I would also like to present a gift to Princess Aaclyde for opening her home to us so graciously."

Eyad procured a small velvet bag from the pocket of his tunic. Everyone watched as his arm disappeared inside the bag, farther than the bag should have allowed. He pulled out a thin leather case and a small mural the size of a sheet of parchment.

The leather case held an ornate white-gold necklace that glittered with sapphires and amethysts. Garridan heard a gasp from his neighbor and found her staring at the necklace, wearing a look of childlike wonder. Eyad explained that it was an heirloom from King Edric's family vault, stored there for almost fifteen hundred years.

When Edric introduced the priceless piece as one owned

by Queen Aloria of Aliquis, the faerie monarch let out a cry of pleasure. The sorcerer provided Edric with the perfect gift idea for the immortal queen; a relic from a favored ally and friend, all those centuries ago when human and fae had interacted.

The sorcerer entertained the room when a sweep of his hand turned the small mural into a full-sized painting, fit for one of the walls in Aaclyde's palace. A renowned Aliquis artist had portrayed the gardens of a gorgeous outlying town as it looked before the Erepos came. Garridan had not been aware that the sorcerer carried anything during their long journey, much less a precious piece of jewelry and a five-hundred-year-old mural of that size. It was the first true evidence he had witnessed of Eyad performing magic, and he almost doubted his own eyes.

After the gift giving, Queen Emilia sat across from King Edric with Princess Aaclyde at her right.

Eyad addressed the room as everyone took their seats. His grand gestures were those of a proud father addressing his children at a wedding banquet. "I give my deep thanks to all the princesses and commanders who traveled so far to be here for this momentous occasion. I would like to thank the king and his men, as well, for allowing an old man to lead them in a merry romp through the rainforests of Miranda."

Soft laughter traveled around the table. Garridan used the opportunity to look around the room, and he realized that not all were amused, most notably the little group in the right corner comprised of the Princess Liana, the male and female faeries from last night, and the redheaded princess. Liana's lips were pressed together, her face blank, and Garridan recalled her departure on the path. The black-haired faerie did not look at Eyad at all, but stared down at the table as if his words made her uncomfortable. Her male friend drank deeply from his goblet and then watched with an unimpressed air. Garridan did not know what to make of their reactions.

"In my long life," Eyad continued, "I have not seen a meeting with more promise and potential; I am proud of each and every one of you for taking this historic step. I foresee great things for those willing to leave the past in the past and look ahead toward a brighter, safer future for all. Thank you, Your Majesties."

The sorcerer sat, and the Faerie Queen smiled faintly. "We thank you, as well, Eyad, for your guidance and assistance."

Rehearsed, Garridan thought suddenly. Their speeches sounded so carefully delivered. Not just from Eyad, who probably looked forward to this day for centuries and had the speech prepared two hundred years ago, but also from the queen. How many times had one as old as she spoken such words? Edric responded with real enthusiasm, but she proved difficult to read. Garridan was not sure what her true feelings would look like.

"King Edric." The queen turned to the elderly monarch. "Forgive my memory. Long has it been since I turned my attention to the outer world. How many years have you reigned?"

"It has been thirty years now, Your Majesty."

Amusement shone through the depths of Queen Emilia's blue eyes, and Garridan wondered if she found the three decades laughable. "Let us become acquainted with one another. Who have you brought to our table, Sovereign of Aliquis?"

Edric introduced Tiberius and Kiryk, speaking briefly of their qualifications as former treasurer and city trade regulator, respectively. Garridan tried not to let the weight of many stares daunt him when the king named him as captain of the royal guard, the same guard Darson and Mourin occupied.

"If you please, I am most curious to hear about the countries the princesses in this room hail from," Edric said after he finished.

Emilia smiled in an indulgent manner. "Of course. My ladies, would you be so kind as to introduce yourselves and our wondrous lands?"

Garridan paid close attention to each princess as she spoke, absorbing the information they gave on geography, what they said with their tone and body language, and anything regarding Erepo activity. The princess next to Tiberius ruled a country called Triton, an area of vast freshwater lakes and seasonal forest, with mountains to the south no doubt protecting her land from heavy Erepo activity.

She appeared sympathetic to their plight, as did the young, enthusiastic faerie in the blue dress who ruled from the heart of the kingdom. A princess with brown hair braided into a crown and a pale complexion, moss green eyes, and an angular, foxlike face regarded them rather coldly and said little about her home of forests that resembled the ones he knew.

Princess Tatyana, who sat next to her, did not mince words, either, but she did not sound motivated by dislike. She had sharp, watchful grey eyes, deep brown skin that made him think of twilight, and black hair pulled into a simple tail. Her timbre was confident, concise, and while she mostly gave the king her attention, she also made sure to include Garridan. She volunteered information on her military and spoke with an intimacy of the subject that suggested a warrior princess. Her country was geographically the closest to Aliquis.

Garridan paid special attention to Anann, the princess with hair that didn't know what color it wanted to be, leaning toward light red made even brighter by her porcelain skin, because she governed Hesperia. She was Commander Arrian's princess. Anann made no comment on his absence, making him wonder if something had gone awry in Hesperia; something serious enough to call him away.

When Garridan's neighbor introduced herself, he did not expect her to turn to him and smile as she did. "I am Dahlia. My country neighbors Miranda and is well protected by her mountains and the Hagan Sea. Do you know where that is, Captain?"

Garridan nodded, growing more uncomfortable the longer she singled him out. He ignored the low chuckles coming from Kiryk's direction.

"I never knew its name, but I was aware of a body of water in that area. Is your country comprised of islands?"

She beamed at him as if he were a prize student. "Yes! My country has white sands, clear water, and…" Princess Aaclyde cleared her throat, and Dahlia looked about the table lazily. Much to Garridan's amusement, she rolled her eyes. "Needless to say, Erepos hardly trouble us. I have never even seen one."

Garridan wouldn't have been more surprised if she had slapped him. In his thirty-two years, he'd encountered and killed an untold number of Erepos, and she had never *seen* one?

"Next." Aaclyde stared at Dahlia sternly, and she hunched her shoulders in mock apology, giving Garridan another amused look that barely registered as he tried to recover from her offhanded comment.

Princess Liana spoke briefly of her home country, repeating what she had said on the jungle path about it being a land of sand dunes. Garridan learned that the male faerie's home country neighbored Liana's to the south and shared the same desert landscape. His name was Dacian; the redhead was his monarch.

Learning of Dacian's status as a high-ranking commander—second only to Arrian in the entire kingdom—made Tiberius turn the unflattering shade of a frostbitten toe.

The young raven-haired princess next to his reluctant ally from last night gave Edric a hesitant smile before she spoke. Her voice carried the high, youthful notes of an adolescent human child. "I am Princess Rees, of Deimos, the southeastern rainforest. Nevada," she indicated the black-haired faerie, "has commanded Deimos's troops for far longer than I have ruled."

Nevada. Garridan had already assumed she was a commander, but hearing it confirmed was something entirely different. Women were not allowed to be soldiers in Aliquis, and here a female was not only in the military, but occupying the highest military position in her kingdom.

The princess's last comment inspired curiosity in Garridan. Was it normal for fae royalty to step down and allow their children to succeed the throne at such a young age, or had something disastrous occurred? Or could Nevada be older than he thought?

After Aaclyde finished the introductions, offering brief

words on Miranda and the protection the terrain offered from Erepos, Emilia moved the discussion along. "Tell me, Edric, what ails your people so that you seek the help of those whom your kingdom shut out for so many centuries? What has become of the human territories during all this time?"

Edric told her of the growing threat of Erepos, how the borders to the neighboring kingdoms of Ferox and Virtus had been shut down decades ago in an attempt to keep travelers between the kingdoms from dying. When he alluded to losing soldiers and civilians alike to the Erepos through bite and disease, a few of the princesses paled. The queen's countenance remained composed as the king spoke of the growing food shortages, loss of soldiers, and the thinning spread of their guard units as they tried desperately to protect their citizens.

"The Erepos' presence continues to hurt Aliquis," King Edric finished, "even more than the neighboring kingdoms."

"And what of those kingdoms?" Princess Anann asked. "Is there no hope for communication and reconciliation there?"

"Travel is far too dangerous," Edric answered. "For my people as well as theirs. Virtus has been dealt crippling blows through ordinary disease, and Ferox is unreachable."

"Ferox is fractured," Liana said slowly, "is it not? It absorbed kingdoms until it could no longer hold what it had assimilated. I imagine they did not handle this new enemy well."

"No, Your Highness," Edric agreed, eyebrows raised in surprise that mirrored Garridan's. *How did she know the problems a kingdom like Ferox faced?* "It did not. Ferox is a kingdom dark; we know not what has transpired in their lands since we shut down trade and moved civilians to safer locations. We believe they have suffered a civil war in addition to Erepo attacks. As far as we know, they have no known leadership."

"Trade is out of the question, lest we bring their troubles to our people," Kiryk said. "Moreover, trade is growing increasingly difficult within our own borders."

"I can imagine." Emilia's blue eyes were sad. "Nothing is more frustrating and heartbreaking than watching innocent people suffer while under your care."

"No," King Edric agreed quietly. "Nothing. At the rate the Erepo infection spreads, in a few decades their kind may even outnumber us, as more civilians fall prey to their plague."

Garridan watched the faces of the princesses and saw mixed emotions. Some, including Liana and Rees, looked sympathetic; others like Tatyana and Aaclyde were stone-faced. Still others shut down completely as Aliquis's additional need for supplies and goods became apparent. His neighbor, Dahlia, paid more attention to the contents of her wine glass than the proceedings. Garridan's faint hope began to fade.

The king appeared to sense the dissension in the room, but he continued. "In the past twenty years or so, we have noticed an unprecedented surge of Erepo activity. May I ask if the faerie kingdom has seen the same rise in activity?"

"Commanders?" Aaclyde asked, nodding to Dacian and Nevada.

The pair exchanged a look, and the latter inclined her head, gesturing to him to speak first. The male stirred, like a great cat unfurling, resting his arms on the table and maintaining a professional, controlled air. The same charged energy from the prior evening simmered just under the surface of that calm lake. The water rippled when he looked at them, and Garridan tensed when Dacian looked at them.

"I can only speak for my country; I do not hold the authority to discuss the terrain other commanders protect. I can tell you, in the past few decades, there has been a rise in attacks along my southeast border." His voice held a lazy, commanding edge as he spoke in flawless, unaccented Vinculum. "They are growing bolder, more organized, pressing harder."

Garridan frowned at *more organized*.

"It is an interesting modification for them. They do not have the luxury of increased numbers as they do on your side of the world, yet they somehow manage to multiply. Their tactics, if you could call it that, have changed, but we have adjusted." Dacian drummed his fingers on the table. "If only we could teach them a little respect." He smiled blandly at Tiberius.

Garridan couldn't help but appreciate the dig as the advisor pretended not to understand the remark.

Dacian gestured to Nevada to speak, and she straightened and exchanged a glance with Princess Rees.

She turned to the human party, as cool and professional as her male counterpart. "Deimos has seen a similar rise. Centuries of weather have compromised the natural defensive border of the mountains. We have adjusted accordingly and delegated more aid to the borders, moving civilians to centralized, northern locations. However ..."

The faintest falter in her formal tone and demeanor caught Garridan's attention.

"We, too, have felt the press of their growing coordination. Recently…" She paused, almost to collect herself. "Five years ago, the random attacks turned into raids and ambushes, and we suffered losses as well as severe topographical damage."

Garridan noted the reactions of everyone at the table; they were in varying degrees of upset and were then quickly masked. Rees's eyes fell to the table, and she crossed her arms over her chest protectively. Garridan looked at Nevada, and witnessed a gesture he was sure had been intended for no one's eyes as Dacian rested his hand briefly on her wrist.

Garridan suspected Nevada had not shared the whole story. She glanced at him, and whatever she saw on his face froze her features as if she were afraid of what else he would read.

"I am so very sorry for your losses," King Edric said solemnly.

"Thank you," Princess Rees answered for them both.

"Your Highnesses," Tiberius began, his tone gruff with nerves. "Is it true that your people are not affected by an Erepo bite?"

"We do not turn," Aaclyde corrected. "Our physiology is sufficiently dissimilar that we are able to recover from a bite."

"The bite is not without its effects," Liana said. "It acts like a poison. We experience the same initial symptoms as you, and if it is not addressed in time, it has been known to kill."

"Am I correct in assuming you use medicines derived from native plants and herbs for treatment?" Kiryk asked.

"We have nothing that treats it, per se," Aaclyde said. "There are certain plants and oils that ease symptoms and speed recovery, but nothing can cure completely." She seemed to sense where Kiryk was heading with his comments because she added, "We are able to tolerate higher levels of certain secretions from plant life that could be fatal to you. I have no recollection of anything that works for humans, and I cannot think of where to begin searching for such a miracle."

"That was far beyond our expectations, Your Highness," Kind Edric said sincerely.

"If I may be forthright, Your Majesty," Queen Emilia said politely, "What are your expectations? What had you hoped to accomplish? After this meeting, what do you hope to be different?"

"I hope for our kingdoms to be on their way to better relations," the king answered. "Open communication so that we may join forces against the stain upon our lands. We are, after all, smarter and more capable then they are, and forces separated and alone are always weaker than those forged together as a united front. A superior fighting force thrives here, and the brave young men who fortify our cities could benefit from your wisdom and experience and pass that knowledge on to future generations."

Garridan looked to the commanders to gauge their reactions. Nevada's face was a mask of concentration, but Commander Dacian looked pained. He reached for his goblet, but dismay crossed his face and he set it back down, reaching for Nevada's instead. He wasted no time draining it of its contents. Garridan did not know whether to be amused or worried.

"It is also my hope," Edric continued, "to find a way to help my people recover from the loss of trade, crops, and homes. It is true we do not have much of value to give in return, but what we do have we freely trade.

"It is my wish that, several years from now, we may find a comfortable position on trade and assistance when an enemy threatens. My ultimate hope, though perhaps a foolhardy dream, is to build a relationship that will benefit both our peoples as we fight against our enemies. We will take anything you are willing to share; even information is a gift we will treasure and use to preserve the lives of our people."

The king spoke confidently in a room full of beings older than any of the humans present could fathom. Eyes that had seen thousands of years of battle, strife, and experience looked at the mortal king. Eyad's eyes shone with triumph.

Garridan had never been more proud of his king.

The Faerie Queen smiled. "Not foolhardy, Your Majesty. Hope is the wood, mortar, and stone used to build dreams and make them reality. I commend you for doing all you can to help your people. If you would but use these next days to tell us precisely what you need and the practical executions of those needs, then we will consider what we can give. Your Highnesses; let us see if we cannot help the king build the foundations of his dream."

Chapter 16

"You are the only one who does not appear thoroughly disgusted," Darson noted as soon as the door to their suite closed behind them.

Garridan frowned at the door. "Kiryk is feeling the effects of three glasses of wine—he is not upset," he said.

Perhaps disgusted was not the right word; disappointed fit better. Not that anything terrible had occurred; nothing at all had occurred, really. He did not enjoy this separation from the king, even though Eyad had shooed the three soldiers to their suite so he could speak with the king and advisors privately. They were to reconvene in two hours for dinner, and Eyad left instructions to "scrub clean and dress proper" for the formal gathering.

"I think everyone assumed the discussions would last much longer," Darson said. "I did, at any rate."

"We really thought there would be further discussion after introductions, but the faeries kept to the schedule Eyad announced at the start of the day." Garridan sat on his bed, idly noting that each bed was made, the coverings stretched taut and smooth. "I am assuming the brownies worked their magic while we were gone."

"They cleaned our clothes, too." Garridan heard the

scowl in Darson's voice as the lieutenant rummaged in the wardrobe cabinet. "I don't know why that bothers me. It would help knowing what they looked like, what with them touching my clothes and all."

"Did you remain in the waiting area the entire time?" Garridan asked.

"No," Darson said. "The boy servant took us on a tour. He could not explain much, since his Vinculum is so broken, but I think he just wanted to impress us with the palace."

"Were you impressed?"

"There is a huge pool of water inside the building," Mourin chimed in.

"For … water consumption?" Garridan asked.

"For recreation," Darson said. "They don't drink it, they frolic in it."

Garridan digested that information with bitterness.

"Can you tell us more of the meeting?" Mourin asked.

Garridan nodded and gave a brief summary. "The king presented our plight well. The princesses had mixed reactions. The queen is stunning and an exceptional public speaker. She seemed very gracious and sympathetic."

"*Seemed*," Darson parroted. He pulled out a light leather jerkin and frowned at it. "Too warm for this, but I don't have much choice," he muttered to himself.

Garridan sat up, propped his elbow on his knee, and wearily rubbed his hand over the stubble on his cheek. "Right. I couldn't get a good read on her. She let the princesses do most of the talking. They all seem to look to Aaclyde as an authority figure, more so than their own queen. I have a hunch that if Edric can convince Aaclyde, a good number of the others will follow.

"Oh," he continued as he recalled the biggest piece of news that would interest—or alarm—the two men, and smirked. "The faeries from last night were there. Nevada, the woman, is a high-ranking commander in a country similar to this one."

Darson's eyebrows rose. "I suppose it shouldn't be such a shock, since women run this kingdom. Why wouldn't they be in command of the military, too?"

Mourin plucked at a loose strand on the bedding instead of participating in the conversation.

"Her friend was also present," Garridan added nonchalantly. "Dacian is not just a commander; he is second to Arrian as the most esteemed in the kingdom."

Darson barked out a laugh. "What did Tiberius have to say about that?"

"He looked ready to lose all bowel control."

The trio laughed.

"We have a meeting with the commanders tomorrow," Garridan warned. "The monarchs will discuss trade while we catch the commanders up to speed on Aliquis's military situation and let them know what it is we are asking for."

They discussed various approaches while they prepared for dinner, using the communal bathing area down the hall; two small pools, heated like hot springs, cut into the marble.

When they returned to their room, Darson pulled out a small leather-encased book and began scribbling down their plan with a graphite stick, Garridan said, "You really did bring a journal to give to your mother."

"Quiet. It's useful now, is it not?"

* * *

When Eyad collected them for dinner, they met King Edric, Kiryk, and Tiberius in the hall, and the six followed the sorcerer to a different area of the palace.

Garridan's mind still looped around could not stop thinking about the fresh water sitting unused in a palace filled with enough wealth to feed and protect every individual in the four largest cities of Aliquis. He carried those bitter thoughts with him as they entered the massive banquet room.

It opened to a large domed ceiling that sat atop three walls of glass windows. Paper in a dark honey color, swirled with ivory and delicate hints of carmine, covered the walls. Blazing lanterns and candlelight illuminated flecks of gold in the paper, and Garridan wondered if he was again looking at real gold threads. Ivory pilasters separated each window, and decorative dentil moldings connected the arch of the windows.

With the sun near setting, the tall trees of the rainforest outside the windows were dark and impenetrable. A lawn of green grass, cut through with stone paths carved out and lined with bushels of wildflowers and shrubs, surrounded the area outside. As he watched, a light rain began to fall; the drops streaked the windows.

In each corner of the room sat round pools of water, encompassed by raised marble structures. In their centers rose a sweep of marble shaped like bowls and filled with copious amounts of delicate ferns, green ivy, and vines. Garridan instantly disliked them.

In the center of the room stood a great fountain with four large, impressive animal statues, their majestic forms upraised, tusks in the air, ears back, and long snouts lifted to spout water in a babbling rush. Five round tables draped with deep red tablecloths formed a rough circle near the bank of windows.

The finery was too much. The stunning craftsmanship was almost too perfect to be real, as if he touched any of it—the marble, the grand fountain, the carved, flowering centerpieces—it might crumble or evaporate like a dream. Garridan was overwhelmed by the ostentatious display of wealth, yet envious and repulsed as well.

"I suppose if you have all the time and money in the world, you would reach a point where you think of gold threads in your wallpaper as a good investment," Darson murmured to Garridan, who snorted softly. "I am trying to keep in mind that these people have had a *lot* of time to amass so much, but this," Darson waved his hand over the room, "is a bit ridiculous. The most extravagant thing about Edric's castle is how tall his bookshelves are. And that fancy chair."

Fae guards escorted the king to the round table in the center, directly in front of the windows, to take dinner with the queen, Eyad, Princess Aaclyde, and a few faeries who Garridan assumed were high-ranking members of the monarchs' cabinets. Darson and Mourin were brought to the table and introduced to the queen. Garridan watched faint sweat gleam on Mourin's forehead as he met her. Darson's smile did not reach his eyes, though he displayed enough charm to make one of the unknown faeries smile.

Before leaving for their table, Garridan drew close to Eyad. When the sorcerer leaned in, Garridan murmured, "I ask that you ensure the king's safety during this dinner."

Eyad appraised him and then nodded. "Of course, Captain. I assure you, his safety is of the utmost priority to me."

Garridan ignored the stares he and his party earned during

their walk to their table. Kiryk was typically flattering, smiling broadly and complimenting the female faeries; Tiberius masked his discomfort poorly but said nothing.

The princesses sat at the other three tables, mingling with more faeries Garridan thought must be from Aaclyde's court, based on their dress. He noted the commanders sat at the table to their far left with the desert princesses and Dahlia. The fair-haired princesses were together at one table, and he caught Princess Tatyana and the faerie with the foxlike face staring at them occasionally from the last table. Darson, too, gazed around, but Mourin sat rigidly in his chair, staring blankly at the table dressings.

"Gentlemen, do not look so *stiff*," Kiryk admonished them, with the easy tone of one a touch inebriated. "Excellent food awaits, I can feel it."

Servants—older this time—delivered the first course, a sweet, brown, broth-like soup. The servants also filled their goblets with a crisp, mildly sweet white wine. The next course was a medley of shredded cabbage and fruit topped with chopped nuts. Placed on each white napkin were pairs of slim, delicate pieces of wood.

Darson picked them up with dismay, exchanging a puzzled look with Garridan.

"Do we stab our food?" Tiberius asked irritably.

Garridan watched a few of the princesses eat with effortless skill. Feeling somewhat self-conscious, he clumsily mimicked them, grabbing a few slender pieces of cabbage and the tart fruit between the two sticks and eating before the food fell. "How do they make it look so easy?" he asked.

Darson scooped food in-between the two sticks with both hands and looked proud. "I think they want us to look ridiculous, so they didn't tell us how to use these."

"That *is* a side benefit. We cannot let it be said that we would miss an opportunity to poke fun at you."

The group turned toward the source of the voice.

Wry humor lit the face of Princess Liana, who stood behind them. She had changed from the pale purple dress Garridan remembered from the meeting into a brown embroidered skirt with a purple, short-sleeved top. A scarf of the same color draped around her neck and nestled in the crook of her arm.

"I would do the same," Darson admitted, and then almost looked surprised at his quick response. He cleared his throat. "But you will have to forgive us if we pretend your … eating sticks … are spears for the meal's duration."

"I can give you a quick lesson on the proper use of the 'eating sticks.'"

Garridan offered her his seat, and she thanked him. The captain noted Darson's faint flush when the princess slipped between them to perch on the edge of the chair, nipping the sticks from Darson's grasp as she sat.

Darson appeared to be surprised that the princess from the path was sitting this close to him. As she positioned the pieces of wood in his fingers, he noted the faint lace detail of her dress, her earthy scent of flowers and spices, and the pale gold paint on her nails. She showed Garridan, too, while the advisors looked on and attempted to mimic her movements.

"I can put in a request for utensils you are more accustomed to," she offered, a hint of amusement in her voice as she stood to give Garridan his seat back. Darson's fingers slipped, and he dropped his food.

"Please, do not trouble yourself. I find it unacceptable

that I cannot master two small wooden sticks; I will suffer through it," Darson replied.

"He means to say he will eat with his fingers when you leave," Garridan said.

* * *

Darson held his breath as his chest constricted at the musical sound of Liana's laughter in response. She stayed until both Garridan and Darson managed to use the sticks properly to pick up food; when servants began to deliver the main course, she bid them good-bye. Her scent lingered, and he felt bereft at her absence.

"Reevaluating your opinion of them, Dar?" Garridan teased, as plates of spicy noodles, crispy pork, cooked vegetables, and an entire baked fish stuffed with herbs and spices were placed in front of them.

Darson would have agreed if Mourin had not chosen that moment to shout with alarm. Darson jerked out of his seat when Mourin leapt up as if a snake bit him, knocking over his goblet and soaking the tablecloth and Darson's arm with white wine in the process. The soldier's chair tipped back and fell with a crash to the marble floor.

"Mourin!" he exclaimed simultaneously with Garridan, who stood along with Darson; Tiberius and Kiryk stared in surprise from their seats. All the color had gone out of Mourin's face, his eyes stricken with terror. Kiryk was saying something, but Darson didn't catch it as he followed Mourin's gaze to the source of his fright.

A female servant stood feet away from him, stopped in the act of walking away after delivering the dinner plates. She stared back at the soldier with a startled expression. Her reaction and Mourin's did not match, and Darson did not know what was wrong.

"Easy," Darson said, as if Mourin were a spooked horse. He was painfully aware that the entire room had become silent, and every pair of eyes was on them. He glanced quickly at the queen's table and found King Edric and Eyad on their feet, concern written across their faces. Eyad moved as if to cross the room to them, and Darson shook his head slowly; he knew the sorcerer's presence would only further upset Mourin, who shook as he gaped at the servant. The terror morphed into confusion as his eyes darted back and forth from her to Darson. He looked wild-eyed, as he had in Hesperia when he'd run and the female guard hauled him back.

Hesperia.

Darson bit off a curse as it clicked. The female guard. The servant was a brunette. Mourin must have mistaken her for the guard.

A hand pressed lightly on Darson's shoulder as a female voice asked, "Is everything all right?"

He stiffened at the unexpected touch. He dared to take his eyes off Mourin to look; it surprised him to see Princess Liana. Before he could say anything, Mourin spoke.

"It was—" he began weakly, then faltered, his eyes flickering again from the servant to Darson and the princess. Darson could feel Garridan behind him, and gestured with his hand for his captain to let Mourin finish. The soldier could not string the words together to make sense; he seemed to choke on every syllable. "Dar, I s-s—"

The lieutenant watched Liana's gaze move from Mourin

to the servant, whom she looked at intensely, almost speculatively, for a moment. The servant spoke to the princess in Fae. Liana nodded once and replied in the same tongue. The servant curtsied, glanced once more at Mourin, and then hurried away.

"No harm done," Liana said, as if every human and faerie in the room were not staring, as if Mourin had done nothing worse than spill the wine. "Perhaps you would like to step out for some air." She moved closer to Mourin, but the soldier started violently.

Darson truly did not know if Mourin was in the throes of a hallucinatory episode, if he perceived the princess trying to help him as a threat. He watched Mourin's shaking left hand hover dangerously close to the knife hidden in his breeches. *No, Mourin, they would kill you.*

"Your Highness, please step back," Darson said, in a low voice. He did not give her a chance to comply and instead stepped forward, blocking her from Mourin's vision. She said nothing, and watched him with an unreadable expression.

"Mourin, it is all right," he said in a firm, reassuring voice. "The princess merely asked if you would like to sit down somewhere else. But there is a perfectly good seat behind you, and if you want, we can right it and you may sit."

Darson moved to right the chair as Mourin watched him and Liana with the look of a child waking from a nightmare. Bright splotches of color rose high on the soldier's cheeks as he finally came back to himself.

"Mourin, sit," Darson said quietly. "Thank the princess for her assistance."

He sat stiffly and stammered a thank you, unable to look

at her.

Darson looked to Garridan, only just realizing that Garridan had spoken at some point, to the room or the advisors, he did not know. Behind the captain, the two commanders watched Mourin like hawks.

Darson edged as close to Liana as he dared and said softly, "We sincerely apologize. Thank you for trying to help." He noticed the slight trembling in his own hands.

She placed her hand over his and squeezed lightly, then pressed a napkin into his palm. As he wiped up the mess from the wine, he wished he could tell her how deeply he appreciated the simple kindness and lack of judgment in her eyes, but words failed him.

"I am sure the chair will recover," she said with a trace of humor. She offered him another goblet a servant passed to her, filled with water instead of wine, and Darson took it, thanking her. He watched her return to her table, saying something in Fae loud enough for the room to hear; voices murmured as normalcy began to return, though some faeries still stole glances at the unstable humans.

"Well, lad, you livened up this party, to be sure," Kiryk said, raising his wine glass. "Cheers."

* * *

"Mourin."

Darson watched the man's shoulders hunch at Garridan's voice, like a pup expecting a smack after soiling the floor. After Mourin received a verbal thrashing from the king following dinner, it was no wonder. The captain sighed and ordered softly, "Take first watch."

Visibly relieved, Mourin nodded, and silently slipped out of their room.

"Hold on." Darson tossed his journal on his bed and followed Mourin out. The two stood alone in the hall, Mourin eyeing Darson warily.

"I know what you thought you saw," Darson said. "I know what happened in Hesperia still affects you."

Mourin looked at his feet. "It was her," he said, as if he could barely believe it himself. "She said, "I can also show you how to eat with those," and I looked up, and *it was her*. But then—" He shook his head, confusion crossing his face once more. "Then it wasn't."

Pity and impatience warred in Darson's heart, and a slight twinge at the word *show*, although he sought to smother it in favor of common sense. "Is it logical, Mourin, to think a Hesperian border guard would also work in Miranda's palace as a servant?"

Mourin's face took on a pinched look. "No."

"Is it possible that your mind tricked you?"

"Of course it is." A flash of self-disgust darkened Mourin's light blue eyes. "I … I am truly sorry. I should have handled that better. I promise you and Captain Garridan that there will not be another incident like this."

"Keep in mind that it is highly unlikely that Eyad would allow anything to happen to us while we are here," Darson said. "He is much too excited for this to work to risk our safety. And honestly, I believe these faeries do not want to be here, either. I would bet they want this over as much as we do, no matter the outcome. They are not fantastical beings with magic powers; they are very old creatures that do not care for us and want us off their land as soon as possible."

Mourin's mouth quirked upward in a smile. Darson squeezed Mourin's shoulder and the soldier promised once more to make an effort to endure. Despite the promise, Darson's heart remained troubled. The gratitude in Mourin's eyes did nothing to dispel Darson's concern or the queer feeling of *wrongness* that dogged him. He wished he could remove Mourin from the environment that triggered such strong hallucinations and responses.

When Darson returned to the room and shut the door, Garridan stood by the window, fingers buried in his thick, dark hair. "I am ready to pull Mourin out of tomorrow's meeting," he said tiredly. "But I cannot leave him alone. Did he give you any indication as to why he chose that moment to have a breakdown?"

"He did not tell me much, but said he truly thought the servant was the Hesperian guard. He should never have come," Darson said bluntly. "Whatever happened when I was unconscious in Hesperia has plagued him ever since."

Garridan grimaced. "I only hope Mourin can keep it together for the meeting tomorrow—and for the duration of this trip."

Chapter 17

The humans were late, and Nevada blamed Eyad.

No doubt the sorcerer was taking his time to show off the palace, playing host in a home that did not belong to him. Then he would dump the soldiers—one of whom was unstable—on her and Dacian. Liana said little about the incident last night at dinner when she returned to their table, but Nevada could not forget the raw fear on the soldier's face.

And here they were, about to have a military conference in the underground levels of the palace. In the weapons room. Dacian's sense of humor ran to the macabre.

She looked at the desert commander who waited with her outside of the main conference room. He sipped fragrant coffee, his countenance fresher than she expected at such an early hour.

"Perhaps the room change was not a wise move," she murmured.

"Of course it is," he replied, taking a longer drink. "If he cannot handle it, he should not be here. I will not go out of my way to coddle a human soldier."

He was right, although she was less worried about that and more impatient for it all to be over. She did not relish the thought of hearing how many fae soldiers the humans needed to gain control over their situation. She did not want to imagine those precious immortal souls dropped into a territory teeming with Erepos, surrounded by humans who did not understand—and would probably fear—them.

Nevada felt downright surly when the humans and Eyad arrived. The sorcerer greeted her cheerfully, and she barely kept the irritation out of her voice when she acknowledged him. Dacian said nothing to any of them, but gave Eyad an unfriendly look as he motioned for the three human soldiers to follow them, leaving the king and advisors with Eyad.

She eyed the soldier called Mourin; he looked withdrawn and a little colorless, but otherwise fine; she hoped he stayed that way. The captain said little as she and Dacian led them down a flight of stairs to the lower wing. The man Liana had helped last night looked around with polite interest.

Nevada almost cracked a smile at their reaction when they entered the weapons room. Not one mortal looked thrilled with the choice … but Dacian looked pleased.

* * *

Garridan wanted to know if Eyad had picked this room, or if the culprit was the smug male commander with an apparent sadistic streak.

He was betting on the latter.

The room was on a lower level of the palace, like the unused dungeons in King Edric's castle, and windowless, with damp air that tasted like metal. Weapons hung decoratively from the walls. Daggers and swords gleamed; wickedly barbed instruments and small metal projectiles flashed like teeth. A tall metal object, just wide enough to trap a body inside, stood in a corner. Garridan was positive it was a torture device of some kind. He wondered if the faeries still brought it out from time to time.

After everyone took their seats at the long table and sat in an uncomfortable silence that hummed with a life of its own, Garridan felt his morning coffee sour in his stomach.

Commander Nevada shifted, and the thin black cloth of her shortened, loose pants whispered as she crossed her legs. The refreshing smell of her loose hair drifted to Garridan as she ran her fingers through it. Instead of bolstering him, the blast of sweetness in the stale air made him ill, like the scent of flowers at a gravesite.

The dead air broke as the heel of her shoe clicked against the chair leg.

Click.

The sharp sound pierced Garridan's brain like a wooden shard.

Click.

He took a careful breath; he was done waiting for the fae to lead the way. "On behalf of my king, Lieutenant Darson, Mourin, and myself would like to thank you again for allowing us this opportunity."

Commander Dacian was quick to respond. "We had little to do with the decision, but we will pass the sentiment along."

"Of course," Garridan agreed. He watched as Dacian eyed him. "We understand our request is unusual," he said. "And uneven. We do not, as of yet, have the resources to make this a fair trade."

"We have not had a need for your assistance," Dacian said, maintaining the same forthright tone Garridan used. "It never would have occurred to any in our kingdom to seek out your aid, so you are correct: it is an uneven trade."

Garridan swallowed back a flush of anger, even though he knew the words were true. "Be that as it may—"

"I am curious." Dacian interrupted him. "How *do* you intend to repay us for whatever services you need rendered over the course of, what, a few decades? A century?"

Garridan locked eyes with Darson and then responded. "All of you have the gift of eternal youth and longevity. While we may not have the means to repay you right away, it does not discount any aid or trade we may be able to give in the future. Our king had hoped to facilitate an alliance that would last well after his immediate heirs took the throne. We would need time to spread the advanced training fae soldiers could provide."

"So for half a century, we can expect no recompense for sending our soldiers to your Erepo pit, no matter the potential casualties or how much it will cost each country in money and lives?" Dacian smiled humorlessly. "You are anticipating long campaigns, are you not? Years of service for each fae soldier?"

"We would happily agree to whatever arrangement would be best for you," Garridan replied carefully.

In a low tone, as if she intended it to be for his ears only, Commander Nevada said, "Dacian, their issues derive from—"

"Yes, yes, I know." Dacian waved off her comment impatiently. "I am aware their mortality and immune systems exacerbate their problem with the Erepos. But as talented as our soldiers are, we cannot wipe the Erepos from the face of this land; if we could, we would have done it by now. I simply want to know what you think we can do for you that would turn the odds in your favor besides kill Erepos and stretch our numbers to the breaking point."

"We are not asking you to kill Erepos *for* us," Garridan explained. "We are asking to learn from your experience and expertise so we know how to better deal with the problem ourselves. Training. Avoiding infection. Gaining our territory back. Enlistment in our forces has been down for four decades now, and handling the Erepo problem has been made more difficult by the retirement or deaths of veteran trainers and soldiers and having no one to replace them. If—" he swallowed, feeling conviction color his voice with an ardor he hadn't wished to show, lest he seem like an overexcited school boy. "If we are able to show the people and the soldiers of Aliquis that others, like you, do not believe our situation to be a lost cause, I know it would make a world of difference."

Darson joined the conversation. "It cycles back and benefits you if you are able to assist with keeping the mortal kingdoms from falling. You understand it would be catastrophic were that to happen. The Erepos are turning *people*, Commanders, who in turn infect more people, who will eventually come to your corner of the world."

Dacian kept quiet, and Darson continued. "Obviously, that mystical wall of yours does not keep them out, and your kingdom is not cushioned from the outside world as well as you assume it is. Our problem *will* become your problem, if given enough time, and let me assure you, you do not want the carnage we face on a monthly basis."

Nevada's eyes widened and then fixed on the smooth dark wood of the table, as if she didn't quite know how to react.

Her response piqued Garridan's curiosity.

Dacian leaned forward in his seat, eyes narrowing, irises a storm brewing in a fiery sunset. His voice chilled the room as he said, softly, "You have no idea what you are talking about."

Garridan felt Mourin shift, and he was sure he could smell the man's fear. He let his attention stray to the soldier. He did not like how Mourin's hands clutched the sides of his chair, or the look on his face as he gazed at the two faeries. He waited for Mourin to acknowledge him, and wasn't satisfied when the final response was a convulsive swallow and an insincere, nervous smile.

Hold it together, Garridan willed him silently.

* * *

In a distant sort of way, Nevada appreciated Dacian's biting comment. Had she not been preoccupied with the massacre her mind's eye recalled, she would have fabricated a response to the lieutenant's words by now. Yet it would not come. The reminder—*you do not want the carnage we face*—delivered a hard punch, and she was having trouble catching her breath.

She worked hard to hide her anger, bringing it out only when she was alone, but Dacian wore it openly, like a bleeding wound. Nevada gave him a warning look, but even that felt ineffective; she was suddenly so *tired.*

"I am protecting you," he said in Fae.

"I know, but I am fine," she replied in kind. She cleared her throat, and said to Garridan, "Let me test my knowledge of Aliquis's military operations with you, so we may better understand your structure and where help would be most beneficial. If I may."

Nevada watched Garridan's shoulders relax. "Absolutely," he said.

"Forgive me if my information is outdated. Aliquis's guard is still split into six divisions, correct? The four corners, the reserves, and the king's guard?"

Her knowledge of Aliquis's military organization surprised Garridan, and apparently Darson, as well, though Garridan noticed he hid it hastily. Mourin looked worried. Had Aliquis's military organization changed so little in a thousand years? Garridan thought on it, reaching back in his history education, before the Erepo surges. Yes, the organization was largely the same, as far as he knew.

"You are correct," he said. "Although the reserves are known as the home guard or the internal unit."

After a moment of silence and a scrutinizing gaze, Dacian asked, "As members of the king's guard, what are your duties?"

"Investigate situations of the king's interest throughout the kingdom," Garridan answered. "We have unrestricted jurisdiction and act according to the king's wishes in any part of Aliquis. We may do anything from extracting a person of interest from a dangerous situation to evacuating a village during an Erepo breach. We aid villages in tightening their security when we can, and we deliver supplies.

"I gather your ways of dealing with the enemy are different within each country," he continued "As a whole, do you utilize quadrant divisions?"

"We have three divisions," Nevada said. "Border guard, internal division, and royal division. As of right now, the majority of the southern countries have transferred considerable resources to their border guards. I would like to procure a map so we can have a visual of our most problematic areas."

Captain Garridan nodded. "Yes, that would be beneficial."

Before long, Nevada laid out a map nearly as wide as the table that narrowed its focus to the three mortal kingdoms, the Wild Territories, and the faerie kingdom. Garridan had never seen such a complete map, although it was a bit outdated; he informed the commanders of Ferox's issues, where the kingdom had collapsed, though he knew his information could be inaccurate since Ferox no longer communicated. Garridan and Darson pointed out the hot spots of Erepo activity within Aliquis, and towns that had been destroyed or evacuated. Nevada marked the map as they made comments. He liked the way her narrowed focus brightened her face, turning her violet eyes brilliant with intensity as she absorbed the new information. He preferred it to her distracted, lost expression from earlier.

Garridan did not know why he was drawn to her. He could not say where his interest came from, only that he appreciated her presence and the way she spoke. He had looked for her at dinner, as he would no doubt look for her again. Something about her settled him. He wished he had time to figure out why.

He easily figured out the reason for her momentary distraction after Darson reminded them of their vulnerable borders. Nevada alluded to a major attack recently. He wondered about the nature of it, and how he could ask questions about it without losing both commanders to anger.

Nevada marked high Erepo activity areas along the fae kingdoms' western borders where they met Aliquis, and none of it surprised Garridan, least of all the activity she noted on the very southeastern edge of Aliquis. "We cannot even access those areas any longer," he told her. "Those communities were some of the first to be evacuated or lost altogether."

"What can you tell us regarding the Wild Territories?" Nevada asked.

"Little," Garridan admitted. "The activity there is not documented well. We rarely venture into the Territories any longer."

"Erepos are less of a problem compared to the pockets of rogue humans," Darson said. "Cast outs from the three kingdoms. They observe their own laws and customs. I would argue they pose as much of a threat to travelers as Erepos."

"I would agree with you," Nevada said.

Garridan did not want to risk rehashing the scene from earlier, but something was bothering him, and if he did not ask soon, he feared he would not get the answers he needed.

"You mentioned something peculiar yesterday," he said to Commander Dacian, keeping his tone politely curious. "About Erepo forces growing more organized. We have seen the same behaviors. They are leaving more victims alive instead of just eating them. As if someone were giving them instruction to help them increase their numbers." He looked at Nevada, whose face had grown rather grave, yet still attentive. "The attack on your kingdom. Did it feel random?"

* * *

Nevada felt, more than saw, Dacian stiffen. She ignored him, and willed her face to remain blank, although her stomach began to churn. She said, "The ambushes were carried out efficiently. With purpose."

Captain Garridan leaned forward. "Ambushes, plural? Coinciding with one another?"

She breathed out slowly. "Yes. Over a series of days."

His blue eyes sparked with an intense desire for more information. *No. You cannot have it all. You cannot have even a fraction of the details.*

"How many days?" Lieutenant Darson asked. "Do you feel there were any deliberate targets among the casualties?"

Nevada was acutely aware of Dacian, who was giving off enough tension and anger to heat the room. Her fingers tightened in a hard grip on the material of her pant leg.

"It—" She painstakingly chose the right words. She struggled to stay objective, to form a simple answer to a simple question. "It lasted four days."

Such a simple phrase to sum up the four most hellacious days of her long existence. Four days that felt like four years, an eternity played out over and over; the same events, sometimes in sequence, or sometimes not.

Sometimes she didn't even remember. Sometimes, all she had were holes, and too many hours unaccounted for.

She felt Dacian watching her.

She could not look at him.

"We came to the conclusion that yes, the civilian population was a deliberate target." The strength in her voice made her proud. "Instead of rushing up from the southern border, this particular group traveled as far north through the mountain range as possible to reach the central part of Deimos and attack from there. The strategy was highly unusual for them."

"Deliberate," Garridan began. "Although they are hardly capable of deliberate actions and tactical maneuvers. Commanders, would either of your experiences lead you to believe that someone or something was controlling them? Thinking for them?"

Nevada and Dacian looked at each other. She could tell the human captain was excited, as if he were on to something that would magically explain the Erepos' actions and move them one step closer to defeating them.

Dacian pursed his lips and said, "It is not out of the realm of possibility."

"It is just a theory," Nevada corrected, frowning slightly. "We have considered it, but we have no evidence to support that theory. As of right now, their behavior is as much of a mystery to us as it is to you. They have not grown smarter, individually. But their behavior in large groups has changed, as I just described."

"Was your capitol attacked?" Darson inquired.

Nevada's chin lifted, and she swallowed. Dacian hissed.

"Yes, it was," she answered.

"Were there any attempts on your princess?" Garridan asked, and he almost looked guilty for posing the question, as if he knew it was a sensitive subject.

Nevada glanced at Dacian as she considered her answer. She suppressed the urge to fidget at his volatile expression.

"Yes." She kept her response curt and matter-of-fact. "Successful attempts. On my previous princess and prince. Princess Rees is, as she informed your party yesterday, very new to her position."

"Is—"

"I believe we have discussed this enough," Dacian interrupted, his tone effectively shutting Garridan down.

The captain blinked at him. "We are merely trying to understand—"

"Nothing. You understand nothing. Let us discuss, then, the actual reason we are all here. What incident brought *you* to our doorstep?"

The humans hesitated, and Dacian raised an eyebrow as he tilted his head. "Come now. Something had to spur your monarch into action."

"Think of it as an accumulation of incidents," Lieutenant Darson replied. "Every few days, across the kingdom, for decades. You have not seen what goes on in our world."

"Enlighten me." Dacian's words came out as a dangerous growl.

With an intensity that rivaled Dacian's, Darson replied, "We have lost a third of our men in the past four years—half of those soldiers are still wandering the countryside, and as their families grieve for them, the only thing on their minds is the taste of flesh." His face flushed with anger as he continued. "Another century of this and the human race will be completely consumed by Erepos. When you have to look in the eyes of someone you love and bury a sword in their neck before they eat you alive, then consider yourself *enlightened.*"

Well. The human has claws, too. And while Darson swiped at Dacian, Mourin seemed to shrink in his seat, as if he were a child witnessing his parents fight.

"Lieutenant," Captain Garridan said sharply. The cool, calm waters of his eyes rippled with the first hint of actual anger. "Let us get to the point. To fully answer your question, Commander Dacian, there *was* a specific incident, two months back. The infected soldier was allowed to walk inside Laurus's walls because of our oversight, where tens of thousands of civilians live. Do either of you know what the symptoms are for a bitten human once the change begins?"

Of course we do, Nevada thought deprecatingly. She answered, "Chills, fever, clammy skin, extreme pallor. Aches that turn to excruciating pain, vomiting."

"He went to the infirmary with these symptoms. The incubation period for a bitten human is twenty hours or so. The soldier turned in the middle of a crowded sick room and killed one of our most beloved healers, then proceeded to kill and eat three other people before one of my men, himself injured, slew his comrade. Had it gone differently, Laurus would be a dead city."

"Thousands of new Erepos," Darson said, quieter. "Thousands more enemies, wearing the faces of loved ones. Men. Women. Children. Fifteen towns over the past decade have been lost that way; we watched many of them burn, the people quarantined or slaughtered before they could turn. The carnage repeats on an endless loop, year after year. All three of us have been forced to kill someone we knew, or loved, to save them from a life of eternal hell."

The room went silent. Nevada empathized with the suffering they witnessed and what they were forced to do; despite recent events, she knew how lucky her people were. She remembered the trials humans faced, trials that did not touch the fae—hunger, disease, aging, poverty. A part of her grudgingly admitted they presented their cause well. She gained respect for them, too. She did not envy their lives, filled as they were with blood, heartache, and death. They were so desperate to see an end to it that they appealed for help from beings they did not know or understand anymore. She watched Captain Garridan's face, the steady blue of his eyes. A warrior caught up in a war he could not win in his lifetime looked back at her.

If Dacian felt the same sentiment, he did not show it. "There are not enough fae in the world to keep your people from turning. What do you expect us to do about that?"

Nevada ground her teeth together as anger crossed the Garridan and Darson's faces. Mourin still looked rather ill. "Was that necessary?" she asked in Fae.

Dacian's eyes zeroed in on her. "Since when are you such an advocate for their kind? I have heard what you really think about mortals, and it is not as flattering as you would like them to believe."

Furious with Dacian for bringing her personal views into the discussion, Nevada abruptly stood, aware of Mourin cringing as her chair scraped back against the stone floor. "Excuse us," she told the humans.

"Come here," she ordered Dacian in Fae. Without waiting, she moved closer to the wall of weapons and farther out of earshot so she did not lose her temper in front of the mortals.

She sensed Dacian following her, and when he neared, she whirled, her words flowing out in a fuming rush. "This meeting has *nothing* to do with my personal opinion. You are out of line and losing focus."

His eyebrows rose. "Losing focus," he said flatly.

"Stop disrespecting them," she said. "This meeting would be over sooner if you would cease to goad them. It took a lot for them to say what they just did, for them to even be here.

They are making an effort, and you are demeaning them at every opportunity. If you could be professional—courteous, even, if you could manage—I would appreciate it."

Dacian stared at her for a long moment, a muscle twitching along his jaw, as he stood stock-still. "Are you done?" he finally asked.

She smiled then, all teeth. "If you are."

They returned to the table, the air frigid between them. Captain Garridan ignored the entire incident and captured Nevada's attention with a soft inquiry. "May I?" he asked.

She glanced at Dacian one more time, as if to assure herself of his good behavior. He gave her an unfriendly look. "You may," she said.

"I know you may not care what happens to us," the captain said. "You may very well throw us out and forget we ever came here. We will leave, but our crisis will not leave us. A century from now, our problem is not something your children or your children's children will inherit; it is what *you* will inherit. We are asking you to help us—and also help yourselves in the long run."

Darson added, "Look at this as an opportunity to stop that from happening one day, because while the years of our lives are limited, yours are not."

Nevada felt wrung out, as if she had not slept for days and the end of her strength was near. Her anger at Dacian abated enough to let Garridan and Darson's words sink in. After a brief, uncomfortable look at Dacian's stone-cold expression, she could see in his eyes that he understood the message, too.

She could see the future Garridan painted in broad, bloody strokes. More ambushes, droves of Erepos and turned humans—more tragedies like Deimos. She found herself nodding as she thought, and then said, "What are you asking for to help your military?"

"Our soldiers number in the tens of thousands," Garridan said, almost apologetically. "Our units are substantial and cover a great deal of ground. To train and assist each unit, we discussed requesting eighty fae soldiers per each of the six units—"

The number hit Nevada like a blow to the stomach.

"—and a time period for maximum potential of that aid, I would venture to say ten years. We do not expect the same fae soldiers to stay for all ten years; if you are willing, we propose a rotation. We hoped it would ease the burden on the countries that assist."

Dacian had brought his hand to his face, fingers pinching his brow as he brooded in silence. Nevada was amazed he did not have an automatic reaction at the 480 soldiers the humans asked for. His shoulders shook once with laughter. He dropped his hand and leaned forward. The humans tensed, and Dacian eyed them with a hint of dark humor. "I am going to forget about that number for the time being. We need a better idea of your skill level before we can guess at a *hypothetical* number that would do you any good and one we could live with."

The captain nodded carefully. "Of course. We would be happy to show you."

"You will each spar with me, as well as Commander Nevada," Dacian said firmly. "Commander, are you willing?"

She nodded. Already, her limbs felt lighter, poised and ready to unleash the energy that appeared from hidden reserves at Dacian's suggestion.

Dacian stalked to the wall and grabbed a curved sword. "First, I believe it would be beneficial for you to see how *we* operate. Then, you will show me on this wall what weapons you are familiar with, what you routinely use against Erepos, and then we will test your proficiency with them. Then we will spar." When the soldiers remained seated, he sighed. "Gentlemen, we will need to move that table."

The three mortals stood pushed the table closer to the wall opposite the weapons. Nevada removed her shoes, put them on the table, and walked barefoot to the weapons wall as she pulled her hair back with the leather tie at her wrist. She selected a sword similar to Dacian's.

With the humans standing against the wall and watching in rapt attention, she and Dacian stood three yards apart, adopting ready stances. Nevada felt the weight of her weapon, and could not wait to take out her frustration and anger on the other commander.

And he knows it.

Dacian grinned at her. "Take notes," he told the men. "And prepare yourselves." He saluted Nevada.

She sprang forward and attacked.

Chapter 18

Garridan's body hurt.

The hot bath he was relaxing in soothed like a balm, but he suspected he would hurt for a day or two more, given that his muscles still ached twenty-four hours after the training session.

He considered himself in near excellent shape for his age; he had to be in peak condition for his job. Training with his men and other units—on the rare occasions he was home to take advantage of it—never completely sapped his strength or endurance. It invigorated him and kept him sharp.

But the faerie commanders had shown him how little he knew of stamina.

Witnessing the tension between the two explode in combat training yesterday reminded him that, as mortals, he and his men could not match the centuries of training and stronger physiology of the fae. It had been hard to watch Dacian fly at Nevada, barely holding back the punches as he tried, like a fierce, relentless wind, to blow through her defenses.

She held her own. Garridan had been coiled with antic-ipation, rooting for her each time her lithe frame slipped through Dacian's grasp as sand slipped through fingers; a grim satisfaction lit her countenance as she refused to allow

Dacian to dominate the sparring. Garridan had never seen anyone move with such fluid grace. Dacian's speed and agility defied logic, and Nevada met his movements with the same frightening power. It was exhilarating, terrifying, and mesmerizing to watch. Garridan and his men were not accustomed to seeing women in combat, let alone with such skill, and he had to quell the urge more than once to assist when she failed to block a hit. Yet she fought marvelously, moved like a dancer, and defended herself better than most men in the Aliquis military.

Nevada enthralled him.

He told himself to put that thought to bed. It was one thing to find her attractive, considering she was intelligent, a soldier like he was, and gorgeous—but quite another to let those thoughts occupy too much of his attention.

His thoughts turned to Commander Dacian. To his credit, he had watched Garridan and his men perform with a critical, constructive eye, quickly and accurately assessing their strengths and weaknesses. It was humbling to work with him and know full well Dacian held back a great deal to avoid breaking bones. Both faeries proved that Aliquis's soldiers had much to learn.

Garridan leaned his head back against the cool tile, breathing in the steam from the heated water. The warmth chased away his distress from today's meeting with the commanders and the monarchs. He could not say what specific part aggravated him. He felt as though they had accomplished nothing and nothing had been agreed upon—except for a party.

A *party*.

Proposed by Princess Dahlia, in the spirit of repairing

relations and learning about one another, she said. A celebration. Eyad pounced on the idea like a man looking for a raft in a raging sea. Garridan wasn't sure whom he disliked more at that moment.

His faith in the sorcerer—what little there had been—sputtered and died like a weak flame in a strong wind. The princesses and the king unsuccessfully discussed trade, and the military discussion was derailed by misgivings and arguments. It seemed as if the celebration was merely a delay before the end of the talks, and they would leave with nothing gained.

He had no desire to play a significant role at tonight's festivities. He desired even less to see more extravagance and displays of wealth—not after such a trying, difficult afternoon. All he wanted was for the faeries to come to a decision so his group could return home. He only hoped Mourin handled the festivities well, but no structure, free-roaming faeries, liquor, and music meant many triggers for the soldier. The evening needed to go smoothly.

Garridan heard footsteps approaching the bathing room's doorway and sat up, wincing at the ache of the tender muscles in his lower back.

Darson entered, journal in hand. "Are you quite done soaking? I am exhausted from watching the advisors preen for this evening, and I would like to bathe, too."

* * *

Princess Liana basked in the silence of her suite.

Back home, the simple quiet of her room was tempered with the wind traveling over sand dunes, tossing handfuls of sand at the windows as it passed. Here in Miranda, she heard pattering rain, birds crying to one another, and leaves ruffling in the breeze.

She wished for time enough to rest her eyes before enduring an evening of minutiae and pleasantries with the human delegates, Miranda's court, and the other princesses. The heat of the desert dictated her normal sleep schedule; in Creo, she would just be rousing for the evening, and her day would end with the morning sun. Her body felt the lack of its normal routine, and she longed for it, which made her hate the impromptu revelry all the more. Liana enjoyed a good celebration—just not one so hastily thrown together to smooth over the strain of the past few days.

The day's arguments lingered like an odd, unpleasant odor, and she wrinkled her nose as she slipped on the maroon skirt and matching embroidered top, enjoying the cool air on her bare midriff and upper back. She walked barefoot through her suite, tidying up the parchments scattered on the bedside dresser, floor, and a small writing desk. Copious notes from three days of meetings mingled with collected information and documentation from Creo. Names of the mortals caught her eye, and she thought of their discouraged, aging faces.

I know how hard your lives are, Liana wanted to tell them. *I know your food is scarce and so is safety*—but getting help to you is not easy. During the meetings, they had spent hours exhausting every possible way to conceive potential trade routes, getting the humans' hopes high only to realize that the danger of roaming Erepos and turned humans would hinder any efforts. The plan would take time and care to implement, and Liana was afraid the mortals did not have the time to spare.

And Eyad acted as if he had no idea what it required to assist the human kingdom.

Liana returned to the washroom and ran a horsehair brush through her unbound blonde hair, harder than necessary.

"Using the Rausa River is a sound idea," Eyad had argued. "Is this not an acceptable option?"

You are not a stupid man. Liana watched the anger darken her eyes in the looking glass's reflection. *Yet you act as if the past century of activity—in either kingdom—is a mystery to you.* What *have you been doing?*

She knew what he did *not* do five years ago.

The memory hurt. She shook it off, took a deep breath, and perched on the marble counter. She carefully applied black eyeliner eyelids and a touch of color to her lips, humming a Creoian folk song to help bury the ugly memories stirred by Eyad's very presence.

The princess heard the door to her suite click open followed by the faintest sound of bare feet over wood.

"Liana?"

She smiled at Nevada's soft voice. She finished applying the kohl and turned to greet her friend. The commander lounged on her round bed, rumpling the cranberry silk sheets, bare toes dug into the carpet with her shoes on the floor beside her. Outside the rain still fell. In the distance, thunder rumbled.

Nevada took a long drink from a clear glass bottle with slices of mango swimming lazily inside.

Liana eyed the bottle. "How long have you been working on that?"

"I just started. I would like to get to the mangos. Would you like some?" She turned the bottle this way and that in an enticing gesture. The yellow fruit churned dreamily. "Pretty dress. You hardly wear that color anymore."

"It suits my mood. And no, thank you, the mangos are all yours." Liana sat next to her, noting Nevada's relaxed demeanor, a stark contrast to her reticence during the meeting.

"Your bruises are nearly gone," Liana pointed out, tapping her finger on the right side of Nevada's cheekbone.

She smiled. "Dacian got lucky. I gave him that black eye as repayment."

"I noticed." Nevada had never been able to give Liana details about the military meeting, so she said, "I heard King Edric say something about five hundred soldiers?"

Nevada groaned. "Can you believe it? And I do not think they are exaggerating their need. Not after listening to the captain and lieutenant speak. After we sparred with them, we spoke more, and they gave us specific examples of why they are here. One concerned a town called Porphys. A unit found a little girl wandering alone, presumably bitten and left outside of the village walls to turn."

Liana winced.

"The soldiers brought her back in, not realizing—although Captain Garridan did not sound sure about that. Everyone died. Every soul in the village, every soldier, one of whom was King Edric's grandson."

The princess sighed and uttered a curse. She *really* was not in the mood for a celebration.

"'I could give you a hundred more examples if you'd like,' he said. I couldn't stand to hear anymore. They nearly lost Laurus, too. One of his own men came inside with a bite and turned while in the infirmary. And there was our answer.

The threat to Laurus prompted them to act, and Edric must have been sitting on this idea ever since his grandson died."

"It is not as if we want to shut them out," Liana said, feeling wretched. "No one disputes their need. But of course, the history between the races came up and all of our past inequities were thrown in our collective faces, as if that alone constitutes whether or not we should provide assistance. I won't even go into how The Severing became a topic of conversation."

"That did nothing but stoke the fire," Nevada agreed. She took another drink from the bottle. "Perhaps this party is not such a bad idea. After three consecutive days of meetings, we could all use a release. A night to forget what we have done to each other and interact in a non-formal setting. An opportunity to get to know them as individuals instead of obstacles."

Stunned, Liana stared at her. "What an impressive change of heart!"

"You should have heard those two men yesterday," Nevada said. "They spoke more eloquently about Aliquis than the king's advisors. They were not begging—they were dignified, and formulated a strong argument. They seemed ... worthier, somehow, than I initially thought. Though this rum might have something to do with my changed perspective and improved mood.

"Now lace me up, please, so we can join the festivities?" Nevada shifted to the side and pulled her hair to the front. The black, finely made satin corset gaped open in the back, the laces loose.

Liana complied and began lacing up the corset. Her heart wrenched when Nevada said softly, "They asked about

Deimos. For details. Over and over."

Liana stopped lacing to smooth her hand down Nevada's hair. "They could not have understood the significance of those questions."

"I know. Dacian handled it worse than I did."

"He cares. His first instinct is to bite instead of reason."

There was a long pause, long enough that Liana dropped the laces and moved to sit in front of Nevada. The commander's head was down, her eyes narrowed and troubled.

"I did not handle it well, either," she whispered. "I wanted to leave, to do anything to stop remembering, for just a moment."

"And for the humans to ask so many questions," Liana commiserated. She laid a hand on Nevada's shoulder, ignoring the needle pricks of pain as her own memories resurfaced.

Receiving the letter, hastily written to raise the alarm and plead for help, *days* after the attacks began; riding into Deimos to find the country in ruins, the princess dead, her children missing … and Nevada missing, too. More days of searching the living and the dead, and all the while silently pleading for Eyad's help to locate her, using the connection he gave her as a child. Liana had never begged so hard in all her life.

All her pleas fell on deaf ears.

The princess reflexively reached for what was not hanging from her neck, and then dropped her hand, irritated with herself.

Nevada looked up at her, violet eyes moist with tears. "I cannot freeze every time it is mentioned. I need to move on, but I do not know how."

"You will, in your own time. Do not be upset with yourself," Liana soothed. "There is no time limit for grief. And it does not help you when Dacian prohibits any talk of it. He needs to be comfortable discussing the subject, too. We all do."

Nevada wiped her eyes. "I need to be stronger than this."

You need to heal, Liana thought sadly. She embraced Nevada and rested her head on her shoulder. "You are doing so much better; you have made real progress these past few years." *You do not remember how you were in the aftermath of Deimos; you are greatly recovered from that broken, lost faerie.* "Now, let us bring back some of that zeal and have a wonderful time tonight. Surely kicking Dacian in the face a few times made you feel better, at least?"

Nevada laughed. "The sparring did help. The humans were not bad. Your new pet is quick, and he adapts to new techniques remarkably well."

"My new pet?" Liana asked, as she moved to continue lacing up Nevada's corset.

"The lieutenant you helped. You said he had lovely eyes."

"He does. And good for him."

"He was one of the initial messengers who came through in Hesperia. You can imagine who they chanced upon there."

Liana chuckled. "I would love to hear details of *that* encounter."

"Arrian appeared quite fond of him."

"Have you heard from Arrian?"

"No, but I plan to ask Anann if he sent her word. She has not mentioned anything, but I would not doubt she is withholding information." She sighed. "Liana, I feel as if Arrian should be here by now."

"The delay could mean nothing," Liana replied. "I am sure

he is all right. Hesperia looks to him for so many things. Countless concerns could detain him, especially with Anann gone."

Of course he is fine. Liana respected no faerie more than she did Arrian; he was excellent at what he did, a wonderful friend, and a fantastic cook. Whatever reason he had for not yet returning was sound, and they would see him soon. She smirked as she tried to picture the lieutenant and Arrian in a room together. If that handsome mortal could keep his wits about him with Arrian as he had when he controlled the situation at dinner the night before last, then he possessed mettle she could admire.

"The lieutenant handled the troubled soldier well, did he not?" Liana asked as she undid some of the lacing to correct a mistake.

"He kept Dacian and me from coming over to drag his unstable comrade out of the room and away from you."

Liana scoffed at the idea that she had been in any danger. "I could have handled it. At least he and the captain had the foresight to keep Eyad out of it."

"Eyad has been useless since his arrival," Nevada said wryly.

"*Utterly,*" Liana agreed. "You know, that is another trigger issue we need to work on."

"No."

Liana bit her lip. "Making peace with him would go a long way, Nev."

"No. I am not ready. Can we go back to being aggravated and disgusted with him? Was he as irritating in your trade meeting yesterday as he was today?"

The princess hissed under her breath. Her fingers began to jerk on the laces, which jolted Nevada. "More so. How can he act as if he does not know what an upheaval this alliance will cause?"

"He's blindly hopeful," Nevada said derisively. "His optimism is not helping. I cannot understand why he fills that king's head with grand visions of everything we can offer them, but does not think once of the vast changes this kingdom will have to endure to accommodate the hundreds of thousands of mouths to feed and defend in Aliquis. Not to mention how unprepared those humans will be—they do not even know their king is *here.* I doubt many know we still exist; how will they handle faeries coming into their cities and directing their military?"

"*Thank* you." Liana pulled viciously on the laces, and Nevada gasped. "He is so ecstatic over the whole business that he forgets how much of an adjustment it will be for everyone, when all he has to do is mediate."

"All right," Nevada breathed. "Maybe you could—"

Liana barely heard her. Now that she had started voicing her grievances, she could not stop. "Initiating trade between two races after having no contact for millennia is not an easy process, yet he acts as if it will be no problem. This is a step in the right direction," she mimicked in imitation of Eyad's deep voice, all the while brutally tightening Nevada's laces.

"Guidelines and policies must be created for trade routes, on both ends, not to mention regulations between countries. A dozen valid points and problems were brought up, and Eyad—as well as Edric—dismissed it as something easily remedied." Liana reached over, plucked the rum bottle from Nevada's tight grasp, and helped herself. She shuddered as the strong liquor burned its way down, and then gave the bottle back to Nevada.

"Liana, I think my laces are tight enough," Nevada said when the princess moved to pick up where she'd left off.

Liana inspected the laces with dismay. "I will loosen them. I apologize." She calmed herself with a cleansing exhale and loosened Nevada's laces. "Tonight we will mingle, and tomorrow we will revisit these issues. I can see how my pet is doing," she joked. Nevada laughed, and Liana patted her back. "Are we ready?"

"Almost. I want the fruit first. Help me."

Liana gave her a wicked grin and took the bottle from Nevada's outstretched hand.

Chapter 19

The lights floated.

Darson tilted his head back to look up at the ceiling. Candles and lanterns hung suspended in the air as if on invisible strings. Flames flickered and swayed, creating a dazzling atmosphere and drenching thc ballroom in soft gold tones.

"Open your mouth any wider and you will catch a wasp or two," Garridan said.

Darson leveled a look at him, but his eyes quickly drifted back to the candles. "Did Eyad do this?"

"I assume so."

The vaulted ceilings disappeared into darkness far above the floating lights. Soaring windows lined three walls; the tops of massive trees swayed gently outside, their dark greenery caressing the glass midway to the ceiling. A blanket of rain clouds obscured the moons and Parna. Rain fell in sheets, battering leaves and windows.

The massive room was divided into two levels. The first level curved like a lazy smile, separated from the second half by a waist-high oak banister. A wide staircase led down to the lower half, where a large middle area was cleared for dancing, with the exception of a marble statue placed strategically in the center: a handsome, bare-chested winged faerie with grapevines wound around his arms, a crown of leaves resting on his head of curls, and a goblet of wine in hand.

In a far corner by the windows, faeries played drums, the harp, violins, the reed flute, and tambourine. The slow rhythm of the drums gave the music a sensuous edge. Faeries danced close together, arms and fingers entwined, smoothly transitioning from one dance to another as the musicians quickened the pace of the music or slowed it down.

Garridan wished he felt that carefree. He had no desire to join the dancing; he preferred the placid atmosphere of the main level, where prominent-looking faeries and conference attendees mingled among clusters of couches and chairs. Long tables held food, and servants brought samplings to the king, advisors, the queen, and Eyad.

"Lads, you look entirely too serious for such an occasion."

Kiryk had wandered from the group; the lights of the vestibule masked the gray in his hair and gave it the burnt gold sheen of his youth. He patted the captain and lieutenant on their elbows. "Escort an old man down to the dance floor, will you? I am ambassador to the faeries, after all, and I must mingle."

Garridan hesitated and glanced at the king. Edric nodded and waved them both off after gesturing to Mourin as well as the handful of guards surrounding Emilia, who glanced at them with a neutral expression. Her vibrant blue eyes skirted over them and settled off into the distance, barely paying the mortal king any mind. She looked distracted. It struck Garridan as odd given the atmosphere, but the observation slipped out of his thoughts when the aristocratic group went out of his sight as he and Darson escorted Kiryk.

They walked down the carpeted staircase to the wide expanse below with the advisor between them. When they reached the bottom of the staircase, Kiryk turned to them. "Do not hover."

"Kiryk, it is our job," Darson said dryly.

"Hover by the bar, then, sweet lieutenant. I will stay within sight."

Darson stared at him, speechless, as Kiryk turned and struck up a conversation with a female faerie descending the steps. She stopped and regarded Kiryk with surprise. The advisor offered her an arm, complimenting her dress with enough charm that her face settled into a look of bemusement. She slipped her arm through his, and the pair wove into the crowd.

"Come along, then, sweet lieutenant," Garridan said wryly. "Let us do as the man said."

Darson laughed, and they stayed nearby to keep an eye on him. They walked toward the long bar to the left of the dance floor past faerie couples sitting together on small couches who stared, their eyes dark with curiosity, as the men passed.

The male faerie preparing drinks watched them approach. He leaned against the wide, smooth wooden surface. His hair, swept back from his face, was so black it shone with blue highlights, and a few strands fell into his obsidian eyes.

"Gentlemen. What would you like to drink?"

Garridan and Darson looked at one another. Although they drank wine at dinner and in the meetings, it did not feel right to drink here, with so many unknown faeries interacting with the king and advisors. "Water is fine, thank you," Garridan said.

"Surely you did not come here for water? Ale is the drink of choice in your corner of the world, is it not?"

"It is," Darson said. He hesitated and added, "However, we would do ourselves a disservice by sticking with what is comfortable. Perhaps we should try one of your specialties." He gave Garridan a look indicating there was no harm in accepting a drink. Play along, he urged his captain silently.

"I like to hear that."

Darson watched the barkeep mix their drinks and, as if he knew of their reservations, explained everything he put in their glasses: lime, coconut milk, basil, and liquor made from fermented rice. Something in the faerie's sure, quick movements made Darson think he was more than just a bartender. His eyes flicked between them and the crowd too often for him not to be military trained.

"Are we witnessing a typical royal celebration...?" Darson raised his eyebrows, fishing for the faerie's name.

The male grinned. "Talan. It has not even begun, my friend. As for whether the celebration is typical, Princess Dahlia orchestrated it, so no. Mind the food. One can never tell what Dahlia has done to prolong the enjoyment." Darson raised an eyebrow, and Talan added, "Were we in her country, this would go on for days. With no rules." He set two full glasses of the clear drink in front of them, infused with green leaves and garnished with lime slices. "Enjoy."

The pair moved away from the bar and toward the dance area. Darson frowned down at his drink and heard Garridan sigh.

"One beverage should be fine," the captain said.

The lieutenant smirked and sipped. He closed his eyes and savored the delectable flavors. Upon opening them, he spotted Kiryk dancing with the stunning brunette faerie, attempting to show her a few traditional dances from Aliquis. He could think of one particular faerie he would love to dance with, but it was a silly, boyish wish.

His eyes shifted to the staircase as he raised the glass to his lips again.

He froze, staring at the two figures descending the steps, one of which he was sure should exist only in a dream. A flush of heat spread up from his neck. He let out a long, slow breath. "Have I told you lately how jealous I am that you are in her company every day?"

"Who?" Garridan followed his gaze to the staircase. He sucked in a breath. "Oh."

Princess Liana and Commander Nevada walked down the stairs. They were the sun and moon embodied, the left a golden sunrise wrapped in deep ruby red, and the right a midnight sky with the deep purple of twilight for eyes. The princess spoke with fluttering hands, the midriff-exposing outfit far more risqué than anything Garridan had seen her in previously.

Nevada's hair was loose; dark waves around her bare shoulders. The black corset and skirt bared just enough skin to make Garridan feel uncomfortably warm for even looking too long. He was not at all accustomed to such attire.

The captain closed his eyes and focused on his breathing. He opened them as Nevada reached the foot of the stairs. When it looked as if her attention would stray in his direction, Garridan's forced his gaze away almost guiltily.

Neither man spoke as the faeries walked to the bar. They glanced at each other.

Darson tapped his glass. "I will definitely need another

one of these."

* * *

"Liana, your pet is here," Nevada said, tilting her head to the left as they reached the lower level.

The princess did not bother correcting her. She made an appreciative noise at the sight of the two mortals. "Quite a fetching pair. Should we say hello?"

"Later." Nevada looped her arm through Liana's and tugged her toward the bar. "Let us see what delicious brews they are serving first."

She was taken aback once she realized who was tending the bar. She tilted her head as she watched the gorgeous faerie's face light up in a smile as a patron approached.

What an unexpected surprise.

Now, what need did Aaclyde have of Talan's particular skill set? It certainly did not include his ability to mix a drink.

Shoulders back, she threaded her fingers through her hair and sauntered toward the bar with Liana in tow.

"The mortal advisor, Kiryk, seems to be having the time of his life among our people," Nevada overheard Talan tell his patron as she approached. "Watching him is akin to watching a stage comedy."

"And you with front row seats," Nevada said.

Talan smiled at her winsomely. "I would not miss this for the world. Commander, it has been ages." He leaned across the bar to kiss her on the corner of her mouth, and she reciprocated. "How are you?"

"Better since the last time we crossed paths. May I introduce Princess Liana? Liana, this is Talan."

Nevada appreciated Liana's swift recovery from recognizing Talan's name, her eyebrows merely raising once before her face smoothed into a friendly smile. Her smile widened with good humor when Talan took her hand and kissed it as he bowed slightly.

"A sincere pleasure to meet you, Princess."

"I feel the same," Liana said drolly. "You look quite comfortable in this position."

"Yes," Nevada said brightly. "You do. Is this what we are tonight?"

Talan only grinned and offered to make them drinks. Nevada wanted to know more, but she lost the opportunity when a certain redheaded royal approached to place an order.

"Princess," Nevada greeted coolly. "How is your evening?"

Anann acknowledged her with a curt nod, her pale green eyes remote. "Commander," she said with a faint chill. "Over soon, hopefully."

Blunt, as always. "I wanted to ask if you have heard from Arrian."

"No. Nothing. In fact, I had planned to write another letter in the morning. I can … let you know when I do hear something," she offered. Her tone made her displeasure apparent.

"I would like that."

"It worries me," Anann confessed after a brief hesitation. "He promised frequent communication to keep me updated. I have not heard a word."

"He may have become sidetracked and decided to provide a full report when he came back," Nevada suggested, hoping to ease her worries along with Anann's. "He knows how busy we all are with this conference. If there has not been anything of note, he might not have bothered."

Anann flashed Nevada a small, grateful smile, which the commander half-heartedly returned. The cheerful façade faded when the princess bade her good-night and left with her drink.

Talan leaned toward Nevada and said, "She did not even tip me."

"You do not deserve it," Nevada said playfully.

The commander jumped when Liana's arm wrapped around her tense shoulders. Liana leaned in. "Set down your worries, my love. Talan has made us something delicious."

* * *

Tiberius and Mourin retired with the king, the advisor complaining of an upset stomach from the rich dinner fare. Queen Emilia left shortly after, and as the hour crept toward midnight, Darson and Garridan noticed a subtle change in the atmosphere.

The flickering lights hanging in the air dimmed. While some faeries took their leave, many others came in. Clothing became scarcer, mere wisps of silk and satin draping agile bodies. Low, sensual voices and laughter filled the air. The men remained apart from it, keeping an eye on Kiryk, who showed no signs of retiring for the night.

Princess Dahlia's arrival caused the largest transition in the mood of the room. She sauntered down the steps in a scrap of a dress that made what she'd worn at the first meeting seem modest. Her dark eyes gleamed as she looked out over the crowd.

Commander Dacian and Princess Sunara accompanied her, the royal looking more dazzling than ever clad in a black dress. Dacian slung an arm across her shoulders, his gesture speaking of familiarity as he leaned in to speak to the composed, bright-eyed princess.

Enthusiastic greetings met the trio, and the dancers pulled them into the growing crowd. The music grew louder as the drums beat a slow, rhythmic tune for the tambourines and violins and urged dancers closer together. Faeries with bells jangling on ankles and wrists danced, arms raised above heads as they spun lazily, their skirts twirling and shoes tapping. Couples of the opposite gender and the same gender pulled each other close, caressing each other intimately as the music moved them like sensual marionettes on a string. They left sprigs of flowers at the feet of the statue in the center of the room.

Garridan had never seen anything like it. Never before had he witnessed seduction lacing the air so thoroughly and brazenly. A part of him wanted to join the dancers, and the desire only increased when he caught a glimpse of Nevada's raven hair and violet eyes. He kept his distance as the celebration escalated, but he was always mindful of Kiryk. The advisor's distinct, robust laughter hit the air more and more frequently.

Garridan knew he should leave soon to sleep and let Darson finish the watch on Kiryk. He had to relieve Mourin in a few hours, but he could not seem to bring himself to take a step toward the staircase.

He found himself looking for her in the crowd.

* * *

Darson leaned on the banister from the upper level, watching Kiryk's movements. He scanned the large room for the twentieth time that hour and stared hard at each flash of dark golden hair. When he did spot her, his stomach muscles clenched, and not wanting to understand his own reaction, he looked away, only to be drawn back.

Finally, his brown eyes found her golden ones, but Princess Liana was looking elsewhere as she laughed with Commander Nevada. The deep scoop of the red top's back exposed delicate shoulder blades. He tried to picture her with wings.

"Lovely," he murmured absently to himself.

"Who is?" Garridan had come up behind him, eating something; he'd apparently raided the refreshment table.

"No one."

A faerie holding a tray of glasses containing a dark, berry-colored drink passed, and Darson took two from her and then handed one to Garridan.

"Kiryk has danced with almost a dozen faeries in the past two hours," Garridan commented.

"Nine. I've been counting."

Not long after, the advisor in question ascended the steps with a female faerie on either arm, chatting cheerfully with them as he attempted to negotiate the steps.

"I think he intends to leave with them," Garridan murmured. He headed the group off and began trying to reason with Kiryk, using words like *inebriated*, *bed*, and *alone*, to which Kiryk did not react well.

Darson moved to help Garridan and used the promise of food to keep Kiryk from leaving the party with unknown faeries. He listened to Kiryk's drunken prattle for a while, shooting Garridan dirty looks when the captain smirked at him. After fifteen minutes of hearing about Kiryk's adolescent days and the dalliances both he *and* his wife had indulged in, "so I can pursue one of those lovely faeries with a clean conscience," Darson had had enough. He left Garridan to deal with Kiryk; it was time to fill his own empty stomach.

He helped himself to the feast laid out on tiered silver platters, selecting all manners of small, bite-sized cakes that oozed chocolate, mango, and lemon creams and were sprinkled with cinnamon, sesame seeds, or drizzled with honey.

A slim figure glided up next to him, and he only vaguely noted the arm reaching over to pluck an egg tart from a platter as he licked honey off the pad of his thumb.

"These are my favorite; forgive my reach."

The smooth, warm voice bolstered Darson like a wind into a sail. He turned, eyes wide, to stare at Princess Liana.

Eyes the color of the honey he'd just licked off his thumb smiled at him as she bit into the small tart.

He covered his mouth as he swallowed before attempting to speak. He felt that ridiculous flush creep up his neck again. "I will not fight you for them. The little treats with the coffee beans, I might."

"I gathered as much. What was that, eight in fewer than two minutes? Not that I watched."

Darson smiled self-deprecatingly. "Somehow I doubt I could replicate it back home, so I am getting my fill now."

Liana eyed the cakes. "I would give you permission to hoard and take some home, but I do not believe they travel well."

"I will remember you said that when they catch me trying to leave with stolen desserts. Do not put it past me to use your name if I find something that would last the trip." Her infectious laughter made him smile.

A faint blush spread across his cheeks when she leaned against him in her merriment, and a feeling he could only describe as giddiness swept through him. He felt sixteen again. *Calm down. She is unavailable. Because she is a* faerie princess.

He thanked her again for her assistance with Mourin; she asked after the soldier's well-being, and sympathized with his poor acclimation to the fae. Before long, they were sampling more food, the princess identifying ingredients. After eating their fill, Liana wrapped a warm hand around Darson's bicep. "Do you dance, lieutenant?"

His grin was honest and quick. "If I did not before, I do now."

* * *

Nevada wove her way through the crowd with more grace than she thought she would have at this stage in the evening, and headed for the bar.

Talan eyed her as she slid into a seat. She propped her elbows on the wood and gave him an easy smile.

"I know that smile. What can I do for you, Commander?"

"Never fear, I have not come for anything but water."

"I had no intention of serving you more than that, for what it is worth." He filled a glass with water and gave it to her. She drank greedily. "I do not need a top military official tumbling to the floor. Besides, you never know what could happen—we need you on your toes."

"Is that a legitimate worry, soldier?"

Nevada reeled back in her chair at the sound of Princess Aaclyde's smooth, even voice. Nevada made a quick grab for the bar's edge, teetering precariously as she croaked out a greeting.

Talan looked away to compose himself. Aaclyde raised her eyebrows at both of them.

"No, it is not, Your Highness," he responded. "They are harmless. Absolutely boring. Mourin left with the king and Tiberius, who is ill from dinner; Kiryk is still making himself at home. I do not expect trouble from him, but I sent one of my own to preoccupy him regardless. If he leaves here with anyone, they will report back to me. I served the lieutenant and captain an hour ago."

Princess Aaclyde looked over her shoulder at the crowd, a thoughtful expression on her face as she leaned against the bar. In contrast, Nevada sat ramrod straight a mere foot away. Her cobalt wings, folded against her back, made the high collared moss green dress she wore appear plain. "Anything from those two?"

Talan shook his head. "My informants told me that Garridan is taking the next watch over the king. Darson is amusing Princess Liana. You look lovely, Your Highness."

Aaclyde looked askance at him and did not bother to acknowledge the compliment. She glanced instead at Nevada, silently judging her response to his observation of Princess Liana.

The raven-haired faerie shrugged, quailing under the scrutiny of the most venerated royal below only the queen herself. "Liana will be fine. Darson appears enamored."

"I see," Aaclyde murmured, almost to herself. In a rare moment of candor, the princess sighed, ran her hand through her short pearl grey hair, and closed her eyes. "I will be glad to see them gone."

Nevada bit her lip and stared at her hands as the cheer of intoxication was slowly robbed from her. "Even if they leave, and an agreement is made, we will not be done with them. Eyad will make sure of it. He wants this alliance so much, it is sickening."

Aaclyde's next words made Nevada and Talan glance at one another. "We shall see about that."

They watched her leave. When she disappeared into the crowd, Nevada groaned and rested her head on her arms. "She makes me feel one hundred again."

"She has that effect on everyone. You look tired, Nev."

"I am ready to retire," she admitted, as desire for sleep overtook her. "It was good to see you, although unexpected."

"Your presence is always a pleasure."

As Nevada turned on the bar stool to stand, Talan had to steady her when she wobbled on the seat.

"Are you certain you will not wind up in someone else's room?" he teased.

"You could always come with me to be sure," Nevada said, brightening at the sudden thought.

Talan laughed appreciatively. "I am tending the bar, Commander."

She rolled her eyes. "Quit taking your job so seriously. You are not a real bartender."

He clutched a hand to his chest in mock hurt and adopted a wounded expression. "Such an accusation! I am a real bartender. It is just not my main job. But..." Talan bent forward, closer to her ear, "under different circumstances, I would accept your invitation."

She was disappointed for a moment, and then shrugged. "Understood. Enjoy the rest of your shift." Then, as an after thought, nodded her head in the direction of the marble statue older than her and added sarcastically, "Don't forget to thank Vignon for a party well thrown. Although this is tame for his standards."

Nevada abandoned the bar stool, and after a few steps, chanced a look behind her at a pensive Talan.

He raised his hand. "Wait. Give me a minute."

Nevada smiled.

* * *

She was at the bar, chatting with Talan. The fact that she was perched unsteadily on her barstool did not escape Garridan's attention, nor did the way her movements remained graceful despite her obvious intoxication. He thought now might be a good time to speak to her. Perhaps he could even offer to walk her back to her quarters, as Darson had a few minutes ago with Princess Liana, he told himself.

Her dark hair tumbled down past bare shoulder blades, legs impossibly long under the even shorter black skirt. Her shoes sat on the floor, and bare feet moved lazily to the beat of the drums.

Garridan walked forward, heart drumming. The bartender leaned over to say something in her ear. She stood and backed away from the stool.

Here is your moment.

And suddenly Talan was leaving his side of the bar, clapping a hand on the shoulder of another faerie taking his place.

269

Deflated, Garridan watched the pair walk up the stairs, Nevada leaning heavily against the taller, muscled faerie as he spoke to her.

Damn.

He sighed, and decided it was time Kiryk went to bed so he could, too.

* * *

Candles flickered along the wall of the darkened hallway, illuminating some sections while throwing others into deep shadow. The couple wandering down the hall kept their voices hushed, mindful that many had already retired for the night. Occasional laughter echoed softly.

"*That* is what brownies are?" Darson asked. "Little old people?"

"They would not look old as *you* know old age to look." Liana strolled next to him, dangling her shoes from one hand by the straps. "They look like an extension of their environment. The brownies in countries like Miranda, it is as if they sprouted from a tree. The ones in my country are like the lizards that blend into the sand. I hardly see them. I *hear* them, to be sure, but they are skittish. They like to do their work and be left alone. The only reward they ask for is sustenance."

Darson shook his head, still trying to wrap his mind around the concept of the invisible creatures. "If I had not seen their work for myself, I would say you were all lying to make us feel like idiots. 'Let us see if we can make the humans believe we have invisible housekeepers that look like trees.'"

Liana stifled her laughter. "When I was a child, and I traveled through the mortal kingdoms, it always baffled me when I would wake up and everything would be as it had been the night before. We are truly spoiled."

"Where have you traveled?"

She listed every human kingdom, and others Darson had only seen referenced in history books. He once again marveled at her youthful appearance and the idea that her true age spanned centuries. She spoke with an animation and candor he did not expect from a princess, and she spoke freely in his presence. She asked him about Laurus and how the city coped with the rise in the number of Erepos and commended their ingenious methods for sustaining water and food supplies.

After answering, he watched her for a moment, and then decided to chance another subject. "May I ask you a serious question?"

"The question about the brownies seemed to be serious business."

Darson smiled faintly. "No, it is about certain ... talents I have noticed that faeries possess."

She inclined her head.

"I have heard that faeries can project things. Images, into other people's minds. To make them see things that are not there."

Liana gave him a long, assessing look. "We can create simple illusions that trick the brain into accepting a falsity for a period of time."

"Nothing prolonged? Do you ..." he began and then paused, carefully choosing his words so he would not offend her. He didn't want this evening to end, and he certainly didn't want it to end with this fragile connection between them severed. "Is it sometimes used to scare people?"

Where on Hylla did he gain that notion? Liana wondered. Was he confusing her people with Eyad's? What he described sounded far worse than anything they could do. She shook her head slowly. "Never to frighten in the way you're describing. That *is* a terrible abuse, and we are careful of it. It is meant for mischief, and as a means of escape in a tight spot to distract the eye of an enemy. Here, let me show you."

Liana saw him tense, and worry sparked in her heart. It reminded her of Mourin and his obviously frail psyche. Were Darson's questions and that incident linked?

She chose a basic illusion, focusing on the hall in front of them. She constructed an image in her mind and then pushed it out, flexing a muscle in her mind she rarely used. She knew the image would be a poor one—fine detail took serious concentration, which is why it was now something of an art form, and she did not wish to tax herself on a demonstration. A simple picture would have to do.

Darson's eyes widened when a large brown rat shot out from behind a tall vase and scurried toward his feet before vanishing. Liana exhaled in a rush; she was sorely out of practice. It was passable, but not her best.

"It can be handy, but it is not something we use frequently," she explained. "It is not a weapon. Did Eyad tell you about this?"

"No," Darson answered. "My source—"

"Mourin?" she guessed.

"I believe he may have come across a faerie capable of vivid illusions when we entered Hesperia," he said slowly.

Liana looked skeptical. "Then you would have noticed

that same faerie utterly taxed after playing such a trick. It is exhausting to conjure something vivid for a long period of time; he or she would have shown the strain. Perhaps the stress of the capture amplified what he thought he saw?"

"Perhaps," Darson allowed. He didn't recall seeing the faerie tired after playing with Mourin, and his confusion grew. What had happened in Hesperia?

The soft click of a door opening broke his train of thought. For a disorienting moment, as the heavy wooden door down the hall swung open, Darson thought Liana was giving him another demonstration.

The door opening appeared to puzzle her. When the perpetrator exited the room, though, Liana's features lit with sly humor.

Darson was surprised to see Talan come into the hall and shut the door behind him, raking a hand through somewhat mussed hair. He strolled in their direction and smiled widely when he spotted them.

He glanced at Darson, and then gave a little bow to the princess and exchanged a knowing, amused look with her.

"Have a satisfying evening, Your Highness," he said.

"Continue to have one of your own, Talan," Liana replied dryly.

He flashed Darson a grin as he meandered past, humming as he disappeared around the corner.

"I am now doubly convinced he is not just a bartender."

"Talan has a number of talents."

As the hall settled back into stillness, Darson picked up the trails of his previous thoughts; he had a dozen other questions for Liana. To his dismay, though, she stopped in front of a door.

"I thought I would be the one to pepper you with questions, and here it is the other way around," Liana said. "It has been so long since I traveled in your realm; I have so much to ask."

"I would tell you anything," Darson said automatically, surprised to realize he meant it.

She smiled. "We have a few more days together yet. I may request your presence on the morrow. Thank you for escorting me back."

He bowed, wearing a grin not unlike Talan's. "It was my pleasure, Your Highness. Thank you for the tour of the gardens earlier, and the exquisite company."

Liana stretched on her tiptoes and kissed the corner of his mouth.

Darson's brain marveled at his body's willingness to give in to what he was about to do. He had no idea what made him do it, but they were alone, and she was the most gorgeous creature he'd ever seen, with a laugh like silver bells.

While she was still close, he slid a hand up the satiny smooth skin of her jaw, tilting her head up. They kissed in the quiet of the hall, ignoring the minutes ticking by. It was as lovely and sweet as the night had been.

Liana could not deny how long it had been since someone affected her the way this mortal did. What a marvel it was, and how unexpected. She loathed seeing that bright, young mind and able body go.

Another kiss was in order. As she nuzzled her nose against his, making him smile, a chill in the air passed over her skin. Accompanying it was a certainty that they were no longer alone in the hall. Although she saw no one, she still felt oddly exposed.

In her hesitation, Darson skimmed his hand over her hair.

"Shall I bid you good night, Your Highness?"

She scanned the hall on either side of them and found nothing. He picked up on it, tensed, and did the same. He said her name questioningly, with an edge of apprehension. Liana could not express what triggered her body's reaction, but she did not want to overreact—nor did she want him walking anywhere alone until it passed.

"It is nothing," Liana said. "But perhaps you should come in. I could answer a few of your questions now, before you return to your quarters."

His warm brown eyes lit with delight. She opened the door and motioned him in. Liana took one last look up and down the dimly lit hall. An old dread reared its head in her heart, shaking off the dust of centuries. Threatening to turn every dark corner and shut door into a foe.

No. It was preposterous. Aaclyde's palace was safe; she need not fear for herself or for Darson. There was no room in her life for that sort of fear; not anymore. She refused to fall back on old habits from more dangerous times.

Liana locked the suite door.

Chapter 20

Nevada felt a stirring in her mind, a seed growing and unfurling slowly into a flower. A soft surface supported her; her head lay on a luxuriously thick, warm pillow. She tried to coax sleep back, keeping still and hoping to return to a dreamlike state.

She stretched her legs, sighing as the lingering dream spoke her name.

"*Nevada*. Wake up."

No. Not a dream. Nevada's brow furrowed. She opened her bleary eyes.

As soon as she registered the silhouette of a person in the dark, her hand slid under her pillow, grasping for cool metal as coldness touched her heart.

"Talan?" she tested.

There was a long, disapproving silence. "It is Anann," came the clipped response.

Anann? Nevada relaxed her arm, pulled her hand out, and dragged it through her sweaty mess of black curls. Not who she wanted entering her room in the middle of the night. She did not even know how long she had slept. What hour was it? "What are you doing in my quarters?"

"I require your assistance."

Nevada noted the trace of drying tears on the princess's cheeks, the hastily pulled-back pale red and blonde hair, her nervous, tightly clenched hands, and her attire. She was dressed for riding, wearing a long tunic over thin leggings tucked into boots.

"Whatever for?" Nevada asked, puzzled. The remnants of sleep added to her confusion.

"I need to return to Hesperia. Now. I need you to take me."

Now? Why? Keeping her eyes open proved as difficult as lifting two boulders with her bare hands. Somewhere in the foggy exhaustion and alcohol clouding, Nevada's brain knew the answer to that, and it filled her with a distant worry. "Why?"

Anann's eyes flashed, alight with barely controlled panic, worry, and blind determination. "There was an attack on a village by the western border. Arrian was injured. Bad enough to take him off the field. It was a *Mauvah*."

Oh God. *Arrian.* Nevada rose on her elbow and pressed the heel of her hand to her forehead as the horror of that realization pummeled into her. They did it; those bastard creatures actually crossed over the border, and *of course* Arrian had met one head on. Images of shattered, mutilated limbs swamped her, and she shook her head to clear them. "How is he? Are there casualties? Is—"

"I do not know," Anann said fervently. "I hardly know anything; I just know he is hurt. I need to check on Arrian, and I need an escort. I have been told the ambush is contained, but I cannot be sure unless I see for myself. She said it is, but—"

Nevada sat up slowly and went over Anann's stilted speech carefully, gleaning as much information from it as possible.

"Who is *she*?"

"The queen."

"Where is Arrian? Did the messenger say?"

"He has been moved to my palace. Nevada, I need to leave *now*. We could be there before nightfall. I have a terrible feeling about this."

Nevada swung her legs to the floor and scrubbed at her face. "Is the messenger still here?"

"No, I think it was by bird. The message was given to Emilia."

"You do not have the message?"

"No, I do not," Anann exploded. "It hardly matters—I am relaying it to you as I heard it, and I require your escort."

"I doubt the queen meant for you to leave in the dead of night," Nevada mumbled against her palms. Slivers of rational, coherent thought started to take hold. "Aaclyde has soldiers who would take you."

"They do nothing without her or their superior's consent," Anann snapped. "I would not be able to leave until morning. You are close to him, and I *thought* you would understand the urgency." The princess added bitterly.

I cannot do this with you now. "The conference—"

"Can go to hell, for all I care," the princess said. "The plight of the humans means nothing. I care about the well-being of my people and my commander. I need to go to him."

Nevada apparently did not answer quickly enough, because Anann continued. "And you should care, too. He dropped everything for you; now it's your turn to do so for him."

Her words made Nevada feel like she had been plunged into an icy lake. Nevada's first impulse was to snarl at the princess for such an underhanded comment.

Instead of giving in, Nevada attempted to regain her composure. Anann was manipulating in the only way she knew how; as a princess, she needed an escort, and she preferred a subordinate she could order about. Nevada only answered to two individuals in the kingdom; she did not face the complicated chain of command of Aaclyde's military. Nevada answered to Rees, whom she would not wake up in the dead of night to drag into this; but a princess of a different country could also demand temporary fealty in regards to personal safety. Hesperia's princess counted on Nevada remembering that detail.

Yes, a large part of Nevada wanted to ensure Arrian's well-being with her own eyes. Anann was using that against her, too.

"I will escort you," Nevada said evenly. "But I am not doing it for you. I am doing it for Arrian. He would not want you to go alone."

Anann nodded curtly. "I will go ahead to the stables and ready the horses while you change. Five minutes."

"Your Highness," Nevada said, her jaw tightening around the title. She made sure Anann looked straight at her as she spoke. "We are checking on him and immediately returning. You are not using this as an excuse to avoid this entire meeting. I *will* bring you back here to finish the talks."

"Speak to no one on your way to the stables," the princess shot back. "You will not confer with Miranda's soldiers upon my orders."

Nevada's jaw clenched. She nodded sharply, and Anann left the room.

The commander heaved a sigh and dragged herself out

of bed. She dressed as quickly as her fuzzy mind allowed, shucking off her nightshirt and trying to find her clothes: boots, tunic dress, belt, sword, and a set of daggers. She only stumbled twice, and blamed the dark for that. Never mind that her head still swam now and again; she prayed the ride into Hesperia would clear her mind.

There was no conceivable way the queen had sanctioned Anann leaving at this hour. Why on Hylla did Emilia even tell her about Arrian, knowing that blasted princess never handled these situations well? Nevada thought irritably. When had Anann *ever* acted rationally during a crisis?

Arrian is all right, she thought as she left her room. It was ridiculous to think otherwise—he was made out of forged steel. He could recover from damn near anything.

She should not be worried.

* * *

Garridan's shift was not halfway over, and he was counting down the minutes. He paced to shake off the creeping edge of fatigue. He mentally went over the bills he owed and the items he needed to pick up from the market when he returned home. He always cleaned out his cupboards before assignments, and always regretted it the first night home, mourning the sparse pickings that awaited his return. Then he would end up eating at Idavida's with Darson until he replenished his stock. He was actually looking forward to that.

Company. Unit. Home. He had forgotten to pay his rent up to date before they left on this mission no one knew about. Well, it was not the first time that had happened, and sure as hell wouldn't be the last. Thankfully, his landlord was tolerant of Garridan's erratic schedule.

His thoughts turned back to Darson, and Garridan realized he had not seen the lieutenant since he brought Kiryk back to their quarters.

Could he still be with Princess Liana?

A door creaked. Garridan braced his hand on his sword. "Captain?"

He relaxed. "Mourin. What is it?"

The soldier stepped into the hall. "It grows late," he said quietly. "Darson hasn't returned yet. I can't help but worry."

"I was thinking the same," Garridan admitted. "I will look for him. Why don't you cover for me for the next little bit. I will have him back here within half an hour, I'm sure of it."

Mourin's smile was tinged with relief. "Be careful, Captain."

"Of course."

Attempting to remember the way to the ballroom was a challenge with his mind still sluggish from drink and lack of sleep. Standing in one position had helped, but moving around now disoriented him enough that finding his way took extra concentration. His brain could not quite keep up with his movements.

It helped that the hallways weren't completely dark. Flames danced in sconces of twisted metal, bathing the walls in a golden light that made him think of cozy hearths and warm cots.

He came to himself in front of a break in the wall, where he could see a garden beyond the glass.

Garridan could not remember how he got there. Or how to get back.

"Focus," he breathed, pinching the bridge of his nose as he squeezed his eyes shut. As busy as the palace was during the day, he had not seen a soul as he walked. Now, he stood in an unfamiliar hall with lavender and green whorled wallpaper.

He contemplated cutting through the garden, thinking perhaps the ballroom was on the other side. Tall fronds framed the glass door, and small candles sat along the edges of the path creating pinpoints of light, like stationary fireflies. Far above, Naula lent some extra light; the rains had stopped.

The captain turned, changing his mind. Maybe he could hunt down a servant to point him in the right direction, or just put the request out to have the lieutenant retrieved.

His thoughts dispersed as he collided with another figure.

Garridan grunted in surprise, and then tried to catch the stumbling person, which he discovered was a female. "I am so sorry," he apologized. "I did not see you coming around the corner. Are you all right?"

He did not recognize her long, wavy dark hair at first, and the voice cursing in a foreign language did not sound familiar. He assumed it was cursing, at any rate. As pretty as it sounded, the way she spit the words out, it couldn't be anything good.

She abruptly switched to Vinculum with a grumble. "Might not have seen me, but you must have heard me."

Words died in Garridan's throat as he took a step back and released Nevada as if her skin were on fire.

Commander Nevada lost her balance and caught herself on the wall, and Garridan's hand reflexively shot out to catch her again. She looked up at him in sleepy agitation. "What are you doing here?"

"Searching for Lieutenant Darson." He looked at her more

attentively and noted her sword was at her hip, and she was dressed for riding. "Where are you going at this hour?" he asked, realizing the moment the words were spoken how inappropriate he was to question her. But it *was* late, and she could not possibly be out for the same reason he was.

Instead of answering his question, she turned around and continued on her original path.

Garridan set out after her, his search for Darson temporarily suspended. "Commander—"

"Nowhere," she called behind her, and waved her hand back in a clear signal for him to mind his business and leave her alone.

He would not be shaken so easily.

"You are going nowhere dressed like that?" he challenged.

Nevada whipped her head around to shoot him a look him what she thought of his question. "Nowhere that concerns you."

She lunged at an intersection as if turning the corner had been a last-minute decision.

His gut strongly suggested he pursue to find out more information. Her evasiveness did not sit well with him, and he began to believe something was truly wrong.

He continued to follow her, jogging down dimly lit halls, straining to match her swift pace. The occasional flutter of other movements caught his eye, and more than once he witnessed small faerie palace servants watching him from around corners and behind half-closed doors.

She nearly gave him the slip after a quick turn at an intersection that boasted four ivory statues of slender, winged faeries in each corner, when an unexpected voice came from his right.

"Garridan, what are you doing here?"

"Darson!"

The lieutenant appeared from the right corridor.

"Well, I started off looking for you," Garridan explained, "but now I am trying to follow Commander Nevada. I will explain later. You can go on back to the rooms—Mourin is waiting, and I will be along … at some point."

Instead of leaving, Darson followed him. *"Garridan."*

As they turned another corner and found Commander Nevada halfway down the hall, Garridan raised his voice and asked her again, "Where are you going?"

Nevada hissed, whirling and glaring daggers at him. Her gaze flicked to Darson angrily. "Leave!"

"No," Garridan said. "What is going on, Commander? Has there been an attack? Has something happened that my king needs to know about?"

"No. I am escorting Princess Anann to Hesperia," she answered in a huff. "There is a problem she needs to tend to, and she cannot go alone. Now that you know where I am going at this hour, you can return to your quarters. *Please.*"

"Only the two of you? How long is the ride to Hesperia?" he asked.

Her expression grew colder. "Yes, Captain. The ride is ten to twelve hours. We will return by the day after tomorrow."

She and the princess would ride alone for twelve hours? What if one of them became injured? Was there any guarantee help would be nearby?

It is not your place to do anything about it, Garridan told himself. Their ways were not his. Yet his heart strongly objected to walking away.

Could I pretend I did not witness her leaving? Am I obligated to report this to someone? Even if I did, would there be enough time to make a difference? What if I left them, and found out later that something happened during their journey? His thoughts collided with each other, moving faster as his anxiety about the situation increased. The only thing he knew for sure was that if the princess or commander was injured or worse, he could not live with himself.

If there was ever an opportunity to show solidarity, this was it.

"I believe a princess requires more than one escort," Garridan said carefully. "Since you do not appear interested in inviting another faerie as an escort, I will accompany the both of you."

"Excuse me?" Darson asked in disbelief.

"No. I did not *ask* for your assistance," Nevada ground out. "You are in the middle of a conference—"

"So are you," Garridan observed. "All the more reason to assist. Think of it as an act of good faith. I cannot, in good conscience, let you and a princess ride off into the night. As you and I have both learned, there is little safety to be had even deep within our own realms."

Nevada stood before a set of doors and stared at him for a long moment. She pulled one of the doors open and slipped out without another word. Garridan slapped a hand on the door's edge and hurried to follow her into the night air, gulping down the oppressive humidity as they approached the stables. Lights burned in the windows of the long, narrow building.

"Darson, go back to the suite," he said.

"I will *not*, Captain."

Garridan turned to see the growing agitation on Darson's face. He leaned in to the man while tugging him along, and in a lowered tone, explained what he was thinking. "I cannot let them ride off alone. I will see them there safely and be back by tomorrow, the day after at the latest."

"Why are you doing this?" Darson asked. "Why are you following her?"

"We can use this to our advantage, Dar. We've had nothing to offer them for all that we ask, and here is an opportunity to do some good."

"Truly?" Darson asked, disbelieving. "Can you honestly look at me and tell me that if it were any other faerie, you would have the same reaction? Have you even cleared this with the king?"

Garridan hesitated as he watched Nevada disappear into the stables. "No, I have not. Please let the king know of my whereabouts—"

"I will accompany you," Darson said, looking disgusted. When Garridan began to argue, Darson held up his hand and added, "I am doing this not just as your friend, but as your second-in-command. You know I'm going with you no matter what you say."

Garridan did not like the thought of potentially putting Darson in danger, but he did not have time to argue. He knew by the look in his closest friend's eyes that he would not back down.

The two men entered the stables. "You ready the horses," Garridan told Darson, "and I will leave a note for the king." Garridan approached a faerie attendant in the aisle to ask for quill and parchment.

"*Why* are they here?" Princess Anann's sharp voice cut through the moist air of the stable. Anger bloomed on her pale cheeks.

"They insist on accompanying us," Nevada answered. She approached the magnificent gray-blue stallion tethered near the princess's caramel-colored mare.

"No, they will not," Anann said. "They will slow us down."

"Is this not the purpose of the conference? To aid one another in times of need?" Garridan asked while he finished writing the note to his king.

Anann cut him off, her words sharper than shattered glass. "We are perfectly capable, and you do not know the territory. Stay put, and stay out of our way." The princess swiftly and expertly secured a saddle and leapt onto the mare with fluid grace. "Nevada, hurry."

Nevada cursed under her breath as Annan dug her heels into the mare, and the horse clattered out of the stable. The commander quickly secured her own horse's saddle, ignoring the men as they readied their own horses. "If you cannot keep up, then you need to stay behind," she said to them.

"Understood," Garridan replied.

"I am thrilled to return to Hesperia," Darson said sardonically as he secured his horse's harness.

Nevada ignored them as she mounted and took off after the princess.

"You owe me," Darson said lightly.

"You will be getting a marvelous birthday gift from me this autumn," Garridan promised. He hefted himself into the saddle atop his gelding.

Darson urged his horse forward, and they trotted out of the stable. "This adventure might be gift enough."

* * *

The men caught up with Nevada at a gated exit on the southwestern side of the palace grounds. The guards let them leave without question, nodding to the commander as the gates swung shut behind them.

The dark jungle soon swallowed the palace, obscuring it completely behind a wall of tall, spindly trees, underbrush, moss, and vines. Minutes down the path, they found the princess.

When she saw them, Anann fixed both men with a contemptuous look. Her silence was loud with dissension, but it was silence nonetheless.

The night around them offered no respite from the cacophony of sound soaking the jungle air. Monkeys howled and called to one another; larger animals rustled in the brush. The inky blackness of night gave the jungle a sinister, living quality, as if the foliage itself were alive and malevolent.

The commander and princess appeared unaffected by the noise or potential threat hidden in the trees, but Garridan could not relax. The terrain was difficult for Erepos, yes, but he could not ignore their surroundings.

Some time later, Garridan mustered the courage to speak. "What happened in Hesperia?"

Darson gave him an incredulous look, silently reproaching him for only just asking the question.

"Commander Arrian has been injured," Nevada called back. "In an ambush. I was told the situation is under control."

"Then why are we traveling now?" Darson wondered.

"You are more than welcome to find your way back to the palace alone," Anann continued, her voice still coiled tight. "Arrian is of vital importance to his country and his princess, therefore I am going to him."

Garridan watched Nevada's back straighten. Her elegant fingers tightened on the reins of her horse. "Princess Anann did not have permission to leave," she said coolly. "I have been commanded to aid her, and that is why I am here. And as I said before," her voice sharpened, "I do not support the decision to leave at this hour. However, I will do as I am ordered."

Garridan held his breath, watching the tension between commander and princess grow. He glanced at Darson, who also watched them with curiosity.

No one spoke again for a long while. The smothering darkness of the jungle proved distracting enough. Pale, misshapen tufts of fog sat atop still waters along shallow, wide creeks. As moisture saturated the air and dawn drew closer, the fog crept from the creek banks through the trees, further obscuring the dark forest floor. The horses' hooves disturbed the thin layers as they trotted along.

Darson broke the tense silence some time later. He did it quietly, for Garridan's ears. "Not how I envisioned this night ending."

"Me either," Garridan murmured. "I was out looking for *you* when we collided, you know. Were you with Princess Liana the entire time?"

"Most of it."

"What were the pair of you up to?"

The dark-haired man smiled slowly. "Nothing to concern yourself with, Captain."

* * *

Below the forest canopy, the darkness gradually lessened,

turning the air a dirty gray as morning approached. The color of the jungle changed from inky black to dark greens and purples.

The horses sloshed through narrow streams, leaving the path occasionally to pick their way past rotted, fallen trees decomposing into the earth. The four stopped at a slow-moving creek to fill their pouches and let the horses drink.

Continuing on, they saw no one and heard nothing but the din of shrieking birds and howls Garridan did not recognize. He felt an eventual incline in the path, a subtle shift in his center of gravity. Muscles bunched in the horses' shoulders and hindquarters as they climbed the path. Light broke through in wider beams, blue sky showing in uneven patches high above the swaying boughs of leaves. The jungle was thinning; it was still thick and busy by Garridan's standards, but less oppressive.

Garridan spotted a hut, and realizing what he was looking at, he pointed it out to Darson. The first faerie home they had seen was nestled in the trees with a thatched roof, secured on all sides by thick limbs, shielding leaves, and hanging vines. He couldn't see any movement.

"Garridan." Darson sounded peculiarly awed.

The captain looked ahead. They had reached a break in the rainforest. The path sloped sharply down and to the right.

Ahead lay sheer magnificence.

Hundreds of feet below rolled the gentle, rounded hills of a valley carpeted in green, groves of trees spread out like a wide, lush blanket. A narrow river, coming down from the hills ahead, snaked its way through the trees. Fog rolled lazily through the trees in the lower dips of the valley. Their path, after curving right, followed a ridge cupping the valley, trailing along toward the series of hills on the other side. Beyond it, drenched in light, laid the golden fields of Hesperia.

The beauty of it was so striking and wild that Garridan's heart ached, and he was stunned into awed silence. As he and Darson coaxed their horses down the path behind the faeries, it began to rain.

* * *

The downpour ceased an hour later. Moisture filled the jungle with an even stronger aroma of damp earth, fresh rain, and flowers. After a time, the path widened and became firmer and less muddy; clearly well traveled as it cut through the higher hills toward the neighboring country. A lukewarm breeze whistled across the path and chilled their wet skin, hair, and clothes.

It took another hour for the swells of grassy foothills to come into view along the path.

Darson shifted uncomfortably in his saddle as he watched the open country loom closer. To distract himself, he wrung excess water out from the tails of his shirt. He wore a pained expression.

"Dar?"

The soldier shook his head. "Cannot believe I'm back here again. Mourin would be horrified."

The mention of Mourin made Garridan flinch. Bits and pieces of last night's celebration began to return to his memory: leaving Mourin at the king's door while he searched for Darson, telling the soldier he would return in half an hour.

"The king will understand," Garridan murmured to himself. Although it was too late to change his mind, he could not help but doubt his choice. *I am doing the right thing. Good will come of this.*

"You better hope he will," Darson said.

Nevada turned to address the group. "Once we cross the foothills, we will give the horses another chance to drink, and we will check in with the border guards. Then it is straight across the plains to the palace."

They crested the first foothill, and Garridan got a look at the country before them. Darson didn't look impressed as he squinted in the sudden flood of sunlight.

Tall, lush grasses swayed in a strong breeze. Far in the distance, golden wheat fields met the bright blue of the horizon, absorbing the late morning sunlight and glowing with health. Oddly shaped trees with sparse vegetation dotted the land, providing little shelter from the hot sun. The air carried a clean, dry smell, free of the heavy, humid perfumes of Miranda. The beauty was simpler, less complicated. In the back of Garridan's mind, he did not understand how such vastly different terrain could nestle up against one another, but he would have plenty of time later to ponder that oddity along with the other pile of magical peculiarities he had witnessed so far.

Nevada led the quartet to a shallow creek winding through a narrow valley between softly rounded hills dressed with small purple flowers. They filled their water skins as the horses drank.

"We waste no more time," Princess Anann said, mounting her horse.

She led them into Hesperia.

Chapter 21

Liana did not know what to expect when she left her room. Emilia had ordered everyone to attend an emergency meeting for which she'd had them awakened in the wee morning hours. Liana was alarmed and thought thc worst, and crossing paths with Dacian on the way there had not helped. She hoped to learn more from Nevada, who had already left her room.

She did not expect to see the mortals in the conference room when she arrived. Yet there they were.

She halted in the doorway at the sight of them, as did Dacian. He had not expected them, either, if his muttered cursing was any indication.

If the matter involved the humans, then perhaps no assault had befallen the kingdom, and her paranoia had no foundation. Emilia would never sanction their attendance at a meeting discussing private devastation.

Neither Queen Emilia nor King Edric was in the room. She heard Aaclyde tell a servant to deliver Her Majesty and King Edric more refreshments. The two monarchs must be convening elsewhere, she mused.

Liana sought out Princess Rees, who stood close to Saffron's young princess. She did not see Nevada with her, or anywhere in the room. She scanned the faces of her fellow royals and found an assortment of mild confusion, unfocused concern, and irritation at the early hour.

A different story wrought itself on the faces of the mortals. Captain Garridan was not with them.

Yet Dacian and presumably Nevada were called down. Liana then noticed Mourin's presence, and her mind began to race. *Where is the captain? With the king and Emilia? If Mourin is here, then Darson should be here, too.* The thought of the lieutenant made her heart skip a beat, even as his absence troubled her.

She studied Mourin, who was the picture of misery. He held on to his composure by thin, fraying strings. Sweat dampened the strands of hair at his temples and forehead. His eyes appeared sunken from a lack of sleep, worry, and guilt.

Guilt.

Did Darson make it back to his room? Could the three absences be a coincidence? What is going on? The jumbled pieces of information did not fit into a clear picture in Liana's mind. Her head ached too badly to make sense of it. *Nevada should be here.*

Dacian stood next to her, scanning the room. When he glanced at her, the look in his eyes mirrored her thoughts.

"Anann is not here, either," he said.

At a loss, Liana stood while the princesses took their seats, listening to their nervous murmurs.

The sight of Eyad caught her attention. "I know someone who will give us answers," she said, nodding to the sorcerer as he mingled with the mortals.

"He will not tell us anything," Dacian said with disgust.

"What makes you sure he even has any information?"

"He knows something." As Eyad's gaze rested on her, Liana felt it with conviction. The sorcerer stood by an unhappy Tiberius, speaking to him in a low, intimate tone and wearing an expression designed to set the advisor at ease. *It is not as bad as you think*, that expression said; *this problem can be solved.* Liana had been on the receiving end of that pretty lie enough times to mistrust his intentions. Next to Tiberius, Kiryk looked grave and awake despite his drinking the night before.

Liana could tell by his expression that Eyad knew exactly what had transpired. "He will tell me," she said. She walked past Mourin and ignored the advisors as she fixed Eyad with a hard stare to let him know she required his presence immediately.

"Excuse me, gentlemen," Eyad said, and followed the faerie to the side of the room and away from listening ears.

"Why are we here?" she asked. "And don't tell me to wait until Emilia makes an official announcement." She lifted her chin and gave him the same firm stare she used on disruptive subjects and reticent sorcerers.

With a look of reluctance, Eyad said, "Anann received word last night of a small ambush on the Hesperian border. Commander Arrian was injured."

"Injured?" Liana echoed. "How badly?" She unconsciously clenched the useless pendant around her neck. She could not remember the last time Arrian sustained a notable injury.

"He will recover," Eyad assured her.

"From what? I should like more information than that," Liana said, keeping her voice low. "A *small* ambush?"

"So the message says. Liana, dear, do not worry; he will be

fine. He is a hardy fellow."

His words stoked the fire instead of soothed. "What struck him down?"

"I do not have specifics, but I am sure we will receive more information as the day continues. Princess Anann, however, would not wait to go to him. She left for Hesperia and took Nevada with her as an escort."

"Why Nev?" Liana whispered, torn between fury at Anann's impulsiveness and a grudging understanding. "How do you know this?"

"Because Captain Garridan and Lieutenant Darson went with them," Eyad sighed. "The captain wrote a note that reached the king early this morning."

Liana barely had time to process that revelation before Queen Emilia and King Edric stepped into the room, prompting the start of the meeting. Frustrated, Liana left Eyad and sat with Dacian, taking odd comfort in the commander's presence. He looked intensely at her face, as if her expression would reveal the entire story to him.

She murmured what she learned and watched the commander's face darken with disbelief.

"Injured how?" Dacian mouthed as the room fell quiet for the queen. Liana could only shrug, which angered him further, and he shot a glare in Eyad's direction.

"Thank you all for gathering so quickly," Eyad addressed the room, remaining on his feet along with Queen Emilia and King Edric. "We have had some developments during the night that would be best cleared up with everyone present, putting us all on the same page until further information is acquired. Your Majesty?"

"It appears as if my dear Anann has let anxiety and impatience dictate her actions," Queen Emilia stated calmly. "Last night, I made Princess Anann aware that her commander sustained an injury during a small battle in Hesperia."

Murmurs of concern echoed around the table. "He is all right," the queen soothed.

"Along the border, Your Majesty?" Princess Tatyana asked. "Does Hesperia need assistance?"

"Near a border town, yes," the queen answered. "We have not heard of any fatalities."

"Should the need arise, I am prepared to send soldiers for support," Aaclyde said.

"As the matter stands, that will not be necessary," Emilia countered. "The message I received indicated the situation is under control."

Liana frowned as she observed the strain between the queen and the princess dearest to Emilia's heart. Aaclyde did not appear pleased with the answer. *It would be easy for Miranda to send help, and Aaclyde offered. Is Emilia softening the matter due to the mortals' presence?* She glanced at the humans, and found them struggling to remain silent.

"Our Anann is exceptionally fond of Commander Arrian and took the news badly," Emilia continued. "I never intended for her to leave Miranda, nor did I give her permission to, as the matter was not one that would require her to leave. She decided to, regardless, and asked Commander Nevada to escort her."

Princess Rees wilted in her seat. Liana heard noises of irritation rise from her peers in response to Anann's rash decision.

"We are here this early because Anann left in the middle of the night?" Dahlia asked incredulously.

"Not merely the two. Captain Garridan and Lieutenant Darson accompanied them," Aaclyde continued.

Dacian and Liana looked at one another as the room broke into confused conversation.

"Why?" Dacian asked the question simultaneously with his princess, although he directed it at Liana instead of the room.

"Yes. How in God's name did our men end up with them?" Tiberius asked angrily.

"Captain Garridan went looking for Lieutenant Darson when he did not return after the celebration," Eyad explained, looking to Mourin for confirmation. The soldier nodded.

"Where was Lieutenant Darson?" Kiryk asked.

Liana's eyebrows rose. Dacian gave her a pointed look. She straightened her shoulders and said to the room, "I was with Lieutenant Darson until around three this morning."

Everyone's attention turned to her. Out of the corner of her eye, she saw Princess Dahlia lift her glass in Liana's direction, though she chose to ignore the cheeky gesture. She kept her attention on King Edric, who gazed back with a chillier expression than she had ever witnessed. "I left the party at one-thirty, and he saw me to my door after I gave him a tour of the gardens."

"And you do not know where he went after?" Edric asked.

"I assumed back to his room," she said smoothly. "I have not seen him since."

"Why would our lieutenant and captain *voluntarily* accompany your princess and commander in the first place?" Tiberius asked, unable to keep the question from sounding reproachful.

"What are you implying?" Dacian asked, amusement

coloring his voice.

"They are protected within these borders," Eyad said, looking earnestly at King Edric and the advisors.

"We do not know why your soldiers accompanied the princess and commander," Princess Aaclyde said evenly, answering Tiberius's question. "But we can assure you that their safety is a priority, as is yours. The king expressed concern over the validity of Captain Garridan's note, and I have called the soldier who delivered the message to me this morning in an effort to dispel any confusion."

As if summoned by her words, the main doors opened. Liana watched in surprise as Talan entered. He was dressed casually, hair raked back yet still appealingly rumpled from sleep. He bowed to the monarchs, his face impassive as he looked at Aaclyde.

"The lad tending bar last night?" Kiryk murmured.

"Talan is one of the most trusted members of my military," Aaclyde answered with authority as she turned to Talan. "Who delivered the note to you?"

"The stable worker who retrieved Captain Garridan's and Lieutenant Darson's horses," he answered. "I checked with the royal guards at the nearby entrance, and they confirmed that Princess Anann, Commander Nevada, and the two mortals left by the southwestern gate three hours before dawn."

Liana wondered if Captain Garridan and Darson decided to join on their own—really, it was the only way it made sense. Nev would *never* ask them to come along, and neither would Anann.

"Why on Hylla would the men end up accompanying them?" Liana wondered out loud.

"What is wrong with Anann?" Dacian muttered. "I would bet a month's wages she said something ridiculous and stupid to convince Nev to take her."

"She always says something ridiculous and stupid," Liana replied. "I just *cannot* figure how both agreed to the humans going with them."

When Emilia reassured Edric again of his men's safety within fae borders, doubt tugged at Liana. Everything she heard indicated the Hesperian attack was small, contained. Arrian was recovering, and Anann overreacting. And yet, something did not feel right.

"Is it not possible to retrieve them?" Tiberius's voice disrupted her thoughts. "Could Miranda's soldiers stop them at the border?"

"I have patrols on the lookout," Aaclyde said. "There is no guarantee they will be found before they pass into Hesperia. The forest is not kind to trackers."

"When will they return?" Kiryk asked.

"The note your lieutenant left indicated a few days," Aaclyde said.

"In the meantime, gentlemen," Emilia said, "please do not fret. We will continue to discuss what we can. All will be well."

The mortals did not look satisfied, and Liana found herself agreeing with them. She stared at Eyad once more. It disturbed her that he would not meet her gaze.

* * *

Darson did not know what to expect when the princess said something about reporting in as they entered Hesperia. He recognized the small, hut-like station ahead as they left the foothills for the flat plains. The small, thatch-roofed building that looked identical to the one he'd seen a few weeks earlier appeared deserted. As they neared the hut, the door opened, and a single guard stepped out.

He didn't know how loose the security was between inter-country borders and if it differed from the kingdom's border security. Because they were close to a mountain pass, though, he thought finding only a single guard was peculiar.

The soldier lifted a hand in greeting as the four horses halted in front of him. A brisk breeze swept his fine, blond hair back from a square-jawed, handsome face. Darson likened him to Arrian and instantly wanted to dislike him.

The guard flashed a cheerful smile and squinted up at them, arms folded across his chest. "Good morning, Princess. I was not expecting to see you come through here."

"I am accompanied by two mortals along with Commander Nevada," Anann said shortly.

The guard looked Darson and Garridan, tilting his head like a curious cat. "That is most unusual. Where do you hail from, gentlemen?"

"Aliquis," they replied in unison.

The soldier brightened even more. He was more relaxed than other faeries Darson had encountered, and he wondered why he and Mourin hadn't run into *him* when they'd first crossed into Hesperia. He did not sound like other faeries, either. His voice was raspier, less smooth. He sounded more common.

"I've been there," the guard was saying. "Eons ago. Who is king now?"

Garridan exchanged a look with Darson, and then glanced

at Anann, who practically vibrated with anxiety. "Edric is king. I am Captain Garridan, and this is Lieutenant Darson. Do you need any other information from us, sir?"

"Aren't you going to document this?" Nevada asked, giving the soldier an inquisitive look.

"Oh!" The guard chuckled to himself and then held up a hand to indicate they should wait a moment. He jogged back to the hut.

Anann cursed in Fae and twisted her reins as if she wished they were around the guard's neck.

"You know Arrian put the rule in place that all non-Hesperians need to be checked in with the border patrol," Nevada said dryly.

"What stops non-Hesperians from ignoring the hut and coming right through?" Darson wondered.

Anann shot him a withering look. "The land knows." Her mare's hooves danced in the dirt, echoing her rider's anxiety.

The soldier returned holding a journal and a writing implement. He shot them another smile, coyer this time. His shoulders appeared to shake from suppressed amusement after glancing at Anann again. It did not escape Darson's notice that Nevada was watching the guard closely. "How do you spell Garridan?"

Darson had to bite his lip and look away as Garridan spelled his name for the guard, and he was positive Anann was ready to leap off her horse and strangle the border guard. He carried on as if they had all the time in the world. She began to turn as red as her hair.

Darson liked this soldier.

"Daaarson. Is there an H in there?"

"No, just d-a-r. One S."

"So what brings you to Miranda?"

Nevada cut off the idle chitchat. "Can we move this along?"

"Of course; just a few more questions," the soldier said cheerily.

"I am not waiting," Anann said flatly. She slapped her horse's flank and the mare whirled around, galloping into the plains.

"Anann!" Nevada shouted.

The commander seethed and glared at the guard again. She did not miss the grin on his face as he scribbled something in the register. When he looked up again to study the group, she tried to pin his gaze, staring into dark eyes that only seemed to reflect the pale sky rather than reveal any depth. Something nagged at her about him—he must be familiar. It had been a while since she trained any of Arrian's soldiers. Maybe his name was escaping her.

But that was not it, either.

He looked back down at the register, flipping through a few pages. Nevada's ground her teeth audibly.

"Are any of you bringing in livesto—no, apparently you're not." His voice dropped to a mumble as he checked something off on the page. "Except horses. Naturally. Any fruits, vegetables, plants—"

"No!" Nevada said. Anann was close to disappearing on the horizon.

The guard's eyebrows rose, and he peered up at her, surprised at her outburst. "All right. Liquor? You look like you've had some, Commander."

Nevada glowered at him. As their gazes locked and she tried to crack the mirror image surface of his dark eyes, she had an unsettling moment where the good humor rippled, just for a second. Beneath the soldier's exterior a colder, darker core looked back at her with sardonic understanding. She had the brief sense that she was staring at the *true* him. She could not look away.

He smirked, and the ripple smoothed. "Done. Thank you for your patience."

Nevada blinked, breathing hard all of a sudden. "Thank you."

"May Toth grant you safe travels," the soldier said, stepping back and waving as they turned to leave. Nevada looked back sharply one more time. It sounded strange to hear the common travel blessing coming from him. The male stood in the field, head tilted, his dark, laughing eyes on them as they rode off. That nagging tickled the back of her mind, but she beat it back as they rode after Anann and into the heart of Hesperia.

* * *

Nevada's head throbbed with a dry ache in the morning sun, easily ignored as she shifted to functioning automatically, letting the pain fade to the background like the distant droning of angry bees. She could hear little else beyond the ringing in her ears.

Breathitt's firm, muscled body undulated beneath her, steady and strong in ways she did not feel. The palace was not far away.

It had not taken Nevada long to catch up to the princess—a testament to Breathitt's lineage and speed. Anann was an excellent rider and rode only the finest specimens Hesperia offered, Breathitt belonged to similar stock; the last time

Nevada set foot in Hesperia had been to retrieve him. She'd kept an eye on his lineage for some time, and news of his birth ended her search. Breathitt was in his element on the open plains.

The mortal's mounts were unable to keep pace with the Hesperian horses, and the men fell back about five hundred feet. Nevada watched for other fae soldiers or wayfarers, but the gentle hills and acres of even ground yielded nothing but animals.

An hour passed, and they alternated speeds for the horses' sake. Nevada looked back to check on the men and found them keeping pace with them. They were beginning to earn her grudging respect. They looked overheated and exhausted by the unbroken morning sun, but did not ask to stop. The heat enveloped her like a heavy, suffocating blanket, worsening her headache and sharpening the light to a fine, unbearable point.

The two mortals continued to follow close when Anann urged her horse into a gallop again and Nevada followed suit, gritting her teeth as the ground lost its even surface and Breathitt negotiated inclining earth.

Beneath the thundering of hooves and the rush of wind, Nevada's ears managed to pick up subtle, distorted noises. For a startling second, what sounded like a harsh, shrill Erepo cry drifted from elsewhere, like an eerie phantom from a nightmare. She saw nothing but grass and brush, and shook it off; she had heard noises like that in her sleep and while awake for the past five years. She had learned to ignore their mimicry of real battle.

A mammoth of a hill lay before them, and Nevada urged Breathitt to move faster. She knew, once they reached the top of the hill, the palace would flash white and tall in the distance.

Almost there.

* * *

As Garridan watched Nevada and Princess Anann crest the large hill looming in front of them, Nevada's horse suddenly reared. The commander pulled back on the reins sharply.

Anann screamed, halting her horse, and he heard the mare whinny in protest.

"Stay back!" Nevada yelled to them, her voice nearly lost in the wind. "Back!"

Garridan slowed his horse, but he and Darson pushed ahead to see what had stopped them cold.

He could hear an unmistakable screeching.

Hundreds of Erepos swarmed the field below.

Blood stained the grasses red.

The clamor of battle ripped the air apart.

Chapter 22

The raging torrent of cries and deeper, throatier shouts swallowed up Anann's horrified yell. The carnage spread before them like a rampant, gruesome disease.

"Back!" Nevada shouted again, pushing the order out of her closing throat.

Erepos' pale white skulls flared under the sun as they loped after the Hesperian soldiers who intermixed with them in the field. Some on two legs, others on all fours in twisted parodies of mad dogs; all were frightfully fast. They launched themselves onto the faeries, latching on like bloodsucking parasites.

Horror mutated into self-hatred. *How did I not hear this? You did, and you assumed it was the hell of your nightmares.*

As soon as the thought struck, her memory attempted to overtake her. For long, torturous seconds, the scene was not Hesperian fae fighting for their lives; it was her own people. Nevada froze and fought an internal battle to move or to react.

Blind with memory, horror, and disbelief, she was surprised when Darson shouted in her ear, his firm grip on Breathitt's reins. "Commander! They haven't seen us yet—if we turn around now, we can get help."

The world, which had been muted of sound and smell as the past grabbed hold of her mind and shook it to jumbled pieces, rushed back. She breathed deeply and immediately regretted it. The stench of blood filled the sweet air, its heavy, rotten perfume moving up the hill. Her stomach turned.

Something nagged at her again, a snatch of remembered conversation with Arrian before he left, and with Anann too, but she could not summon it from the dredges of memory. Rationale uttered one loud demand.

"Anann," Nevada called roughly.

The princess's horse danced away from the carnage, nostrils flaring. The redhead stared blindly; tears wet her cheeks.

Nevada did not want to leave the struggling soldiers, but her primary duty was to Anann, and Anann was not safe here. "We need to leave," she said, as Anann's wild eyes landed on her. "Before we are spotted. You—"

No sooner had she spoken her fear than a lone figure racing up the hill caught her eye.

Erepos might not have seen them yet, but a Hesperian soldier had.

"Commander!" the male soldier called hoarsely. She vaguely recognized him, but blood covered half of his face and silver helmet. Nevada dismounted to meet him, clasping his arm to steady him. "Did not think anyone would come," he said. "Our unit leader is dead. So glad you are here. Half our forces are dead or injured. They poured out of Cypress, to the south, the town burns—we came to aid the forces here, but we did not know how bad—we need help. There were too many. The creatures flee for the palace."

Nevada felt pulled in different directions, her heart pulling her to the ground forces, her mind enforcing her pledge to Anann.

She stared into the Hesperian soldier's pleading, tired eyes. "Take my horse," Nevada told him. "Take the princess to the palace, keep her safe. I will stay."

"Yes, Commander."

Nevada helped him mount Breathitt.

"You cannot stay," Anann cried. "They are slaughtering—"

"Let me help your people survive," Nevada said. "Send any help you can when you get there."

When Garridan slid off his horse, she shook her head sharply. "No. You will both go with them."

"I will stay. Lieutenant Darson will go with Princess Anann."

"I am *not* leaving you here," Darson said.

"You are weaponless," Garridan countered.

The Hesperian soldier unsheathed a short sword with a curved blade from his belt and handed it to Darson. The lieutenant took it somberly, reaching over to clasp his hand, and thanked him.

Garridan turned back to Nevada.

"This is not your fight," she said.

"Is this not the purpose of an alliance?" Garridan challenged. "We are doing exactly what we came here to do. Our job—all of our jobs—is to rid *every* land of these creatures."

"I will not have you bitten," Nevada argued.

"That is a risk we take every day," Darson said as he dismounted.

Nevada cursed. She did not have time to fight with these mortals. A glance down the hill confirmed a handful of Erepos circling, climbing the hill on all fours, smelling the horse, human and fae flesh. In Fae, she ordered the Hesperian soldier to take the human's horses with them, and then whispered to Breathitt in a softer voice. She slapped the flank of Anann's horse. A single shudder went through the mare, and she leapt into motion, followed by the fae soldier on Breathitt. The four horses tore off to the east, arcing away from the bloody field below.

The men watched Commander Nevada sprint down the hill before either of them could react.

A moment of silence fell in the space between them as they stared at one another before racing after her down the hill and into the fray.

* * *

Years ago, Garridan's unit had come across a settlement almost decimated by a bitten farm boy. The townspeople had taken matters into their own hands, gathered everyone who'd encountered the boy, bitten or not, and had quarantined them inside the church.

The townspeople asked him and his soldiers to take care of the situation.

Garridan saw it vividly in his mind: the mindless snarls and growls coming from the church. The loud thumps of bodies hurling themselves at boarded windows and doors.

Take care of it, they had pleaded.

Two of Garridan's best marksmen climbed to the roof. They broke in through a high, painted-glass window, perched on the rafters, and shot everyone inside with arrows. One by one, the shrieks went silent, like a macabre version of birds in a forest gradually quieting as danger passed.

Garridan never forgot the overwhelming stench of death, coagulated blood, and rot that greeted them when they opened the sanctuary's doors. Sixty bodies, either struck with arrows or torn apart from trying to eat one another, lay on benches, the center aisle, and the altar. He remembered the sounds of his men retching. It was the worst carnage he'd ever seen in such close quarters.

Until now.

The memory paled in comparison to what greeted him here. Rushing into the battlefield was like stepping into a living nightmare. Garridan knew without a doubt that in following Nevada, he had given himself a death sentence. But as the cries of rage and animal hunger tore through the air, as he watched Nevada disappear into the madness, he knew he would have followed her in regardless.

Garridan sidestepped an Erepo running for him, swinging his blade low to catch it in the gut. His mind focused on a few simple commands: Do not get taken to the ground. Do not let their teeth come anywhere near you. Watch Darson's back. Find Nevada.

Darson was to his left, lips curved in a feral smile as he viciously cut down Erepos. Hesperian soldiers continued to fight, barely registering the two humans that joined them. Darson caught his eye and whooped. Garridan grinned.

He could not deny his flash of adrenaline in the thick of it. Hatred for the Erepos consumed him. He did not mind dying out here in battle—as his father had, as Darson's father had—if it meant less abominations. One less Erepo to bite and turn a child, a spouse … a child's mother.

A lunging Erepo forced him to duck, crouch, and then roll out of its path. His arm shot out and gripped its leg.

He grimaced at the cool, oily flesh under his fingers, then pulled and sent it crashing to the ground. Garridan leapt up, slamming a boot into its torso to keep the wriggling, spitting creature in place. It shrieked as Garridan drove his sword deep into its chest.

Something heavy slammed squarely into his upper back. Fear spiked as the Erepo's fingers grabbed his shoulders, pushing its weight down on him. Garridan stumbled but stayed upright, lungs burning as he tried to breathe. He did not dare try to reach back and pull it off with his bare hands.

"Off!" he gritted out, hearing it shriek. Pain exploded at the crown of his head as the creature bash its head against the back of his skull. Terrified for his neck, he dropped his sword and somehow managed to pull a dagger from his belt. He thrust it back, driving the sharp blade into meaty flesh. The move only angered the hissing Erepo, forcing Garridan to change tactics. He lunged forward, crouching down as if he were diving for the ground, and used the momentum to throw the creature into the dirt.

It almost worked. The Erepo pitched sideways, and one of its hands flailed and grabbed for purchase. Its sharp fingernails dug into Garridan's ear, temple, and the sensitive skin below his earlobe and pulled. Hot pain seared around his ear, and he felt blood trickle down his neck. He tackled the Erepo before it could right itself, pinning the creature to the dirt as he tore its hand off his ear. Garridan raised the bloody dagger high.

A cry of satisfaction tore out of Garridan's throat as he pulled the blade out, leaving the dead Erepo to retrieve his sword. The whole upper left side of his head burned. He searched for a familiar face among monsters and fae.

Where are Nevada and Darson?

* * *

Screeches sounded in Nevada's ear as she darted around a boulder, spinning with her sword to catch an Erepo in the neck as it rounded to chase her. Her left arm stung from a short but deep cut high on her shoulder, thanks to a sneaky little bastard who looked like he had been turned at thirteen.

A border soldier she briefly teamed up with wheezed out more information. The mob of Erepos showed up two days ago. They attacked a small town by the border, massacring over a third of its citizens before a unit of Hesperian soldiers large enough to defeat them arrived. The Erepos moved to the next town, and then the next—Cypress, the one a few short miles from the bloody field. They did not come alone: the Hesperian force's downfall came from the creature even the fae had difficulty defeating: that same downfall met Arrian and took him off the field.

They were what Nevada had forgotten. The interlopers Arrian alluded to before he left.

She had not spotted one yet, but it was only a matter of time. She needed to find the humans.

Her mind slipped, now and again, when an Erepo lunged, when she fell to the ground and saw the vacant eyes of a dead soldier. Nevada did not know how long she could stay in the present.

She moved throughout the field to regroup the Hesperians, take the injured away from the worst of the fighting, and keep the soldiers from becoming isolated. Every time a Hesperian called her by name, she heard the voice of one of her own soldiers, now dead for five years.

She fought around bodies of faeries mingled with Erepo carcasses in the beautiful wild grasses. Some bodies were still intact, flesh whole, hair still gleaming with life recently robbed; but others were desecrated. Uniforms were torn open, blood pooled on the ground, lapped up by the eager, starving monsters. The flesh and muscle tissue of capable, ageless beings felled and feasted upon by depraved, devilish creatures. Deep in her core, Nevada suffered for every member of her still and lifeless brethren, who had been debased in a way so alien to the fae.

Another Erepo lost its head to her blade, and as she watched a female soldier struggle with two Erepos yards ahead, Nevada's vision blurred, and she lost her focus as her mind took over.

Her nightmares came alive again before her eyes.

Warriors, *her* warriors, hanging limp from the trees, eyes sightless, the smell of blood mingling sharply with fresh, heady flowers.

No. *No.*

Nevada bit the inside of her cheek to banish the memories. Sharp cries of pain from the past mixed with the ones hurtling through the air in the present. Her heart pounded wildly, and hot sweat poured down her face and neck. Her hands trembled.

You are not home, she thought forcefully. *This is not Deimos.*

Hesperia. You are in Hesperia.

The female soldier fell to her knees, and Nevada sprinted for her, tackling the Erepo clawing at the brunette's face. Her mind finally clear, she dragged the soldier to her feet and scanned the immediate area.

Nevada shoved back her growing worry for Garridan and Darson as the sun climbed higher in the sky. She concentrated on estimating how many fae remained. The hundred or so left were not doing too poorly; many fought with severe injuries, but sheer determination and rage kept them going. Nevada joined them, using a hot spring of hatred to cut down every Erepo who dared come near her.

She was relieved to run into Darson soon after. He managed a quick grin, saluting her with a bloody short sword. Blood darkened his shirt sleeves; his hair was messy, and his muscles tensed under sweaty skin.

"There are other creatures here," she yelled to him as he closed in on another Erepo. He barely tilted his head in her direction. "Do not engage—they are too large and fast. It is the same creature you encountered on your first visit to Hesperia."

Darson's expression grew grim, and he nodded in acknowledgement. He stayed within sight, easing Nevada's mind enough that she could take her eyes off him and help a soldier with a trio of Erepos. After finishing off the last one, the male faerie's knee buckled. Nevada knelt in front of him and found a long, deep gash tracing a path from the back of his knee to his thigh. When he tried to stand, the skin gaped open, and pale bone gleamed under torn, mangled muscle.

Nevada ripped at his tunic, intending to make a tourniquet, but he shook his head fervently, pushing her hands away. "Go. I will see to it," he said.

She ignored him and dragged him to a small outcropping of rocks. There a group of fae had crafted a makeshift infirmary and were tending to the severely wounded behind a line of soldiers. A soldier took the injured faerie from her, and Nevada returned to the battle, taking out her anger and grief on Erepos's brittle bones and shrieking forms. It went on until Nevada could not remember what the day had been like before the killing began and could not see an end to it. There was no end to it. But she could make an end of them until her body failed her.

If her mind did not fail her first.

* * *

The sun burned hot and high in the sky. Sweat and blood soaked Garridan's clothes. He felt the strain of battle between his shoulders blades, in his arms and legs. The heat threatened to sap his remaining strength. His throat was bone-dry, and he'd lost Darson. As he moved toward the hill they had crested so long ago to look for his friend, he found Nevada.

He only watched for a few seconds as she fought. Commander Nevada moved with a grace not of the world he knew. Each footfall was carefully placed, each swing of her arm like a movement in a dance; the sword was a mere extension of her. Her hair whipped around her as she crouched, leapt, and attacked the creatures around her. She was bloody and sweaty, but that did not dim her fierce glow. Her face was radiantly beautiful, alive with fury and determination.

He understood why faeries hardly ever suffered such losses.

Her eyes fell on him after she killed the last Erepo near her. "You are not bit, are you?" she called. "I would hate to have to kill you after all this."

Garridan smirked, hobbling across a clear stretch of grass to her, trying not to favor his right leg. "I would not be offended if you felt the need to check."

Nevada raised an eyebrow.

"Be thorough, if you like."

His comment startled a laugh out of her. She was more relieved to see the captain whole than she cared to admit. Blood streaked down his left cheek from the mess of his ear. He had a few minor gashes on his arms, but he was on his feet.

"Do you think Princess Anann made it to the palace?" he asked.

Nevada pursed her lips as she stepped to Garridan's side, crouching slightly as she watched the underbrush for movement. Smoke began to curl through the wheat stalks around them as fires burned Erepo carcasses nearby. "She is a renowned rider. I think she did."

Pale flesh moved in the brush close to them, but Nevada's concentration was drawn away as a din startled cries reached her ears.

Garridan burst into motion toward the tall grasses and attacked the Erepo lying in wait. Jerking his sword out of the still, pale body, he heard the cries, and his eyes roved over the field before fixating on something in the distance. He gestured toward the south. "What in hell are those?"

"Mauvahs," Nevada spat.

"What? Mauv—"

"Run!"

Garridan did not question her. He trailed after her, his right leg cramping with pain.

A horrific roar tore through the air. Wide, clawed feet

flung up dirt and ripped through grass as a creature, tall as a horse, lumbered toward them with frightening speed, its muscles rippling under mottled skin and matted, short hair. The creature resembled a large, misshapen dog, but Garridan got a good look at its face while it slinked through piles of dead bodies and gnawed on Erepos. It did not have the face of a dog.

He knew what the face looked like. Knew it, but could not accept it. He could not make sense of what he saw.

Limping behind Nevada, he gasped out, "How do you kill it?"

"Spine, neck, head—only way!"

Garridan narrowly avoided a crouched, feasting Erepo and headed for a small cluster of short trees. He was surprised when Nevada stopped, turned, ran back toward him, then moved right past him.

What is she doing?

The commander veered right, directly into the creature's line of sight. Drawing its attention away from him, and to her. To save him? Protect him?

He was not going to let her do that. Garridan searched the ground for any dropped weapons. If he could just find…

There! Garridan swooped down on the bow clutched in a faerie's limp hand. He nearly broke the male faerie's fingers to pry it loose, but soon enough Garridan had the weapon. He found a quiver with six arrows on the dead male's back.

Nevada was closer to him, carefully backing away from the Mauvah as it stalked toward her. Powerful muscles bunched and wicked teeth protruded from rotted gums dripping with saliva. Its growl was as terrible as a dozen wolves descending on prey. Nevada leapt forward, sword swinging.

The Mauvah roared and ran straight for her.

Garridan nocked an arrow, drew the string back, and aimed for the creature's head.

The arrow flew and sank into the Mauvah's neck. The beast howled, enraged, and Nevada leapt onto its back as it stumbled. She shoved her sword deep between its shoulder blades. The creature's legs crumpled.

"There will be more," Nevada said to Garridan as she jumped to the ground and he joined her. "Thank you."

"Where do they come from?"

Nevada shook her head. They froze as a group of Erepos, their pale torsos streaked with black blood, noticed them. The creatures began approaching, slowly at first, but gaining momentum at the sight of fresh meat. They reached the Mauvah carcass, and a few Erepos stopped, and began to feast. "We do not know," she finally said.

With wild screeches, the remaining Erepos ran toward them. As Garridan met them in combat, the thundering of hooves in the distance told him that help had arrived.

* * *

The aid Anann sent ensured the Erepos died faster, but the day was not yet over.

His head throbbed as the long afternoon marched forward. The sun beat down ruthlessly, drying the blood on the side of his face and burning his eyes and his skin. An Erepo stabbed wildly with its sword and sliced his collarbone. Garridan forced its head away, gripped its neck, twisted, and listened with satisfaction as bone snapped dully.

Garridan's mind prickled with sharp, needle-thin points

of heat and pain as he squinted against the unbearable brightness. He watched for a moment as horses traveled through the thin smoke whirling in the air and the additional fae soldiers focused on hunting down the Mauvahs as per Nevada's orders. He spotted a blood-covered faerie, one knee to the ground and teeth bared as he fought off an Erepo. Garridan limped over.

He buried his sword into the back of the creature's neck, slicing through the vertebrae and spinal cord and almost severing it. The faerie struggled to his feet, his eyes on Garridan. He said something that might have been a thank you, and the captain nodded.

And then the faerie's eyes widened. He shouted something unintelligible.

Garridan turned to see an Erepo lunging toward him, limbs outstretched in a grotesque version of a flying hug. Feeling his utter exhaustion, Garridan knew with the certainty the Erepo would take them both down and have plenty of time to go right for the bleeding wound at his lower neck.

All right, he thought. *That is all right. As long as it dies, I am—*

A dark blur moved in front of him. The Erepo disappeared as something crashed into Garridan. He grunted in surprise as he fell back and hit the dirt. His breath left his lungs in a huff as something landed on top of him and then rolled off as the Erepo landed on *her.* Garridan stared at Nevada in utter shock.

The Erepo latched on with a screech, hands clutching at her battle dress. Its head lowered to her shoulder as she bucked to throw it off, and its teeth snapped and clattered.

Nevada jammed an elbow into the side of the Erepo's jaw

and felt her skin tear when its head whipped to the side.

Garridan struggled to get up. Nevada straddled the Erepo under her before Garridan could reach her. A dagger flashed, and she drove it up under its chin.

Her chest heaved as she rose to her knees. Her left shoulder blade was on fire as she pulled the dagger free. Sweat stung her eyes as she looked into the field beyond, aware of Garridan safe next to her.

She would have turned to check on the man if she had not seen them. Everything around her seemed to slow to a crawl. The battlefield drifted around her like a hazy nightmare as she narrowed her focus.

Two males stood in the field.

Not Hesperians. They wore no uniforms. Erepo carcasses and dead faeries filled the grasses around them. Erepos ambled past as if ignorant of them or not bothered by their presence. The pair stood frozen amid the carnage with an eerie stillness. A tall, powerful male with short, dark hair looked down at the bodies, face impassive. And then, as if sensing her eyes on him, he turned his head to look at her. The other male was younger. His pale blond hair fluttered in the breeze. Nevada stared hard at him, ignoring everything around her. I have seen him, she thought. *Where have I seen him?*

Nevada felt her heart go cold.

A hand closing around her arm jolted her attention away. She took her eyes off them for a second as Garridan helped her to her feet. Nevada swiftly looked back.

They were gone.

"Are you all right?" Garridan demanded. "Did it bite you?"

"Grazed me," Nevada said absently, still staring at the

empty space the figures had occupied. "I will live." The unspoken *you would not have* hung in the rank air.

He wanted to check the bite, but he was not sure he should touch her. She had a nasty gash above her left eyebrow, and when she walked, she held her arm close to her left side. She looked exhausted. Angry with her for taking such a risk, Garridan was still by her side when two more Mauvahs wandered into the area.

He and a group of faeries worked to take down a particularly large, snarling beast. A warning bell ringing of unknown disease or infection went off in his head when the claws punctured the skin of his bicep, breaking through as easily as teeth puncturing a grape. The pain set his arm on fire. Garridan stumbled to a clear grassy section and let his twitching, sore leg have a break as he knelt on one knee to examine his arm.

Nevada and a female Hesperian soldier approached him after killing the Mauvah. The soldier sank down to take a look at his wound. He flinched when she lightly touched the reddened skin around the bleeding claw marks.

"They are not like Erepos," Nevada said. "You will not turn," she added.

"You do not know what they carry," Garridan said, his voice strained.

"Not when it concerns humans," the female faerie admitted. "But I think it will be fine. We just need to get you to a healer."

Garridan snorted, looking around the battlefield. The Erepos were dying off, but this place of death did not hold much hope for the living.

Nevada and the female perked up suddenly, looking off into the distance. Their faces flooded with relief.

"More help," Nevada said. "It is nearly over."

Garridan did not bother quelling the flood of hope her words gave him. He locked eyes with Nevada and said, "I need to find Darson."

* * *

Darson lost Nevada earlier and ended up near the middle of the field helping a pair of faeries with a mob of Erepos. The rush of adrenaline that had carried him all afternoon started diminishing as fatigue set in. Sweat dripped from his forehead and chin, his dark hair slicked back with it as he avoided another mouthful of rotted teeth and slammed the hilt of his sword into its chin.

The lieutenant jumped when he felt an arrow whiz by his ear on its way to thudding into something solid behind him. Darson whirled. An Erepo slumped to the ground, the arrow embedded in its neck.

The faerie soldier nocked another arrow, barely pausing to give him a curious look before turning her attention to the creatures. She shot another arrow into the eye of an Erepo.

Hope lit a small fire in Darson's heart when he noted the dwindling population of Erepos. He looked forward to returning to Miranda. Spending another evening in Liana's company sounded all the sweeter after the hellish day he had endured.

He knew it was not yet over when the screams began.

Faerie soldiers ran past him heading west. Something that sounded like horse hooves pounded into the earth behind them. Darson watched the female's eyes widen in horror.

"Mauvah!" she shouted. She nocked an arrow as she

backed away quickly. She kept the arrow trained on the creature running toward them.

Darson watched with revulsion as the beast came their way, snarling like a wolf, gnashing its teeth at anything that got in its way. Its face looked smashed in, nose crushed and flat, cheeks wide, human-like pink lips stretched to reveal sharp, jagged teeth. There was something grossly human about that face, especially the dark, beady eyes. The firm jaw line, too, was something more human, not like the features of a wolf or a dog.

This *is the creature that stalked Mourin and me.*

The female warrior let an arrow fly in the Mauvah's direction, catching it in the upper left flank. It bellowed at her, tearing toward her despite the arrow stuck in its shoulder.

Darson pulled a knife from his boot, took a step back, aimed, and flung. It whistled through the air and buried hilt-deep in the Mauvah's other flank. The creature stumbled, but did not stop.

Darson and the faerie turned to run at the same time, sprinting for a rock outcropping a dozen yards away. The ground vibrated with the force of the Mauvah's speed and weight.

"Turn!" the female suddenly shouted to him. "Turn left! To your left!"

He did, a yard before they made it to the rocks. He saw what she had already spotted—another Mauvah leapt from a crouch on the other side of the rocks, roaring as it soared over and slammed into the other Mauvah. Darson did not look back at the snarling animals as he and the faerie ran for safety.

They heard shouts and saw faeries running to the east. The young brown-haired faerie suddenly grinned as they ran, her eyes flashing to him. "Our help," she shouted. "Over soon. More reinforcements."

When they were far enough away from the Mauvahs, Darson slowed to catch his breath. His muscles screamed as his blood oozed out of a few wounds. Knowing the end was near gave him the confidence to rest a minute, assess his wounds, and catch a second wind. He rested his hands on his knees, gulping in air, as the wind shifted.

Smoke from the fires lit to burn Erepo carcasses crept into the area. The smell of roasting, rotted flesh burned in his nose. It hung in a thin haze and blotted out some of the afternoon sun, decreasing his visibility. The acrid taste and smoke choked in his throat, and he gagged.

Darson could no longer see the female faerie, and he did not know her name to call for her. He could see maybe thirty feet through the shifty haze, and when a particularly strong wind blew in more smoke, all he could see were more obscure figures.

One foggy figure stumbled toward him. Darson brandished his sword, his heart pounding, as he waited for it to come close enough to strike. It moved like a lame Erepo, hunched over slightly. He edged closer, ready to swing.

The wind shifted again. The swirling smoke dissipated.

Darson watched the brown-haired faerie stumble toward him, holding her side, which was missing a massive chunk of flesh. Blood poured copiously over her fingers as she took each step. She gazed at him in agony, unable to speak, and then collapsed to the ground.

Darson stared at her in frozen horror, imagining the teeth

that had ripped a hole that huge in her side. He crouched to help her.

A growl rose from behind him.

Something slammed into his chest as he turned, knocking the breath out of him and pitching him back onto the faerie.

Darson's horrified scream pierced the air.

Chapter 23

The field no longer sang the horrid tune of active battle, clanging metal, and angry cries. Instead, Nevada heard the somber, broken melody of injuries and mourning.

Nevada weaved through the handful of healers who tended to the wounded and lifted the prone forms of injured faeries onto litters. Thankfully, the second wave of aid had brought medicine, transportation, and horses. Breathitt stood among them, and Nevada felt the horse's dark eyes on her as she moved about the field with able-bodied fae. Her mind focused on the present: clearing the field, helping a healer tourniquet a thigh wound, assigning the Hesperians to different tasks.

The Hesperian soldier who had taken Anann to the palace returned with the litters, and he confirmed that Anann had safely arrived. Nevada set the messenger to work moving the injured, while others dragged dead Erepos and Mauvahs through the grasses and threw them into growing piles of burning carcasses.

The smell of burning flesh polluted the air as Nevada walked past one of the piles. Without warning, panic seized her by the throat again. In her mind, she saw a hut in the jungle in flames, whole villages—

Gasping, Nevada turned away from those around her. She crouched down and fought off the parallels her mind made, reminding herself she was in Hesperia. *Hesperia*, not Deimos.

She took shallow breaths with eyes closed, and brought herself back with the sounds of the Hesperian soldiers' voices and footfalls.

"Commander?"

The healer's voice startled Nevada, and she opened her eyes and stood. He told her about the overflow of wounded at the palace, and proposed relocating some to the nearest town. She could barely process what he said as a pulsing headache gripped the base of her skull. She was further distracted by the dancing ribbons of smoke rising from the nearest town in the distance, a brown bead on the horizon. Nevada gave him what seemed to her to be appropriate responses, but the healer stared at her with growing concern.

"Commander, you must be seen to," he said. "In fact, I feel it might be prudent to look at you before you ride. Have you had a head injury?"

He moved toward her, asking where the source of the pain was.

"I can ride," Nevada argued. "It is a simple headache." When the healer looked skeptical, she added firmly, "I know my limitations." She glanced over his head and spotted Garridan.

Searching the field. Alone.

Where was Darson?

She felt cold despite the sweat on her skin. "Excuse me," she said faintly.

* * *

"Dar!" Garridan shouted hoarsely; on the fifth and sixth tries his voice cracked, strained from smoke and overuse. The captain stared in the face of each faerie passing by, glancing longer at any with dark hair and a build similar to his closest friend. He fought off panic. Surely Darson was caught up helping someone and didn't hear his name being called?

He saw Nevada the field a few yards to his left, calling Darson's name every so often as she continued to seek him out, too. After a while, he caught her looking at him with a careful expression, as if she were on the verge of saying something he did not want to hear, and he flushed with anger and denial.

Darson is here on the field somewhere. That fool is just too preoccupied with whatever he is doing to pay attention.

"Darson!" Garridan hollered, cupping his hands. His blue eyes roved over the bodies in the field, even looking down in acceptance that Darson had possibly sustained an injury and was unable to get up.

Nevada stopped to help an injured faerie, casting another look at Garridan before assisting the female into a sitting position and inspecting her stomach wound. He lost sight of her as smoke moved between them. His eyes burned, and his throat itched.

Garridan moved on. He could barely swallow as he stumbled through the field. His right leg throbbed. His left ear was engulfed in pain, inflamed as if it were ablaze, as did his bicep from the Mauvah injury. The pain distracted him from suffocating panic as he shouted Darson's name again.

He could not find him.

"Dar!"

He is fine. Injured, perhaps, but alive. Unconscious? What if he is bitten? What if Darson is alive but bitten, and then what?

Garridan wanted to crawl out of his skin as the fear took hold. Childhood memories of a spring afternoon and another beloved face warped with the change surfaced in his memory, and he balked. When he tried to call his friend's name again, the two simple syllables would not come out.

He did not know what made him stop to look at the dead faerie. She was on her side, curled as if to protect the vital organs now exposed and spilling out of a gaping, jagged hole in her middle. Wispy, light brown hair lay across her pale cheek, hiding her face.

Her hair struck him cold. For a moment, as his heart constricted further, the brown deepened, and it was not a faerie curled on the ground. It was his mother, blood spattered, vulnerable and still. Garridan squeezed his eyes shut, hands shaking. He opened them again.

The faerie lay in front of him. And he finally noticed what lay next to her.

The hair was much darker. A deep, rich brown, damp with sweat. The male torso was eaten into; jagged rips larger than an Erepo could manage were torn into the flesh. Pink tissue exposed to the daylight gleamed amid the blood red mess of his side and chest. An arm was gone; only a bloody stump was left at the shoulder. He thought one of the legs was gone, too.

Garridan could not see the face, not under the scratches and blood. The head was horribly bent sideways, the neck mangled. The tattered shirt …

The shirt was familiar.

"No, no … It is not—"

Garridan tasted vomit in the back of his throat. He tried to speak Darson's name, but he choked. He did not sit so much as collapse when his legs refused to support him anymore.

He leaned forward and retched, his chest heaving as he expelled what was left of the food and drink he'd had the night before. When nothing else came he sat, muscles trembling, gasping, tears of horror and grief overcoming him. He stared at the mangled body and could not reconcile it with …

Darson.

In his mind, the scream built as it banged around the confines of his skull, railing with the terrible, all-consuming grief that rattled its way through his bones. His stomach turned again. He barely held down a dry heave as the stench of what was in front of him hit. The small, logical part of his brain still functioning vaguely noted that Darson was dead. Beyond that, it cowered in the face of grief this huge.

Garridan looked away, blind with tears, unsure of what to do. Something glinted in the bright sun a few feet away and caught his eye. An arm lay in the grass, and on the middle finger was a ring set with a small ruby.

That small, logical area of his brain spoke again. He did not know what the faeries would do with – with … but this, now, was his. He would not give it to the battlefield. Garridan crawled over and, with shaking hands, touched the still-warm flesh and pulled off the ring, grasping the limp fingers tightly. Darson's father's ring. Garridan sat on his haunches, cradling the treasure in his hand. He could not feel his wounds anymore.

He could not feel anything.

* * *

Nevada heard him screaming. The wretched, hopeless sound traveled up and down her spine with razor sharp teeth. She found him next to what she knew now to be Darson's mangled body. Garridan cupped something in his hand.

Grief she had not expected rushed through her like water from a broken dam. I should have watched Darson more carefully, Nevada thought, angry with herself. *How did I let this happen to him?* Sorrow weighed on her even heavier than before and clogged in her throat, as she stared at the defeated curve of Garridan's broad back.

Nevada carefully rested her hand on Garridan's shoulder. He did not move or flinch. She prayed silently to Patris, to Hesperia's protector Inaana, and tried to distance herself from the devastation, the inexcusable *waste*.

The light touch of his fingers on the back of her hand surprised her. She watched as he squeezed her hand.

Take care of him, she told herself. *Get him away from here.* "Your arm needs to be looked at, Garridan." She kept her voice gentle and neutral. "You do not want an infection to set in. You need to see the healer and get some water. And we will go to the palace." She continued saying directives in a soft, firm tone, and felt relief when his back muscles flexed. She pulled her hand away when his head rose.

Garridan got to his feet like an old, feeble man. Nevada knew he might not appreciate assistance, so she stepped back. He stood, dazed, his profile to her.

She said his name again, and this time he looked at her.

She flinched at the wreckage reflecting out of those blue eyes. "I will make sure he is taken care of," Nevada said, her voice trembling.

He did not respond.

Nevada caught the attention of a healer and had Garridan led away from Darson's body. She remained, trying to compose herself. Anger at her own carelessness washed over the grief—for letting them stay, for letting them come in the first place. She was responsible for this, and did not know how to right it. She could not right it.

The awful guilt ate away at her. Darson had died here, defending a country and a species not even his own. She saw the captain yards away, staring into the distance as a healer tended to him. This would stay with Garridan for the rest of his life. And she bore the weight of that responsibility.

When two soldiers came to collect the female faerie's body, Nevada stopped them from collecting Darson's. It had been a long time since she'd bothered to study human culture, but she did not imagine their rituals for death had much changed. Humans were not buried. The least she could do for Garridan was give him something to return to Darson's family.

"This—he is human," she said hollowly, gesturing to the pieces. "Take him and burn the remains. It is a human custom," she explained at their puzzled looks. "Put the ashes in an urn, and bring them to me." When they did not move, she snapped, "It is not a suggestion, it is an order."

Nevada did not watch them collect Darson. She went to Garridan as the healer bandaged his arm and told him he could be properly stitched up at the palace. Nevada could not look at his vacant, hopeless face for long, and instead busied herself by speaking with one of the head healers and a few soldiers about the remainder of the clean up and removal. She informed the healer that she would leave to take the captain to the palace and report to Princess Anann.

When she returned to Garridan, he stood like a puppet whose strings had been cut. "We are going to ride to the palace," she said to him, using the tone she had once used with a devastated Princess Rees in the days after her parents' deaths. She applied gentle pressure to his shoulder to prompt him to move, and he followed wordlessly, obeying her instructions when she told him to mount a horse. As they rode out of the clearing, Garridan never once looked back.

Neither said a word during the ride. A handful of soldiers traveled with them, and a few litters lagged behind with their loads.

Anann's beautiful, sprawling home grew on the horizon. The white stucco palace, protected from the vast plains by a tall, black enclosure, opened its gates to the riders. The group traveled down a long, white cobblestone pathway cut through a brilliantly green lawn sprinkled with decorative trees and clusters of blue and white wildflowers.

Nevada noted the healers flitting around the injured soldiers out on the lawn, the latter resting in makeshift beds. The scene marred the tranquility of Anann's courtyard. The massive black front doors opened, and palace staff, healers, and soldiers descended to receive the newcomers.

Nevada dismounted, handing Breathitt's reins to a palace servant and ignoring another servant holding out a bowl of cool, damp towels, the Hesperian customary greeting for guests. She looked back at Garridan as a healer approached him. The faerie spoke to the captain, and from the look of faint bewilderment on Garridan's face, the healer must not have realized he was human. She started in his direction to help him.

"Nevada!"

The commander bristled at Anann's voice. The redheaded princess descended the palace steps, her loose hair flying and her face pale. She looked distressed, and she pinned Nevada with her harried gaze.

"How many injured are left?" Anann asked. She looked past Nevada, toward the front gates. "Are there more litters coming?"

"Five more litters that I know of, and there are more yet in the field. I do not know the exact number of wounded. Have you been to see Commander Arrian? How is he?"

Anann hesitated. "Recovering," she said.

"You have spoken with him? Is he aware of what occurred today?"

"He was asleep when I looked in on him," the princess confessed. "I did not have a chance to speak with him."

Of course, Nevada thought irritably.

Anann must have sensed Nevada's displeasure, for she stiffened and snapped, "Do you realize how utterly awful it has been here, as well? I have been dashing around like mad, I hardly had time to do more than look in on him. I *cannot* believe this is happening," she ended with a frustrated cry. "I did not expect this *at all*. *How* did this happen? I do not understand it."

Out of the corner of her eye, Nevada watched a servant cautiously approach her and the distraught princess, holding a bowl of damp towels. "No," she told him.

"My lady, if you would like to wash up—"

"No," she repeated. Realizing she had neglected Garridan since Anann's arrival, an idea struck her. "Take it to that man, there." She pointed Garridan out. "Make sure he is tended to—he is injured. He is mortal, and a Mauvah wounded him. I want a healer who speaks Vinculum to look at it. See to his comfort, and make sure he eats."

"Of course. But really, please, your hands—" He waved a damp towel at her.

Nevada snatched it irritably. "Go, now."

"Yes, my lady."

"Do not let him wander the palace," Anann called after the servant. "I have enough to deal with." She turned to Nevada, exasperated. "Where is the other one?"

"Darson," Nevada gritted, furious. "Lieutenant Darson lost his life fighting for *your* country." Anann's eyes widened, more likely at her disrespectful tone than the revelation.

"I told you they should not have come," Anann said.

Nevada gave her a vicious look. "I am going to speak with Arrian about what happened today," she said coldly.

She stalked off to enter the palace even as Anann tried to talk to her, leaving the princess calling her name. Nevada wove through the bustling fae rushing to bring in more soldiers and move them to the infirmary. She finally pressed her hands into the damp coolness of the towel, and she had to admit it felt wonderful against the hot, scraped, and bloody skin of her hands. Nevada's hands began to throb as she finally cleaned her cuts and scrapes. She found Raust, Arrian's second-in-command, in the foyer as he prepared to leave, and he told her about the substantial damage the Erepos had left in two towns directly south of Cypress, where the masses of Erepos in the field came from. He appeared as harried as Anann, delivering the news to her rapidly and promising her more information upon his return from the field.

She stood still after his departure, her heart throbbing as badly as her hands. She did not want to repeat Raust's numbers to Arrian.

Another palace staff member approached her with more towels. She dispensed the used cloth to him and grabbed a fresh one.

Nevada had not wandered Hesperia's palace in a few years, and possessed only a vague recollection of the guest quarters. Arrian did not live on the grounds, but he had his own room for visits. After losing her bearings twice, she found a stretch of hall that contained a familiar series of black and white paintings.

She stopped at the half-closed door and then stepped hastily out of the way as a healer's aide exited Arrian's room.

"He needs his rest," the female said softly.

"I will only be a moment," Nevada lied. As an afterthought, she thrust the dirty towel at the nurse.

Nevada braced herself for what she would find beyond the doorway.

The open windows let in a cool breeze, but it could not quite banish the heat of the closed-in room or scrub the air of the faint yet unmistakable smell of blood. Nevada's hand gripped the doorframe. Feet that carried her on doggedly throughout the battle refused to budge as she surveyed the room. A bowl of blood-tinged water sat on a wooden table, and damp washcloths lay in the still pool.

Commander Arrian's carefully wrapped leg lay elevated

on mounds of pillows. Blotches of blood saturated the white cloth of bandages at his upper thigh. His pants were largely cut away to let the wounds of his right leg breathe. More bandages wound around his bare chest, protecting what she assumed were broken ribs. Those mended easily enough for their kind, re-knitting in a matter of days, but she knew the deeper wounds at his stomach and leg had been more horrific two days ago. Healing cuts covered in salve littered his chest; she could smell the herbal concoction, sharp and earthy. The skin had mended, but angry red welts remained, and claw marks raked down his chest and into the muscles of his stomach.

Yet even like this, Arrian retained the powerful aura he wore like a second skin. The body in the bed was not shriveled up and wasting away; it was a lesser god sloughing off the hurt and horror. Soon, he would be whole again.

His face was not peaceful; he was not asleep. His eyes squeezed shut, and his fingers gripped the bed sheets.

The door creaked as she shut it behind her. She inhaled and willed herself to be strong for him. He had done it for her, and it was time she returned the favor.

Arrian's eyes, dark and hazy from pain and medicine, fluttered open. It took him a second to notice her. When he did, the transformation was instantaneous. His eyes widened, shock disguising his discomfort.

"Nev?" his low voice croaked. "What are you—" He looked at her carefully, his eyes slowly clearing. She fidgeted, knowing when he figured out where she had been.

"Why are you here?" he rasped. "Nev, what happened?"

"I came with Anann—"

"Anann?"

The sharpness underlying his utter confusion closed her throat. She raised a hand and began to explain, but he cut her off.

"Anann is *here?*" He furrowed his brow, and his hands clenched the sheets tighter. "Why would you both come with Miranda's soldiers?"

Nevada's head reared back in surprise. Miranda's soldiers? A pang of sympathy squeezed her heart when he reached up with a shaky hand and rubbed the bridge of his nose, struggling to make sense of what she told him.

"We did not come with soldiers from Miranda," she said slowly. "I came down with Anann this morning; she wanted to check on you, and she asked me to escort her."

She could not read his expression as he stared at her, and she grew more uncomfortable. "You did not see *any* Mirandian soldiers? Nor Charon's forces?"

"No," she answered, although her confusion dissipated as the nature of the miscommunication grew clearer. She hesitated, knowing the impact her words would have on him. "If you were expecting reinforcements from Miranda, Arrian … there were none. There was no indication, when I left, that reinforcements were needed. And if any were coming after, they would have arrived long before now. Anann heard you were injured late last night. The queen told her. When did you send a message requesting aid?"

"Once I knew we were losing the border town where I was injured. I sent two messengers: one to Miranda and one to Charon." His voice was devoid of emotion. "She never reached the palace, did she? My messenger?"

Nevada watched as some of the pieces began to fit together in his mind. "No," she said. "Not that I know of. Arrian, I am sorry." She crossed the distance to his bedside. She did not know *how* to tell him the death toll of his soldiers, of innocent Hesperians, and the devastating news she had learned from Raust.

He had thought help was coming, that reinforcements were brought to aid his people, but there had been none. None. She barely held on to her fragile composure, keeping the flood of tears at the back of her throat.

Arrian stared at her for a long time. She squirmed and wished she had washed up before coming in here. "You have been fighting," he said. The implication of it darkened his eyes. "I know the route. Are you telling me Erepos moved that far north? Where were you? Where was Anann?"

"We came upon fighting an hour's ride from the palace. I sent Anann here with one of your soldiers as an escort, and she sent back reinforcements."

"You sent Anann off with one of my soldiers, and you stayed to fight by yourself?" Arrian asked.

"No," Nevada admitted. She cringed on the inside. She wanted to spare him this, too. "I ran into Captain Garridan and Lieutenant Darson, of Aliquis, on the way out of the palace. They insisted on coming with me. The two of us traveling alone did not sit well with them, and I allowed it because I was under the impression that I was merely escorting Anann here and back. I thought it would only be a matter of two days. They would not—" Her rushed explanation halted abruptly, and she looked up at the white whorled marble of the ceiling. The words hurt as they moved past the aching mass in her throat. She could barely manage above a whisper. "They would not leave me when we ran into the battle, either. Insisted that was the whole point of the alliance."

"Where are they?" Arrian asked.

"Garridan is in the infirmary, but his wounds are not severe." next words. "Darson did not survive."

She watched a flash of emotion she could not place cross his face. She knew he did not want the blood of a human soldier on his lands, especially a human soldier that had died aiding his forces. Arrian did not speak for many minutes.

Nevada had expected him to regain his composure; instead, anger darkened his face and warred with the pain in his eyes. "How did this happen?"

"I—"

"Stop." The serrated edge of his voice cut her like a knife. "You let two of the six human ambassadors in this kingdom go into battle with you. One is in my infirmary and the other is dead. How did you let this happen?"

"Had I known the situation, I would have never allowed them to come," Nevada said. "I lost track of him, and I take full responsibility for that." She felt a great pressure on her chest, and her pulse fluttered faster. "I could not protect him, as I could not protect all of your soldiers."

Arrian sighed. "Was it a bite?"

She raised a trembling hand to her throbbing forehead. "Not an Erepo. A Mauvah. Captain Garridan was with me near the end, and when the second round of aid came, and he went to find Lieutenant Darson. We looked and looked, and the captain found him—"

Darson's torn body and Garridan's slumped shoulders flashed through her mind.

His screams—

The massacre of Arrian's soldiers … it was just like

Deimos—

Nevada stared out of the open windows at the wild, clean grasses below. The scenery blurred as her eyes filled with tears. Her mind retreated as she contemplated the horrible truths she was about to reveal to him.

Jungle hotter than the air of the room took the forefront of her mind's eye. She smelled the blood, stronger than ever, among the pungent smell of flowers and plants. The devastation of her home. The crumbling stone of the palace. The still pools of blood on the marble floors, on edges of glass in broken windows. Bodies everywhere, soldiers and children and people she knew and loved, out of her grasp and gone forever. Trees caught on fire as a hut burned and the screams from inside—

"Nevada!"

She gasped when a warm hand closed over her wrist and squeezed. She stammered out an apology and attempted to pull away, but Arrian held her fast.

He peered closely at her, as if he could bore his way into her thoughts. "Are you all right? What happened? Is it your head?"

Nevada let her gaze drop to his grip. His hands were huge, his grip firmer than she thought he could manage. "It does not matter," she said, her voice unsteady.

"Yes, it does," he replied. He let go of her wrist. She tried to shy away, but he gently gripped her chin and forced her to look at him. "Did this happen on the field?"

She wanted to look away again, but he called her name and demanded her attention. "Do not treat me like a stranger, or a fool. Stop hiding from me. Did you have these flashbacks in the field?"

"Yes," she said in a small voice. "More than once."

Arrian cursed. "Nevada, you were not ready for this. It has only been five years—"

"*Stop it.*"

"No. Five years, and no situations in between to prepare you for a major battle."

"I had no indication it would happen," Nevada interrupted. "How was I supposed to know?"

"I could have told you," he said. "You do not remember how you were after the palace raid, but I do. I was *there*. We said it then, that you needed help processing this, and a slow integration back into the field. What happened today was too soon. You have not properly dealt with those events. Of course something similar would trigger your memories."

"I had no idea what I was riding into," Nevada said hotly, backing away. "I did not expect it anymore than I did the first time, how *dare* you—"

"How dare I care?" Arrian asked. "A flashback at the wrong time, a bad reaction of any kind, could have killed you. You were not able to control what happened today, but you can from now on. We want you well, but until then, you should be off the field." He softened his voice and added, "I did not know until now how deeply the raids still affect you. I wish I had known. You still have people who love you and want you to heal. Liana, Dacian, and I know what you have been through; you can talk to us. We will help you."

"I know," she finally whispered, not knowing how else to respond. She did not look at him as her throat ached and hot tears slipped down her cheeks. The sun's light slanted through the window as it dipped toward the western horizon.

When he sighed, Nevada raised her gaze from the floor and hastily wiped her cheeks. Their eyes met. She was shocked to see tears in his green eyes, too. "Nev," he started, and then stopped. He gestured for her to come closer.

Nevada shook her head, knowing she still had more wounds to inflict. "Arrian … I came here to tell you—"

He nodded slowly. "What happened?" he asked thickly.

Nevada's face crumpled, and she fought to stay strong. "Your soldiers fought brilliantly, you would have been proud. But it was—they were overwhelmed."

"How many?" he asked quietly.

It physically hurt her to say it. "Over one hundred, just in that field. Twice that many injured. Many of them are downstairs and outside on the palace grounds. The town of Cypress is all but lost, and at least two others south of there. I spoke with Raust, and he will return with more definite numbers tonight."

Arrian bowed his head. His face twisted with the pain Nevada knew all too well. She reached out and then hesitated, her hand hovering in the air, unsure what to do.

He gripped her wrist like a lifeline. Their eyes met, and he looked right into her and saw everything she did not want him to see. A twin echo of the anguish that overtook her when he delivered the same news five years ago now filled his eyes. An awful understanding. He may as well have said it aloud: *I know now what you went through. I am in it with you.*

Nevada could no longer keep her tears at bay.

The moment her head rested on his chest and her arms wound around him tightly, the sobs began. She felt the tight band of his heavily muscled arms pull her to him with all his remaining strength. His body shook underneath her and she realized he was crying, too.

They held each other and rode out the storm of grief together. Nevada buried her head in the crook of his neck. She could not stand his tears—they only made her grief sharper. She felt him press a kiss to her hair and rub his cheek against her temple. She let his heartbeat ease her out of mourning's clutches, and soon her sobs abated, leaving small, broken hiccups in their place. It had been so long since she had purged she had forgotten how exhausting it was. She felt wrung out. Here in this male's arms was the securest port in any storm.

They remained like that for a long time, drawing comfort from one another.

"I do not know how I will face Emilia," she murmured into his neck. "Or Darson's king. I do not know how to explain what happened. I cannot make it right."

"Do not worry about it now," he said gently. "We will figure it out." He pressed a kiss to her temple, and then settled his forehead against hers.

"Thank you," she whispered.

Reluctantly, she pulled away, but not before placing a kiss on his cheek, and then resting there a moment. She watched his eyes close in contentment, lips hinting at a smile.

"Go to a healer," Arrian said. "No more waiting. This," he lightly touched the gash above her left eyebrow, making her flinch. "Needs stitches."

"I will. I need to check on Garridan, too."

Nevada's hand found his, and she squeezed his fingers tight, fighting again for composure. She slowly stepped back from the bed, her smile a little shaky. He did not let go of her hand until it stretched his arm. She gave his fingers one final squeeze before letting him go.

"We will rebuild from this," she heard him say quietly as she left the room.

Chapter 24

Healers tossed her into a makeshift wash area set up in a corner of the palace's front foyer, refusing to mend her until she washed off the filth of battle. Nevada's body ached as she carefully washed her hair and cleaned what cuts and gashes she could reach. The gash in her eyebrow needed stitches, and the healers applied a thick, herbal salve to wounds on her arms, neck, and back. The commander mourned the absence of the medicine of Triton. It was a pulp created from the petals of a rare plant that grew only in a small area of higher elevation; that flower possessed powerful qualities that greatly reduced the effects of an Erepo bite on an immortal, and its limited quantities made it precious.

She asked for Garridan after the healers were done tending to her. A servant led her to the infirmary. Most of the small, private rooms were at triple occupancy. The servant took her to a half-open door, and she quietly thanked him.

Now that she was outside Garridan's door, her apprehension returned. Nevada slowly pushed open the door and watched him.

Garridan looked exactly like what he was; the only human in a country of fae. His back was bowed under the weight of the day's events. He wore clothes from the infirmary: clean, dark pants and a plain shirt. His dark, wavy hair was damp and pulled back. A thick, white bandage covered the Mauvah's claw marks on his arm, and he was barefoot. He stared blankly at the wall, oblivious to everything beyond his open doorway. She was sure she could walk in and stand in front of him, and he would not notice.

Some of the peace of mind she found in Arrian's presence crumbled. Nevada knew it would disappear entirely if she looked into his lifeless, glassy eyes. He should not need to be alone with his thoughts.

But he looked exhausted. He probably had not slept the night of the party, and had used what energy he had to get through the day. Sleep would not come easily for him after what he'd witnessed. He could use a draught to help that along and ensure he rested well into the night.

Nevada located his healer and suggested the sleeping drought. "Put him in a room on the second level, near my quarters," she told the healer. "He is a guest of the princess and myself."

She looked in on Garridan one more time, noting that he had not moved at all. He still stared at the wall, arms slack at his sides. She wanted to go in and say something, but nothing adequate came to mind.

Nevada left his room and moved toward the foyer. She ignored the furious grumblings of her stomach as she passed by cots that lined the opposite walls; healers tended to the soldiers and civilians from the ambushed town. She recognized one of the soldiers as one she had trained during a cross-training exercise three decades earlier; he had a splinted arm and a nasty bite on his leg.

"Commander Nevada!"

She watched warily as a bronze-haired, mud-splattered soldier approached her with an air of relief. "Can I help you?"

"We have at least two dozen more soldiers coming in from the fields. Where do you want them?"

"I do not—" Exasperated, she asked, "Does Anann not have head staff members for this? Why are you not asking a healer?"

"We are trying, Commander, but there are so many wounded and everything is in shambles. We need all the help we can acquire. The soldiers are due here in ten minutes."

Nevada sighed. Resigned, she agreed to help and headed to the courtyard.

* * *

The hour crept to midnight when she finally left to retire to her room, released by Raust's return. The foyer and courtyard had settled into some semblance of order; she had coordinated the delivery of more salves and supplies from the nearest town that had not suffered an attack. She finally left as Raust sent birds to Charon and Miranda requesting aid for the damaged towns.

Nevada did not see Anann again, and ceased looking for her as she was overcome by exhaustion. She walked up the flight of steps to her room, mindful of her aching bruised ribs. Her body eased with the prospect of sleep, but a sickly edge of foreboding teased of the brutal response from her injury to come. She needed it to hold off for a few more hours—long enough to look in on the captain and then fall into a hard, dreamless sleep before rest was impossible.

* * *

Garridan awoke in the cool darkness of an unknown room. For one blissful moment, he could not remember anything of the past day.

He did not bask in that ignorance for long.

They must have given him something to help him sleep, since he only vaguely recalled being led by the arm up the stairs and to the wide, comfortable bed he was now in.

He wanted to sleep again, but his mind and aching body would not allow him to.

The silence of the room was oppressive.

Most of the opposite wall was glass. The open windows offered a peaceful view of distant wheat fields and grassland. A sweet-smelling breeze drifted in, rustling his hair and bringing with it the pleasant whisper of shifting grasses. Compared to Miranda, the Hesperian palace and its area were less complicated, almost sparse. What little Garridan actually noticed of Anann's home, dressed in simple blacks, whites, and fresh greenery, gave the impression of under-stated grandeur. Everything else was a blur of hallways, healers, and injured faeries.

He had not seen Nevada since arriving at the courtyard.

The sense of displacement was overwhelming. He was stranded in a palace he had never been to before, separated from the two people he barely knew, and was now the only human in the entire country. He had not heard more than three sentences in Vinculum.

I need to get out of here.

And then what? Garridan's eyes slid shut as his heart sank. *Go back to Miranda and face the king? Let them know that Darson is dead because you decided to leave in the dead of night and allowed Darson come with you?* The sheer stupidity of his decision was almost unbearable. It had been his decision to come; he should have been killed, not Darson, who only wanted to ensure Garridan's safety. He did not even care if he lost his job over this; at this point he would willingly hand over his uniform. He did not deserve to wear it. He imagined going home to Aliquis, and what he would do then; he drew a blank. His future was an empty canvas.

What am I going to tell Idavida?

Garridan stared at the dark ceiling as a sharp pain dug its thorny, razor edge through to the center of him. The thought of sleeping slipped away. Garridan rolled onto his side and stared out at the night sky as he felt a pain far greater than any physical wound could inflict. He felt Darson's passing like a hole carved out of his core. Instead of bleeding, the hole was empty and bone dry; happy memories turned brittle and left him with nothing but torment. He squeezed his eyes shut and pressed his fingers against his eyelids, feeling hot tears slip past.

Despite the cool breeze, Garridan started to sweat. In an attempt to push off the sheets he aggravated his right leg, and he ground his teeth together in pain. Gingerly, he sat up and pushed the sheets down. His ear began to throb, and it felt as if the Erepo was digging into his skin anew. The rest of his skin felt too dry, too tight; he could hardly stand to be trapped in it.

Garridan carefully left the bed and limped across the cool marble floor. The captain swept a hand through his sweaty hair, and then just stood, wishing for—what, he did not know. Peace. Sleep. He wanted Darson, unable to sleep either, to walk into the room, hating this country and wanting to go back home. He wanted it all to be a hellish nightmare.

Anger and grief climbed their way through him with ragged claws. If he did not do something, he would end up screaming or tearing the room apart. Garridan's feet moved forward, his leg protesting. He opened the door and peered out into the wide hallway.

Nothing looked familiar.

The dark, empty hall held none of the clutter and finery of Aaclyde's palace, nothing to weigh it with history. He had thought coming across a faerie would answer all his questions and ease the pressure in his chest, but now he wanted to see no one, nor did he want to deal with a language barrier while trying to explain himself. He had no idea what he wanted.

Garridan retreated back inside his room. He walked slowly to the balcony, opened the glass door, and stepped into the cool night air.

He saw small glowing blotches low on the horizon. Fires from the battle.

He closed his eyes and rested his forehead on the cold metal railing.

It was going to be a long night.

* * *

Nevada watched Garridan return to his room. In his distracted state, he did not notice her enter the hall. He left his door ajar, giving her the perfect opportunity to peek in on him.

She slipped through the door, making enough noise to signal her entry.

The captain stood on the balcony, the glass door open wide, letting in a breeze that carried the slightest suggestion of smoke from faraway fires. She watched his shoulders tighten as he became aware of her presence; he turned his head to catch her in his peripheral vision.

Nevada stood next to him, her arms crossed as she leaned on the metal railing. His face was impassive, but the vulnerability in his posture and the way he favored his right leg stirred her sympathies. He nodded to acknowledge her but kept his peace; she could sense puzzlement at her appearance. The skin around his left ear looked swollen and angry; salve glittered beneath a bandage that protected the larger gashes. The thin, simple shirt he wore was damp with sweat at the neckline, his hair disheveled from a deep, drug-induced sleep. He did not look rested; he looked wrung out, scorched by harsh sun, the battle, and losing Darson, a scalding that reached all the way to his core. His hands hung loose over the railing; his knuckles were cut and bruised. He wore Darson's ring on his left hand. The ruby looked black under the stars.

She cleared her throat, and, although she knew the answer, asked, "Did you sleep well? I had the staff assist with that. I hope you do not mind."

"I gathered," he said, devoid of the humor she imagined he strived for. "I slept fine." He added a distant "Thank you," almost as an afterthought.

"How are you feeling?" Nevada touched her own ear. "How did your leg handle walking?"

"Poorly." He looked down at it, then at her, as if still perturbed by her presence. "It's stiff. My ear is … tender. But I will heal."

Garridan's ear felt drenched in hot, viscous oil, but he did not want to acknowledge the pain; it had less power over him if he ignored it.

What was Nevada doing here? It was strange to see her now. The agile, deadly warrior from the battlefield had withdrawn, and a quieter, introspective faerie stood next to him. The moonlight turned her olive skin pallid, and cast a sheen over her long black hair, clean and loose around a shirt that must have come from the infirmary.

Why was she checking on him at this time of night? Because she felt obligated? To appease a sense of her guilt for allowing him to come along? They were not friends. What could motivate her to attempt conversation, if not out of a sense of guilt or duty? Because Darson died?

He did not want her here if it was forced. Political. Out of pity.

She had lapsed into silence, staring out at the fires. He could be judging her harshly and assuming too much. He remembered the weight of her hand on his shoulder when he found Darson, and her calm, measured words. The gash at her brow was knit together with stitches; a few smaller cuts and scrapes were barely showing, a testament to the faeries' ability to heal; the larger wounds hid under bandages around her arms, and high on her collarbone. He could see the outline of bandages wrapped around her middle.

She had not asked for this, either.

"Are you in any pain?" he asked.

Her gaze shifted his way, eyes glittering like purple jewels under Naula's pale glow. "Not presently."

Liar. He remembered the Erepo bite hiding under the borrowed shirt. "Thank you for sparing me from—" A fate worse than a clean death. The fate of countless friends; the fate of his mother. "Thank you for saving my life."

"I could do nothing less," she said quietly. "But you are welcome."

She found his word choice unsettling. The thought of his fate had she not acted in time rolled queasily in her stomach.

He had dead to bring home with him, too. Darson would be delivered to a kiln by morning.

She thought of his remains, and stared at the distant fires. Her heart thudded; dread sickened her stomach as, in her memory, she saw a hut, a home she knew so well, lit up with flames, and she was too late, too late.

Nevada closed her eyes, and her sharp inhale was like a punch to her ribs. She gripped the railing and bowed her head, waiting for the memory let her go.

Like surfacing from underwater, his voice suddenly hit her. "—all right? Nevada?"

She turned and stared at him; he had not touched her, but concern drew his brows together and darkened the blue of his eyes. She took a few careful breaths and then nodded. "Yes," she said, exhaling. "I apologize."

"Do you need anything?"

"Just a few moments, please." She felt his eyes on her, and debated being truthful with him. She imagined delayed reactions like hers were not new to him. "Today triggered memories of my home for me. What we lost, what happened."

He said nothing, giving her time to continue. Her fingers squeezed the railing. "Powerful memories. Debilitating, and at the wrong time. I still struggle with Deimos more than I care to admit."

Garridan said, "I have experienced what you are describing. It is not a sign of weakness. We cannot always process what happens to us, not right away—and sometimes never. The smallest things can trigger those memories, but there is nothing shameful in that. It has happened to me often."

His voice was soothing. The tightness in her chest loosened. Nevada released her grip on the rail and looked at him, seeing calm in his eyes for the first time since the battle; there was a depth to him she had not taken the time to notice before. "I thought it was over." He nodded, as if it did not surprise him. But she had not come here to talk about her issues; she had come to see that he was all right. She did not know the repercussions the field would have on Garridan.

Before he could continue, she added, softly, "I will take the necessary measures to deal with it. Will you?"

Garridan's face was sober. "I will have to."

Nevada felt rotten. For him, for her; for the weeks to come. For Darson.

"I would like to apologize for not keeping track of Lieutenant Darson during the battle," she said abruptly. "Had I done so, the outcome might have been different. I am sorry beyond words for the loss of his life. For your loss."

He said nothing for a long moment. Cricket song and wind tussled wheat filled the silence. Nevada looked at his profile. His jaw clenched as he gripped the railing, the tension running up his arms and giving his muscles stark definition. Moonlight glittered against the tears in his eyes. She looked away and gave him time.

Garridan finally cleared his throat and said, "No one is responsible but the creature that killed him."

His tone exposed the lie of his words; she heard guilt, and the hint of an accusation directed at her, even if he was not conscious of it. She did not know what to say, but he spared her the effort by talking more freely. His voice was pained. "He was here because of me."

"How long did you know him?"

"Six years. His father died battling the Erepos. Both of our fathers served in the military; my own died when I was nineteen. I lost someone the year Darson and I met, and it was … effortless to talk to him. Over time, he showed me I could trust him, not just with my life in the field, but as a friend. He listens well—" Garridan paused, "—listened well, and offered sound advice, whether you wanted to hear it or not."

Garridan pushed off from the railing with a grimace. Some of the shadows left his expression, and he began to use his hands as he talked.

"He grew up relatively affluent, given our situation. His father's family was well known for occupying higher military positions. I believe his grandfather successfully evacuated a village of four or five thousand with less than one hundred casualties, and his mother comes from a long line of historians, great assets to the monarchy and to preserving our history."

The commonalities between Darson and Dacian were uncanny, Nevada thought, amused.

"It was just him and his mother, Idavida. He had an older sibling that died, and I think there may have been another child who died at birth. He adores her." Garridan's voice softened. "I treasure her, too. My mother died when I was thirteen, and Idavida took it upon herself to fill that role for me. She is a remarkable woman. They had an enviable bond. He wouldn't leave her, although he's had opportunities."

Nevada's eyes stung. "Family, whether by blood or bond, is our greatest reward in this life. And a precious gift to protect." She saw him wince again, and said, "Would you like to sit?"

He silently acquiesced by limping into the room and sinking slowly down onto the bed. Nevada sat next to him. He talked more of Darson, and she let him while Naula made her dreamy way across the sky. Sorrow weighted her heart when he tried to explain the hole Darson's passing left behind.

"I have lost many people, but none like him," he said hollowly. "He had more to live for. It would have been—"

He stopped himself, and Nevada looked at him sharply. "How so?"

Garridan shook his head. He could not explain it to her. Darson was more connected to the world; people were made better by his presence. Idavida needed him. How could he explain the certainty he felt that it would have been better if he had died instead of Darson? Darson encouraged people with his life, with his words and actions. Garridan would trade places in a heartbeat, and give the one who would be missed a second chance.

How to explain to her that this trip changed his life, utterly and irrevocably, and for the worse, and he could barely live with it? He was unmoored in a foreign sea, with no idea how to find shore and no sense of direction. The only piece of driftwood he had sat next to him.

He looked at the touch of despair and sadness hiding in the planes of her cheekbones, around her small, straight nose, and in the deep well of her eyes. He felt that he knew her better now; she was no longer the distant commander from the conference, nor was she the fierce soldier from the battle. He remembered the reason she had escorted Anann to Hesperia in the first place. "How is Commander Arrian?"

She stared at him, seeming unsatisfied with his lack of response to her question. "Healing. Sedated; otherwise he would attempt to help despite a broken leg and fractured ribs."

He heard familiarity and affection in her voice, and Garridan realized the two of them must be close. "I am glad to hear it. And your bite?"

"I can ignore it, for now. By morning, the repercussions will … preoccupy me for a few days."

"You mentioned it was similar to our symptoms before infection."

"Yes. I will be down the hall should you need anything. We must stay for two or three days until I am well enough for travel." She did not like the prospect of leaving him unattended for so long, but it could not be helped. "Do not hesitate to ask the staff for anything."

"Do not worry over me. Concentrate on recovering. I will not bother you. Is there anything I can do to assist in the meantime?"

Nevada shook her head. "No, Garridan. You have wounds of your own to contend with. But thank you for the offer."

His brow furrowed. He pushed his hair back from his face, his eyes anxious. "I would rather be useful than sit in this room and..." Think of Darson. Grieve. *Give me anything to keep me away from my memories.*

He could see that Nevada read the thought as if he had spoken out loud, for she glanced down, her brows furrowing. "It would help me to know you are safe," she said carefully. "You have already done more than you should for this country. I do not know what will become of this alliance, but we will not forget what you and Lieutenant Darson contributed today. Rest, and when we are both well enough, I will escort you back."

"Take your time. I have no idea what to say to my king upon my return."

She groaned. "I do not want to face a single person in Miranda, either. I am not entirely sure Anann will come back with us."

"I can understand why."

Nevada nodded.

"What is your protocol for attacks like this?" he asked. "To the best of my knowledge, they seldom happen on this scale. What will Hesperia and the kingdom do?"

"Arrian will station the majority of his forces at the borders," she said, her voice slipping into a detached tone. "More heavily in the south. What countries can spare it will send aid. The towns will be rebuilt. It is slow work, as you know, but—"

"Necessary. To move on."

"It will be hard for them," she said softly, almost to herself. "Hesperia has never suffered an attack of this magnitude. Arrian's military made Anann's country a safe haven for so long."

"Was it like this in Deimos?" he asked quietly.

She did not answer right away, and he regretted asking.

He wanted to prompt her to explore the relapses she had and how they tied in to Deimos, but he thought perhaps he had pushed too far. He was surprised when she answered.

"Yes," she whispered. "The damage was more extensive. Closed in, less spread out. You could not get away from it."

"Did you lose anyone? Anyone close to you?"

"I did," Nevada said. "I worked closely with Rees's mother, for many years. Friends in various units."

There were more, he knew; he could feel it. "I am sorry," he said. She nodded.

They sat in silence, close enough that they leaned toward one another.

Nevada sighed, and then slid her hand along the left side of her ribcage. Discomfort flashed in her eyes, and she asked, "Can I get you anything to help you sleep?"

No, but you can admit you are wounded and take of yourself, Garridan thought. "No, thank you. I will manage. You should try to rest before you become ill."

"I will." She smiled a little crooked smile, just a touch broken. "Remember, I'm down the hall, if you need anything."

"Of course. Sleep well, Nevada."

"And you."

On impulse, Garridan reached out and lightly squeezed her shoulder before she rose. She returned the gesture with a gentle pat and bade him good night before leaving him alone with his memories.

He suspected neither of them would sleep at all, let alone well. With the warmth of her presence gone, he had nothing to distract him from the nightmare landscape of his mind.

* * *

Garridan spent the next three days alone and mostly in his room. He heard from the healers who checked on him that some of the injured were being moved to other locations or given clearance to return home. His world became the marbled, airy room he was in, and the brief flashes of hallways when the room became too much for his wounded psyche to bear and he grew tired of waiting. He only spotted Princess Anann once. He did not see Nevada at all during that time. He asked the healers about her condition, and received nothing more than a simple "The infection is running its course. We are keeping her hydrated."

On the morning of the second day, Garridan could not stand the four walls of his room any longer, and his brain hounded him with images of Darson and vivid auditory fragments of his voice. Garridan followed the servant who removed his breakfast tray down to the kitchens. The kitchen staff paid him little notice and seemed unconcerned with his presence, so he came in randomly to fill himself with Hesperia's fare.

If the giant wine cellar was any indication, Hesperia apparently supplied the kingdom with a great deal of its wine. One of the cooks with a firm grasp of Vinculum was eager to let Garridan sample a few of the wines the country was best known for. Garridan snuck some of the wine back to his room and let the liquor dull Darson's voice.

It was a watered down distraction from the heavy tide of Garridan's grief. He'd lie in the dark, staring out at the stars, struggling to process this new reality without Darson.

He could not.

Garridan's eyes were dry during the day and night when sleep would not come, but when he woke in the morning, the pillows were damp.

Chapter 25

Nevada's sickness wreaked havoc on her body for three days. Hours felt like days; her stomach violently rejected all but the smallest sips of lukewarm water. Her dreams were strange, filled with the jagged teeth and claws of monsters, of golden fields and rivers of blood. She felt pulled out of her own mind as the infection raged through her until her body's defenses wore it down.

But none of that mattered. She had to return Garridan to Miranda, whether her body was truly ready or not.

Cleaning up exhausted her, but Nevada finally left her room with washed hair, scrubbed skin, and clean battle dress, leaving the pallor of sickness behind. Her near-empty stomach rumbled with hunger pains and the distant stirring of nausea. She was unused to prolonged periods of standing; her muscles quaked. Dizziness slowed her steps, but it was the best she had felt since the early morning hours after her talk with Garridan.

Heat prickled at her skin, and Nevada suppressed a shudder as she reached Garridan's door. She took a deep breath, straightened, and knocked.

A tired, pale, shell of a man answered, looking as if he

were fighting off an illness similar to hers. His skin appeared to have grown thinner in the past few days, and she could almost see the weariness of his soul. He looked her over, and she saw distress in his eyes; she knew she looked no better. His eyes sought hers, silently asking after her health.

Never mind myself, she thought. He had never looked so *mortal*. "I am recovering," she told him. "How are you feeling? The healers tell me your Mauvah injury is on the mend."

"Yes. I should be completely healed in a week. Have you been able to eat?"

"I kept down everything I ate this morning."

His expression remained concerned. "I am glad to hear it. Are we to leave soon?"

"Now, if you are ready."

His eyebrows rose. She knew he did not think she looked fit to travel. Either his feelings were particularly transparent, or she was growing more attuned to what the captain did not say. "Are you positive?"

No. "Yes. We must," she said. "How is your leg?"

Garridan's lips thinned. He looked down at the offending limb. "Stiff, but manageable."

You will be in agony after hours of hard riding, Nevada surmised. "We will set a pace we are both comfortable with."

The pained look that crossed his face almost made her smile. He murmured that he needed to collect the few things he had brought. She waited just inside the room while he grabbed his belt and scabbard, cinching them around a waist that looked much narrower than she remembered. He wore the clothes he came in. Nevada scanned the room and saw a cluster of empty wine bottles at the foot of the bed.

She sighed sadly. "Ready?" she asked quietly.

He nodded.

They walked together, a fine pair of limping, broken toy soldiers. Garridan's face remained impassive as they walked down the stairs, his limp growing more pronounced as they reached the bottom. Nevada only had to pause twice, clenching her teeth as a foul metallic taste filled her mouth.

The courtyard was completely different than it had been three days earlier. The soldiers were gone, and the lush grasses were pristine. She had heard from the healers that attended her that some of the wounded had healed quickly, and others were taken to infirmaries closer to their homes. The remaining wounded were now within the infirmary walls. Order had returned to Anann's palace. Nevada had sent a message to the princess regarding their departure, but heard nothing. She assumed Anann had no intention of leaving with them.

At this point, she was not complaining.

Nevada's spirits brightened at the sight of Breathitt moving restlessly on the white stone, black mane and tail fluttering in the cool, early-morning breeze. Garridan's horse stood next to him, as did Darson's mare.

And a tan gelding with a black, braided mane.

Her eyes narrowed, and she searched the courtyard to find the horse's owner.

"Excuse me," she said.

Garridan watched Nevada walk off with more vitality than he thought possible. He wandered toward the horses, pained by the presence of Darson's mare. The worn saddle would remain empty until she was sold to another owner. He greeted his horse, smoothing his hand over the gelding's velvety nose. He did the same with Darson's glossy brown mare, almost as an apology.

He dreaded their return. He could not stand the thought of leaving Hesperia without Darson; could not stand the thought of going home with only his horse. The despair that clutched him in the dark hours of the night gripped him again.

He looked for Nevada and found her by a tall, impressively built male faerie wearing riding clothes.

Commander Arrian.

Was he returning with them?

Next to the commander stood another male faerie in the loose, bright blue garb of the infirmary healers. The color contrasted with the dark brown of his skin, and the sun shone on his shaven head. He did not look pleased with either Arrian *or* Nevada.

Garridan's mind flashed back to the first time he saw the pair of commanders together, by the steps of Princess Aaclyde's palace. He remembered Darson's voice in his ear as he speculated about the conversation occurring between the two then unknown faeries. How different they looked now. Standing by Arrian made Nevada seem small and slight. The confidence she had radiated a few short days ago diminished under a shroud of poor health. She already looked as if she needed to sit down.

He was reminded again that her suffering was a direct result of his weakness. And never mind the small, ugly voice that had whispered to him late at night. The one insisting that he should have died in Darson's place.

He drowned out the voice by talking to his horse, lavishing attention on the steed while he waited for Nevada.

* * *

"I am returning with you; so is Princess Anann. She will join us soon," Arrian said calmly.

"You cannot be serious," Nevada said flatly. She stared into Arrian's foggy green eyes, saw the faint sweat at his temples, the woven tunic hiding Mauvah injuries she knew were not yet fully healed. She looked again, accusingly, at Arrian's healer. "You see nothing wrong with this?"

The healer folded his arms and gave her a withering look. "I see everything wrong with *both* of you engaging in strenuous activity. I have, however, been reminded of my commander's extensive background in medicine, which he received from *me*, and informed that my opinion is valued but otherwise will be ignored."

"Your opinion matters greatly," Arrian said patiently, "but I must do this."

"Ten hours of travel," Nevada said, frustrated. "You are all but guaranteed to set your progress back."

"I am aware of my limitations." Arrian paused, and looked at her intently. "Speaking of limitations, I have not seen you in days. Are you feeling well?"

"Of course," she said. Her stomach twisted at the lie. "I was more exhausted than I thought, and I wanted to stay close to the captain and monitor his progress."

"Exhaustion."

"Yes," she said tersely.

"Why are you lying to me?"

"I beg your pardon?"

"My body is injured, not my brain." Agitation filled Arrian's face and his green eyes flashed. "You have lost weight since

I saw you three days ago. I can see it in you; I have *treated* bites, Nevada. Did you think I would not piece it together? That Sofus would not tell me?"

She looked away. "You had your own rehabilitation to focus on."

"Yet you are traveling to Miranda. You are in no position to stop me from doing the same."

Nevada glared at Arrian. "You have made your point. But can you not wait a few more days?"

Arrian sighed and turned to the Sofus. "Will you please excuse us?"

The healer left, muttering under his breath. Arrian pinned Nevada with another unreadable look. "You are fully aware of the protocol after attacks of this magnitude. Everyone gathered after Deimos. Everyone is gathered in Miranda now. We need to discuss this, and I wish to do so while the humans are still here. I would like to speak with their king. And I want to know what went wrong. Why there was such a gross miscommunication between Miranda and Hesperia."

She knew he was right. And yet something about his tone when he mentioned the miscommunication made her pause and stare at him with speculation. "What are you suggesting?"

Nevada bit off an oath when Anann walked down the steps to join them, and Arrian shook his head, mouthing *later* to her.

"Ten minutes," the princess said curtly to Nevada. The redhead shot Arrian a mildly unfriendly look, as if the idea of going back to Miranda had been pressed upon her.

"I need to retrieve something first," she said to the princess. "Arrian, can you—"

"I will speak with him," he said, knowing what Nevada needed to do.

She nodded her thanks and left.

* * *

Garridan watched Nevada leave just after Princess Anann appeared; she was dressed for riding in dark brown leather, her light red hair pulled into a coiled, braided bun. A small part of him was relieved, even though the princess looked agitated; truth be told, no one seemed content with returning except for Arrian.

The faerie commander's skin was a little sallow; bandages peeked out from loose shirt, and limped from the healing fracture. As Garridan studied the faerie, he found himself under the male commander's same quiet scrutiny.

"You are one of Edric's captains," Arrian stated, his voice carrying. "Nevada has spoken of you."

Garridan frowned. He was not sure he wanted to know what she had said about him. "It was an honor to fight among your soldiers, Commander. I was sorry to hear of your injuries, and am glad to see you are recovering."

Arrian nodded and then walked toward him. Garridan saw sympathy in the faerie's dark green eyes. It was too much. Garridan looked away.

"I met your lieutenant when he first delivered your king's message," Arrian said. "I wanted to tell you how sorry I am he lost his life here. His sacrifice will not be forgotten, nor was it in vain. I regret not having the chance to know such a courageous soldier, as you did. You loved him."

"As a brother." The words tasted bitter, but something in

Garridan eased at the acknowledgment.

"He will be honored as such. Your actions, as well, will resonate further than you may realize. I speak on behalf of my country, my soldiers, and myself when I thank you and Lieutenant Darson for your service." Arrian bowed, grimacing as he rose.

Moved at such an eloquent, unexpected show of gratitude and solidarity, Garridan returned the gesture. He felt that if Darson had been given a chance to look beyond a bad first impression, he would have liked this commander.

"May I ask, Captain, what will become of his horse?"

"Pardon?" Garridan frowned with confusion. The question was unexpected. "She will be sold," he said slowly. "Probably to another soldier."

"Hesperia has something of a reputation for horse breeding," Arrian said, raising his eyebrows to indicate the understatement. "Horses are well cared for in this country. I would like to make you an offer. Rather than risk the journey home riderless, I wondered if you would let us keep her, where she can retire comfortably. I would have her among my personal stock, for the services her master rendered to my country. I would like to negotiate a price."

"I could not take your money," Garridan said automatically.

Arrian said nothing, and reached past him to stroke the forehead of Darson's mare. She closed her large, dark eyes and leaned into the commander's touch, chuffing softly. "Some other form of payment, then," he said, before switching to Fae as he talked to the horse.

Any preconceived notions he had of the commander scattered to the four corners of Hylla. Respect and gratitude swelled in Garridan's chest, and he mulled over the offer, the loss of Darson's mare, and the physical reminder of Darson's absence for the entire journey home. Yet leaving her behind, however well she would be cared for, would be bittersweet. "You may keep her." The words were difficult to say, and he paused. "No payment required. He would appreciate it."

"The pleasure is mine. I have something for you as well, Captain; I would give it to you now lest I forget later." Arrian reached into the pocket of his breeches and produced a small ivory envelope, closed with a red wax seal. Garridan took it from his outstretched hand and read the writing on the front.

Idavida.

Garridan's heart clenched. He stopped breathing.

"Please give this to Lieutenant Darson's mother for me."

He could not speak for what felt like ages. He sensed Arrian waiting patiently for him to regain composure. After swallowing hard against the lump in his throat, Garridan met the commander's gaze and thanked him, voice trembling, and he wondered: how had the commander known her name?

Nevada. I told Nevada her name.

As if conjured by his thoughts, Nevada returned with a soldier carrying a small wooden ladder. "If you cannot get on that animal with this ladder," she called to Arrian as he walked to his horse, "then you have no business traveling." She watched with a critical eye as he managed to do so.

Garridan noticed she carried a small vase made of smooth, glossy wood. When she handed it to him, he looked at it and then her, baffled.

"To take home, for Idavida," she said. She hesitated. "From what I recall, burning is customary for your kind." When he didn't respond—couldn't—and just looked at her, Nevada hesitated. "I had them collect his ashes."

Garridan cradled the vase in his arms, speechless for a second time. A memory surfaced, of Darson telling him the fae buried their dead. Nevada had remembered the difference. Somehow, despite the battle, and though she was gravely ill, she had found time for this, found time to tell Arrian the name of Darson's mother. And then Arrian took the time to write to her.

As tears blinded him, Garridan embraced Nevada. Feeling her arms hesitantly return the gesture freed some of the tightness in his throat, enough for him to whisper, "Thank you."

Nevada squeezed his arms, touched the back of his head, and pulled away. She held his gaze long enough to silently acknowledge his thanks, and then busied herself with Breathitt as Garridan looked away, everything blurred by his grief and gratitude. He stood for a long minute, eyes squeezed shut, fingers pressed against his eyelids, feeling the weight of the vase in his arms.

Garridan wiped his eyes, collected himself, and carefully stowed the vase and letter in a small pack secured to the saddle. He whispered a good-bye to Darson's horse before a servant led away the last living reminder of Darson's journey to Hesperia.

* * *

The four left the palace with two soldiers to accompany them to the border. Because of their slow pace, it took longer to reach the border.

Arrian spoke little during the trip, spending most of

it clenching his teeth and painstakingly controlling his expression. When they stopped to rest at the border, Arrian took medicine for the pain and Garridan had a chance to stretch and rest his throbbing leg. Anann spoke only to her horse, content to ignore everyone. Nevada excused herself for a long while and came back pale and wracked by tremors.

The commanders fared better in the hills of Miranda's jungle, where the terrain forced them to slow down. Their preoccupation with their own illnesses gave Garridan ample opportunity to study them. He had assumed there was a close relationship between them when he first saw them in Hesperia, and their hours on the jungle paths reinforced the notion. He was almost envious of the support they had in one another; a support he was painfully aware he lacked.

Miranda's humidity and jungle pressed in on them late in the afternoon. Hours into the thick forest, thunder rumbled in the distance and they quickened their pace. Clouds darkened the hills and valleys, creeping closer to the rainforest as they entered the last half of the trip. Nevada, unwilling to travel in a downpour, pushed them to move as quickly as they could handle and as the jungle would allow. She was attentive to Arrian's condition and preoccupied enough with him and the impending weather that she barely spoke to Garridan or Anann.

He could feel an end coming. The loss of a fledgling connection.

But at this point, it paled in comparison to what he had already lost.

Chapter 26

A bottle holding a few scant inches of rice wine stood between two seated figures. Dacian's goblet sat empty next to a plate of crumbs as he stared out at the forest canopy. Clouds gathered in the southwest, piling on top of one another and gradually stealing the remaining light. The long balcony off the third floor dining area contained chairs, but Liana and Dacian sat on the wide, flat surface of the balcony's railing, feet dangling.

Liana swung her bare feet and stared pensively out at the jungle. Her vision zeroed in on the movement of every rodent, monkey, and snake creeping through the trees. She played with the thin gold chain around her neck. A half-full wine goblet and a berry tart sat next to her. They faced the front courtyard of the palace, and she watched it empty as faeries headed indoors in anticipation of the storm.

The pair anticipated something entirely different.

It had been four days too long.

Four days, and no word of Nevada's whereabouts.

Word from Hesperia, certainly; the country had requested aid for attacks on a scale that could very well rival the horror that had befallen Deimos. This had not been confirmed, naturally; but Liana's instincts told her otherwise. Aaclyde sent troops, and the rest of them were left waiting, forbidden to leave, terror in their hearts as they anticipated the death toll. The damage. Anann was accounted for; Arrian still lived.

Not a word on Nevada, or Captain Garridan, or Lieutenant Darson.

It made Liana sick to her stomach.

In the past, four years could lapse before Liana saw Nevada, sometimes longer—even a decade or more. Despite the dangerous nature of Nevada's chosen path, Liana seldom worried, confident in her friend's extraordinary abilities and unshakeable nature. A period of silence was hardly noteworthy.

Until five years ago.

Nevada disappeared then, for three days.

When they found her, she was not the same. She had not been the same since.

Liana's anxiety levels climbed with the mounting storm, though her hands were steady, her composure a matter of habit. She did not think she was overreacting when she assumed the worst in this scenario, not with so little information. Days of silence had meant catastrophe for Deimos. And now, each passing day of more nothing, more silence, as it had been when Nevada was missing before, filled a little eternity.

The parallel affected Dacian, as well. Perhaps that was why she gravitated toward him, and vice versa. Not one other faerie in the palace understood the magnitude of these long days. It hurt to think of Arrian, too. Alive, but in what condition? And what of Garridan and Darson? They were so much more fragile; anything could have happened to them.

Liana picked up her goblet and drank.

Neither she nor Dacian had spoken since they left the claustrophobic meeting where Aaclyde informed everyone of her decision to send another small troop to find their missing conference members. The suspicions, the relentless reminders of Deimos, and the palpable fear—even from the humans—had become too much. Emilia's nonchalance about the entire business, an air put on partly to appease the humans and keep them calm, grated horribly.

Liana was well versed in the art of politics, but even she needed a break from the forced decorum now and again. And she drew more relief from brooding on the balcony with Dacian than driving herself into a panic alone in her room. Alone, she would be drowning in her own suspicions and letting the fear play into her theories, fueling them and driving her obsession.

She could not fall into that trap. Not until she knew Nevada was safe. Not until she had more concrete answers. Her research was best left alone, tucked away in her suite.

But Dacian would understand, even if she had no intention of telling him what she thought could be going on with these vicious, elaborate attacks. Liana took comfort in the stiff set of his broad shoulders. It made her feel less alone in her assumption that all was not right, less preposterous for the conclusions her research forced her to draw.

One could trust so very few these days.

She felt Dacian looking at her, and knew he watched her smooth her finger over the blue pendant. *He will bring up Eyad,* she thought. *He cannot help it. His hatred of that wizard far surpasses Nevada's.*

"I have not seen *him* in over a day."

"He has been spending a lot of time with the mortals," she answered lightly. "Reassuring them while they wait."

"He has more than one way of reassuring everyone."

Liana looked down at the pretty blue gem unhappily. "He will not. Or cannot."

"Semantics do not change the outcome."

She glanced at him out of the corner of her eye.

He raised an eyebrow. "You and I both know it is true. What is the harm in checking?"

Liana's chest tightened. "His limitations are … strange. Whatever rules he has, he cannot bend them." Rules that, during all those years, he had never explained to her or Nevada; teleportation was still a talent of his that neither of them understood the mechanics of.

"Well, of course," Dacian said bitterly. "He refused five years ago, why would he possibly care to investigate Nevada's well-being now?"

The reminder cut something in Liana's heart open. The old wound began to bleed again, as it had not done since the last time Liana had pleaded. *Make sure she is all right, tell me if she is alive, find her, please find her.* And he had rejected her pleas. Eyad, the one who had all but raised them both, had ignored her. "We have to remember there is a reason for it," she said distantly. "It is not because he cares any less."

"How often do you have to keep telling yourself that?" Dacian's maroon eyes narrowed at her.

Her hand fell from the necklace. "Stop."

"I—"

"The situation is more complicated than you realize," Liana said, cooling her tone. "I did not come out here to discuss him."

Uncomfortable silence settled on the balcony. Thunder rumbled in the empty air. Dacian drummed his fingers on the railing but said nothing. She felt his stare again, and turned to reciprocate, raising her eyebrows in a silent question. Something in his face relaxed her posture, and as quickly as the space between them grew uneasy, it drifted back to a comfortable, shared gloom.

Did he not think it frustrated her, too? That it did not make her feel angry, helpless, and cast aside? Eyad's preoccupation with the mortals, his distance from her these past few days, only added to her irritation at their inability to do anything. Emilia had tied their hands until Anann returned, or until Aaclyde's troops sent back information. A part of her wanted to ignore every order and leave the palace for Hesperia. She could find Nevada herself; Liana, Dacian, and Arrian had found her without help the last time.

A tickle on the back of Liana's neck alerted her to the air stirring behind them; a disturbance filled the balcony at the presence of another being. The pendant warmed against her skin, and then cooled when the transition completed. The change was so subtle Dacian had not yet felt him, but Liana was used to the comings and goings of a Craft member.

Not for the first time, she wondered if he knew when they spoke of him.

She turned her head as Eyad's robes fluttered in the breeze, and Dacian first stiffened and then did the same.

"Why are you here?" Dacian asked. Liana detected a hint of disgust in his voice.

"It has been a trying four days." Eyad looked more tired than Liana had seen him in ages. A part of her was pleased to see it.

"Yes, it has." Dacian looked expectantly and unkindly at the sorcerer.

Eyad sat down on one of the stone benches. Liana watched him, as it was the first real sight of him after three days. He could not hold her gaze for long. A sudden gust of wind whirled around them, whipping through their hair. The smell of rain saturated the air; a flash of lightning and a loud clap of thunder startled cries out of whoever sat on the balcony below theirs. She realized Eyad had been avoiding her.

"They could get caught in the storm," she said softly.

The older man's gray eyes looked as dreary as the sky. "And it would be a tribulation they could triumph through. As I have seen you both triumph over many things without assistance."

Fury boiled into a sudden storm inside her. "Do not give me a generic, placating response to a simple request," she snapped. "I am not a politician you need to appease. Talk to me like I am the surrogate child you claim me to be, and tell me the truth."

"Liana." Eyad's voice was sad, and kind. "You know I—"

"Cannot be bothered to even tell us if she is alive?" Dacian cut in. "We have gone through this before. If you have nothing substantial to give us, then you can return to the humans you have spent all your time with. Why did you come out here?" Without giving the sorcerer a chance to answer, he gestured to Liana. "To ask for her continued understanding? Her patience, her *forgiveness?*"

Ire sparked in Eyad's eyes, and Liana could not immediately respond to Dacian's passionate words. The past and present flooded her in a heated rush.

A commotion in the courtyard kept her from doing more than meeting Eyad's gaze as the sound of horses' hooves struck the stone below.

Suddenly, Dacian's hands came down on her shoulders, and he was pulling her off the balcony ledge and to her feet.

"She has returned."

* * *

The few faeries still remaining in the courtyard stared at the group as they dismounted. Joyful, relieved staff rushed from the stables to receive the horses, and two servants dashed toward the palace to alert the queen. Arrian would not have made it up the stairs without leaning on Garridan, and Nevada took his other side. The exertion after such a long journey made her muscles quiver and her stomach clench. Arrian shrugged them off when they reached the dais, determined to walk in of his own volition.

The doors were thrown open, and as the storm broke behind them, Nevada entered the palace with Garridan on her right and Arrian and Anann just behind them. She watched Dacian run across the expansive floor with Liana a step behind him. Her body remembered its fading aches and pains more when Dacian smothered her in a tight, crushing hug. The flood of emotion did not hit her until his smell wrapped snugly around her, like home.

Nevada had barely squeezed Dacian to her before he pushed her back and framed her face with his hands. She watched him register all of the healing cuts on her face and neck, the raised, angry sore on her brow. "You were in combat."

"We ran into fighting." Nevada started to babble, picking up speed as she continued. "Mauvahs ran wild; the number of Erepos might have been something Arrian's soldiers could handle, but they all just kept coming. It was a disaster." Her voice trembled. "So many died. I could not help them all. It was overwhelming."

Dacian's grip was so firm he nearly shook her. "Do not leave again without telling me. Or someone. You know better. You *know* better."

She nodded automatically. Her throat hurt at the tears welling in his eyes and the faint tremor in his tone. "I did not mean to—"

"Shh." He kissed her forehead roughly and leaned his head against hers. She reached up and wrapped her hands around his forearms, feeling the awful tension in them. "Thank you for coming back to me again," he whispered.

Nevada squeezed her eyes shut. Distantly, she heard Liana murmuring to Arrian, and then Arrian's deep voice, softly requesting to speak with Liana later, in private.

Dacian let Nevada go, and she watched him swipe at his eyes and look at the disheveled, bandaged Arrian. "It looks like you finally learned your limitations," Dacian said.

Arrian laughed humorlessly. As the two commanders embraced, Liana hugged Nevada, tears streaming down her face. Nevada burrowed her nose in Liana's dark blonde tresses, and her whole body sighed with contentment at having her lifelong friend in her arms. "I am so glad to see you," Liana said, her breath hitching.

"And I you," Nevada whispered, as Liana's hand moved up and down her back. Over the princess's shoulder, she saw Garridan, alone, off to the side, watching the far end of the hall.

As Nevada released Liana, she caught sight of Queen Emilia and Princess Aaclyde coming toward them from the throne room. Aaclyde's relieved expression turned to one of mild shock at their appearances. She turned to a servant, murmured a few words, and sent him off, no doubt to summon the mortals.

The queen had not yet reacted, her features frozen like a beautiful porcelain statue. Then Nevada saw a flash of something—irritation? Sadness?

Princess Aaclyde's voice broke through the reunion. "Princess, Commanders; we are relieved to see you alive and well. Did any of you encounter my troops?"

"Yes," Anann said. "They arrived two days ago."

"Why did we not receive word?"

Anann flushed and began to offer excuses related to the chaos of the aftermath. Nevada's attention was divided between her words and the queen's expression, which had grown cloudy.

"Where is the other mortal?" Queen Emilia asked with a deadly calm.

"Lieutenant Darson gave his life assisting my soldiers," Arrian said after a brief glance at Garridan. Liana gasped, her hand flying to her mouth.

"Both he and Captain Garridan were assets during the attack," Nevada added. She glanced at Liana, who appeared to notice Darson's absence for the first time. The sorrow in her eyes bruised Nevada's heart anew.

Emilia was silent for a moment. "I am very sorry to hear that," she said slowly. "I believe answers are in order. We must know exactly what transpired in Hesperia."

"That is the reason why I made this journey," Arrian stated as he stared at the queen. "I am afraid my knowledge is also limited; this seemed to be the best way to remedy that."

"Of course," Aaclyde agreed. "My healers will tend to you all, and you may bathe and change before—"

"No," the queen said coolly. "Fetch the princesses; we must talk of this now. There are far too many unanswered questions. King Edric will want answers."

As do we, Nevada thought.

Aaclyde was frowning thoughtfully at the queen. "Emilia, I think we can let them clean up and then gather afterward. They appear to have had a difficult journey. Does that sound reasonable?"

Emilia's presence seemed to swell at being challenged. The entire group held their breath as her blue eyes held the promise of retribution. Dacian glared in the sovereign's direction; Liana looked surprised that Emilia would consider denying such a request.

Before the queen could speak, King Edric appeared with the advisors, Mourin, and Eyad. Nevada and Garridan glanced at one another as they each steeled themselves for what was to come.

Chapter 27

Nevada felt like she was suffocating.

The room had lapsed into silence, but the air was heavy with confusion, anger, and grief. Her stomach twisted, the nausea rolling as angrily as the storm outside. She wanted to excuse herself to be sick, but she did not want Garridan to face the accusing looks and wrath by himself. He needed someone who could corroborate his story and share some of the blame.

Garridan sat across the table from Nevada. Every time she looked at the captain, she felt King Edric's gaze pierce her. Disbelief and anger sparked in the monarch's eyes. Tiberius sweated and dabbed his flushed face with a small cloth, his mouth set in a bitter line. Kiryk was on his second goblet of wine; Mourin was a pale ghost next to him, looking toward the door to avoid any one person's gaze.

Nevada did not know how it happened, but Liana had been separated from her and sat farther down the table. It hurt to look at the princess try to process Darson's death quietly. Her face was composed, but her eyes were grave and sharp. Her gaze always came back to Nevada, as if reassuring herself Nevada was still there. She occasionally leaned in to murmur something to Rees; the younger monarch's expression was pinched and pallid.

Eyad commanded the room, and the novelty of it would have amused Nevada if she were not so tired of his entire existence.

He had not once glanced at her, nor had he greeted her in the foyer earlier.

"I am aware that everyone wants answers," Eyad said to the silent occupants of the room. "We will have them if we maintain order. One person at a time will speak; please wait until the speaker has finished before addressing the room or the individual. Let us clear the air, arrive at an understanding of the events, and move on from there. King Edric, I know you have questions."

"*We* have questions," Princess Tatyana snapped. "What of our people in Hesperia? How extensive is the damage?"

"In due time," Princess Aaclyde said with a reprimand in her voice. Her wings fluttered with agitation. "Aid has been dispatched, and Commander Arrian assured me earlier that the situation is under control. But the attack on Hesperia is not the purpose of this meeting; now, we are here to discuss the captain and lieutenant's involvement." After a satisfactory amount of nods from those in the room, Aaclyde said smoothly, "King Edric, you may ask your questions."

"I wish to know," the king began, his voice trembling, "how it is that the lieutenant of my royal guard died on these *secure* fae lands? We came here under the impression that you were protected—"

"Do we blame *you* for the dilapidated state of your Erepo-infested kingdom?" Dacian lashed out. Nevada felt uncomfortable, and her stomach pains worsened. She desperately wished for a cool bath or a damp towel.

After a chilly pause, Edric repeated his question. "I would like to know how my lieutenant and my captain ended up in battle."

"A question that will be answered if we trace their steps, my king." Emilia's smooth voice made Nevada inwardly cringe. The queen's stoic expression worsened Nevada's nausea. Something in her posture and her eyes—glassy blue, like a mirror surface with no depth—made her anxious. Her words did not match her stilted, rigid demeanor. Out of the corner of her eye, Nevada watched Dahlia look away from the queen uneasily and rub her arms as if she were cold.

"Anann."

The Hesperian princess looked positively terrified at the attention. In a rare moment of solidarity, Nevada could not blame her. Every eye in the room fixated on the princess.

"Yes, Your Majesty?"

"Explain to the room why you chose to leave when I explicitly told you to remain in Miranda until the morning."

The princess flushed. "The message about Arrian held so little concrete information, Your Majesty, that I felt compelled to see what had occurred. I did not intend to disobey you—"

"How else would you describe your actions?"

Anann fell silent. As she hesitated, thunder rumbled outside the palace walls. Nevada knew she was wringing her hands underneath the table from movements of her arms and shoulders. When the princess's words came, they were defensive. "My commander was injured. I will admit, Your Majesty, that I panicked and reacted rashly."

"Rashly enough to take the time to choose an escort, one you were sure would indulge your whim because of the injured party?"

Nevada straightened in her chair. Next to her, Arrian radiated displeasure at the queen's choice of words. Emilia turned to her. "Commander Nevada, why did you allow her to do this?"

"I followed protocol—it was a command, not a request," Nevada replied. She ignored Anann's burning stare. I will not shelter you, Nevada thought angrily. "Truth be told, Your Majesty, the task seemed negligible and quick. The information the princess gave me indicated Commander Arrian's injured status and that the situation was under control. I did not agree with the impulsivity of her departure, but not to the extent that I would have roused the royal quarters. It was not wise, but the hour and the princess's distress made me more compliant."

Nevada was proud of herself for piecing together a coherent explanation for her actions despite the cramping of her abdomen. Sweat gathered at her temples, and she hoped her illness did not show as she endured Emilia's penetrating stare. She could feel Dacian looking at her as well, and did could not decide whose scrutiny was worse.

The queen asked, "Why did you allow Captain Garridan and Lieutenant Darson to accompany you out of Miranda?"

Allow? Garridan shifted uncomfortably at Emilia's wording. He should be defending his own actions, not Nevada.

Bracing himself, he spoke before Nevada could. "I *insisted* that we accompany her and Princess Anann to Hesperia. I was searching for Lieutenant Darson after the celebration, and I came across Commander Nevada as she was leaving the palace." Garridan looked over at Mourin and met the soldier's grief-stricken gaze. More than any other person in the room besides the king, Garridan wanted Mourin to understand the reason for his actions. "I have learned through my time as a soldier that there are few safe places left, and I could not, in good conscience, walk away while they traveled in the dark across country borders."

He felt helpless as they stared at him. Dacian's expression was severe; his princess's face was stony; Princess Dahlia looked ill at ease. He focused on Nevada, who looked pained *for* him. How to explain it to them any better? "They were leaving quickly. Lieutenant Darson and I did not have time to formally announce our departure. It was either leave then, with them, or remain, and the thought of anything befalling them on their journey because I did not follow my instincts was unacceptable. Lieutenant Darson felt the same." The small lie stuck in Garridan's throat, and he swallowed hard. "Commander Nevada is not the only one responsible for our presence. I am at the helm of my own actions."

"Then we may blame the captain of the royal guard for the death of his lieutenant," Tiberius said flatly.

"Yes," Garridan agreed. He did not know what to say after that. His body was miserable with fatigue, and his stomach rumbled with hunger. His leg felt twice as heavy as normal and bloated with pain. The atmosphere of the room was smothering, and he retreated mentally for a stretch of time, missing entire chunks of questions and accusations.

"Why Darson?"

Garridan winced at Mourin's quiet voice. The soldier looked at his captain with betrayal and grief filling his face. "Why include him?" he asked, his voice thick.

The captain felt two inches tall. "I did not want him to take the risk. He felt—"

"That it was his duty to see to his captain's safety." Nevada's voice was firm as she addressed Mourin. He met her gaze with all the anger of a broken heart. She softened her tone when she said, "Lieutenant Darson performed the duties of his role by accompanying his captain. I would have expected the same from my own second-in-command."

"Did you feel the same when you allowed them to fight?" Aaclyde asked. "As representatives of a neighboring nation, their safety is a great priority; why did you not prevent them from fighting?"

"I have never walked away when Erepos are attacking," Garridan said flatly. "I was not going to walk away then. There was nothing to do but act to save lives. It is what we are trained to do."

"Captain Garridan ordered Lieutenant Darson to leave with the Hesperian soldier to see Princess Anann safely to the palace," Nevada said to King Edric. "He refused to leave his captain. Both of them behaved admirably."

Garridan felt undeserving of the praise. After meeting Nevada's eyes and silently thanking her, he found himself staring across the table at Princess Liana. "We all know the risks we take when we accept positions like these. It should not have happened, but Lieutenant Darson died in battle, doing what mattered to him: protecting others."

The princess from Triton who sat next to Tiberius in the earlier meetings caught Garridan's attention, her eyes—as blue and deep as a mountain lake—filled with genuine sorrow. "May I ask, Captain, how he died? Have we discussed that? Did he suffer?"

"A Mauvah killed him," Nevada answered quietly. "He did not suffer long."

"What is a Mauvah?" the king asked warily.

"Mutations of a wolf ancestor, or so we believe," Liana answered. "They originally migrated to our region from colder northern locations a long time ago."

"None of you have ever seen a Mauvah?" Aaclyde asked King Edric.

"No, never." He looked to his advisors for confirmation, and they shook their heads, baffled.

"As far as I am aware, Your Majesty, Mauvahs have rarely, if ever, traveled to the human kingdoms," Eyad said. "Erepos have laid such a heavy claim to Aliquis and some of the kingdoms farther north over the years that the Mauvahs have not bothered with them."

"What do they look like?"

"They are difficult to describe, Your Majesty. They are the size of horses," Garridan told Edric. "They appear to eat anything in their path, including Erepos."

"Be thankful you know so little of them," Dacian said to Edric, his tone dark.

"I cannot believe this turn of events," Edric said quietly, almost to himself.

"None of us can," Arrian said. "It should not have happened this way." He looked pointedly at Nevada, Garridan, and then Princess Anann. "None of you should have been there. No one here knew what Hesperia was enduring, but they should have. I cannot fathom how a message about my health made it here successfully, yet those concerning the attacks did not. I sent Elsbet north to Miranda and Roth east to Charon; I am willing to accept that neither of them made it to their destinations alive. But I also sent letters by bird. And I was not aware a letter solely addressing my injuries was delivered."

"I already have staff looking into this issue, Commander," Emilia said. "As well as the whereabouts of your missing foot messengers."

When Rees cleared her throat, Nevada looked at her with surprise.

Aaclyde nodded to her. The princess took a deep breath. "Has anyone considered how similar these attacks are to what happened in Deimos?"

A murmured chorus of uncomfortable agreement filled the room. "Deimos had the same communication issues when they were attacked," Tatyana mused.

No. That was not right. Nevada curled her hand into a tight fist beneath the table as her stomach cramped. "Deimos's aviary was destroyed. Hesperia's was not."

"Three days of silence," Tatyana continued. "Did you notice any parallels between Hesperia and Deimos, Commander Nevada? Did their tactics appear to be similar?"

"Do you mean in jungle terrain versus grasslands?" Nevada asked sharply. "I think it is safe to assume their tactics would be different."

"This is a discussion that should occur at a later hour," Emilia admonished.

"When?" Princess Sunara argued. "The similarities are too coincidental. We *must* discuss this. I am sorry for the loss of King Edric's lieutenant, but we must look to our own losses before we shift our focus elsewhere."

"I am also curious, Your Majesty," King Edric said to Queen Emilia. "I have heard Deimos referenced more than once now. May I ask what happened there?"

"Of course," Eyad answered. "Hosts of Erepos infiltrated

the southern and eastern borders of Deimos via the mountain passes, taking many civilians by surprise. By the time additional forces reached the southern villages, many were already burned; the spread of the fire was unusual for a tropical forest, but I believe the area was experiencing a mild draught that season. A few groups of Erepos used the passes to continue north. Deimos's palace lies close to a river, and they swam through and climbed the palace walls. The royal guard did an admirable job defending the palace, but the attacks were continuous, and they breached the walls on the second day of the siege. The surrounding inhabitants were evacuated, but from what I understand, the evacuation was hindered by the alarming number of Erepos and the chaos of survivors from the south traveling north for shelter that did not exist."

Nevada stared at Eyad and saw a stranger. Who was this man, discussing the greatest tragedy she had ever experienced as if he were reciting figures from a history text that held no personal meaning for him? She knew he could have easily obtained this information from any Deimos soldier after the fact, or from someone in Saffron. Everyone knew the details in the months following, when aid poured into Deimos and the whole kingdom struggled to cope with the losses. But his clinical delivery of the details of the attacks disturbed Nevada on a visceral level.

She was there the night they scaled the walls.

Princess Niobe had entrusted Nevada with her children; she had trusted Nevada would take them to safety if the creatures used the trees to drop onto the roof.

She and her soldiers met some of the terrified, weeping villagers, who fled on foot carrying their wounded children.

The screams still haunted her.

Eyad did not look at her or at Rees. Liana had placed a soothing hand on Rees's back as the princess tried to appear brave while unshed tears filled her dark eyes. Liana glared at Eyad with an echo of the rising anger and choking sadness that gripped Nevada. She barely registered the shock and grief on the faces of other princesses, as if they, too, were unnerved by Eyad's rote account of such a deeply delicate subject, like prying open a grave and exposing the rotted remains inside. Arrian was motionless; Dacian vibrated with fury. The muscles in his arms were rigid from his grip on his chair. Nevada placed her hand on his arm, shaking her head. She could not handle a scene. Her insides were already roiling.

Nevada did not hear the rest. She knew Eyad was talking, but his words blended together into unintelligible sounds. All she heard was the hard beating of her heart. She fought off panic and the urge to vomit. She heard Arrian say something in a tight voice. Dacian, unrepentant, glared daggers at the sorcerer. Garridan looked trapped in his own hell, appalled by Eyad's words.

Drowning, Nevada sought out Liana. The princess stared back, her eyes gleaming with the hint of tears. Nevada tried to use the strength of their bond to keep from crumbling, but it was not enough. Liana's gaze shifted to her right, but Nevada did not follow it.

She heard Edric ask about the death of Deimos's monarchs, and Eyad reply.

Torn between the present and the past that never left her, Nevada's attention fragmented. Pain as fresh as an open wound reflected back at her from the eyes of her young princess. How was it that the worst memories were the brightest and the easiest to recall? Her stomach turned, and queasiness rolled through her like a slow-moving wave.

"Nevada."

She closed her eyes and took a deep, shuddering breath as Dacian's voice murmured in her ear. "Do you need to step out?" he asked quietly.

"No," she whispered.

Garridan could not stand the renewed tension in the room. Eyad, the source of it all, sat to Edric's left, looking as if he had no idea the effect his words had on nearly every faerie present. There was a wealth of information Eyad did not share; Garridan had gleaned that much from the faces of the commanders and Princess Rees. What Eyad did say was upsetting enough, yet he did not stop. Garridan found it distasteful. He shifted uncomfortably, watching Nevada's pallid countenance, and all but sagged with relief when Princess Aaclyde cut off Eyad's narration and thanked him.

"The Erepos took considerable measures to reach the palace in Deimos," Edric said slowly. "Could they have attempted the same thing in Hesperia?"

Nevada startled when Arrian placed a hand on the small of her rigid back. She drew her shaking hands into her lap and clasped them together. Dacian unexpectedly covered his hand over hers and gave them a brief squeeze.

Arrian replied, "I cannot imagine how they would even know where to find the palace. It was never conclusively confirmed that they deliberately targeted the palace in Deimos, either."

"Perhaps they took advantage of a momentarily leaderless

country with easy terrain and an absent commander," Kiryk commented. "Commander Arrian was originally supposed to be here for this conference, correct?"

Liana ran her fingers through her hair and pulled the blonde mass off the nape of her clammy neck before she argued, "How could they have known about this meeting?"

"My own people do not know of this meeting," Aaclyde added. "I trust the nature of this meeting was kept secret. Am I correct in assuming this, Your Highnesses?" A murmur of agreement rippled through the room.

"We did not inform any in our kingdom of this conference, either," King Edric said. "No one but my advisors and the soldiers here knew of it."

"To take advantage of an opportunity implies a measure of intelligence," Garridan pointed out. "The Erepos are one shaky step above rabid animals. How could they possibly have any purpose beyond feeding?"

Dacian nodded in Garridan's direction as he sat forward in his chair. "We are discussing Erepos as if they are an intelligent force capable of planning an attack. As if they are sitting in a war room grunting strategy to one another and plotting our deaths. Have we ever established that Erepos possessed the brain power to coordinate tactical maneuvers of any kind?"

"They may have more than basic instinct," Eyad remarked. "Acting against their inclination to feed themselves is quite a feat. But not impossible."

Dacian narrowed his eyes. "There is a considerable gap between instinct and premeditation. What are you saying?"

Liana looked from the commander to the sorcerer. She hesitated, not sure what to do; tempers were high, and the air in the room was dripping with moisture. At first, she said nothing to keep from disturbing the room. But the frustration and annoyance on Dacian's face and the misery on Nevada's pushed out the words. She added, "It begs the question of how they are able to organize themselves to achieve specific ends."

Eyad regarded her as a teacher would a disruptive student. She did not know whether to be pleased at his annoyance, or worried. "Do you see that level of organization frequently enough to justify your suspicion that those creatures possess specific goals?" he asked mildly.

Liana narrowed her eyes at the challenge in his voice. She felt a rush of heat born from indignation and paranoia, but she willed her features to give nothing away. Every individual in the room stared at her, but she kept her attention on Eyad. Did he know? Was he deliberately testing her?

"I would not necessarily say that it is Erepos who have specific goals. I would theorize that perhaps there could be an external force causing them to act in such a manner."

"What sort of external force?" Edric asked suspiciously.

She hesitated. *Tread carefully.* "It is only a theory, based on very little evidence. I know, as does every faerie here, that fae do not have the ability to control Erepos nor play the role of a herder, manipulating the flock to maneuver in a certain way. Neither do humans, or elves. An individual possessing Craft or Craft-like abilities, however..."

All eyes swung to Eyad, but Nevada looked at Liana speculatively. Liana subtly shook her head; she would speak to Nevada later.

Before Eyad could respond, the Queen did, her voice

dripping with disapproval. "Liana, that is quite an accusation to level at Eyad's people."

"Oh, no," Liana disagreed. "It is not an accusation; it is, to me, a logical conclusion." That sounded terrible. Nearly everyone in the room looked between her and Eyad with growing alarm.

"Explain," Emilia ordered.

Liana blanched as Princess Aaclyde gave her a cool stare as well. She hoped they did not interrogate her extensively; she had not meant to present what she had uncovered in such an abrupt fashion.

"I have a decent grasp of what Craft members are capable of," Liana said, mainly for the mortals' benefit. She refused to give them any more than that. "From what I understand, controlling Erepos is well within their repertoire—if they were unscrupulous and immoral, of course. But it is still merely a *theory*," she stressed. "An attempt to understand the startling patterns of late."

"What are you implying?" Aaclyde asked.

Liana's nerves fluttered. She fought the urge to jump at a crack of thunder from the storm. She quelled the urge to comb her fingers through her hair and pull it off of her neck again. It was so *warm*. "Certain members of the Craft have, historically, shown an ability to control the movements of other species that possess lesser intelligence. It…" No, too much, she thought, panicking. Emilia's attention burned into her, and Liana, for reasons she could not untangle, felt a trill of fear in her heart. She could not decipher the look in the queen's eyes.

She barely kept herself from stammering. Liana did not know where to look, so she looked up, toward the honey whorls etched into the chocolate-brown walls. She could feel Nevada looking at her intensely, attempting to work out what Liana was not saying.

Liana recovered with a lie. "I spent a considerable amount of time around Eyad when I was younger, and I gleaned some of this information during that time. It is just an attempt to understand the sudden organization and peculiar movements of Erepos in the past half-century or so. I have been trying to form connections that make sense."

Dacian fixed Eyad with a viperous look. "There is a great deal we do not know about you."

"We have never had the privilege of meeting other Craft members except your predecessor, Eyad," Arrian added. "It invites speculation."

"Your kind can control Erepos?" Tiberius asked the sorcerer dubiously. The other humans looked uneasy, eyeing the older gentleman warily.

"The capacity is there," Eyad admitted. "None of the Craft—at least the good, productive members of our kind—would dare attempt such a nefarious use of our ability. But ... there are others who blatantly disregard our laws and freely break them for selfish reasons. Others who have left our society, either willingly or forced, who might still possess full Craft abilities."

"Others," Aaclyde said flatly. "What *others* do you refer to?"

Eyad hesitated, and Aaclyde pounced. "Now is not the time to protect the sacrosanct ways of your culture, particularly if you suspect someone with your ability is behind these organized Erepo attacks."

"That is not what he said," Emilia stated calmly. "He simply confirmed some of Princess Liana's assumptions concerning their abilities."

"How long have you carried these suspicions?" Edric asked the sorcerer guardedly.

"You must understand, Your Majesty," Eyad answered, "that this type of matter is taken care of within our own community. It is neither a fae nor a human matter."

Garridan wanted to leap across the table and assault the sorcerer for such an ignorant comment. Anger numbed his bodily aches, giving him renewed energy. Countless human beings, torn to pieces or turned, dead faeries, decimated towns. Yet it was not *their* matter?

Princess Sunara echoed his thoughts. "And yet faeries and humans are dying. Eyad, with all due respect, this is a matter that deeply affects all of us."

"I assure you, I will do everything within my power to investigate your theories."

"Where exactly does this leave us?" Dacian asked. "What are we supposed to do while you *investigate*?"

Arrian's jaw clenched, and he leaned forward, bracing his arms on the table. "The only way to prevent more organized attacks on our kingdoms is to discover who is organizing them. We need to be proactive."

"Because as faeries die here," Nevada said, "more Erepos are created in the mortal kingdoms. Soon their kingdoms will have higher Erepo populations than human."

"Precisely," Tiberius snapped. "Our people die not just from Erepo attacks, but from illness and starvation. And here we have a *friend* of the kingdom who has gone from wielder of harmless magic to someone with the power to harness Erepos." He glowered at Eyad. Beneath the veneer of blustering anger Garridan saw a sliver of fear.

"I am not implying it is him," Tiberius continued, "but how can we continue to entrust him with sensitive information if he will not do the same with us?"

Garridan looked from the king's pensive face to Eyad, the latter careworn in a way he had never seen. He felt no sympathy for the sorcerer.

Eyad cleared his throat. "As I stated earlier, I will look into this. For now, there is nothing I can impart to you that will change the current situation. What you can do, in the meantime, to protect one another, is *form this alliance*. Share information, aid each other, and ease one another's losses."

Aaclyde was shaking her head before he finished speaking. "It is never that simple, Eyad. King Edric, I am sorry for the loss of your lieutenant. I truly am. But we have sustained substantial losses of our own, and we must tend to our business before we can offer aid outside of the kingdom."

"Perhaps in a few years we can reconsider this alliance," Emilia added, her face sad as she addressed the king. "This does not mean we will cease communication with one another. It does mean, however, that we simply do not have the resources to offer full military aid, much less begin to reestablish trade routes. I would also ask that we cease idle speculation, allow Eyad to do his job, and focus our energies on the devastation within our borders."

Garridan's heart sank into the pit of his stomach. He looked at Nevada, but her eyes were on the table; her complexion more sallow than he had ever seen it. Arrian looked preoccupied and troubled.

Garridan knew now they would leave with nothing. He would lose what precious little he had gained here, though he had already lost the most valuable thing in his life. Darson's death was slowly choking him.

"King Edric, you will be compensated for the loss of your lieutenant," the queen said.

Compensated. Garridan's hands fisted at his sides. She said it like the king lost a caravan of goods. He saw the same incredulity transform Mourin's face. *Can you turn his ashes into a fully formed person? Can you resurrect the dead? Then there is no compensation that will suffice.*

"We will see to it that you return home safely," she continued. "I will arrange for soldiers to escort you to our borders. We must use what remains of this evening to grieve, and to plan recovery."

"May I say something before we dismiss?" Arrian asked.

The tone in his voice, suspiciously light and empty, made Nevada turn to stare at him. His eyes flashed to hers for just a moment but gave away nothing as he waited for the queen's permission. She could not think past the exhaustion and nausea of her body to fathom what he planned to say.

Emilia pursed her lips, and then nodded tersely.

With a scrape of his chair, Arrian rose slowly from his seat. Nevada fought the urge to steady him as she saw him favoring his injured leg. He braced himself with his hands on the table.

He said, "Communication is worthless if the Erepos are slowly eradicating their species."

Nevada had the pleasure of watching Queen Emilia's face contort.

"If they are denied assistance of any kind, there will be no one to communicate with in a matter of years." Arrian did not look at the mortal king as he spoke; his eyes were on the queen. "What they experience on a regular basis is comparable to what has happened to my country." He paused and took a breath. "Commander Nevada told me of Lieutenant Darson and Captain Garridan's bravery on Hesperia's fields—of the fae lives they saved. They assisted my soldiers without thought of their own well-being. They risked, and lost, their lives to fight for Hesperia, and we should be willing to do the same. *I* am willing to do the same."

Garridan stared at him in astonishment.

"There will never be a time I cannot offer military support to Aliquis after what they have shown me; surely, it cannot be an unacceptable time for anyone else. An alliance is *not* impossible. This is when an alliance is the most appropriate, the most necessary. The Erepos are more aggressive, so *we* need to be more aggressive. We need to maintain a united front. Together."

During the stunned silence, Arrian stared pointedly at Anann.

She stood slowly and then grudgingly added, "Hesperia will lend its support to an alliance."

"Creo also lends its support to the formation of a proper alliance." Liana rose to her feet, giving Arrian and Nevada a small smile.

Nevada met Rees's gaze from across the table, and the princess nodded. They both stood as her high voice chimed in. "Commander Nevada and I would also like to vote in favor of an alliance. We have benefited from the aid of our sister countries; we would like to extend the same courtesy to those in need in Aliquis. We do not have the resources to give at this time, but when we do, we will offer our military aid."

Garridan watched as each princess stood and offered her support to the alliance, some wholeheartedly, some grudgingly when it become apparent that the majority stood in their favor. A beautiful sort of pain seized his chest; abruptly, tears stung his eyes. He wanted so badly for Darson to be here to see this. He glanced to his left, and watched the king cough to hold back his own tears, hiding it by looking away for a long moment.

Queen Emilia surveyed the table, and Garridan thought he saw displeasure in her eyes. "You are all in agreement on this?" she asked evenly.

Princess Aaclyde folded her hands together on the table and studied the room solemnly. "I understand everyone's position. Due to the recent events, and the theories presented today, it appears as if an alliance would be sensible."

"The question of who can spare the soldiers at this time remains," Dacian added. He casually reached around Nevada to grab Commander Arrian's arm, all but forcing him to sit back down. The blond's large frame trembled with the motion, and Nevada followed.

Princess Dahlia hesitantly raised her hand. "I can. Hesperia needs immediate help from the countries around her. I can send soldiers to Aliquis in the meantime."

"Well, King Edric." Queen Emilia smiled slightly. "It appears as if we have reached a unanimous vote for your alliance."

"The only words I have to honor this show of support are thank you." Edric looked to Commander Arrian. "I grieve for your country. And I am devastated to lose an exceptional soldier such as Darson. He paid a heavy price for this hour to come, and I wish I could thank him. I extend thanks to my captain, as well, and I am humbled by everyone's pledges."

"We have much to accomplish in a small amount of time, now that this has been decided," Emilia said. "We will allow the military representatives to retire for the evening after a few more details have been resolved. Princesses and advisors, you will remain: we will devote the rest of the night to determining the terms of the alliance. In light of Hesperia's plight, I am afraid we have no time to lose."

One hour later, the faerie commanders were dismissed, along with Garridan and Mourin. Garridan lingered as Dacian and Nevada helped Arrian out of his chair. He was only feet away from Nevada as the doors opened. He wanted to say something, but the faeries spoke among themselves, and Nevada did not look his way. Dacian positioned himself in the middle to support Nevada and Arrian. Garridan wanted to help, but he did not know if his presence would be welcome. He felt his connection with her snap.

When he and Mourin walked in silence to their quarters, Garridan attempted to speak to the soldier.

Mourin did not look his way or reply.

Garridan felt like he was suffocating.

Chapter 28

The storm continued late into the night as the fae rulers drew up a contract for the alliance. The heavens unleashed sheets of rain in a thundering orchestra. Treetops swayed violently in the wind, wet leaves whipping against glass windowpanes. Lightning illuminated the maelstrom outside in wicked, irregular flashes, jagged bolts hiding in the bellies of clouds as the eerie light filled the night air. Thunder cracked, only to die away in a protesting, distant rumble.

Nevada watched the storm from the safety and comfort of the large bed in Arrian's suite as she squeezed a goose-feather pillow in her arms and cringed at the flashes of light and booming thunder. Though most of her childhood fears had disappeared, this one persisted. The only good it did her now was to distract her from her quaking, empty stomach.

A bowl of untouched broth lay on the bedside table. Arrian offered her some of the rice from his bowl, but Nevada had thrown up before washing up in her quarters and was not eager to eat. She considered requesting a cup of hot tea, but that required movement and effort she did not want to exert.

Arrian was stretched out next to her, his leg propped up on a mound of pillows, echoing the soft heap propping her up in a seated position. He ate slowly from the bowl of food in his lap, eyes unfocused as he stared at the ceiling and ignored the storm in such a complete way that it invoked Nevada's jealousy.

The hours of hard travel combined with the unpleasant meeting had sapped what little strength either of them had left. She ached. Sleep waited in the wings, eager to take the stage and sweep her under for the night. Processing the evening's meeting proved challenging and bothersome for her foggy mind.

She was grateful that Arrian did not appear keen to discuss the meeting, either. Every so often his eyes would darken, but he never voiced his thoughts.

"Did you see your sister while you were at the palace?" Nevada asked.

He hummed a yes. "She stayed for two days. Despite the circumstances, I enjoyed the few hours we had. Her training takes her all over the country, sometimes to Saffron, and our schedules have not allowed for much contact besides letters. I was grateful to Sofus for bringing her."

"*He* brought her? Did she give him a choice?"

Arrian smiled in response.

"Typical."

Nevada saw him looking at her out of the corner of his eye, his lips twitching. She almost continued to tease him, but a wave of nausea gripped her, and she curled to protect her stomach while letting out a slow breath.

"Would you like some tea, Nev?"

She shook her head no. "It will pass." Nevada remained motionless until the nausea and cramping subsided. When it dulled to a low level of discomfort, she sighed and reached carefully for the thin sheet at her feet, pulling it up to her middle. She moved to lie down and curl, facing Arrian, then listened to the steady drum of the rain. It lulled her into the hazy state between sleep and awareness, where reality blurred and memory could slip in like a brownie, cleaning the cobwebs and bringing old experiences up to the light for clarity. She remembered being small, waiting out storms in strange inns and towns, drawing comfort from Liana and the shaded windows that blocked all but the most persistent bolts of light.

Nevada's mind drifted to Garridan, who she knew must be lacking comfort.

Frowning, she replayed the last few minutes of the meeting in her mind's eye and focused on the figure of the captain. The dogged loyalty; the gaunt shadows that haunted his tired face, the sorrow stripping his eyes of all but the palest hue of blue. She had wanted to say something to him, but he had already walked away with his grief-stricken soldier.

She felt as if she had let him down somehow. Or perhaps she was misplacing a sense of guilt as she sat in comfort with a friend, while he no doubt faced the hell wrought from personal choice and circumstance. His hell would follow him home.

A home he would journey to tomorrow.

It was very likely she would never see him again after he left.

The idea was more troubling than she cared to admit, and she tried to banish the thought of tomorrow from her mind. The storm obliged her as thunder splintered the air and Nevada jolted, ripped her from her thoughts.

Arrian chuckled. "After all these years."

"Quiet."

"Why not stay here tonight?"

"Quit making—" her sharp tone faltered when she realized there was no teasing in his voice or face.

"I am not a child," she mumbled.

"I meant only to say that you are not feeling well, and you are comfortable where you are. Stay."

Nevada nodded. She reached for the broth on the table and had a few spoonfuls before the last of the warmth left it. Then she tried to eat a few pieces of roasted vegetables from Arrian's bowl. The decision proved to be a terrible one; she left the bed to use his washroom, afraid of becoming sick again. Once the cramps passed, she felt more stable than she had all day. Nevada returned to the bed and sat upright, turned away from the windows as she listened to Arrian talk idly, murmuring occasionally in response.

The blessed quiet was marred when the door opened. She knew who it was before she opened her eyes; he carried such a powerful presence. Dacian ambled in, wearing looser clothing, his dark hair damp. His expression was thunderous. She held her breath and saw Arrian doing the same. They shared an exasperated, amused look as they waited for Dacian to shatter the silence.

The door clicked shut firmly.

"What is *wrong* with Eyad?"

Arrian dropped his head on his pillow and closed his eyes. Nevada laughed soundlessly.

"I wanted to gag him and drag him out of the room. He spouted half-truths and vague comments that helped no one. Did you hear him in there?"

"I heard him," Arrian murmured. "Did you, Nev?"

Instead of responding, her smile widened as Dacian threw Arrian a foul look before addressing her. "I knew he was a self-serving bastard, but he didn't have to do that to you. It is not his place to air out our business like he did. Not in front of humans. And Emilia *let* him." He stalked over to the bed, the neck of a bottle of liquor tight in his grip. Despite the flurry of energy radiating from him and disturbing the tranquility of the room, Dacian lacked none of his surprising gracefulness, and he sat smoothly on the edge of the bed. He offered the bottle to Nevada, who shook her head to decline.

"Of course it would not matter to Eyad," he said, pausing to take a drink. "He was too busy ensuring his precious alliance went through. No thanks to *you*." Dacian glared at Arrian. "I cannot believe you. Do you realize what you've started?"

"As a matter of fact, I do," Arrian replied.

"*Do* you?" He gestured emphatically with his hands. "She was ready to send them home! Now Eyad can strut around with his satisfied smirk because he obtained what he came for."

"And you think I spoke to please Eyad?"

"Even if you did not, your words did not help." Dacian scowled at the rain outside. "He was infuriating when you were both gone. He spent all of his time with their decrepit king and any questions were met with placations and assumptions that everything was *fine*. How he can live with himself is beyond me."

Nevada did not want to hear about Eyad. Dacian kept ranting, and she tried to let the storm drown him out. Lightning flashed, and her chest tightened. She cursed under her breath when thunder cracked and then rumbled down the windowpanes. Rain drummed angrily on the balcony;

Nevada was sure the gardens in and around the palace must be flooded. It would be hell to ride home.

Nevada found Dacian looking at her expectedly. She raised her eyebrows.

"Have you eaten?" he asked.

"No. I would rather not."

He studied her in that consuming way of his, absorbing every detail of her expression, complexion, her bearing—nothing ever escaped his attention. "You looked terrible during the meeting."

"Thank you," she replied dryly.

"What is wrong with you?" he demanded. "Our supposedly intelligent foes did not have weapons of a certain metal, did they?"

"… No. During the battle…." she sighed.

"She was bitten." Arrian elaborated before she did, and Nevada wanted to kick him in his lame leg. Dacian's head shot up.

"It just grazed me." She gestured to her upper back.

Dacian's lips formed a thin, unhappy line. "Show me."

Reluctantly, she turned to the side and tugged at her shirt collar, exposing the bandage that covered the wound. It was still bruised an ugly purple and sickly yellow around the edges.

"Captain Garridan would have been infected if she had not acted," Arrian said. "You should be proud of her."

Dacian's eyes darkened to a murky red. "I do not care about *Captain Garridan*. I care about you. And the fact that you risked your life for a mortal."

Nevada gave him a black look. "I was not going to watch him get infected after all he did for Hesperia."

"Can you absolutely tell me that the Erepo would not have latched on and ravaged you given the chance, or snapped your neck, or taken you down—"

"No one knows that for certain, Dacian. You will not sit here and make me feel terrible for a decision I do not regret."

"Do you know what feels terrible? Sitting here for three days not knowing how you are or what you are doing, or if you are even alive. *Again*. You disappeared in the middle of the night, just as you did before."

Nevada felt the color drain from her face. She wanted to be indignant—how *dare* he lash out and blame her for a situation out of her control—but a part of her flooded with shame and the guilt that had not left her for a single day over the past five years. She was speechless as she struggled to form a defense against his personal attack.

"Dacian, enough," Arrian said with a quiet forcefulness.

"No," Dacian countered with a shake of his head. "We are at a point where leaving without backup, in any situation, is stupid and foolish. What happened in Hesperia did not just bring up memories for *you*. It is too soon after Deimos to act so bloody blasé about putting yourself in harm's way for humans who do not even matter. In the past five years, Nevada, two of the three countries with the most well-known commanders have suffered massive assaults. Who is left, Nev? *Who?*" Across from him, he gained Arrian's full, unadulterated focus, the commander's eyes narrowing.

Nevada's jaw clenched, and she stared at him. "Dacian—"

"Do you think I liked sitting helpless for a second time? And wondering when it is going to be my country, or when they will try for either of you again?"

Arrian's deep voice cut through the air. "It is never going

to be Acacia."

"A week ago it was never going to be Hesperia," Dacian said, his voice reflecting his exhaustion. He raked a hand through his hair, and his shoulders slumped as the anger slowly leaked out of his bunched muscles. "Our world is changing, and we are not in the times anymore where rash decisions—even the ones I tend to make—are acceptable. We need to adjust our mindsets and our tactics and be diligent. And *you*." Dacian pointed a finger at Arrian. "I *know* you did something you were not supposed to do—probably something heroic and stupid—to get an injury like that."

"Is that what you think?"

Dacian is scared, Nevada realized as Arrian defended his actions. Furiously grasping for anything or anyone to take the blame, any way to relieve the stress and displace the fear. He showed fear so rarely that his ability to *be* scared always took her by surprise. She imagined him waiting for her and not knowing, all over again, his anger and frustration having no one to fault but her and Arrian. She remembered his face when he found her after days of searching in Deimos, his tears of panic and relief.

Now he had nearly lost her again, and he faced the possibility of a major attacked to his country.

She squeezed Dacian's hand, capturing his attention. "I hear you," she said.

"Good." He squeezed her fingers and then drank from the bottle. "No more of this. I was trapped here with every princess in the kingdom and the *queen*, and I will be damned if I am left behind again."

"You did not have to travel ten hours with a wounded leg, I do not want to hear your woeful tale of lounging in Aaclyde's palace with royalty."

Nevada smiled weakly at Arrian's retort, and lost the rest of their conversation as she mulled over the idea of an architect designing the attacks on their kingdom, using Erepos as fodder for aims she could not fathom. Assassinating monarchs. Sabotaging alliances. Dacian was right to be paranoid if what Liana had said turned out to be true. She heard the steady rainfall increase to a dull roar of sound, muting out the rest of the world. It gave her the impression that they were quite alone in this part of the palace, a few feet of stone and glass away from the tempest outside. Broad leaves and branches smacked the walls. She stared out at it moodily.

"Can we discuss tonight's meeting?"

Nevada's gaze swung to Dacian, and then she exchanged a pained glance with Arrian.

Arrian said, "We'd rather—"

"I do not like what I heard tonight. Did you know about the Erepo connection with the Craft, Nev?"

Nevada sighed and sat back, knees up under the sheet. She searched through her long memory, into her childhood, for anything like what Liana had suggested, and found nothing. "Eyad rarely ever disclosed the extent of his abilities with either of us. If he performed magic, he did not explain it. Liana did not learn it from our travels with him." And if Liana was not yet ready to identify her sources, it was an easy enough deception. To this day, the other princesses were mystified by the strange upbringing the two of them had shared.

"I would like to know where she obtained the information, and how long she has been investigating," Arrian said, voicing

Nevada's thoughts. "She has said nothing to you?"

"No. But she wouldn't unless she had verified information and a solid foundation to work from. She was not ready to speak of it tonight."

Although Nevada was not entirely sure Liana *didn't* want to address the possibility of a nefarious external force. Eyad's presence must have been the prompt; here was a Craft member who could confirm or deny her suspicions. But Nevada was hardly surprised that Eyad raised questions more often than he provided answers. Liana gave him chance after chance—when was she going to realize that the Eyad they'd known in their youth was gone?

And something about the mood of the room had made Nevada nervous for Liana. It was more than Emilia and Aaclyde's chilly stares. In their youth, Eyad had been adamant that their exposure to the Craft remained minimal. To this day, neither of them had a clear picture of Craft capabilities beyond what Eyad had shown them. What were members of the Craft really capable of? *What is he hiding?*

Nevada pulled the sheets up to her chest, twisting the material in her fingers. She wished Liana had consulted her before speaking out at the meeting, especially if Liana had put herself in harm's way to obtain the information.

Nevada worried about the unwanted attention Liana could garner because of her probing.

"I will certainly speak with her soon," Nevada murmured.

Lightning bathed half the room in an eerie blue light, and she almost expected the candles to flicker in their sconces.

"Could she be right?" Dacian asked.

"Possibly," Nevada replied after a pause of consideration. "I hardly know anything about the Craft. We met a few other

Craft members when we were young, but they were outliers, or so I thought. Eyad never trusted us with any information regarding his people. We know so little. If Liana has done substantial digging into their culture, it worries me. I was always under the impression the Craft operated like a cult, and his secrecy encouraged distrust. And to be honest," She said with a smile that felt brittle, "I cannot say I trust him anymore, either. I have not for years."

Dacian patted her knee and then reclined against her legs. She lightly scratched the back of his head, her fingers twining through his thick brown hair.

"How could anyone obtain the information they need to help them stage such attacks against our countries?" he asked.

"A traitor?" Arrian suggested.

"Or more than one," Nevada added. "If this Craft member exists, I do not doubt he could manipulate, bribe, or threaten a faerie to get the information."

"We *have* met a few faeries who would sell their child for the right price," Dacian said darkly.

Arrian grunted in agreement.

Could there be a traitor within the walls of Miranda's palace? Nevada shifted uneasily, sifting through her memory, thinking of all the staff and visitors she had come across since her arrival. The possibilities within Aaclyde's home were endless. Or perhaps someone in Hesperia. It had been a long time since there had been a traitor in the kingdom. But a defector of this magnitude was a different beast altogether.

"Now what do we do about it?" Dacian mused.

"First, we learn what Liana has uncovered," Arrian answered. "I would like for us all to meet again, soon, in a different location to have a more in-depth discussion. We are missing a few who need to be aware of this. In the meantime—"

"Hesperia is a priority," Nevada said. "We will get your country stable, and then discuss this to pieces." She wanted to speak with Liana before anyone else had the chance.

The rain fell in waves, slapping the windows and balcony doors and then receding again as the wind whipped it through the air. Dacian's body heat warmed her legs, and she leaned forward to rest her cheek on his shoulder, drawing comfort from his warmth.

Arrian, wearing a thoughtful expression, stared off into nothing, and Nevada asked about his thoughts.

He shook his head, troubled. "I was thinking of Elsbet and Roth. I was not happy with Emilia's vague response about their disappearance. I expected more. And I would also like to see this message about my health that I did not know existed. Perhaps it would be worth it to meet with her privately."

"I have never gotten far with her in private meetings," Dacian said.

"You are brusque," Arrian said mildly. "She has never appreciated it."

"My conduct is fine," Dacian shot back. "If she does not care for me, she can hire someone else."

"I would wait to speak with Emilia," Nevada said, stretching her legs to move Dacian off of them. "I think this alliance upset her. I am not sure she even wanted it. Aaclyde seemed on edge, too. The night I left, she made a comment to me that she would be glad to see the humans gone. The mood was strange tonight. And I just could not read Emilia. She had an odd reaction when we arrived; there was something about her face."

"I noticed that, as well," Arrian said.

Nevada felt uncomfortable discussing Emilia and Aaclyde in the rooms of Aaclyde's palace, although both were holed up in another wing drafting the alliance. The subject of the discussion was disquieting. Despite the noise of the storm drowning out their conversation, any passersby in the hallway could stop to listen.

Nevada's skin prickled and itched. Her gaze drifted to the dark windows, and she stared out into the tempest. The jungle beyond was indiscernible through the heavy rain, but flashes of lightning illuminated a ridge of thrashing treetops in the distance.

"Emilia behaved oddly the entire time you were gone," Dacian said. "Did you know she would not allow outgoing letters?"

"Perhaps she wanted to minimize the rumors until she heard what happened," Arrian said reasonably.

"Liana said something to that effect, too, but it still did not sit well."

Nevada could not pinpoint the source of her agitation, but she focused on the glass door leading to Arrian's balcony. Lightning lit up the dark in rapid succession, and Nevada could see the outline of the balcony and the slim, concrete bars of the balustrade. Something darker than the driving rain blotted out the center of the railing. Pursing her lips, she stared at the spot, trying to identify what broke the line of the railing. Had a limb fallen onto the balcony?

"And I can understand Aaclyde's point of view," Dacian continued. "She could very well be preoccupied with what is occurring in our own borders, as she should be. But then you opened your mouth." Dacian looked at Arrian. "Why the speech? As if you do not have enough to worry about. They were two humans. You let sentimentalism and misplaced gratitude make you hand over soldiers and drag everyone else into it."

"It is not a matter of sentimentality, it is about showing solidarity. Besides, I hardly twisted their arms," Arrian argued. "A good number of the princesses must have already seriously considered the alliance if my words tipped them in the mortals' favor. They just needed a reminder of how beneficial this could be."

She wanted to quiet them both so she could focus. Lightning flashed again, and her body tensed. Yes, the center of the railing was still missing, hidden behind *something*. It did not look like a tree limb; no leaves slapped against the ground, and she could not see any crooked branches sprouting from the limb. The lightning died, and all Nevada could see was their reflection in the glass, the male commanders behind her deep in discussion.

Arrian's words filtered through despite her preoccupation. "And one of *those humans* died defending my people. That may not matter to you, but it matters to me."

Lightning lit up the balcony again, and Nevada leaned forward, bracing a hand on Dacian's shoulder as she fixed her eyes on the railing.

The spot shifted almost imperceptibly. She crawled toward the edge of the bed, as if she were leaving to use the washroom. *Is it an animal?* Large jungle cats jumping on balconies were not unheard of, but Arrian's room was fairly high up for a cat to risk a jump. And it had not paced, or twitched a tail—she would have caught that, no matter how well the animal blended in with the storm.

"You are willing to risk fae lives to repay that favor?"

Arrian scoffed. "Think proactively, Dacian. Divided ..."

The rest of the debate faded into static noise as Nevada slid off the bed and padded over to the glass doors. Her heartbeat was slow but heavy, pumping dread through her veins courtesy of the storm she hated and the peculiar feeling of something not ... quite ... right. Another flare of lightning arced through the sky, and her nerve endings twisted as if struck. No, it was not moving. It was not an animal, either. Her breath hitched as she approached the glass.

The world flared white.

Rain beat down on broad, wide shoulders, and dripped down a thick neck, off long sleeves and dark pants. Frozen in horror, she looked up into a pair of flat, cold eyes.

Staring directly at her.

Nevada gasped, and the world plunged into darkness. Her reflection stared back at her in stark terror. Lightning flashed a second later, burning away the shadows.

The male was closer to the glass.

Chapter 29

Nevada shouted in alarm. As she stumbled back from the doors, expecting the figure to crash through the glass, she heard Arrian bark something in the background.

She retreated too quickly and screamed when her back hit something rock solid. Fingers gripped her arms, and before another scream could bubble to the surface, Dacian moved past her, pushing her back.

"Balcony!" she yelled hoarsely.

Arrian left the bed more smoothly than Nevada thought possible, pulling a serrated knife from underneath the mattress. As Dacian stalked to the doors, Arrian called his name and tossed him the blade. Nevada remained motionless, her heart racing, her insides whipping into a frenzy of cramps.

"Wait," Arrian ordered as Dacian unlocked the door. He doused the lamp on the table to dim the light in the room and reduce the glare on the glass. "Watch the balcony, Dacian," he said as he approached her. "What is out there, Nev?"

"Male," she said, dropping her voice. "Large. Facing us. I did not see his features clearly. Short hair, at least six feet. Burly."

Dacian slid into the long drapes that framed the doors; the material drifted around him. His eyes narrowed as he peered into the blackness outside. Nevada eyed the door's handle, bracing herself for it to open and the intruder to let himself in.

She did not feel like a commander. Caught unaware and unwell, she felt as unprepared as a novice or a child. Her heart thundered as they waited for more lightning; who could it be? How had he scaled the walls in this weather?

A spider-like bolt of lightning crept through the sky. The trio tensed.

The balcony was empty.

"No. I *saw* him," Nevada stressed. "Standing right in the front of the doors."

"Check the balconies above and below," Arrian ordered. "He could be in a corner. *Careful.*"

Dacian opened the door.

A fierce wind blew in, throwing rain into the room as Dacian almost lost control of the door. He slipped out into the storm. Nevada moved to the doorframe, wiping water from her eyes. Her heart thudded an irregular beat as she watched Dacian, soaked through to his skin, search the balcony, his knife glinting in the dark. He jumped onto the balustrade, crouched and peered down, and then disappeared.

"What was the intruder doing?" Arrian asked tersely.

"Watching us," Nevada whispered. "Staring in. As if he were listening, or waiting for the right moment."

Dacian returned, swinging over the railing and landing as neat as a cat on the slick pavement. He looked up toward the balcony above, positioned asymmetrically to the right, clenched the knife between his teeth, crouched, and then sprang up effortlessly. His fingers caught the ledge, and Nevada saw his legs swing once and then disappear. In the breathless moments of his second absence, her fingers curled into fists so tight that her nails dug into the flesh of her palms.

They waited.

Even knowing it was coming, Nevada still gasped when a dark figure dropped from the sky. She shrieked when she backed into Arrian, who gripped her shoulder when Dacian landed in the same crouched position he began in. He rose, shaking his head at them.

Arrian and Nevada moved back into the room as Dacian slammed the door shut behind him and locked it. "Gone," he said, wiping the water out of his eyes. "You are positive?" he demanded of Nevada. A puddle spread on the carpet at his feet.

"Yes." She shook her head, pulling damp hair back from her face. "There was someone out there, I am sure of it. I do not know how long he stood there, but he was *there*."

"I could not smell anything but rain and lightning," he admitted. "They mask everything else."

Arrian nodded. Nevada pulled at her hair again, pressing the heels of her palms in front of her eyes, willing her heart to stop thundering. She could not scrub the image of the intruder out of her head; where had he gone?

"He was there," she repeated.

"Is it out of the realm of possibility that the storm and the stress of the past few days could—" she gave Arrian a withering glare. He held up his hands. "All right. I am not trying to—"

"I have been in stressful situations," she interrupted flatly.

"And I am sure none of them have caused me to hallucinate. Arrian, there was someone on your balcony."

"We're not calling you a liar, Nev," Dacian said. He hesitated and then took another long look outside, his nose to the glass as bolts of lightning lit up the empty balcony a few times. "If you are right, who could it be?"

A memory surfaced in Nevada's mind, breathtaking in its clarity, of a sunny afternoon on a blood-soaked battlefield. Of two mysterious figures in the field; one tall, dark, and menacing, one slighter in stature and blond. Nevada suppressed a shudder. "I do not know," she whispered. "He was menacing. I saw his violent intent."

Dacian gave her a blank look and tucked the knife into the waistband of his wet trousers. His tone was softer when he said, "If he meant harm, he could have broken through that door. Why would he leave? And where would he go?"

"I cannot explain his disappearance. But did we not just discuss the possibility of a traitor or someone having a Craft-like ability to appear and disappear on a whim?" Nevada latched on to the theory with fervor, hoping it would soothe her frayed nerves and justify her panic. Somehow, it was worse to think she saw a figure her overtaxed mind conjured out of thin air versus a credible threat to their safety. "We do not know how long he stood there; perhaps his only goal was to obtain information. To listen."

She hated the way Dacian looked at her. Anger made her throat hurt. "Maybe he could …it is too much of a coincidence, with the three of us in here, and what we were discussing, what I—"

Nevada faltered, and Arrian cocked his head. "What?"

Maybe you are *hallucinating. And not recovered enough from the bite. Did you really see someone on the balcony, or those males on the battlefield?* It was not uncommon for faeries to hallucinate after a vicious bite. And then there were her vivid flashbacks.

She barely checked her frustration. Her hands curled into fists again, and she tried to take deep, measured breaths. "Nothing," she finally said. She took another deep breath because their careful, concerned expressions made her feel unstable.

"Nev," Arrian said, as he went to the bedside table and lit a match to relight the lantern. "We had a terrible week. You experienced a lot of things that brought up bad memories. You are recovering from a bite. Think carefully over what you saw, and if you truly feel someone was outside watching us, then we will bring it to the attention of Aaclyde's palace guards. When the storm is over, Dacian and I can look again."

Exhausted, Nevada rubbed at her face. Her stomach was furious with her. She shut her eyes and replayed the images again, suppressing another shiver as the fear welled fresh. She thought she had seen the shape of a male, but could it have been an animal crouched on the balcony rail? Was the battle so fresh in her mind, the bite's infection still potent enough, to distort the image and make the simple shape of an animal seem like something more sinister? "It could not have been an animal," she mumbled doubtfully. "I know I have…"

She remembered the battlefield, and how the strength of those fits of memory blocked out all reality, cloaked every shred of her present with visceral scenes from the past. For a few moments on that field, she had not been positive which reality was the truth.

She could not trust her own mind then. Could she claim to trust it now? They were three levels up on highly secured palace grounds, in the middle of a storm.

"We are not suggesting you contrived it." Dacian's voice was as soothing as it ever got, and his hand dropped onto her shoulder. "It is just a hell of a thing to see here, especially during a thunderstorm. The palace walls are not easy to scale. And if there *is* someone out there and he tries to get in," he paused and gave them a cold, anticipatory grin, "we will skin him alive. No one is a match for the three of us."

A pacifying answer, Nevada thought resentfully, but she did not have a retort. Both commanders looked calmer, as if she had given them an unnecessary scare and the danger was over, but her blood still ran hot with suspicion, and the glass doors were never far from her attention.

Nevada was unsure of what to do. She did not want to try to convince them she had seen something when she was still unsure. If she continued to insist, Arrian and Dacian would call Aaclyde's guard, risk interrupting the alliance proceedings, and she would spend the evening in the infirmary with healers asking a dozen questions. If she let it go, she would rest in the company of the greatest soldiers in the kingdom—you are one of them, she reminded herself—and then she could reconsider it in the morning.

And even if he had been there, he was long gone now.

Nevada smiled thinly at Arrian and Dacian. "Good point," she said, her tone flat.

"Would you feel more comfortable in your room?" Arrian asked.

She shook her head.

Arrian walked stiffly to an armoire. He took out another

pair of sleepwear for himself and tossed one of his nightshirts in Nevada's direction. She caught it in one hand. "You will feel better out of those damp clothes."

"I will stay awake for a bit, keep a watch." Dacian acted as if he was going to hurl himself onto the bed, and Arrian blocked him with an arm.

"You are soaked. No."

Dacian rolled his eyes and pulled off his shirt. It slapped wetly on the carpet. "I can get naked if—"

"Borrow a pair of pants."

"I assumed Nev could use a distraction."

Nevada smiled and retreated to Arrian's washroom to change. Her insides, still roiling from the excitement, spiked with pain and nausea, and she tried to be quietly sick into an empty chamber pot.

While she sat on the cool tile of the floor and waited for the last wave of nausea to pass, she became distantly aware of the rain slowing. She could hear Arrian and Dacian clearly now, but paid them no attention; at least, until she heard her name.

"Do you believe her?" Dacian asked in a hushed tone.

The stretch of quiet that met his question twisted Nevada's heart.

"You did not see her four days ago." Arrian's lowered voice was grim. "She had a flashback in my room, and admitted to having more than one on the field. She completely loses her sense of reality in the throes of them, and it could get her killed. She cannot be on the field while these flashbacks continue."

Her hands clenched into fists as a new ache in her chest joined the ache in her middle.

"Have they occurred frequently since Deimos?" Dacian asked.

"You would have to ask her. But I would not be surprised if they have."

Nevada wanted to snarl at them even as a humiliated and scared part of her recognized the truth in Arrian's concern.

"She is not over it," Arrian continued. "I want her to receive help."

"She would never take a leave of absence without a fight," Dacian said automatically.

"What would you suggest? If this were one of your soldiers, what would you do?"

"This is not one of my soldiers. This is Nev."

"All the more reason. I cannot stand by and do nothing."

"The only thing you could do is suggest it to her, unless you wanted take it out of her hands completely." Dacian fell silent. Nevada imagined him pacing, conflicted. "I don't know if I can condone that."

"One more flashback at the wrong time and we could lose her. The risk is unacceptable. I am willing to take it to the queen, if need be." Conviction resonated in his voice.

Damn him. Nevada's eyes filled with tears, blurring her view of the washroom and its splashes of blue and gold along the walls. He had *no right* to discuss her problems in such a manner. Their close friendship did not mean he was her *keeper*. She knew she needed help, knew it was a serious issue, but to hear Arrian consider removing her from making decisions concerning her own life scoured her heart.

"If you want to enrage her, by all means," Dacian retorted. "But if you are truly that concerned, suggest the time off. Have her stay with Liana for a few months and see someone while she is there. Deimos may release some of its hold on her if she has a little distance. And leave Emilia out of it."

"However you might feel about Emilia—"

"Has no bearing here. Leave her out of it. It is Nev's business. If she wants us involved to that degree, she will involve us."

"Then it may never happen. She will not ask for help, and we cannot ignore her situation. Now is not the time for a detached approach, Dacian."

Nevada stood up, wiped her eyes, then grabbed a dry cloth and soaked it in the bowl of clean water that sat on a stand. She pressed the cool, damp cloth to her eyes, steeled herself, and went through the archway that separated the wash area from the suite.

Dacian stood not far from the balcony doors. He looked up at her, startled. Arrian stood by the bed, his eyebrows furrowed in consternation.

"I do not disagree," she said coolly. Dacian's gaze shifted away from her. "But I do not wish to talk about it now."

She walked over to the bed and met Arrian's eyes, willing herself to stay angry despite the regret she saw in his face.

"I would not push this if I did not love you as a friend," Arrian said.

Nevada nodded jerkily and let him enfold her in a hug. She heard Dacian sigh as he embraced her from behind and rested his chin on the crown of her head.

"You should not keep this kind of distress to yourself," Dacian said roughly.

"Can we discuss it at a later time?" Nevada pleaded, her voice watery.

"If that is what you wish." Arrian patted her back. "Let us

sleep. The mortals leave in the morning, and I intend to be there. I imagine you would like to be there too, Nev."

She nodded and settled on her side, facing Arrian instead of the balcony doors. After a while, Arrian extinguished the lamp, pitching the room into darkness save for two small candles on either side of the main doorway. True to his word, Dacian kept watch and did no more than sit on the bed, occasionally rising to pace. Nevada heard his whisper-soft foot treads as sleep pulled her under.

* * *

A thin stack of thick parchment, bound by gold thread and open to the last page, sat on a gleaming oval table, ink barely dry on its pages. Fourteen empty lines awaited signatures.

Beyond the glass windows, birds greeted the dawn. Water dripped from boughs of leaves, soaked the ground, and quenched the flowers. Morning burned away the mists left over from the storm. Outside of the room, the palace awoke, but those inside the room had never gone to sleep.

Liana wanted to feel proud of what they had accomplished. The compromising, arguing, and drafting were all part of why she had agreed in the first place; every decision they made had been in the interest of the safety of immortal and mortal lives. It was unprecedented, at least in her lifetime.

But she did not feel the joy such an occasion warranted.

The many of the faces surrounding her did not reflect that joy, either. Her peers were still resplendent in their gowns, but they looked tired around the eyes. Some seemed resigned, even bitter; others were mute with weariness from spreading the care and resources of their countries thinner;

everything balanced precariously on a teetering plate.

Liana feared the plate would fall and shatter.

And none of them had even signed the treaty yet.

Her eyes fell to the pieces of parchment, the agreement drawn up over the night. They had agreed on terms for an alliance in less than twelve hours.

It was far too hasty for her liking.

Queen Emilia and King Edric stood before the parchment holding quill and ink. A few princesses shot the monarchs sullen glares from around the room. They had said they needed more time to draft this agreement. And truly, beneath Emilia's beauty and elegant façade, Liana imagined she could see some of the cracks from last night and displeasure in her chilly demeanor. Aaclyde's face was impassive as Emilia handed the quill to King Edric.

Eyad beamed behind them, as proud as a new father.

Liana did not bother masking her feelings as her skin flushed with anger. She could not allow Eyad to claim this victory; with a push from a commander everyone respected, the humans had done this themselves. And Lieutenant Darson helped them earn it.

King Edric's hand hovered over the parchment. His advisors looked on; the long night had aged them. "Truly this is a thing out of my dreams," murmured the aging king. "If only these pages had not come at so heavy a price."

If only. Her heart ached for the lost lieutenant. It was a rare individual who could make such an impression on her in so short a time, but he had managed it.

Liana swallowed against a tight throat.

Emilia swept her gaze over the room and met Liana's eyes in passing. A part of the princess wanted to shy away from the attention, especially after last night's proceedings.

"From here on and for all of the forthcoming years of your reign, King Edric, the kingdom of Aliquis is friend and ally to us," the queen began. "We will put aside differences born eras ago and unite in the face of an enemy that seeks only to destroy life—to maim, starve, and contaminate us with its poison. No longer will we face forces alone."

Eyad stepped up to the pair and said, "With cooperation, perseverance, and faith, great things can be achieved. Lives will be saved. Perhaps, one day, we will see an end to this enemy."

Liana pressed her lips together in a thin line. She dismissed Eyad's idealistic comments, but she heard a false note in the queen's tone, hidden somewhere among the pretty words. It could have been as simple as impatience with the proceedings and the situation in Hesperia, but Liana did not think that was the case.

"The night was long, and very few in this room have had more than an hour of sleep," the queen said. "Each of you shall receive a copy of the agreement to share with your commanders." As if waiting for her signal, two scribes from the team of scriveners who had also worked tirelessly throughout the night entered, carrying copies of the agreement. Liana murmured a thank you as she took her copy, and then she opened the contract to reread the main points. She heard a few others rustle the pages of the parchments.

Her finger traced over "thirty days," written in Vinculum on the left page and Fae on the right. Liana's commander would draft a report once a month to deliver to King Edric's head marshal that would detail all enemy movement and activity as it pertained to the borders. And any information Aliquis possessed would be delivered to the faerie commanders through Eyad.

Liana's eyes fell on the meticulous text beneath "military assistance."

Those princesses with soldiers to spare will survey their units to find volunteers willing to train human soldiers in Aliquis. The term of training agreed upon is twelve months, with an option for extended stay in increments of six months should the soldier so desire and permission is granted. The soldiers provided shall number in a minimum of two hundred throughout the faerie kingdom.

She glanced at Princess Dahlia, who read her copy with a grave expression quite unlike her usual countenance.

The queen then gestured to a guard at the door, who slipped out. She turned back to the assembly and said, "As we noted last night, Eyad may not always be available to you, Edric. I have a gift for you in the event he is not."

The guard returned with a small, elegant white bird clutching the leather brace on his arm. Its long, sweeping tail bobbed as the guard brought the bird to the queen and king. A small smile flitted across Liana's lips. The sight of a sylph never failed to lighten her heart.

Edric carefully reached out, his fingers barely grazing the soft feathers of the graceful bird's chest. The bird watched him with small, dark eyes. "What wondrous creatures they are," he murmured. "I am humbled by such a treasure, Your Majesty."

"They are very special to us," Emilia said. "She will do us proud. When you have parchments to send, just give them to her and she will bring them directly to me." She then reached down and picked up the quill pen.

The room was quiet as the quill passed from hand to hand, and Liana watched signatures fill each empty line. The writing tool was given to her, and she dipped it in ink. Her hand was steady as she signed, though her heart remained troubled.

The alliance between the mortal and immortal worlds had begun, and Liana could not wait to leave the room.

She escaped to the hall after exchanging niceties with the mortal king and a few words with Rees and Aaclyde, determined to find the nearest dining area to satisfy her growling stomach. Exhaustion dogged her, although it was not from lack of sleep. Her mind was heavy with worry and politics.

As Liana filled her plate with fresh fruit and bread, a head of dark, wavy hair caught her attention.

Captain Garridan sat alone.

Perhaps he wants to be alone, Liana thought dolefully, her heart dropping with sympathy at the sight of him.

Something in his defeated posture drew her to his table, and she rustled her clothing to avoid startling him. He did not look up, though, until she set down her plate.

"Good morning, Captain," Liana said, keeping her voice warm and friendly.

Garridan gave her a smile that did not quite reach his lovely blue eyes. "Good morning, Your Highness."

She refrained from reminding him to call her by her first name, and instead sat down to face him.

"Was an agreement reached?" Garridan asked.

Liana nodded as she took a bite of mango. "The alliance is in place. Your king should be along shortly, I would assume."

Garridan looked skeptical, and Liana remembered the awful scene of the night before; the king's anger and grief warring with Garridan's grief and shame. It struck her that he could very well lose his job over the journey to Hesperia.

Garridan could barely meet Liana's gaze. The searching flicker of her tawny eyes over the quiet dining hall and her expression told him she was trying to piece together his self-inflicted exile. Perhaps she thought his people had deliberately cast him out in preparation for the journey home alone.

It was not far from the truth. Mourin had guarded the hall the entire night rather than stay in the same room as Garridan. Garridan's sleep was fitful and broken, and his body still ached. He felt empty and worn. He was already feeling sorry for himself; he couldn't handle her sympathy on top of it.

Garridan cleared his throat roughly. "Can I ask you a question about the alliance?"

The princess gestured with a piece of green fruit. "You may."

"Realistically, when will the first batch of soldiers make it to Aliquis?"

"Six months from now," Liana answered.

Well, it wasn't ideal. But what did he expect? She must have seen the concern in his face, for she smiled apologetically. "By the time volunteers come forward from Dahlia's country, and the commanders decide on an itinerary, half a year will easily pass. I wish there could be a faster solution."

"I did not mean to sound ungrateful. Any help at all is welcome."

Liana studied him, and he could only meet her penetrating

gaze for so long before averting his eyes. Her voice was soft when she said, "Your actions played a larger role in forming this alliance than you may realize, Garridan."

"No." Her words stung. "That honor belongs to Commander Arrian and L—and Darson. I merely survived."

He didn't look up to gauge her silence. "I am glad he met you," Garridan said to the linen tablecloth.

"I am glad to have met him," came the soft reply.

He sensed her stand. Liana placed her hand on his shoulder, and he composed himself enough to look up and meet her pained expression. "I will leave you to your meal. See you in the courtyard in an hour."

Garridan nodded. He watched her leave, her airy dress the color of tropical vines trailing behind her. In a perfect world, he thought Liana could be a good friend. In that same world, Darson was still alive. But Darson was dead, and Garridan would most likely never see Liana again beyond the courtyard.

He wondered if Nevada would be there so he could see her one last time, too. He doubted it, as sick as she had been the night before.

But … it would be nice to say good-bye.

Chapter 30

Liana did not find Nevada in her room, but she had an idea of where to find the missing commander. After receiving a note concerning another meeting in the afternoon to further discuss Hesperia, she went to Commander Arrian's room. She lifted her hand to knock and then thought better of forcing Arrian to haul himself out of bed, so she quietly opened the door instead.

Sunshine tried to slant in along the edges of the closed drapes, which gave the room a drowsy, warm ambiance. Liana appreciated the peace and quiet for a moment before inspecting the bed's occupants.

Dacian was there, too.

Should not be a shock, she mused. The three were so close and saw one another so seldom.

Arrian lay closest to the door and flat on his back, sleeping so deeply she grew tired just watching him. Dacian was sprawled out on the other side, sheets tangled in his legs. He slept on his stomach, arms stretched and slipped under the pillow; his trousers were pulled low and exposed the smooth curve at the small of his back. Liana took a moment to admire him before seeking out Nevada, who was curled up in a ball between the two.

Her wild, wavy hair obscured her face. She appeared to be wearing a male's shirt. Liana cautiously approached on Dacian's side to sit on the edge of the bed. She knew the moment he awoke; the muscles in his upper back tensed, and she saw the pillow move; his fingers were no doubt curling around a weapon. She quickly whispered, "Dacian, it is Liana."

He raised himself up, elbows digging into the mattress, and turned to stare drowsily at her.

"Rough night?" she asked, only half teasing. She looked over Nevada.

He snorted, yawned, and dragged a hand through his sleep-mussed hair. "Something like that." His voice was a little hoarse. He sat up and let his feet fall to the floor. He stared at the curtains that concealed the balcony doors. "She did not sleep very well."

"Poor love."

"Poor *me*. She flops around like a fish when she sleeps badly. Backhanded me in the face earlier."

Liana failed to swallow a laugh. She crawled onto the bed to get closer to Nevada. The movement disturbed Arrian, and his glassy, dark-green eyes opened and focused on her.

"So the alliance is in place," Dacian said neutrally.

She hummed in agreement. "I cannot yet say how I feel about it. I am pleased we can help them, but…." she sighed, reached over, and smoothed back some of Nevada's hair, exposing a face that was exhausted, even in sleep. "Maybe my mood is affected by what happened to Hesperia. I do not feel particularly joyful."

"It bothered you," Dacian observed. "About the human."

"Darson," Arrian corrected, voice thick and raspy with

sleep. He looked at Liana curiously.

Her fingers stroked Nevada's wavy hair as she slept. "Of course it did. It was an absolute tragedy. Humans are so easily broken. The reminder was harsh."

"Did we miss the humans' departure?" Arrian asked.

"No," she replied. "They leave within the hour."

Dacian's eyebrows rose.

"I thought it was quite early, too," Liana confessed. "But Emilia appeared adamant that they leave with plenty of daylight, and Edric voiced concern over his continued absence from Aliquis. We have a meeting this afternoon about Hesperia; that could have hastened their departure, as well." She handed the note she received to Dacian, who opened it, read it, and then promptly crumpled it up and tossed it across the room.

She wished the entire mess could be crumpled into a ball and flung into oblivion just as easily.

Nevada felt the soft fingers in her hair before she registered Liana's voice. Opening her eyes took a ridiculous amount of effort. She took in the blurry sight of long, blonde hair, golden skin, and a cool green dress, and could not muster more than a noise as a greeting.

Liana patted her cheek. "Darling, the human party is leaving within the hour. Do you want to be there?"

No. Yes. Nevada looked at Arrian; he was nodding his head. She parroted the motion.

"Do you need help getting ready?"

I need help with a great many things. Nevada dragged herself into a seated position, her body absolutely crying out for more sleep. Her eyes swung to the balcony doors, and she found the curtains drawn, sunlight peeking through. Liana's words slowly sank in, and Nevada did not know how to describe the feeling that coursed through her. Her eyes met Liana's. She could feel both commanders staring at her, too, and she wanted to leave the room to escape their probing looks.

Arrian left the bed like an old, feeble human, upsetting the mattress. "I do not intend to miss the departure." The unspoken *and none of you will either* registered loud and clear, for even Dacian sighed and stood. Nevada followed suit.

* * *

She felt worn and wrung out, like a discarded dishrag, as they walked to the courtyard, though her stomach had calmed somewhat. Nevada wore the same clothes as yesterday. She had washed her face and could have purred like a kitten while Liana combed through her hair and braided a few sections. Nevada did not say a word to her about what had transpired the night before; she wasn't ready to have another person look at her as if she were crazy.

"How did the alliance talks go?" she asked Liana.

The princess's sigh spoke volumes. "Quickly," she said. "It feels … imperfect. I am not sure if I can even articulate why it bothers me so. I am curious to hear your opinion when you receive your copy of the contract."

Nevada could not help asking, "How were Emilia and Aaclyde?"

"Resigned, I think. Aaclyde drove a hard line concerning service restrictions and the accommodations of the soldiers, which everyone appreciated. I believe she will be far more hands-on with future arrangements than Emilia, but who knows. The queen is a maze of mirrors to me." Liana's voice lowered when they reached the grand foyer, though it was not low enough to escape the attention of Arrian and Dacian. Nevada suspected it was not the commanders that Liana intended to exclude. "If you could spare an hour before I leave—I will be heading out late this evening—I would greatly appreciate it. We need to have a long overdue conversation concerning Eyad's people."

"Not here," Nevada said sharply. Liana raised an eyebrow. "Here would not be private enough. Can we arrange a visit elsewhere?"

"Of course," Liana said slowly.

Now we both have secrets to divulge later.

Humidity slapped Nevada in the face when the palace doors opened. The bright sun pierced through her skull like a lance as she took in the harsh daylight.

Emilia already stood at the bottom of the steps with Aaclyde and a small number of princesses. Apart from them and the human party, the courtyard was quiet and scarcely populated. Sunlight played through the dwindling mists that hovered over the ponds; every so often, colorful birds flapped overhead.

The queen was speaking to King Edric when the commanders and Liana approached the princesses and the three soldiers who stood by their horses; Nevada had forgotten about the escort Emilia had promised the king. One of the soldiers stood at attention by a tan mare, and his raven-black hair and bronze skin were a striking contrast.

She *knew* that hair.

"Is that Talan?" Liana breathed in her ear. "Why is he one of the escorts?"

"I was wondering the same," Nevada whispered back.

With the position he held in Aaclyde's military, it was a peculiar assignment to give him, one more suited for a rank he had passed ages ago. Aaclyde did task him with watching the mortals at the party; she may have wanted him to see the mission through properly. Nevada frowned at her own theory, but she smoothed her expression when Talan looked her way and nodded.

She heard Emilia say the king's name; her voice floated across the space between them. "Our talks did not go as smoothly as anticipated, for reasons we could not have foreseen."

Dacian looked ready to comment, but he pursed his lips when Arrian gave him a pointed look.

Eyad clapped a hand on the king's shoulder. The sorcerer looked so pleased that Nevada's anger was roused. "Lieutenant Darson proved an alliance is an attainable goal, realized by a helpful heart and a willingness to act for the greater good. On this momentous occasion, where the futures of two cultures merge and intertwine, his contribution will resonate throughout the length of this new endeavor."

Nevada felt Liana's posture stiffen; her eyes sparked with annoyance at Eyad's ingratiating words. Dacian growled under his breath like a prodded hound. Arrian pressed his lips together in what Nevada knew was disapproval, but his face remained impassive. Nevada could barely stand to hear them reduce Darson's death to a symbol of the alliance, a grand display for the cause dazzled with pretty words. It stripped him of his identity.

She looked for Garridan, thinking of him and how those words might have sounded to him.

* * *

Garridan could not listen to Eyad speak any longer. *Congrat-ulations*, he thought bitterly. *You got far more than you could hope for from Darson. He put this alliance on a platter for you.*

He heard his king respond, acknowledging his pride in Darson and grief at his loss. Then he thanked the faeries for their hospitality. Garridan let the trite comments fall away from his ears as the humidity grew worse and he strived desperately to keep his thoughts as light as possible.

His eyes continually strayed to the wooden urn secured to the king's horse.

"We'll have a hard time breaking this to everyone," Kiryk murmured to Tiberius.

"We could keep our *guests* restricted to military areas only," Tiberius suggested.

"People will find out," Kiryk said confidently. "Can't hide close to three hundred fae spread around the kingdom. It would be only a matter of time. Besides, citizens will have something to talk about besides Erepos for a little while. We can work that in our favor."

"It won't bother them?" Mourin's quiet voice garnered everyone's attention. Garridan was surprised to hear him speak. The soldier's gaze remained on his horse, and his fingers lightly played with the gelding's mane. "Darson died here, and we're welcoming the faeries in our cities with open arms. People won't understand how they can help us. I certainly don't understand," he finished with a mumble.

"It wasn't faeries that got him killed," Tiberius said.

Garridan's jaw clenched. Kiryk glanced at him with a spark of empathy in his eyes. The advisor ignored Tiberius and said, "Don't underestimate simple curiosity, Mourin. We mortals can't help ourselves."

The ache in Garridan's throat was back, and the courtyard became a blur of vivid colors and people and faeries whose names escaped him. He spotted wavy black hair and a familiar uniform, and his relief was so great he sighed a little. Nevada looked as tired and worn as he felt. Dacian and Arrian stood behind her, and Princess Liana was to her left. Garridan turned his attention back to Eyad's speech.

"The road to change is a long one, wrought with obstacles, unexpected twists in the path, and stops and starts. This is the most promising change to come about in centuries. With trust, hope, and unity, we can alter the face of our future and make it a brighter one for both civilizations. Congratulations to all of you on the beginning of a long, promising journey."

A smattering of applause rippled through the gathering. Nevada's smile was more of a grimace and not much better than the faint, distant smile Emilia gave the mortal king. She had seen the queen deliver warmer smiles to emissaries she barely tolerated.

Dacian groaned when a servant began passing out glasses of wine, and he waved off the male with a flick of his hand. "I have heard enough of him to last me a lifetime. I am going back to bed."

"Yours or mine?" Arrian laughed at Dacian's expression.

Nevada looked at Dacian meaningfully, and he sighed a little and nodded, understanding she wanted him to check the balcony.

As he left, Arrian called, "Do not forget the meeting at three."

"What meeting?" Nevada asked.

Liana told her about the note she had received. "I am going to sleep for a few hours first," she said. "After I bid them farewell."

She murmured an agreement as Liana walked toward the human party. Nevada caught sight of Garridan across the courtyard. "I should say good-bye, as well," she said, almost to herself.

She felt a faint pressure as Arrian placed his hand on the back of her arm. "I will go with you. We will say good-bye and then meet with Dacian."

As Edric and Eyad mounted their horses, Garridan looked to the palace steps, silently willing Nevada to draw near. He did not know if he could step away for a moment. The trio of fac escorts approached, and he was certain that walking away would not be appropriate. He realized with a start that one of the escorts was the bartender from the party.

Darson had picked up on the nuances that identified him as a soldier. Seeing the proof of Darson's theory astonished Garridan with a sharp sting of pain.

"Hello again, Captain."

Garridan pulled a smile from a deep reserve of willpower as Princess Liana walked toward him. "Hello, Your Highness. Thank you for your kindness to Darson, your compassion toward me and Mourin." He shook his head. "Thank you. It was wonderful to make your acquaintance."

"And you." She hugged him and said, "Be well." The princess left to say farewell to the king and the advisors, and then Commander Arrian approached him to wish him well and shake his hand.

"Safe travels, Captain," Arrian said. "May we meet again under better circumstances."

"Thank you for everything, Commander."

Arrian smiled at Garridan, and when he moved away, Nevada stood before him.

"Commander," Garridan said with a formality that did not feel right. "How are you feeling this morning?"

"Better. You look like you are on the mend, too."

His dark hair, clean and pulled away from the strong, attractive lines of his face, absorbed the sunlight. It struck Nevada that she did not really know this man; she knew nothing of his past and only a little of his character. Memories from the conference flashed in her mind—his cool head during the explosive meetings, the surprising intensity he hid in normal circumstances only to let it explode in battle. She was sorry to see him go, and sorrier still it had to be under the pall of his friend and comrade's demise.

"Captain, your efforts..." Nevada paused, unsure what to say next. This was the last time she would ever see him. "I want you to know, and I hope you realize, how greatly appreciated they were. Yours and Darson's." She lowered her voice, and he leaned in to hear her. He smelled like a forest from the land he hailed from. "I wish you the best. I hope everything works out for you."

He smiled ruefully. "I'll know when we return. I wanted to thank you again for saving my life, for the injury you took for me. For remembering our customs. It will help his mother a great deal."

I did it mostly for you. "It was the least I could do." Time was slipping away, and she suddenly disliked the reminder. "I think they are ready to go." She nodded in his party's direction; they were all on horseback.

Garridan bowed at the waist. A breeze fluttered the

waves of Nevada's hair, and her scent drifted over him. He tried committing every detail of her to memory. "Farewell, Commander Nevada. It was a true pleasure."

"Good-bye, Captain Garridan. Be safe."

Garridan took his time backing away to leave, and did not break eye contact with her until he mounted his horse.

* * *

Nevada watched the horses clop down the courtyard in pairs; Garridan and Mourin trailed behind, with Eyad leading the way. Garridan's straight, broad back belied all that had befallen him since he had come to Miranda. Nevada hoped there was solace in his future and, perhaps one day, peace of mind.

The rainforest soon obscured the horses and riders, as the path twisted toward the edges of Aaclyde's property.

And then he was gone.

Nevada jumped when a warm hand curled around her arm. "What a week," Liana murmured.

She snorted. "I would trade my week for yours in a heartbeat."

Liana lightly squeezed Nevada's arm. Nevada noted that Eyad had not said good-bye to either of them before leaving.

"I will write to you when I return home," Liana said, "and we will set up a visit."

"Yes," she agreed. "Shall we share a meal before you leave?"

"That would be lovely."

* * *

Liana left Nevada with Arrian and slipped away from the royals in the courtyard, hoping to avoid any interaction with Emilia or Aaclyde. Her mind buzzed from the meetings of the past twenty-four hours as well as all she had left unattended beforehand. Eyad's words, whether he realized it or not, had helped her envision the path she needed to tread.

Safe inside her suite, Liana locked the door and went to a desk in the corner. A leather folder lay open. The stack of parchment sat in a perfectly stacked pile.

Liana abruptly sat on the chair. She had left the papers a bit scattered, facedown; she had never had a chance to return here because of the meeting. She picked up the parchments and sifted through them, counting the documents with unsteady hands. Notes from meetings; letters from correspondents answering questions no one but she and the letter bearers should have access to.

Brownies, she thought, her heart thudding. *They hate clutter and untidiness. Reasonable explanation.*

No documents were missing. And no one prying would be stupid enough to move the papers and alert her. *Unless it was done as a warning.*

She looked around, listening to the quiet. She was alone; she had to be alone. Nothing else was out of place.

Slowly, Liana replaced the parchments, closed the leather folder, and bound it tight with the leather cord. She carried the folder over to the armoire, opened it, and tucked it in her traveling bag.

Nevada was right. Not here.

* * *

Nevada watched Dacian stand on the sun-dappled balcony, misshapen pockets of shade from the tall, willowy trees decorating his skin. No sign of last night's storm remained. The searing heat had evaporated any moisture from the stone. The balcony was even clear of stray twigs and leaves that had been ripped from their branches. Nothing was out of place.

Dacian leaned over the railing, then pushed off with a long exhale and joined Nevada and Arrian in the room. He shook his head.

She pursed her lips. She did not know whether to feel relieved or frightened.

Dacian shut the glass door behind him, and Arrian began cleaning up, moving around a little less familiarly. Nevada could appreciate that. She was far from comfortable here anymore. A feeling had permeated the room; she felt like she was walking into a stranger's bedroom she had no business in. The space was no longer welcoming.

"Room feels peculiar," Dacian admitted. "As if there is something here I am not seeing."

"I feel the same way, for a different reason," Arrian said. "I need to speak with Anann, and then the queen, before the meeting this afternoon. I want to get back to Hesperia as soon as possible; perhaps one of my messengers has turned up somewhere."

The unspoken *dead or alive* hung in the air, and Nevada inwardly cringed. "I think I will try to rest in my room," she said.

"I will come for you before the meeting," Arrian said, embracing her.

"We will talk after," Dacian added. "I would eat soon, if I were you. You look weak, Nev. I could bring up something for you."

"Thank you, but I can get food," Nevada replied. She left the two commanders with their careful glances and returned to her room for the first time since the party. Instead of falling into the sleep of the sick and exhausted, she sat on the edge of her bed.

What would she do if she could not trust herself? What sort of help could deliver her from the torment of her own mind?

She needed to get out of Miranda and go home. And then … she did not know. She had spent so much time putting Deimos back together that she had ignored the fracturing of her own health. Maybe Arrian was right. Perhaps time away was in order. Even the short break Dacian had suggested. Loosen the uniform she always wore, if only for a little while.

Nevada laid down to rest, but her mind meticulously inspected her memory of the male at the doors last night night, searching for flaws, for any indication he was a hallucination.

For any indication he was real.

Chapter 31

She woke up in the dark, on a stone floor.

Elsbet did not know where she was.

She held her breath, trying to recall how she got here, wherever "here" was, and why the cold, hard floor underneath her was wet.

Muggy air drifted over her skin. It smelled stale. Another scent accompanied it, and she inhaled carefully.

Blood. The air smelled of blood.

Elsbet froze. She moved her fingers, testing to see if her arms were bound. Her muscles were stiff, as if she had been lying in the same position for some time.

How long have I been here?

Her last memory was of riding her horse across the plains of Hesperia toward Miranda. A cry from her horse; a tumble to the ground. She could not remember anything beyond that. She drew a frightening blank, unable to fill in large gaps of memory.

How did I get here?

She could not play dead forever. Elsbet slowly opened her eyes.

Dim lighting barely illuminated the far wall; she could not see a door of any kind in her limited view. The source of light came from somewhere above her, and the way it fell over the floor suggested it reached her through a grate of some kind. Her fuzzy mind cautioned her to not look around.

Am I alone?

Elsbet shifted onto her side with painstaking care and felt whatever moisture coated the floor drip from her cheek. She had an awful suspicion as the liquid trailed slowly down to her neck. With a shaking hand, she wiped at her cheek and held her hand in front of her face.

Dark blood was smeared across her fingers.

Her breath stuttered in her chest. Elsbet drew her legs up, trying hard to beat back the frantic wings of panic. She looked up to find the source of light.

A body hung from the ceiling.

A low, surprised cry tore out of Elsbet as she sat up and scrambled back. The body hung by its feet from a thick rope attached to the grate in the ceiling. The arms, streaked heavily with blood, hung toward the floor, fingers a foot away from brushing the stone. Thick dark hair hung over his face, obscuring it, but Elsbet knew the uniform. He was a Hesperian soldier.

She looked around with wild eyes. The small room was empty. Just her and the dead faerie.

Is *he dead?*

Crawling to stay close to the ground, she edged toward the still body. His chest did not appear to move. Still, her hand shook as she reached between the slack, bloody arms to push back some of the hair.

Wide, empty, bloodshot brown eyes stared back at her.

Elsbet let out a short scream and backed up on all fours; her movement disturbed the body. It swayed hideously, spinning a slow, dreamy circle on its rope. Her bottom hit the stone hard, and she covered her mouth, her eyes wide, her lungs so constricted that every breath was a struggle. She choked on the foul air; bile rose in her throat, and she gagged.

The other messenger Arrian sent to Charon. One of her comrades. It was Roth….

Elsbet gasped sharply as movement in the dark right corner of the room caught her eye. She froze, hand still over her mouth. She could not see …

The faint shuffling of feet hit the air as loud as a hammer hitting a nail. She could just make out clothing. Long strips of something tattered. A dress? What little light the room offered bounced off long, sallow hair.

It was a female.

Elsbet's breath caught in her throat, and a desperate sort of hope filled her.

"Are—" her voice croaked out, rusty, and she tried again. "Do they have you, too? Can you help me? My … my friend." She pointed a trembling finger at Roth. "What did they—where are we?"

The girl did not respond. Her face was hidden beneath long, unkempt hair.

Elsbet didn't know what to do. It occurred to her this girl might not speak Fae and did not understand her, but the total lack of response unsettled her. A little voice inside whispered, *She is not your friend.*

She switched to Vinculum and asked hesitantly, "Can you understand me?"

"I can."

The male voice came out of nowhere, but it was everywhere, bouncing off the walls, and Elsbet gasped and looked around frantically. Her eyes fell on Roth again, who had ceased his awful turning. Except now, he moved sideways, as if—

A hand crept around Roth's side, fingers closing over his still chest and pushing him aside, revealing the darkened figure of a male.

Elsbet wanted to disappear into the floor, putting as much distance between her and the male as she could without risking what else lurked in the darkness behind her, for she could see no door, no way out.

"What do you want?" She wanted to demand it, but it came out trembling, a child's plea.

The girl in the corner shifted and walked toward Elsbet. Her voice whispered through the air, high and feminine. "I can help you."

No, no, I don't think you can. Elsbet scooted back as the girl walked forward, stretching out her arms. She did not appear to have a weapon, but Elsbet knew that didn't matter. But she could not move. Sheer horror shut her mind down, and she watched with a macabre fascination as pale fingers extended toward her. The girl leaned forward, blonde hair falling over a face Elsbet still could not see.

"I'll help you," the girl whispered. Her cold fingers touched Elsbet's temples.

The faerie felt something force its way into her mind. Her eyes stared blindly as obscene images flashed in her head. Blood. Screaming. Roth. Torture.

Elsbet was screaming, the sound echoing off the walls, and she jerked away from the girl, leaping to her feet and running; away from the girl, from Roth, toward the walls to find a door to escape.

Suddenly her feet slid in the opposite direction, jerking her away from the wall as if someone had yanked her back by the shirt.

No one was touching her.

Elsbet tried to lunge forward and reach for the wall, but it was as if she had lost control of her legs. She howled as an unseen force dragged her backward. Through a haze of tears, she caught sight of a thin, bedraggled shadow of a man. His eyes, bright as a rat's in the dead of night, gleamed at her.

All the while, the girl remained where she had first touched Elsbet, with her head thrown back, her laughter high-pitched, joyous, and deranged. Other voices joined in from the darkness. Laughing at her. Elsbet hugged herself.

"Let me out," she cried. "Please, I know nothing. I am only a messenger. I have no information to give. Please—"

"Please," the girl mocked. She twirled slowly, dancing her way to the wall and then back toward Elsbet. "Please, help me."

"That's enough."

Elsbet choked on a gasp as a deeper male voice came from the far left corner of the room.

"Let the poor faerie catch her breath. Have a seat, child."

Elsbet didn't know what else to do. Her eyes flickered to the silhouette of the bony rat man; he did nothing, said nothing. She sank to the bloodied floor in a crouch, arms wrapped around herself. Candles flared to life in the dark, and she flinched. The small, flickering flames illuminated more figures than she would have ever guessed to be in the room. The room wasn't huge, and their presence was stifling, oppressive; they were all so close, less than three yards from her. Her stomach clenched, turned, and she thought she was going to be sick again.

Seven. There were seven of them that she could see, scattered about the room.

A final candle flickered to life, and the hand that waved over it drew back to the side of the tall man who must have been responsible for conjuring the flame. Blond hair gleamed dully in the dim, reddish glow.

"Lovely." His voice was as thin as his body. Thin and wistful. His beady eyes shone out of a pale face. "I wish to have her."

"No." A younger masculine voice denied. "Not you. No need to mar such a pretty thing. I want to pluck that mind clean."

The blond man chuckled. Elsbet shrank from the sound.

"You always get first pick," the female pouted and gestured toward Roth's body. "You got him, and look how long *that* lasted."

"He wasn't a challenge. She has information."

"No, no, I don't," Elsbet denied vehemently. "Please, I do not—"

"Shh, shh," soothed the young, masculine voice, and then its owner sighed. He separated from the wall to circle her. She somehow knew he was the one who had pushed Roth's body aside to frighten her. "Rather presumptuous of you, dear. You do not know what I am looking for." He leaned toward her, and she reared back. Pale gray eyes flashed in the dimness of the room, and his voice dropped to a whisper. "Something to play with. Do you want to play with me as you did yesterday, Elsbet?"

Yesterday? What does that mean?

Her terrified, ragged breathing filled the room, and the

authoritative male voice spoke again in a warning tone. "Bastian."

Bastian obliged. Elsbet watched him walk to the wall, passing another figure leaning against the curved surface. The figure moved away from Bastian, closer to her, and she stiffened. He did nothing, but a clean and refreshing, almost soothing scent wafted off of him—like still waters in a deep wood. It comforted Elsbet for just a moment, even as it disconcerted her, because it was a *familiar* smell. She knew it from somewhere.

He looked at her mutely with eyes as dark as a deep pool of those still waters, and it was almost apologetic, almost intimate.

"None for you?" Bastian asked mildly. The new stranger did not respond.

"You know he gets the leftovers," the blond who created the fire scoffed.

Leftovers? What did that mean? Elsbet wanted to shrink away into nothing, do anything to get away from them, to never find out what he meant.

"Make up your minds," the authoritative voice, who spoke earlier, commanded. "We have actual business to attend to. I know it's very exciting to have one last this long, but let us not overdo it."

"At the rate you're all going, she won't be alive for much longer," the fire conjurer said, as apologetic as a lion over a defenseless antelope.

"What?" Elsbet cried.

"Not yet. I have more things to show her," the female complained.

"Like the human you could not leave alone?"

The girl made a sound like a cat that had found a bowl of cream.

Elsbet remembered the images the girl had shown her, and tears burned her eyes. Who *were* these people? How could this girl put those things in her head? How did the blond create fire out of nothing? Faeries could not do that; these … creatures were not fae. But they could not possibly be human. What sort of species collected people just to torture them? Her throat closed in an effort to keep her mounting sobs at bay. If she cried now, she would never stop.

She knew she would never make it out of this room alive. She pleaded silently that they would let it be quick.

Someone chuckled in the dark. She recognized the voice belonged to the one called Bastian. "Oh, darling. It will not be quick."

Had she said that aloud? No, she had not. Elsbet stared at Bastian as a new level of terror rocketed through her.

He read my mind.

She began to cry.

A few of the figures laughed at her, and the authoritative voice clucked at the group. "Now, look what you have done. You made our guest cry."

"Who are you?" Elsbet choked out between sobs.

More laughter.

"Harbingers of death," the female giggled.

"Your people will know soon enough," the deep male voice answered. "We have already monitored your commander quite closely. He had a visitor last night."

A frigid wind blasted its way through Elsbet's heart. She stared up at him; because of the candlelight, she had a difficult time discerning his features. She felt like she was scrutinizing someone's reflection in a basin of rippling water.

They were watching Commander Arrian? He was already terribly injured. Anger bloomed like a dark sun inside her, and she asked viciously, "What did you do to him?"

"Nothing yet, child." The man nodded to a large, hulking beast of a man to his right. "Why don't you let our guest hear how her commander fares?"

In a deep, rumbling voice, the watcher said, "He recovers. He was with the red-eyed one and the purple-eyed one in Miranda. They conferred late into the night. They speculate a traitor, and talked some of other possibilities; they're not far off the mark. One of the princesses is digging; she bears watching. The alliance is in place as of this morning."

Why are they letting me hear this? Elsbet wondered wildly. Spying on her commander—on more than one—monitoring a princess. How? Were they walking among her people?

What alliance?

"I am aware," was the dour response.

"I'd be willing to take care of them—"

"I can help," said the thin, skeletal rat man. His dark, disheveled hair hid a hungry face, and Elsbet shuddered.

"No," Bastian said, his voice ringing with a note of glee. "I guarantee the commanders would have more interesting things to say than this one, given time."

"You stay away from him," Elsbet spat out, gratefully letting rage smother her fear. She bared her teeth at them and got to her feet. "Touch my commander, and the whole host of the kingdom will tear you apart."

They laughed at her, taunting her bout of temper; although her knees trembled, she remained standing.

"That is precious," Bastian said, grinning at her. "Although

I must divert our attention, briefly, back to you." He pointed at the watcher. "You omitted an error on your part." He tsked. The big man's back straightened. "The Deimos commander spotted you. It was the second time. You are slipping, my friend."

He growled a warning, his eyes cold. "It matters not."

Elsbet's heart sunk with dread at the mention of Commander Nevada. *What are these people doing? And for how long have they been doing it?*

"The storm ensured she would hardly be able to pick him out in a crowd," the fire conjurer added.

"She could pick *you* out," Bastian said. "All but gave her your name. Dear, that wasn't very subtle."

"I didn't intend to be subtle."

"Enough. We will discuss it later. Leave them for now," their leader said to the watcher. "I wish to see them for myself. Keep an eye on all four in the meantime, but stay out of sight. Now choose, the lot of you."

Elsbet didn't know how they chose or what they were choosing. Coming to terms with her own demise, fearing for her people and her commander took the forefront of her mind. She held on to herself as she tried to keep from falling apart. She barely registered a feminine gasp, and then a brief, light clap of happiness.

"Vulvia can join us when she is finished," the leader said. "We have preparations to continue making."

The others left the room through a door Elsbet had not noticed in her frantic search for a way to escape.

Bastian's voice trailed behind him. "Leave her alive for me, sister."

The door shut Elsbet in with the blonde female, who

smiled with sharp, white teeth.

Elsbet's screams echoed off the walls. Woven through the sounds of terror was Vulvia's joyous laughter.

Epilogue

One week later

Garridan looked at the small, russet, cobblestone cottage. The windowsills were alive with bright, vivid flowers and flourishing green herbs. The door was painted an ocean blue; here and there, the original tan wood peeked through at the peeling edges.

Idavida was home. One of the open windows let out the smell of roast meat and vegetables. The faint clinking of cookware reached his ears.

He carried the smooth, wooden urn in the crook of his left arm.

Garridan had pleaded with the king for permission to bring Darson back to Idavida, to tell her himself. He didn't want her to hear it from strangers. It surprised him when Edric relented, after he had stripped him of his duties and title for six months.

A light sentence.

Six months with no wages would chafe, but he barely felt the blow, cushioned as it was by exhaustion. He walked through the familiar streets of Laurus in a fog that had clouded his mind with increasing strength since they had left Miranda's courtyard and entered the heart of the jungle. Now he couldn't see past the thick haze obscuring his vision of the future, leaving it unknown, bleak, and cold.

Darson, I can't do this to your mother.

He moved forward, the satchel of his and Darson's belongings hitting his hip with each step. He watched his traitorous hand reach up and knock lightly, because maybe she wouldn't hear it and he could—

The door opened.

Darson's mother appeared in the entryway, drying her hands on a rag. Her long brown hair, barely threaded through with silver, was swept back into a burnished gold clip. She wore a blue and gray dress he'd seen on her countless times.

She gave a cry of pleasant surprise and threw her arms around his neck. "Hello! Welcome home! Was the mission a success, did they agree? Oh, my dear, I want to hear *everything* you boys saw, everyone you spoke with. Spare me no details!"

Garridan drew in a deep breath and spoke. "Hello, Idavida. They agreed; we have an alliance with the fae kingdom."

"Wonderful!"

She patted his stubbled cheek and drew back, her eyes retaining a glow of happiness even as she looked behind him and the silent question formed on her face. Bands of iron compressed his chest until he could not breathe as she looked down at what he held in his left arm.

Idavida's brow furrowed. She dropped the rag and touched the urn with trembling fingers. "What is this?" she whispered.

A thousand platitudes filled Garridan's head, but he could no more voice them than he could bring back Darson. His mouth was an arid desert, and he choked on the words. "He is in the next place. With his father."

She whispered, "My son," as her eyes filled.

"I am—" Garridan couldn't see past his own tears as she took the urn in her delicate hands and cradled her son's remains. "I am so sorry. I should have … Forgive me, Idavida, I should have—"

She shook her head. The tears fell as she backed up a step and into the doorframe. Garridan felt sick as he gathered her to him, the urn between them. Her last living child taken from her, and all he could offer her was an apology. He stroked her hair as she shook and cried while church bells rang in the distance.

* * *

She fed him roast duck and steamed vegetables. They spoke little during the meal, though her hands trembled and he picked at his food. Garridan cleared the dishes and cleaned the kitchen for her, then brewed tea while she sat motionless at the table.

He placed the cup of steaming tea by her clasped hands and then moved his chair to place it closer to Idavida. Before he sat, he pulled out a small, leather-bound journal from the satchel and set it on the table. Out of the corner of his eye, he spotted the urn on the wooden counter and jerked his attention away as he would have pulled his hand back from a scalding kettle potas if burned. He looked down at his hands, at the ruby ring on his finger.

The memory of finding the ring burned as if he'd laid a hand on that sweltering pot and done nothing but watch the skin blister. A phantom smell of burning flesh clogged in his nose, and for a moment, Garridan couldn't breathe. He fisted his hands in his lap, slowed his breathing, and waited until the moment passed.

Trembling, he pulled the ring off.

After his tremors ceased, Garridan took one of Idavida's hands, turned it over, and placed Darson's ring in her palm.

"Darson brought it to Miranda," he said, amazed at the steadiness in his voice. He pushed the journal toward her. "He wrote in it every night we were there. I haven't read it."

"We can read it together," Idavida said, her voice husky with grief.

I don't know if I can.

As daylight faded, the thought of returning to his cottage made Garridan feel ill. He convinced Idavida to try to sleep, and then realized nothing was stopping him from staying overnight. Darson would want someone to look after her; Garridan would have wanted that for his own mother, had it been him. He could have slept in the small living area, but something drew him to the closed door of Darson's room.

The lieutenant's vibrancy and spirit clung to every object in the small bedroom: the books along a shelf by his bed, the clothes carelessly slung over a wooden chair, the carvings and trinkets he had collected from past missions. Surrounded by Darson's possessions, Garridan comforted himself by imagining that his friend was just delayed, and would return for his things any day.

The letter with the red seal crinkled in his breeches as he sat on the bed and stared sightlessly.

* * *

Garridan could not remember if he had slept at all during the night, or if he had merely slipped into the fog of a sleepless stupor. Before he knew it, dawn crept into the room.

Idavida wandered the small house like a ghost the next day. Garridan found fresh eggs in the kitchen and cooked them over a small fire in the hearth, then stood over her to ensure she ate.

In a voice as dry and bare as kindle wood, she said, "Tell me what happened."

Throughout the day, he slowly recounted what had happened on the trip, factually at first, but he did not have the energy to reveal everything. He narrowed his focus to Darson's final days and hours so she would know, and he would only have to tell it once and then never again.

It replayed often enough in his memory as it was.

She excused herself after he recalled Darson's death. Garridan let her go to her room alone. He heard her weep freely; like a bird answering a call, his heart did the same.

Miraculously, Garridan slept for a few hours early in the evening. When he woke, the house was silent and dark, but upon opening the bedroom door, he spotted light coming from beneath the study door.

He knocked softly.

An hour later the pair still sat in Idavida's study. A little color had returned to Idavida's cheeks, and muted enthusiasm entered her voice when he asked if she wanted to hear a little about the fae. He was glad to distract her with the golden gates of Miranda's palace, the food and décor and sculptures.

He made her laugh by describing Darson's initial reaction to the faeries and his attempts at humor during the trip to Hesperia. She listened with wonder as he told her of Darson's brief connection with the beautiful desert princess.

"How marvelous," she sighed sadly. "How lovely it must have been for him. What were they like? How do they act? How did they react to you?"

"They're not much different from us," Garridan answered. "I forgot, sometimes, how long they have lived, how much they've seen. Some of them are intense and quick to anger, and others hated us on sight. There was one commander …" He talked about Dacian, and Idavida absorbed every word at first and then abruptly made him stop. She sifted through a pile of books on her desk and pulled out a journal, then a writing utensil, and told him to start over.

"Write down everything you remember later, too" she ordered as she scribbled furiously. "I want to add your experience to my ledgers. I want every memory recorded. The jungle and the plains, the faeries you and Darson met. Everything. In fact, take this with you when you leave."

Garridan agreed and reached for the letter in his pocket, hesitated, then took it out. "I have something a little more tangible for you." He handed her the letter.

Idavida took it carefully, puzzled, and glanced at the name scrawled on the front. Her eyes flew to his with surprise.

He let out a long breath. "This is from the commander he met when we made initial contact." Garridan explained Commander Arrian's compassion and kind words as they left Hesperia, and at the final joint meeting. Idavida listened silently, slicing the envelope open with a small knife, handling it and the letter inside carefully.

"'Dearest Idavida,'" she read aloud, "'I wish to express my condolences and sorrow at the loss of your son, Lieutenant Darson. I met him only once, weeks prior; my impression of him then, coupled with his bravery and sacrifice on the fields of my home, give me cause to call him a comrade with pride. He shall never be forgotten in this kingdom. May you find peace. Arrian.'" Idavida put the letter down and covered her mouth, squeezing her eyes shut as tears streamed down her face.

A fierce burst of gratitude, pride, and grief gripped Garridan. He could hear the Hesperian commander say the words as if he were in the room. He wished he could thank Arrian and Nevada one more time, wished it with an ache so great that tears burned in his eyes.

He got up and walked around the desk to hug Idavida. She clung to him fiercely as he said, "All the princesses recognized what Darson did for their people. Arrian made sure of it. Your son's bravery and strength formed the basis of the alliance."

"History will remember him, as it should," she said tremulously. She composed herself and motioned him back to his seat. "Tell me more about this commander and the princess."

Garridan obliged. As he spoke, he glanced idly at the papers scattered about her desk. One old book, its yellowed pages curling at the corners, lay open to a page with wispy, faded handwriting. He had read the passages during the night and had realized it was a very old account of another individual's encounter with faeries. The style of writing, flowing like poetry on the page, dated it back a few centuries. A few lines had jumped out at him: *"eyes of infinity,"* and *"hands were cool and firm, but gentle."* One line in particular struck a deep chord in him.

"We are changed."

It was exactly the right phrase.

"Did any of them make an impression on you?" Idavida looked up at him, eyes bright with a bittersweet sadness and the promise of more tears to come.

He thought of long, black hair that fell in waves. Piercing violet eyes. A selfless, compassionate faerie, fiercely adept at her profession. "Yes. The commander who saved my life. I never could have imagined anyone like her." It hurt to remember her. And although life moved on, a small part of him would forever remain somewhere between the jungles of a faraway land and the grasslands of another, never to be seen again by his eyes. There was a thirst there now, and it would go unquenched.

Garridan left Idavida's the next day. As he lingered in the doorway, Idavida took Darson's ring from her pocket and gave it back to him.

"Keep this for him," she said.

He re-entered the fog that had dogged him since his return from Miranda, finding his way home by memory. His small cottage looked cheerless and deserted, a visual sore among the other diminutive homes decorated with tiny plots of flowers.

Someone sat at his front door.

Garridan approached cautiously, not recognizing the bowed head at first. "Can I help you?" he called.

The head rose. Foster looked up at him, then rose slowly to his feet, still favoring his injured knee. "Welcome back, Captain."

Garridan embraced the soldier and invited him in to talk. His suspension was no secret, and while he anticipated curiosity, he was not ready for Foster to offer to help with room and board while Garridan was suspended without wages.

"After everything you have done for me," the soldier said firmly, "I would be a thankless fool to do nothing."

He could not shake the man off, and Garridan relented days later, still feeling undeserving. Foster had his own demons to wrestle with; he was in good company.

* * *

In the weeks after Garridan's return, the memories continued to wake him. Sometimes, dreams of thick, oppressive jungle and dry grassland tainted with the metallic tang of blood flooded back into his mind, along with the jewel-toned eyes and black hair of someone he swore, only late at night, didn't exist at all. Perhaps he had dreamed her up. Maybe the whole thing was a terrible, beautiful dream.

He could only fool himself for so long, since Darson would never again stop by, and news traveled throughout Laurus that the city was expecting ethereal visitors in a few months. It wouldn't be who he wanted it to be.

But life moved on.